NO PEACE FOR
THE WICKED

Annamarie Delaney

This book is dedicated to YOU the reader. Without you my work would be pointless

CHAPTER 1

The morning after Joe's experimental meal, Jacques and Marie-France came down the stairs together. He went through to open up the bar, she made her way down to the cellar to feed the pups. Now that her offspring were weaned, Galla had taken to sleeping curled up in her old place on the new balcony. Seeing her there, Marie-France experienced a fleeting wave of nostalgia for the cane seat and their shared nights. The moment soon passed, pushed away by her present contentment. She stepped through the archway between the two balconies, peered through the reflective glass. No sign of Joe or of the cushions he'd piled up to sleep on the previous night.

'Must have gone to Lucie's after all,' she remarked quietly to Galla. 'Thought he might have been too exhausted after all his hard work yesterday.'

Marie-France smiled, remembering how Joe had compared his new lover to her. *'Lucie's as insatiable as you are but twice as big. Think I might have met my match,'* he'd said. She'd been uncharacteristically embarrassed at the time, worried about Jacques' reaction. Was that really only yesterday? What a day, and night, it had been.

She walked carefully down the wide wooden steps, holding on to the smoothly varnished rail with her uninjured right hand. Jean-Paul, the physio, had told her she should start using her muscles more naturally but not to overdo it. The previous evening, showing off her waitressing skills, she'd done a bit too much. Her broken arm was aching, so she was wearing a sling to remind herself to give it a bit of a rest.

Ecstatically greeted by eight hungry puppies milling about her feet, scrabbling at her trainers, she decided it was time to start some basic training. Her convalescence was over, so was their baby-puppy stage. Time they learned who they were as individuals. She put food into the communal dish, made sure the littlies were all eating, looked around the cellar where she'd slept during the heat of summer. Since her very short lived marriage when she was eighteen years old she hadn't once spent the whole night in a real bed with a man. Not until last night. A real bed and a real man. With a grin and a self-hug she decided she'd better go back upstairs, to make sure he really was real and not just a figment of her hungry imagination.

She met Eveline and Corinne at the bottom of the stairs, wearing the same clothes they'd had on when they so dramatically left the company the night before. Some might have wondered whether their amorous exit was a staged performance for the benefit of Corinne's nasty ex-husband but anyone seeing them now couldn't fail to believe their feelings were genuine. They were like two beams of early morning sunshine spilling into the dull hallway, filling it with a satisfied glow.

The three women exchanged bonjours and kisses, went through to the café together. To Marie-France's surprise, Joe, looking very relaxed and rested, was drinking a cup of coffee.

'What a bevy of beauties!' he exclaimed, looking and sounding exactly like his grandfather. He smelt like Grandfather Jacques too, Marie-France noticed, as they greeted. His next comment explained why. 'It's a superb shower, that one next door, well stocked with shampoo and soap too. A shame we'll have to demolish it but it just doesn't quite fit into the ambiance of my restaurant plans. Always supposing I'll still be allowed to have one after last night's meal.'

'But it was marvellous, Joe,' Eveline exclaimed. 'And you know me better than to believe I'm just saying that.' 'It certainly was marvellous,' Corinne concurred. 'The experience as well as the meal. Can't remember the last time I enjoyed myself so much.' She looked at Eveline, giggled unashamedly, was rewarded with a grinning hug.

'Coffee?' Jacques asked generally, trying to maintain his usual deadpan expression as he placed the cups on the saucers he'd already laid out. 'But forgive me. I'm not used to serving women in evening dress at this time in the morning. Would you like your coffee at a table, mesdames, rather than leaning up like commoners against the bar?' Eveline picked up a sugar lump, threw it at him, suggested archly to Corinne that they should go and get changed somewhere more convivial. 'Those two aren't exactly making an effort to be discreet, are they?' Joe observed with a broad smile, as Eveline and Corinne downed their coffees and skipped off arm in arm.

'Bonjour tous le monde! I'd like to thank you all for a truly memorable evening, especially the chef. Joe, the food, the whole experience was wonderful. I've sworn Léa to secrecy when she goes back to Paris otherwise all the best restaurateurs will be swarming down to try and recruit you.' 'How is Léa, Doc?' Marie-France asked, totally failing to make the question sound innocent. 'I'm sure she'll tell you herself when she arrives,' Doc replied enigmatically, a twinkle in his eye. 'And how are you this morning, my dear?' He overtly glanced over at Jacques, as if to say two can play at that game. 'I'm fine, thank you Doc,' she sparkled back.

'Bonjour tous le monde!' Dominique breezed in with the usual delivery of bread and breakfast croissants. 'Sorry I'm a bit late but all the people who weren't here last night wanted to hear from all the people who were here about how it went. Sounds as if you excelled yourself Joe, in fact...'

'Bonjour!' A cheery voice interrupted her, one that wasn't often heard so early in the morning. 'Bonjour Lucie. What can I get you?' Jacques, the first to find his voice, prepared himself to manage the potential scene that might erupt between her and Joe. Still a bit bemused by the conversation he'd had about the coiffeuse with his younger brother the previous evening, he knew for a fact that Joe hadn't gone to her for what was left of the night. 'Coffee, please Jacques. Thought I'd give myself a treat as it's Sunday.' 'Sunday?' Marie-France reacted like an alien who'd never heard the word before. 'Is it really Sunday?'

she asked, appreciating for the first time just how out of touch with reality she'd become since her accident. 'Jacques, what's happened to the market stall?' 'Martine and Jules are managing fine. A distinct lack of vegetables, of course, but they're still doing a trade in eggs and baskets. Martine's added a few more of her wares too, now she's closed the shop for the winter. The stall, ma bien-aimée, is one of the many things we need to discuss in the business meeting which *will* take place on Wednesday.'

Marie-France had stopped listening after his endearment, breathed so quietly she'd nearly missed it. My dearest one. She replayed the words, turning them round and round in her heart to see how they felt. Had anyone else heard them? Did they sound sincere or would people just think that some of his grandfather's verbal gallantry had been left behind in the air?

'Guess who I saw just now?' A voice broke into her mental meanderings, as it was meant to do. Lucie wanted everyone to hear what she had to say. No one bothered to answer. They knew she'd tell them soon enough. 'I've just seen Eveline and Corinne!' Lucie exclaimed.

Jacques and Joe exchanged a knowing look, having only recently spoken about Lucie's propensity for gossip. 'Eveline and Corinne,' Lucie repeated, somewhat less confidently. She'd noticed the exchanged look. It set off a train of thought she'd been trying to avoid travelling on. 'They were together, really together, you know, arm in arm, kissing and cuddling and everything!'

Dominique remembered Lucie coming into the boulangerie after the first time Jacques' wife, Eveline, had been spotted with another woman. She'd used almost exactly the same words then. On that occasion Dominique had been at pains to protect Jacques from too much explicit detail, in case he found the picture distressing to contemplate. She glanced over at her old friend. His eyes were laughing!

'Is it true then?' Dominique asked. 'The Wilsons called in first thing to buy a picnic for their journey back to England. They said Eveline and Corinne had left hand in hand but weren't sure whether it was just an act for Corinne's obnoxious ex.' 'Looked fairly convincing to me,' Jacques replied, his dry voice contrasting with his dancing eyes. 'Definitely the real thing,' Marie-France chipped in. 'I was turned on just looking at them together this morning.' 'Looking at a bar stool is enough to turn you on,' Joe commented, attempting to sound sarcastic. 'Just you leave my bar stool out of this,' she retorted, wriggling provocatively. Jacques sighed heavily, Joe grinned, Lucie was completely upstaged.

'Well, I think that's brilliant news,' Dominique exclaimed. 'I like Corinne but she's always been just a bit too nice and sensible. I'm sure a fling with Eveline will do her the world of good. But listen, I was going to tell you about someone else who's come out!'

Jacques looked at her in surprise. The boulangerie was a hotbed of gossip but it was unusual for Dominique to be the one to spread it beyond those walls.

'Georges!' she announced theatrically. 'Georges? Your Georges?' Dominique's husband, the baker, rarely went more than a few paces away from his bread oven. Everyone knew they were a completely devoted couple. A gurgling laugh saved the company from spending any more time trying to contemplate the impossible.

'Yes, Georges. My Georges. He's decided to come out of the bakery to celebrate our twenty fifth wedding anniversary.' Jacques melodramatically clutched his heart, murmuring 'Twenty five years since I was jilted.'

Dominique had vowed undying love when she was ten years old. She smiled at him affectionately before explaining. 'We'd had a sort of half-hearted conversation about a celebration of some sort but by the time we'd listened to the Wilsons, Natalie and Marc all saying what an amazing evening they'd had here the solution was obvious. We want to share our happiness with our nearest and dearest and seeing as everybody *Chez Jacques* fits into that category we'd like to have an intimate party right here. Is that possible?'

Joe, always a large, happy man, doubled in stature, positively radiating joy. 'Depends when,' Jacques replied. Joe tensed. Was Jacques going to be obstructive? 'You see, we're busy this afternoon and...'

Dominique laughed again. Joe relaxed. 'Oh, don't worry, it's not until well into the New Year but I wanted to know if it would be alright in principle.' 'We'd be delighted, wouldn't we Joe?' 'Of course. Twenty five years. That's silver, isn't it?' The chef was already searching through his creative mind for presentation ideas. 'Just tell us how many and when and Dominique....' Unable to contain himself any longer, he lifted the matronly woman off her feet in a bear hug, swinging her around until she threatened to be sick if he didn't put her down. 'Anyway, I'm off. Don't want Georges divorcing me because I'm not tending the shop. Bye all, see you later!'

The Sunday market always brought custom to *Chez Jacques*. People from the locality and beyond, coming in to the village to buy fresh produce for the week, catching up on the neighbourhood happenings. As she was leaving, Dominique held the door open for a gaggle of elderly men. They routinely spent the first part of the morning in the café, drinking coffee, dissipating the loneliness that weighed too heavily if they didn't make the effort to occasionally leave their isolated farms. A new member joined the group this morning. Albert Aubry had taken a second lease of life since Grandfather Jacques' visit. As the tables were being rearranged to accommodate this particular clique, three women arrived, also Sunday morning regulars. The Sabbath was far from being a day of rest for the Lucianis.

Lucie picked up the Sunday edition of *La Dépêche*, the regional newspaper, sat herself down at a corner table, not yet ready to socialise. The deflated feeling she'd experienced at the way her news had been received had settled into her mood, reminding her of the real reason why she'd decided to pay *Chez Jacques* an early visit. Joe.

Lucie watched him moving around the café, greeting people, taking orders, passing the time of day. Not only was he an exceptionally handsome and sexy man, made more so by the stylish hair cut she'd given him, he was also amiably pleasant, cheery with everyone. From the moment she'd woken up that morning in her empty bed she started cursing herself for the way she'd spoken to him the day before. Sandrine, whose account of the way *her* affair with the younger Luciani had ended, had provided Lucie with the ammunition for her attack. She'd arrived unexpectedly the previous evening, bringing a bottle of vodka along with a different version of her and Joe's break up. 'Thought I'd come and keep you company as Joe's working,' she said to Lucie. 'What time do you think he'll be round?' Lucie shrugged, as if she didn't care. She'd laid into to Joe when he'd phoned to explain that he was going to pretend to take Corinne to bed, telling him she didn't trust him, didn't need him, even suggesting she might prefer to have a fling with Jacques.

'You two had a fallout?' Sandrine asked. Was there a hopeful inflexion in the question? Lucie shrugged again, poured them both a drink, sat down on the sofa, curling her long legs up underneath her full length robe. 'Because if you have, well I'm beginning to regret ditching him myself. I miss him. And he's been so good to Benoit, keeping him off the streets by giving him work. It's great he's got a man to look up to, seeing as his shit of a dad doesn't take any interest in him at all.'

Lucie wasn't interested in Benoit. 'What do you mean, you ditched him? I thought you said he'd ditched you because you told him you weren't happy about him carrying on with Marie-France.' 'Oh? Did I say that? Well, it's all the same really, isn't it? And actually I think I was a bit hasty about Marie-France. When I saw the mess she was in after her accident I believe Joe really had been just looking at her. She certainly didn't look fit enough to do anything else.'

During their phone call the previous day Lucie had told Joe, in no uncertain terms, that she wasn't prepared to be picked up and dropped whenever he felt like it, based on what Sandrine had reported. Now it transpired that he'd been the one who was dropped. Lucie had even given him an ultimatum. 'I want you but I don't need you,' she'd said. 'So get here as soon as you can.' The 'or else' was implicit.

Sandrine left Lucie's apartment early, her hostess was rather reticent in filling up the glasses. Lucie changed into her sexiest negligee and waited. And waited. Looked at her phone, willing there to be a message. Waited. Dozed on the settee. And waited. Eventually she crawled into her cold, lonely bed. Realising how stupid she'd been, she determined to go and see Joe as soon as the café-bar was open, to invite him round for a conciliatory meal. Watching him, charmingly flirtatious with everyone - he'd even greeted her with kisses, chaste, polite kisses, without a hint of angst at the way she'd spoken to him - she understood that to tame him would be to change him. Why would anyone want to do that?

CHAPTER 2

Lucie was born and brought up in Labeille. Her parents owned the quincaillerie, an old fashioned hardware shop. A treasure trove for any handyman, handywoman, handyperson, for anyone who loved rootling around in potentially useful bits and pieces. The sort of place to find the screw for the one that had stripped clean during a repair operation. Or one single washer for a dripping tap, avoiding buying a whole packet in the big DIY chain stores. Of course it was more expensive and you had to be prepared to spend the time looking for what you needed. Or waiting for Monsieur Mercadier, Lucie's father, to suggest another way of sorting the problem, as well as hanging about while Madame Mercadier carefully noted in an exercise book the exact description and how many of what had been sold, as part of a complex manual system of stock management. This had to be done before she rang the purchase through the till, as if once it had left the shop it was no longer hers to write about. But the wait was shorter than the drive to the nearest big store and there was never any doubt that if you couldn't find the precise thing you were looking for, whether plumbing bits, joinery, kitchen equipment, you'd leave with something that would do the job. Various services were offered at Mercadier's too. A piece of glass cut to any size to replace the vitrine in the kitchen door, cracked when the wind slammed it shut. Paté, rillettes, jambonneau, ready in the cans provided by the quincaillerie, sealed and heat treated, the last part of the food conservation process after the pig was killed. Any blunted garden tool, knife or saw, restored to a gleaming sharpness in the time it took to explain the job it was needed for.

Mercadier's hardware shop, a hub of constant activity, was where Lucie learnt to socialise. Her parents doted on their pretty, precocious daughter and her self-esteem couldn't fail to be sky high. At school she was an average student, bright-ish but not brilliant, popular with teachers and pupils. But she really came into her own when she reached puberty and discovered sex. She enjoyed it from the first tentative kiss and clumsy fumble, didn't waste any time dreaming about the perfect lover. Variety was definitely the spice in life that she sought. Her friends started going steady, she carried on playing as many fields as she could. Her friends started to live with their men, have babies or even get married. Lucie went on the pill, took herself off to the nearest *grande ville*, became a qualified hairdresser. Much as she relished men she didn't want them around all the time. The hairdressing salon her parents bought her in the village, with the flat above, were her personal territory. She controlled who and when people visited. The place was kept immaculate, the sheets on the bed changed almost daily, the kitchen pristine, stocked with all the food and drink Lucie liked to consume. She enjoyed pampering herself, spending long hours soaking in a scented bath listening to music, drinking a glass of wine, smoking a joint. She liked nothing better than to float around in sexily unrestricting clothes, worn for the pleasurable way they made her feel. Solitary evenings usually culminated in a long, drawn out masturbatory session in her crisply fresh bed, stimulated by fantasies of real or imagined lovers. She was telling the truth when she told Joe that although she wanted him she didn't need him. It was the same with all her men. Although now, watching him, she did feel she'd been too hasty. She had a lot more wanting for Joe left in her yet.

Lucie's organised life extended to the way she selected her lovers. She'd never accept or make advances towards a man living with anyone else in the village. Once a couple had split up they were fair game. Labeille people were a significant part of her clientele, she didn't want to lose their custom, even though she was never short of customers, so good at her job that both men and women travelled to her salon from surrounding villages. Perhaps surprisingly, Lucie had never fallen out with any of the girls she went to school with. Girls like Sandrine, Benoit's mother, Joe's ex-lover. 'Bonjour Sandrine. What can I get you?' Jacques' voice broke into Lucie's deliberations.

Sandrine? Here? She wasn't wasting any time. Lucie, feeling her anger and anxiety rising, made an effort to calm herself, heard Sandrine speaking to Joe. 'Benoit told me all about last night, the meal and....everything. It all sounds very exciting.'

Joe grinned at Jacques, imagining the youngster telling his mum, in the strictest confidence of course, about how his employers had seen off an undesirable man. How they'd seen him off and why he was undesirable was something he wouldn't disclose. He didn't know.

Sandrine did the rounds, greeting everyone in the bar. Lucie continued her musings. In amongst her ravings at Joe she'd suggested that maybe he *should* get together with Corinne while she, Lucie, made a play for Jacques. She glanced over at the bar proprietor, efficiently and courteously moving around the increasingly crowded space. Taking orders, delivering drinks, passing the time of day, totally unflappable, charmingly cool. The previous year, when the news surged around the village that Eveline had left him, he became, instantly, the most eligible man in the neighbourhood. Comfortably situated as the proprietor of the café-bar, very personable, always smart, pleasant, decidedly good looking. Plenty of women thought they might offer him solace, Lucie amongst them. In the early days, he'd become an ice filled replica of himself but looking at him now he'd certainly thawed. He rarely actually smiled but good humour and warmth shone from his penetrating eyes and there was a lightness in his step indicating that once again life was worth living. 'Maybe I should have another go at him,' Lucie thought. 'He wouldn't want commitment either, he's far too taken up with his family, but just a casual association with someone who knows every possible way to relax a man would surely hold some appeal.'

What a coup for her that would be, to seduce the man everybody said held the power in the Luciani family. She glanced at him again, the goose lines around his eyes creased deeply as he shared a pleasantry with Doc. She'd never seen him quite so breathtakingly attractive as he was this morning. Joe bubbled but Jacques smouldered, like a dangerous volcano, just biding its time before it erupted. And what an eruption it would be, if she was in control.

Lucie almost erupted herself as a firm hand squeezed her shoulder. Joe loomed over her, smiling. 'Planning your assault on my brother?' he asked amiably. 'Joe! I ...Listen Joe, about what I said yesterday.'

Here was a man beside her, a man with real flesh that she'd touched, blood she'd roused to boiling point. A man she'd had, in all possible senses of the word. Filled with remorse that she might have driven him away for no good reason, she was also infuriated that he didn't seem even remotely concerned that she might be setting her sights on Jacques.

Joe shrugged off her protestations. 'I had a good time anyway, even if it was Eveline who went off with girl I'd booked for the night.'

Lucie started to seethe. He was goading her, insinuating all sorts of possibilities as to what could have taken place. Had he intended having sex with Corinne after all? Maybe he did. Maybe the three of them... She had to get him back, even if just for one night, to save face if nothing else.

'Bonjour Lucie. You're up bright and early!' Sandrine, beside them, bending down to greet her. Lucie and Sandrine were old friends. They'd been through school together and since had shared more than a few lovers. Though not at the same time, obviously. Obviously? Why was it obvious that they'd not actually, physically shared a lover? Lucie's body starting warming with excitement at the idea that her brain hadn't yet formulated. 'Morning Sandrine. Shall we make it a good one, move onto something stronger after coffee. I've had an idea I'd like to talk over with you.'

Sandrine was intrigued. How could she fail to be? The woman who'd been positively chilly towards her the night before was bathed in a mysterious, warming glow. 'Good idea. A short coffee to wake me up and then I'll be ready for anything.' Lucie's colour heightened even more, her grin undeniably wicked.

Joe moved away to clear a vacated table. Marie-France materialised beside Lucie and Sandrine, waiting to take their order, delighting in the scenario of Joe's lovers, including herself, all gathered together in one place.

'Two coffees for the time being please, Marie-France. It's good to see you back on your feet,' Lucie remarked agreeably. 'It's good to be there,' she replied, moving towards the bar, just as Eveline slipped in beside Jacques. 'Thought you might have given up on bar work,' he remarked, as she picked up the tray of drinks he'd prepared. 'Afraid not. You don't get rid of me that easily,' she replied. 'Good! I don't want to get rid of you.' he said. 'Oh, and Eveline, on that note, there's a business meeting on Wednesday I'd like you to be at. I wonder if you and I could get together first, to sort out a few practical details about our ongoing relationship. Being happy suits you, by the way.' 'You too,' she smiled, giving him a wifely peck on the cheek. The draught from the opening and closing door breezed the kiss away.

Lucien and Marc, appropriately dressed in jeans and shirts, made their way around the room, shaking hands with some, kissing others. They reached Joe and Marie-France in front of the bar, passing on orders to Jacques and Eveline. At the much discussed meal Lucien had been wearing a skin-tight devil suit. It was Sunday. Joe couldn't resist delivering a suitably biblical quotation, before thinking it through. 'Get thee behind me Satan!' he boomed.

Marc buried his face in his hands, Jacques looked skywards, Marie-France smirked. 'Oh, *mon choupinou*, I thought you'd never ask,' Lucien shrieked, moving towards Joe, elegant hands on gyrating hips. 'Lucien, behave!' Marc snapped. He'd hoped this visit might re-establish his respectable public identity, aware that he'd gone uncharacteristically over the top the previous evening, something he tried to avoid doing on his home ground.

'And you behave too, Joe,' Jacques added with mock severity.

'This is a reputable family café. And talking of families, here come the boys.' Jacques and Eveline's sons, Jacqui and Angelo, were mooching across the square, heading for home after spending the night at friends' houses.

Marie-France slithered off the stool she'd been momentarily resting on. 'Joe, get this thing off me!' The urgency in her voice made him respond immediately. She was clumsily clawing at the Velcro of her arm support. He efficiently removed it, without asking why. 'Jacques, stow this behind the bar, will you?' And give me a full tray.' Jacques also complied, but he did look the question. 'For Angelo,' she explained.

Two disastrous events in the recent past had both occurred directly after a special Luciani meal. Jacques' youngest son, a sensitive and exceptionally imaginative seven year old, had decided that not only was there a direct connection between special meals and catastrophes, but also that he, personally, possessed some sort of predictive ability about them. Marie-France's accident was the first of the meal-associated misfortunes. Jacques and Joe immediately understood her plan to break the perceived curse.

'Right mes amis, stand aside! ' Joe called out, clearing the way to the adjoined tables just inside the glass doors that the boys were making their way towards. Marie-France, holding the tray up to shoulder height, strode through the gap Joe had created, making herself as visible as possible. She reached the table just as the boys pushed open the door, as she'd intended. Putting one hand on her hip and a bright confident smile on her face she welcomed them cheerily. 'Marie-France, who mended you?' Angelo asked in amazement. 'What do you mean?' she asked, opening her eyes wide as if she'd forgotten she'd ever stopped twirling laden trays and bouncing her way through crowded cafés.

'Oh, this!' she looked at the tray, started lowering it towards the table, to the bewilderment of the group of men sitting around it, still nursing their first coffees. Jacques, who'd followed in her wake, discreetly took the tray from her, so she didn't have to use her left hand to put it down. 'I am mended, aren't I?' She squatted down so she could look the little boy in the eyes as she spoke. Joe moved in closer, ready to support her if the position became too difficult to sustain. 'Last night mended me,' she explained earnestly. 'You see, Ange, everything was just so much fun. Your uncle Joe made some great food, your dad made sure everything ran smoothly and most of the people that I love were there. When I saw what a good time they were having, eating, laughing enjoying themselves, I decided I was fed up with not being me. I joined in and had fun too and forgot all about being broken.'

The words tumbling out of her mouth were for Angelo's benefit but as she heard them, Marie-France realised they were true. 'You'd have loved it, Ange, it was awfully messy, and I really wished you were there.' The little boy smiled appealingly, cocked his head on one side. Sounding very like his flirtatious uncle Joe, he asked, 'Coz I'm one of the people you love?' Marie-France's laugh bounced around the bar as she hugged him.

A droll voice cut though the merriment. 'Now Ange, while I do appreciate, more than most, that Marie-France is a very important person, don't you think you should say bonjour to your mum too?' 'We've already done that,' Jacqui, the eldest son explained, his tone matching the dryness of his father's. 'We met her on our way back. She sent me a text asking me to get Ange from his pal's house because she was running late. She was with Corinne.'

'Oh?' his dad responded, wondering exactly how 'with' Corinne, Eveline had been. 'We like Corinne.' Angelo supplied the answer. The boys had clearly already discussed their mother's new liaison. 'She lives in Labeille.' Jacqui clarified the basis for their approval. No threat of this relationship taking them away from their father's village, as they'd been before.

Exhibitionist Angelo was unwilling to abandon centre stage. 'So, mum's alright, Marie-France is alright, and dad, you're alright too, aren't you?' His father nodded, gave him a hug. 'And are you alright, uncle Joe?' 'I'm better than alright. I'm the biggest and best super chef there is. I might even decide to put little boys on the menu next time.'

He scooped his screeching nephew into his muscular arms and swung him around, giving Jacques the opportunity to help Marie-France into an upright position. 'Now we know everyone's fine it's time you remembered your manners towards the rest of the people here,' Jacques remarked.

The boys diligently worked their way around the crowded café, shaking hands with the men, presenting their cheeks for kisses from the women. Their father put a hand in the small of Marie-France's back. 'Take a break,' he ordered sternly. 'And by that I mean a real sitting on your backside doing nothing break. In fact, why don't you go and sit with Doc. He's looking at you as if all he wants in the world is to have you close beside him. A feeling I know well.'

The last comment was spoken in exactly the same flat, unemotional tone as the rest of his utterance. Many a one would have missed it, but not Marie-France. She was storing up all the precious gems that fell from his lips to add them to the treasury of her wellbeing. Their eyes met for an instant, long enough to rekindle the spark of desire she was nursing in her mind, sending it shooting down into the depths of her sensuality. The object of her longing was already busy, apologising for the tray of water filled cups, taking orders for another round of coffees, agreeing that it was good to see the wee lassie fit and well at last.

'You're brightening up a lot of lives today,' Doc remarked, as she sat down beside him. 'Including mine,' he smiled, taking her left hand, massaging the fingers, one by one. She shuffled her seat closer, to stretch out the arm that had been so hastily released from its sling. He pushed his chair back so her damaged limb could rest comfortably in his lap, continued the massage, working slowly up over her wrist to the elbow, where his touch became lighter because he knew that was where she experienced most pain. 'You have amazingly soothing hands,' she remarked. 'I think you should become a doctor when you grow up.' 'I have no intention of ever growing up, my dear,' he murmured. 'Have you?' 'Tried my best but I only just made it to one metre fifty and that was in my highest heels.' He laughed too, trying to imagine her in high heels instead of sandals, trainers or boots. How pleasant it is to talk nonsense with comfortable friends.

Jacques was doling out the coffees to the group of elderly men. 'Now there's a woman who'll turn heads wherever she goes,' one of them remarked. Léa Jourdan, walking across the square. 'Her mother was like that too.'

Albert Aubry hadn't said much since he'd joined the group, after having spent most of his retiral secluded on the farm. They turned to him with interest. 'Do you remember her then, the mother?'

'Mmm. A few years older than me, so quite a few older than most of you,' he remarked, acknowledging the dubious privilege of seniority. 'She was Henri and Paul Blanchard's sister. Ran off with the village schoolteacher just after the liberation.' 'Never came back to see her family?' 'No. It was as if she'd never existed. Nobody ever spoke about her, as far as I know. Not that I had much to do with the family.' His tone of voice suggested that this was a matter for regret.

'What about the daughter then? What's she doing here, after all this time?' 'Inheritance. Monique, her mother, is dead. Léa, the daughter, is next in line of succession. Along with the Blanchard sisters. Léa lived here, with her grandmother, during the war. Nearly finished the poor woman off, I seem to remember, when Monique and Jean Guerin, he was the school teacher, took her away. But happily for her the eldest son, Paul came back. He'd been a prisoner of war in Germany.' 'Oh yes, of course. He came back and took over the farm again, didn't he? That was when Henri moved out and set up the garage business. Good thing for the village that he did. Good thing his daughters are keeping it going too. Mind you, they had a bit of a rough patch recently, what with someone trying to put them out of business, didn't they?'

The conversation moved away from the distant past as more recent events were re-discussed, each one telling their own bit of the story as though they'd never told it before, each one listening attentively as though they'd never heard it before, each one adding on a little extra descriptive detail to keep the word picture bright.

'Nicolas, my grandson, was there, the night the Lucianis chased that couple off.' Yet another interesting contribution from Albert Aubry. They were glad he'd decided to come out of hibernation. It was always good to have a new angle on the old tales. Sandrine Cros' father remembered he'd heard his daughter discussing a new one with the neighbour, while she was waiting for him to get into the car so she could drive him to *Chez Jacques*. 'Sounds as if there was a bit of a carry-on last night, right here,' he contributed. 'My grandson, Benoit, works for the Lucianis. Apparently there was a bloke bothering Corinne, the quiet girl who works with Adele in *La Beauté*. Seems Joe and Jacques saw him off in no uncertain terms. In fact, look, isn't that her there, talking to the good looker?'

Seconds later Corinne and Léa entered the bar. Undaunted by the crowd, they made their way around the tables wishing everyone bonjour. Eventually they settled, Corinne with Marc and Lucien, Léa with Doc and Marie-France. In danger of succumbing to sleep if she stayed in Doc's lulling company any longer, she called out to Angelo, heading towards the balcony door. He was beside her in a blink.

'How did you know I was talking to you?' she asked. His podgy face creased into a frown. 'You called me.' 'But how did you know I was calling you?' 'Coz you said my name?' 'Exactly. The name that your mum and dad gave you when you were a baby. But they had to teach you that it was your name, and that it belonged to you, didn't they?' 'I s'pose so.'

He understood this was leading somewhere. Knowing Marie-France, it would be somewhere fun, especially now she wasn't broken any more. 'Go and call Galla in for me, would you?' Normally Marie-France whistled for her dog, but she wanted to make her point. Within seconds boy and dog were beside her. 'How did you get her to come?' she asked, as if she really didn't know. 'I called her, like you taught me.' Angelo's eyes, almond shaped and almond coloured, narrowed. He was beginning to get a notion of what this was about. 'I called her name,' he added. Marie-France nodded encouragingly. 'Mmm. And how does she know her name?' 'Coz you taught it to her?' 'Exactly. Can you think of anyone else who needs to learn a name, one that you gave them?' 'Jambon!' he replied in delight, proud of the name he'd given to the pup who was mainly his. He didn't even mind he had to share her with Uncle Eric on the farm. Marie-France had promised she'd train Angelo at the same time as the pup, very useful if he was going to be a shepherd when he grew up. He was going to marry Marie-France too. Probably.

'Come on then. The first lesson of puppy training is about to begin.' She stood up with ease, well rested. 'Go and get the stale bread from the kitchen,' she instructed. 'The hens are going to have to share it with the pups today. Oh, and there should be plenty of cheese rind left from last night. Ask uncle Joe if we can have that too.' 'We're going to teach the pups their names,' Angelo explained excitedly to everyone he passed, whether they were listening or not. 'Can I come?' Jacqui asked. 'Matt's gone to Marseille for the day,' he explained, making it clear that puppy training would take second place if his best friend was around.

'Of course. There are lots of pups with lots of names so we need lots of people. In fact, next time you see Mathieu ask him if he'd come and do some training sessions as well, would you? He was my first boyfriend here, you know. And Galla's. He taught her how to play with a frisbee.' 'I know. After you rescued him from the river. He told me,' Jacqui replied.

CHAPTER 3

Léa Jourdan, the good looker, appeared to be as cool and elegant as she always was but internally she was irritable and jaded. She'd woken earlier than she'd have liked, with a headache, dry mouth, feeling cantankerous. Of course she was hungover, she hadn't reached her sixties without recognising and admitting to those symptoms. Memories of the previous evening swirled around her aching brain, making her thoughts as sour as her dry mouth. She sat up in the hôtel bed, turned the pillows to make them feel fresh and cool, tried to focus on the causes of her petulance.

It was Sunday. Appropriately a biblical quotation ordered the sequence of her themes. *'The last shall be first'*. Her thoughts were directed to Doc's behaviour after he'd walked her back to the hotel. An identifiable source of disappointment. They'd spent a good deal of time together since she'd been in the village and she'd imagined that the lively evening they'd shared might cumulate in them spending what little of the night there was left in bed together. He was agreeable company and she was impressed by the efforts he'd made with his appearance over the past few days. But at the door of the hôtel he'd kissed her companionably, as he had every evening, and she'd been left lonely in an anti-climax after an over stimulating few hours. Yet that, in itself, surely wasn't enough to have thrown her into such a foul mood? She could hardly count herself as rejected, she hadn't even extended an invitation. In any case, she'd fallen asleep immediately, didn't think about him for a blink, couldn't have wanted him that much, could she?

Léa forced herself out of bed but didn't feel much better after she'd showered, dried and restyled her hair. She carefully applied her facial, the everyday not too obvious look designed to make people wonder 'Is she wearing make-up or not?' Now she didn't look so pale and delicate it was time to convince her constitution that she didn't need to feel that way either. Breakfast, that would sort it.

She went down the thinly carpeted stairs, not wanting to risk the potential lurching of the lift. The waitress delivered a pot of coffee, inevitably taking Léa's mind back to the last time she'd been waited on. Last night. *Chez Jacques*. The uniforms the serving boys and indeed Jacques himself and Joe, the chef, had been dressed in, were very classy and surprisingly effective. But weren't they just a bit up themselves, presenting an image like that in a hick, run down country village? Léa knew exactly where her musings were trying to take her but didn't feel strong enough to follow them just at the moment. She concentrated on the small, bitchy details instead, the individuals, rather than the bigger picture, the café rather than the village, the people within the café rather than the people in her life.

Joe, the chef, she analysed first. True he was a good looking young man but she did wonder if he wasn't rather fatuous, striding about the place with his shoulders flung back and his chest expanded as if he thought he was god's gift to every woman. And as for that ridiculous scar, she was almost sure it was artificial, a clever application of make-up, to give him more of the gangster look his infamous grandfather was known for. The film Lucien had compiled of the old man's arrival in the village had given her quite an insight into that whole business. Grandfather Jacques, everyone called him, to distinguish him from his grandson, Jacques Luciani, the owner of *Chez Jacques.* The old man, according to his illegitimate son, his mirror image, had been in love with Léa's mother, although he'd fathered a child, Eric, with her mother's cousin, Solange. Léa took a long draught of coffee to divert that train of thought. Not ready to face that one yet either, she forced herself back to the present day people she was determined to rubbish. She'd finished with Joe, more or less. He might be a big man in stature but he didn't have much about him otherwise. Although he could cook, she had to give him that. The meal was really quite special, but surely wasted here.

The next contender for scrutiny was Jacques. Léa was a journalist, skilled at extracting information, at reading situations and people, at writing about her subjects perceptively. So, what would she say about Jacques, if she had to report on him? Maybe as some sort of vengeance for the fact that it was his alcohol that had made her feel so rough she decided, on the spot. She didn't like him. An average sized man, with average ability, trying to be Mister Big, not difficult in such a small community, especially when he was able to feed off the legacy of his colourful grandfather. The tartness of the orange juice focussed Léa's concentration. She realised she was being pretty small minded herself, basing her opinions on absolutely no information. Why didn't she like the man everyone else seemed to hold in such great esteem? She allowed herself a self-deprecating sneer. Could it be because she didn't know if he liked her? Throughout her young life, Léa had resented her good looks, paranoic about people not seeing through them to the real, intelligent person inside. She matured, established herself in a profession that proved her intellectual worth and began to exploit her appearance, discovering that it was far easier to manipulate those who were attracted to her. But Jacques was like an automaton, extending the same smooth, unemotional courtesy to all his customers. Was that it? Did she resent the fact that he treated her like a customer when she considered she was something more, a local, a native who'd been dragged away from her birthright by her selfish mother.

The coffee and chocolate croissant were sweetening her up. Léa dunked the remains of the *chocolatine*, watched the chocolate melting and dribbling to the bottom of the cup. She'd almost finished breakfast but was reluctant to abandon her character assassinations. Who else was there? That pretty girl from the beauty salon with her crude ex-husband. Léa still wasn't sure if that business with Eveline was for real or simply a charade. Whatever, it was certainly an effective put down.

Doc seemed benignly amused. Marie-France, an interesting character, thrilled. Léa's internal sight scanned the rest of the tables. Marc, a pleasant, efficient estate agent by day, part of an outrageous double act with Lucien by night. Maître Moreau and his partner. Attractive, genuine, qualified professionals. The English couple who owned a *chateau*. People she'd feel at ease with if she had to share their company. Well-off people. Was that what was niggling at her? She'd been included in what appeared to be an attempt at an elitist meal. Whereas her cousins, Amelia and Emilie, hadn't. Embarrassed at how eagerly she'd accepted Joe's invitation, without any thought that they might think she considered herself better than them, she decided she'd go at once and make up for her crass behaviour. Patting her mouth with the napkin, she pushed back her chair, nodded her thanks to the staff and headed back to her room to clean her teeth and make sure she looked as impeccable as she always did. Her normal aplomb re-established, she was ready to face the world.

The village was busier than she'd expected. She hadn't realised there was a market trading by eight thirty in the morning. Blanchards' garage was open, already doing business. Léa stood waiting for Amelia to finish serving a customer before she greeted her.

'I can see you're busy Amelia, but I wonder if you've got time for a quick word?' The older Blanchard's look seemed to suggest that she was expecting such an approach. She beckoned Léa into the office, confirming the impression when she called out, 'Emilie, Léa's here!' as if they had been anticipating her arrival. The younger sister came through into the shop from the living quarters, wearing an apron rather than the nylon overall that usually protected her clothes when she was on the garage forecourt.

'Bonjour Léa.' She kissed her on either cheek, assumed the same pose as her sister, arms folded, waiting. 'I wanted to catch you first thing,' Léa blurted out, realising as she spoke that her cousins had probably been up and working for hours. 'I didn't realise you opened the garage on a Sunday,' she added by way of explanation.

'Our busiest day in the winter because of the market. But only in the morning,' Emilie responded. 'Oh! Well, there we are. Typical tourist eh? Lazing about while other people are working for a living.'

Emilie gave a rather weak smile. Amelia didn't. 'And, of course, us non-working, touristy people also tend to live it up at night. As I did. Last night. In fact, I had a drop too much and got a bit carried away with the spirit of the event.' 'We know,' Amelia said dryly. 'Doc told us,' Emilie added.

'Doc? Oh, I didn't expect him to be up so early either.' She couldn't interpret the warning, silencing look that Amelia flashed at her sister.

In the early hours of that morning Amelia had been dozing but woke immediately to the sound of the key turning in the lock of the street door. Identifying the footsteps coming up the stairs she waited until she felt, rather than heard, the figure hovering outside her bedroom. She slipped out of bed and pulled a coarse woollen dressing gown over the flannel pyjamas she wore to keep out the wintry chill. The only heating was the wood fuelled *cuisiniere* in the kitchen and a small fire they lit in the salon on the rare occasions when they sat and relaxed. She opened the door. She and Doc exchanged smiles. With a movement of her head she suggested they go downstairs to the remnants of the warmth in the kitchen. He nodded his agreement, raising his eyebrows in a question, glancing at Emilie's door. Amelia's head bobbed, she moved in that direction. Scraping with her nail on the varnished wood she whispered, 'Doc's here. Join us if you want, Em.' A short while later the three of them were sitting around the kitchen table, nursing a bowl of hot chocolate, made even more warming by a generous dash of cherry flavoured *eau de vie*.

'Well?' Amelia asked, when they were all settled. Doc regaled them with every detail of the evening, drink by drink, taste by taste, word by word. The two women were spellbound, murmuring in appreciation, sighing in amazement, smiling with affection. They pattered their fingers together when the raconteur described Marie-France and Galla's entry onto the balcony, frowned and tutted when he reported the Parisian's crude comment about 'that bitch with her bitch,' gave a little cheer at Corinne's dog handling skills, imagining the transformed figure Doc described in Eveline's stylish dress. Their eyes lifted skywards when he told them about Lucien's antics, they nodded approvingly at Jacques' controlling intervention. Three pairs of eyes danced together next, following Marie-France, liberated by the lack of conventional presentation, moving from table to table, taking tasters from other people's plates, popping delicacies into other people's mouths. It was marvellous to hear she was behaving confidently and enjoying herself without inhibition. But Amelia and Emilie did agree that they were glad they'd taken Joe at his word when he'd explained that the reason he hadn't given them an invitation was because he really didn't think it would be their thing!

'The evening culminated in a very interesting fashion,' Doc continued, smiling his acceptance to another drop of eau de vie. 'Marie-France warned me beforehand that Joe was going to put on a show of taking Corinne off to bed, the final put down for the unpleasant ex she wants rid of once and for all. But when it came to the moment it was Eveline who led her from the room. I must say it didn't seem at all like an act, confirmed when they didn't come back down after the ex-husband had left. Jacques sent Jacqui off to stay with Mathieu too, whereas I had the notion he was going to be acting as a sort of chaperone had it been Joe she'd gone up with. So.....'

The two women were quiet for a while, mulling over this latest turn of events. Whilst they made every effort not to be judgemental, it was sometimes difficult to adjust their thinking to the unorthodox way life was conducted at *Chez Jacques*. After a moment, during which Doc sipped serenely at his chocolate, the sisters' eyes met, they gave an almost imperceptible nod, then smiled. Amelia expressed their shared opinion. 'Corinne and Eveline? And why not? Two very nice people.'

'One person you haven't mentioned, dear friend, is the lady you escorted to this extravagant event. Our cousin Léa.'

'Ah, yes, Léa.' Doc flushed, smiled bashfully, shifted in his seat, remembering Léa's lingering look. 'Not quite sure what she made of the evening but she fitted in perfectly, as you can imagine.'

Amellia misinterpreted Doc's embarrassment, thought he was trying to defend Léa, maybe she'd been a bit supercilious, a big city woman in a backwater. 'Aunt Solange warned us, didn't she Emilie, that she didn't know what Léa was like and that perhaps we should be cautious about taking her too much to heart too soon. Not that she's shown any desire to be taken to anyone's heart here, with the possible exception of you Doc, her one demonstration of good taste. In fact, she's just floated about the place, flaunting her indisputable good looks and behaving like Lady Muck looking down on us poor peasants.'

The colour of Amelia's cheeks heightened as she spoke. Doc's face transformed into a smile, his eyes almost disappeared. 'Amelia!' he gasped, when she paused to take breath. 'I've never seen you cross before. You really are a splendid looking woman, you know.' She glared at him defensively. The warmth of his look started its work, thawing her frigid features, his words completed the job. 'I said goodnight to Léa outside the hotel. I, too, have good taste you know.' 'Well come along then,' Amelia responded gruffly. 'Let's get those clothes off you and hung back up in the *armoire* where they belong. Goodnight Emilie.' She kissed her sister tenderly on the top of her tousled head. 'Goodnight Emilie.' Doc repeated the words and the action. 'And I thought you were popping in during the day for extra showers because of a new lady in your life,' she murmured. 'You know I have an eye for the youngsters,' he responded, with a cheeky grin, chucking her under the chin.

'Funny to think of my older, nearly fifty year old sister as a youngster,' Emilie pondered. This thought was followed by a fleeting wonder about the gossip that re-emerged from time to time about Doc and Marie-France, an idea pushed out of place by the amusing notion that maybe her own name might be linked with Doc as well as Amelia's. Finally, with a sigh of contentment, her romantic ramblings settled on Corinne. Corinne and Eveline. It would be great if those two gave each other some happiness, even if it was just over one night. And she knew Amelia would be cheerful tomorrow too. She always was when she yielded to Doc's charms. Emilie decided to complete her night's sleep on the sofa in the salon.

There was nothing yielding about Amelia's expression as she stood squarely by the till with Emilie, both of them facing a discomforted, floundering Léa. It had just dawned on her that Doc might not have been up early. He'd maybe left her to come to the garage. Did Amelia think Lea had been after her man? Her stomach churned and her chest tightened at the unemotional tone and stony face. But she was still sure she could recover the situation.

'Amelia, Emilie, I'm so sorry you weren't there last night and that we haven't had time to get to know each other. Perhaps I could take you to lunch at the hôtel and we can start again.' She poured all her persuasive charm into this invitation. To no avail.

'No thank you, Léa. We won't eat with you at the hotel. Emilie has already started preparing our Sunday meal. It's the one time in the week when we sit down together and relax, after drinking a couple of aperitifs and catching up with the village news at *Chez Jacques*.'

'But if you would like to join *us* for lunch, here, it might be better to, as you say, start again, in private.' Emilie spoke firmly, without apology. In her own way she was every bit as assertive as her sister, who did sometimes dig herself into holes she struggled to get out of.

Léa relaxed, her smile became less tense. All was not lost. 'That would be lovely Emilie dear. Is there anything I can contribute?' 'If you'd like to provide dessert, one of Georges' patisseries, that would be a treat,' the younger Blanchard replied, without hesitation.

'Sorry I'm late!' Léa recognised Guillaume, one of the waiters from *Chez Jacques.* 'I'm impressed you're here at all,' Amelia replied, shaking her part time employee firmly by the hand. 'I thought you'd be needing a lie-in after last night.' Guillaume grinned. 'Got a clearer head than I usually have on a Sunday morning. Jacques says that he pays us to work. If we want to drink *we* have to pay him.'

Amelia nodded approvingly, pleased at how confidently the young lad had started relating to the adults in his world.

'Bonjour Madame Jourdan.' His greeting to Léa was equally self-assured. 'It was a good night last night, wasn't it?' 'Certainly was,' she replied, dredging around in her still sludgy brain for something more to say that didn't sound condescending. Guillaume's next utterance did nothing to order her ideas. 'It's great having the Lucianis around. My pal works at the hôtel, says Corinne's ex left at the crack of dawn, couldn't wait to get out of the village. Eveline and ......' 'Just as Jacques doesn't pay you to drink, I don't pay you to gossip,' Amelia interrupted sternly, glancing out of the window at the two cars waiting for service. 'Come along, we have work to do. I'll see you later, *Chez Jacques,* Léa.' It seemed her morning had been planned for her.

Amelia bustled out with Guillaume. Emilie edged her way towards the door marked *priveé* that led into the kitchen. 'Oh well, nothing for it but to face the rest of the world,' Léa told herself, stepping out of the garage office, setting her sights for Duponts' Boulangerie.

CHAPTER 4

'But if you call them one at a time they don't have to know their own name.'

Jacqui had just put the last of seven out of the eight energetic puppies in their containment pen. They'd all had a good running about play session and Marie-France declared it was time they started work, individually.

'True, but at the beginning they have to succeed, to learn they'll be rewarded so they'll want to do it again. They'll all get a go, one at a time, until they begin to associate the words and the name with the reward. So, Jacqui, you keep Jambon with you, Angelo, you go a few paces away, get down to her level, and call her. But this is work, so you must think out what you're going to say, stay calm and remember to be consistent, use the same command and gestures every time.'

Seven year old Angelo assumed his serious look and considered what he'd been told. 'Like when I call Galla?' 'Yes, but Galla's already trained, don't forget.' The dog in question was watching, listening, pricking up her ears, but not too enthusiastically. She had a notion this wasn't going to be interesting. Her people seemed to be talking about her, not to her. She stayed alert though, just in case she was called on to do something fun. Like herding those wing flapping geese around the garden, for example.

'You and Jambon need to find your own style,' Marie-France explained. Galla dumped her chin onto one of her front paws. She was right, this wasn't about her. 'Now, get down to the pup's level, make a little noise or a small movement to attract her attention. As soon as she looks at you call, 'Jambon, come!' Then, Jacqui, you let her go.'

'Right!' Angelo knelt down on the ground. His fastidious older brother squatted on his heels.

'Wait a minute!' Marie-France spoke again. 'How are you going to reward her?' 'With a treat!' Angelo's response was immediate and confident, his pockets stuffed full of cheese rind. 'Okay, but you can't give her a treat every time she does what you've taught her to do. You need to have a way of letting her know she's done the right thing. Chose a short word, any word, it doesn't have to mean anything but it's a very important word because it's going to be special between you and Jambon so whatever she learns you can tell her she's done it right.' 'Like Good Girl?' Angelo said dubiously. That seemed too obvious. And not special enough. Everyone said that to dogs. Except Marie-France.

'You say something like *moanian* to Galla, don't you?' Marie-France had been born and brought up on the Isle of Skye. She grinned. 'Exactly! *Mo nighean.* Gaelic for 'my girl'. Something not many other people will use here.'

Angelo's pudgy face creased into a frown. Jacqui, getting bored, stood up, wondering what he might look up on his phone. 'Got it!' the would be dog trainer declared. 'Aye!'

At first Marie-France thought he was saying garlic (*ail*) but the intonation was a wee bit skewed. She realised it was the Scottish affirmative. 'Like your dad says,' Angelo explained. 'I like your dad,' he added. 'So do I,' she smiled. 'I like my dad too,' the little boy remarked, not wanting to sound partisan. 'So do I.' The smile broadened. 'And that's a great word, Ange. So let's give it a go. Jacqui, get the girl in position. Call her name Ange, just once. And stay close, so she can't fail. When she gets to you say your magic word and then give her the treat. Ready?'

'Jambon, come!' The whole sequence was carried out faultlessly. 'Can we do it again?' 'No, not yet. We don't want to overdo it and risk a failure after such a brilliant success.'

Jacques had been standing on the balcony, watching and listening. He chose the natural break to speak. 'Marie-France, come!'

At the sound of his voice she almost did! She took in a deep gasp of air, her whole body tensed, her face turned crimson.

Marie-France had been sleeping in Jacques' bed for the past week or so, but the previous night was the first time they'd been in it together. And what a night it had been, a culmination of months of anticipation.

Jacqui smirked, noticing her reaction to his dad's words. He'd thought at the time that maybe he'd been sent to spend the night with his best pal, Mathieu, because of something going on between uncle Joe and Corinne. This morning he'd decided it was because of his mum and Corinne. But now, he wondered. Jacqui, as an eleven year old boy, was more worldly wise than many grown men. He knew about the sounds people made in bed. He'd tried not to hear his mum and Arlette, her first girlfriend, grunting and giggling and moaning, when they'd been living together in that horrible cramped flat. It had been reported to him that Marie-France and his uncle Joe had made so much noise down in the cellar that his dad had had to turn up the music. That didn't surprise him. Uncle Joe and Marie-France were always noisy when they were together, whatever they were doing. They shouted at each other on the forecourt, laughed behind the bar, giggled in the kitchen. Always carrying on like a couple of rowdy kids. He couldn't quite imagine his calm, controlled dad making a racket though, whatever he was doing. But who knows. Anyway, it didn't matter, as long as he was happy. And the way he was crinkling his eyes down at Marie-France and she was simpering up at him it certainly looked as though they'd made each other happy. He thought about sending a text to Mathieu, to confirm that what they'd been betting on forever had finally happened, immediately changed his mind. He'd been thinking about family, what it really meant, since his great-grandfather's visit and his new uncle Eric's acceptance and decided that some family things should be kept private. If his dad had finally got round to taking Marie-France to bed, that was nobody's business but their own.

Seven year old Angelo knew he was missing something but was too immersed in his role as dog trainer to try and work out what was. 'Dad, if Marie-France comes when you call her, you'll have to give her a reward, you know.' 'Oh, don't you worry about that, son. She knows she'll always get a treat from me.' He patted the front pocket of his jeans, where he kept Galla's biscuits. Marie-France's breath released with a shudder. Jacqui turned away to disguise his embarrassment at the blatancy of the gesture. Angelo was unperturbed. 'That's Galla's special sign, dad. You can't use that.' 'Oh yes, so it is. And she's more obedient than her mistress. Aren't you Galla?'

At the sound of her name, a definite, directed-at-her sound, the well-conditioned border collie looked up. Jacques repeated the pocket patting, accompanying it with a tongue against teeth click that came out as 'tut-tut'. She tripped lightly up the broad wooden steps and sat neatly at his feet, waiting for the reward she knew she'd receive.

Marie-France noted that her dog hadn't looked to her to receive permission to go to Jacques, as she always used to do. 'But what can I expect? Since the accident my girl's been looked after by all and sundry. It's time we got back to work, both of us. For a start, I'll phone Eric, see if he can come down in his van tomorrow to collect some of the geese. That should be fun, trying to get them in that little space. And it's time I got myself some wheels and became independent.'

Her stomach lurched. She acknowledged to herself for the first time that she was frightened at the thought of driving again. She'd lost her nerve! She'd travelled the route, up and down, to and from Eric Roumignac's farm, a few times since the crash but someone else, usually Joe, had been driving, quite reasonably as her injuries, especially the multiple fractures in her arm, needed time to recover. But now she was just about recovered, physically, it was time she got her mind sorted out too, time she took control of her day to day life again.

'Although perhaps I'll leave Jacques in control of my sex life, just for the time being.' She gave herself a miniscule hug, although it was a wave of warmth rather than cold that was making her shiver, risked a glance up towards him, still standing on the balcony, watching her with those penetrating eyes that she was beginning to believe really could read her soul.

'Didn't I hear you say something about not overdoing it?' he asked. 'Look, even the pups are flagging.' The bundle of podgy creatures in the pen were piled up on top of each other in various stages of twitchy sleepiness. Jambon, the student, was lying with both front legs stretched out in front of her, as if reaching for the future, flying through a goose studded sky, struggling to keep her eyes open in case she missed a second of her promise-filled life.

'You're right. Ange, pop your girl in with the others and top up the water bowls. We'll give them a break and give Jazzy her first formal lesson later. In the meantime, I'd better see if *Chez Jacques* is managing to function without me.'

Doc, a practised diagnostician, prescribed the coffee cognac that settled Léa's residual physical symptoms. Her mental confusion was rather more resistant and had, in fact, been aggravated.

'Madame Jourdan. May I present myself. Albert Aubry. I knew your mother and having spent the past fifty odd years not giving her a moment's thought find myself curious as to how her life turned out, after she left here.' 'Oh! Well, Monsieur Aubry. She died when she was in her forties. In London.'

Léa didn't want to think about, never mind talk about, her mother, the woman she'd always resented for taking her away from what she thought of as her real life. She'd imagined she would rediscover the childhood self that had been left in Labeille but now she was here, her mother was presenting herself at every turn. And not as the wicked witch her daughter had construed her to be.

'Ah, so she got as far as London, did she? What a woman she was. Did she stick with the school teacher, Jean, Jean Guerin? Brave man that. Kept me out of the war, him and Jacques Luciani. Jean, Jacques and Monique. And Solange of course. Four courageous people. And yet here, after the liberation, all they were remembered for was scandal.'

Albert had been dusting off his memories of those times, since he'd been jolted back to them by Grandfather Jacques' reappearance in the village he'd frequented during the war.

'My mother didn't stay with Jean. We left him in France when we went off to England,' Léa replied, not really wanting to reconsider the school teacher she'd disliked so much but needing to slow down the old man's reminiscences to give her brain time to absorb them.

'Doesn't surprise me. Too much woman for any man, I should think. All us youngsters fancied her like crazy. She was the nearest thing we had to a home grown pinup.' Albert chuckled at the thought of the fusty octogenarian he'd become once being a randy lad, all those decades ago, then realised that perhaps a daughter wouldn't want to hear such things in relation to her mother. 'She did the right thing, Monique, getting away from here, for herself and for you. Would have been a lot easier for her to have left you here, looking back on it. Brave, selfless woman.' Even more unsettling for Léa. She was used to thinking of her mother as the selfish seductress. 'Brave' and 'selfless' contradicted her long held beliefs. She drew breath to argue the case of the seven year old country girl dragged away from the security of the only home she'd known. But Albert Aubry was in full, reminiscing flow.

'It was hard on your grandmother at first, of course, but I'll bet she was grateful you'd gone later on, when Paul came back. He was a difficult young man even before he was taken prisoner by the boche but when he came back his mother had her work cut out looking after him. He was nothing but a big, spoilt boy. She was happy though, having her first born, her favourite, all to herself. Just as well Henri had the brains and the means to get out and make his own way. No way those two could have existed under the same roof.'

Léa blinked. Throughout her life she'd carried the vision of her beloved, devoted grandmother standing in the yard, hands clutched to her breast, leaning on Henri's arm, looking down the track, watching and waiting for her, little Léa, to come skipping back home. Just as well she hadn't, if her kindly Uncle Henri's place had been taken by cossetted, demanding Uncle Paul.

'Good to have some new blood in the village, all the same.' Albert was looking over at Jacques and Joe, standing together behind the bar. 'When Jacques first arrived lots of people thought he'd come with his big city ways to lord it over us poor, ignorant peasants. Couldn't be further from the truth. So far him and that brother of his have given a lot more to the village than they've received from us.'

Léa struggled to contain a wave of nausea, thinking how strange it is that an excess of food and drink makes your system crave more. But it was her brain rather than her body that was provoking her, making her remember the way she'd belittled the Lucianis to herself that morning. Even worse, she was forced to acknowledge that she'd been doing exactly what this chatty old man had described his fellow villagers as thinking.

'Anyway, I see my daughter-in-law's arrived to rescue you from the garrulous old man I've become. Better go, otherwise people will think I'm trying to seduce you!' He roared with laughter at the preposterous notion and, after squeezing Léa's hand, chuckled his way through the crowded bar, shaking hands and patting people on the shoulder as he passed. Wouldn't any man be happy after spending a few moments in the company of such an attractive wench?

The rest of Léa's aperitif session passed without incident. *Chez Jacques* bustled as the locals wandered in. The meal the previous evening was the major topic of conversation. Even though so few of them had been there everyone was keen to congratulate Joe on his culinary success. They all praised Jacques too, although the way his hand was clasped and the knowing way some of them murmured, 'Another job well done, Jacques, I hear,' it seemed he was being acclaimed for something more than efficiently hosting the event. He accepted the remarks gravely, his expression never changing as he shook hands, returned kisses, moved smoothly around his domain. 'A thoroughly professional man,' Léa chided herself. 'Treats everyone exactly the same, even a smallminded incomer like me.'

The Blanchard sisters nodded over to her once they'd finished the two *kirs* they allowed themselves before they went home to eat. She made her farewells, determinedly interpreting the renewed churning in her stomach as hunger, rather than nerves.

CHAPTER 5

The kitchen was simple but cosy. Léa handed over the *tarte aux pommes* she'd selected in the boulangerie. Emilie took her coat, indicating which seat she should take. The guest was rooted to the spot, physically transported back to her childhood for the first time since she'd been in the village, hit with a wave of nostalgia so strong it almost made her cry. At first, being a practical woman, she thought it was another bout of post, over-indulgence nausea.

'Are you alright Léa?' Amelia asked brusquely. 'Oh! Yes! It's just. What is that marvellous aroma?' Emilie smiled. 'Grandmère Blanchard's special recipe for lamb ragout. Meat courtesy of cousin Eric. It might not be as fancy as Joe's food but as a rib sticker it takes some beating.' 'I remember it,' Léa gasped, sitting down heavily in the chair. 'It would simmer on the stove for hours, filling the kitchen with such an amazing smell. I used to pick the herbs to go in it. But I can't remember what they were.' 'Rosemary, thyme, oregano. They still grow around the cottage, although they're a bit woody now. No wonder you're nostalgic about the place if your memories are so strong,' Emilie remarked compassionately.

'Shall we get the business out of the way before we eat?' Amelia suggested. 'So we don't spoil our appetites by mixing financial matters with food.'

Emilie poured them each another *kir* and they sat. Amelia wasted no time on formalities. 'Now, Léa. Are you in a hurry for Uncle Paul's place to go on the market?' 'No, Amelia, not at all.' 'You don't need the money from the sale?'

Amelia was nothing if not direct. Léa was quite comfortable with the straightforward approach, even though she felt like a youngster again, having a first meeting with the bank manager, inquiring about her financial situation before sanctioning the mortgage she'd asked for.

'No, I don't need the money. I have a house in England and a *pied de terre* in Paris, both paid for. And I have enough income from my pensions to maintain my lifestyle. In any case, from what Marc said, the house could take a long time to sell, especially as there's so much work to be done on it.'

Amelia nodded, like a teacher pleased that a recalcitrant pupil has managed to grasp at least some of the basics. 'You'll be relieved to know that there are no outstanding debts to be paid if we decide to accept the inheritance.' 'Amelia kept Uncle Paul's books,' Emilie explained. Léa hadn't considered there might be costs involved. She'd always employed an accountant to deal with her financial affairs. 'And there's enough money in his account to pay the inheritance tax. The funeral was paid for by an insurance.' Uncle Paul didn't need to employ an accountant. He had astute Amelia.

'So, if we don't immediately sell up the only costs we'll incur are the taxes, which are minimal, especially while the property is undeveloped and uninhabited. There are, of course, Maître Moreau's fees. I am the other executor of the will and would be prepared to forgo mine if we can come to an amical agreement. Emilie and I have discussed the matter and have decided that our preferred course of action, at the moment, would be to hang on to the place, as long as you're prepared to take on your responsibility for your share of the upkeep. I can, of course, supply you with all the appropriate figures and paperwork.'

Léa almost giggled. How ridiculous that she'd thought, even for a second, that she was dealing with unsophisticated country folk. Amelia Blanchard, businesswoman, could no doubt buy and sell her without being distracted from filling a car up with fuel.

'Amelia, I am a journalist. In my own field I am competent. In legal and administrative matters such as this I know nothing. Usually I would let a lawyer deal with everything and just sign when and where I was told. On this occasion it seems I am blessed to have you as part of the process. I'm more than happy to do anything you wish to keep the property in the family for a while. From a totally selfish point of view, I'd like to indulge my nostalgia for a little longer.'

Amelia nodded, rather less curtly. Emilie visualised Doc, wondering if Léa was being viewed as a rival in love. 'Good. In that case, let's complete the legal side of the matter with Maître Moreau and put a hold on the property sale for the time being. Quite frankly, our major consideration at the moment is Eric. We're worried he's feeling pressured to make decisions about land before he's ready. His mother took care of all the administrative side of his affairs but, like Eric himself, and his grandparents before him, never thought about developing the farm, only concerning themselves with maintaining its self-sufficiency. And now Eric has not only lost his mother he's also become involved with Marie-France and the Lucianis. We would very much like to give him time to figure out the land use at his own pace, informally, before he commits to anything legally binding. I might be an astute businesswoman, Léa, but, up until your arrival, Eric has been our closest relative and family is very important.'

Amelia's antagonism evaporated with Léa's nod of agreement. Emilie's sincerity was palpable when she said. 'And you're family too Léa, so let's drink a toast to starting again and then we can get on with dinner.'

As Emilie poured them each a glass of sweet white wine – 'To go with the *entrée*,' she explained - Léa reflected that she'd never been part of a real family at all, not since her mother had taken her away from it. She was determined to make the most of this opportunity, this starting again, as Emilie described it.

The starter was served. Léa unconsciously reverted to her big city mentality. '*Foie* gras! They must be trying to impress me!' Amelia's comment soon put her back in her place. 'We're wondering if this batch is going to be the last,' the older Blanchard sister remarked. 'Aunt Solange did the *gavage,* and although Eric still has plenty of geese I don't see him having either the time or the inclination to fatten any of them up for their livers.'

Foie gras. Not a luxury at all. Ordinary, home produced country food. Léa mentally rebuked herself.

'From what Doc said, it sounds as if last night went well.' Emilie's attempt at casual conversation gave Léa the opportunity to clear up any residual doubt in Amelia's mind about herself and Doc.'

'Yes, indeed. Interesting food and interesting company. Marie-France shared the table with Doc and myself. She's an unusual character, isn't she?' Emilie hoped her sister was reassured. 'She is unusual. But at the moment she's a very subdued version of her true self. It will be good for Eric, for all of us, when she's really back to fighting fitness.'

This led on to an explanation about Marie-France's partnership with Eric, her accident, Eric's heroic part in her survival. As Amelia told the tale it struck Emilie that perhaps her older sister had inherited more of their father's story telling ability than she usually allowed the world to see, hiding it behind her bluff, no-nonsense façade. As if she'd been reading her cousin's thoughts, Léa said, 'Tell me about your father, my Uncle Henri. I have a very clear image of him in my mind but of course I was only a child and he was a young man when I last saw him. I always think of him as a busy person, always on the go.'

She didn't elucidate. The image of the young man kneeling down beside his stricken mother as she, little Léa, was dragged away, was not the sort of sour atmosphere she wanted to introduce.

'He was always busy, a very hardworking man. He built this business up from scratch, with very little help from anyone else. He used to love telling stories though, about his young days during the war, especially about Grandfather Jacques. But he never even mentioned Monique, his sister, or you, his niece. Neither did grandmère Blanchard or Uncle Paul, although in his case that's not surprising. He was a tetchy man at the best of times and really only interested in himself. His mother was an absolute saint, the way she put up with him, but she seemed delighted to have it to do. I don't know how many times she told us how good God had been to keep him safe throughout the war and then to send him back to her so she could look after him. Of course, when you're kids growing up you don't really question how things are but as we got older we did sometimes feel a bit sorry for Dad the way he was side-lined. Actually, we spent more time at the Roumignac's with Eric and his maman and papa than we did at Uncle Paul's.

Léa frowned. 'But I thought Jacques Luciani was Eric's father and I got the impression that his mother had stayed single.'

'Oh, of course, you don't know. That's another thing that we always took for granted as kids. Eric's grandparents brought him up and they were always his maman and papa as far as we, and him were concerned. He was a young man before Aunt Solange came back from Toulouse and became part of his life. And he didn't know about Grandfather Jacques being his father until a very short time ago. Poor Eric. His life has been really shaken about in the past few weeks, what with one thing and another.'

There was a pause in the conversation when the main course was served. Léa was once again transported back into the farmhouse kitchen by the taste of the lamb ragout. As they were mopping up the last of the juices with bread Emilie returned to the subject of family.

'We cleared out a load of stuff from the *grenier* after Uncle Paul died. We didn't bother looking at it very closely but the other day Amelia remembered a box of photos. We had a quick look through it to see if there was anything in it that might interest you. And, in fact, there's an album with your name, Jourdan, on its cover.'

Jourdan. Léa's mother was a photographer. A widely acclaimed photographer. Léa had a notion that her father was too. In Marseille, before the war. She didn't know whether to be excited or scared at what this album might reveal but she would have to wait a little longer to find out.

'Goats' cheese, of course. We buy it from Paulette Aubry on the market but we sort of pretend it's from Eric because he does have a couple of milking goats. That's another job he's not used to doing himself. Aunt Solange said they only really kept the goats for sentimental reasons, because her parents always had them. Apparently Eric was weaned on to goats' milk when he was a tiny baby so Aunt Sol could go to Toulouse.'

Emilie chatted away as she cleared the dinner plates and brought out the cheese, two rounds, one a soft *cendré,* the outer cinder-coloured crust making it look dirty, the other a harder *tomme.* Léa picked up on the name of the cheese seller.

'I met a Monsieur Aubry this morning. Albert, I think he said his name was. He said he remembered my mother.'

'Paulette's father-in-law's father,' Amelia confirmed. 'Funny, he's not been around the village much for years. He's never had much to do with us at all, even when dad was alive, apart from using the garage. But since Grandfather Jacques' visit he seems to be popping down all the time.'

'I got the idea he was the same age as your father?' 'Yes, he was. They went to school together, yet after the war it seems they never socialised. Another one of the many complicated stories we were never told about, although we have a notion it was all something to do with old man Jacques Luciani. Not that he was old then, of course. We learnt for the first time during his visit that Albert Aubry played a part in one of dad's favourite stories, but he never mentioned him by name. There seemed to be lots of fallings in and out at that time. I bet half the people can't even remember what they were about now. But that's village life for you. Nothing ever seems to get totally lost in time, just totally confused.'

During dessert Amelia once again revealed her budding story telling ability by recounting an un-melodramatic but amusing version of the tale Georges, the boulangère, had passed on to Joe about his grandfather's encounter with Jacques Luciani during the occupation. Not for the first time it occurred to Léa how strong the old man's presence had remained in the village, despite his physical absence of six decades.

'Shall we take coffee through to the salon?' Emilie suggested. 'Then we could look at the photograph album we found. I'm quite excited to see the photos now, knowing they might be relevant to you, Léa.'

Léa's hands were shaking when she picked the album up from the low walnut table. As a journalist she'd often seen her own name in print, but as she stared at the formal, gilt lettered cover, she realised that the words in some way represented her own beginnings.

Jourdan and son. Photographers. Portraits, Weddings, Christenings by appointment. 41 Place de La Republique, Marseille.

She psyched herself up to look inside the padded book, painfully conscious that it might contain emotionally disturbing images. After a sip of coffee and a deep breath she opened the book, gently lifting the tissue paper page away from the first photograph. It was indeed the start of a new life that led to hers. A wedding photo.

'That must be your mother, Léa. The likeness is quite extraordinary, even though she is so young. What a beautiful girl she was, and so stylish. Presumably that's your father. A handsome man too. What a striking couple.'

Léa barely heard Emilie's chatter as she stared at her parents, the first time she'd seen them together. Her mother's shiningly happy eyes stared back. They seemed to be saying. 'I'm your mother, Léa. Won't you give me another chance?'

The photograph was neatly dated, October 1937. Léa did a quick calculation. Monique Blanchard was nineteen years old when she married Raphael Jourdan, a man considerably older than herself. He was stiff and formal, in a patriarchal pose, facing the camera, no doubt in the hands of his own father. Monique's ebullient personality wasn't supressed by the stylish, calf length clinging skirt or the tight waisted jacket hugging her slender waist. Or the sweeping-brimmed hat, that rather than concealing her lively face, emphasised the tilt of her head and the playfulness in her glance.

'Nineteen thirty seven! Three years before the occupation.

When were you born, Léa?' 'Nineteen thirty eight,' she replied absently, trying and failing to see any semblance of familiarity in her father.' 'Really! That makes you, what, sixty seven? It's hard to believe you're that age.'

'The same age as Doc,' Amelia remarked, rather curtly. Emilie took a sip of coffee to hide the smile playing over her face as she remembered Doc's remark about having an eye for younger women. Like Amelia.

Something about the tone of Amelia's comment drew Léa's attention away from the perusal of her parents. 'Yes. The same age as Doc,' she echoed. 'In fact, he says we were at school together, here, for a short while, though neither of us can remember the other.'

She returned her attention to the photographs. There were a couple more pages of stylised wedding photos but Léa didn't know any of the people in them. There was no one from her mother's side there, as far as she could tell, probably quite reasonable considering the distance they'd have had to travel. Then she remembered how piously Catholic her grandmother had been. This was clearly a civil wedding. Grandmère Blanchard's principles would have stopped her from attending even her own daughter's strictly non-religious marriage ceremony.

She turned another page, carefully smoothing down the protective film of tissue as she did so. The presentation, the whole atmosphere of the book changed, the pictures themselves became far more informal. A few of them were loose, removed from their designated spaces.

Emilie, sitting back on the sofa beside Léa now she'd finished her coffee, leant forward again with renewed interest. 'Look! That's dad with uncle Paul. I recognise them from the photo that was always beside grandmère's bed. And that must be your mother with them in this one, Léa! Look, there's a space where a photo has been taken out, presumably the one of dad and Uncle Paul that was on display. The one with the three of them must have been out on display at one time too because it's not stuck in.

How sad for grandmère, to have had to hide one of her children away like that.'

Amelia came to sit on Léa's other side, the three of them crushed up together like books on a library shelf. 'They are all so young, aren't they? Look, there's grandmère beside your mother, Léa - I suppose we should think of her as Aunt Monique - with a baby in her arms. That must be you. I wonder how often your parents came to the farm? It must have been a very different world from the sophisticated one they lived in in Marseille. Do you know how they met?'

Léa shrugged her shoulders. She'd never had any conversations with her mother about her young life. In fact, she was beginning to wonder if she'd ever had any meaningful conversations with her vilified mother at all.

'And look at this one. Who do you think dad's with? It's hard to make out if it's another boy or a girl.' Amelia peered closely, taking the album from Léa, holding it close to her face.

'It's taken at Roumignac's farm. I recognise the millstone. That must be Aunt Solange! She certainly wasn't a looker like her cousin, was she? How strange that a handsome man like Grandfather Jacques should fall for her and not for your mother, Léa. Although I presume she was a married woman when they met, of course.'

Léa remembered Eric's calm voice when they were in the woods together, telling her what his mother had told him about those times. *'It wasn't my mother that Jacques Luciani was in love with Léa, it was yours,'* he'd said. He'd explained about Jacques and Monique's cancelled tryst and, in the same completely unemotional way, how his mother had asked Jacques to rid her of the potential inhibition of her virginity. That was how he'd been conceived. *'But mother was sure that Jacques always carried a flame for her cousin, Monique. She'd even presumed that they were having an affair during the war in Marseille, which was why she was so shocked when Monique and Jean Guerin went off to Paris together, taking you with them.'*

And why mother was so shocked when she thought Jean had

abandoned Solange, knowing she was carrying his child, Léa had thought at the time. Now, as then, she said nothing. Some secrets were entitled to stay buried.

Emilie was chattering again. 'You know, I've never thought much about photography but presumably each individual does have their own style. These photos are quite different from the earlier ones, aren't they? And they can't have been taken by your father because he's in some of them. Look, there he is, in a fancy looking room, with baby Léa standing on his knee. He still looks very stiff and posed himself but the whole atmosphere is somehow different. Did your mother take photos as well, Léa?'

Monique Jourdan's photography had been the passport that had taken them from France to England after the war, the means by which they'd lived once they settled there. With a stab of shame Léa admitted to herself that she couldn't recognise her mother's work. She'd never looked at it. Peter Knights' career in journalism had been launched by his collaboration with the Frenchwoman - he provided the words to her graphic pictures of the Battle of Marseille. He'd presented eighteen year old Léa with a cardboard box, after her mother's untimely death. She'd driven her motor bike into the back of a London bus. 'I've kept a copy of every piece of work your mother produced,' he'd explained kindly. 'Your mother was her work so I hope this helps you to remember her at her very best.'

The surly daughter took the box, sealed it, wrote *'ma mère'* on the top. She carried it around with her, un-examined, putting it under the bed every time she moved home, as if it was an urn of ashes. Léa felt no affection for the life it contained.

'Look, lots of snap shots at Blanchards' farm.' Emilie had lifted the album off Léa's lap. She seemed to have retreated into her own world and lost interest in it, but the sisters were eagerly poring over the pictures of places and people that they knew.

'These are lovely, aren't they? They're so full of life. There's dad, as a kid, pulling faces behind uncle Paul's back. And here's one of you as a toddler Léa, standing beside grandmère. You look so cute dressed in an identical housecoat. You must have had it for a while though, it barely covers your dress!'

With a lurch Léa remembered how upset she'd been when her mother had given that very garment away during their journey through France after the occupation. One of the many episodes she'd stored in her memory as reasons to dislike her mother, believing she'd chosen something that her daughter was sentimentally attached to on purpose, just to upset her. Could it have been that she knew that she'd have been even more upset when she could no longer fit into it? Albert Aubry had described the Monique he remembered as a brave, selfless woman. Was she? Was Léa the only one who didn't know her? What had she done in Marseille that was so brave?

Léa had come to Labeille to find herself, the self she'd left here when she'd been forcibly taken away by her mother. She'd always believed, deep down inside, that the true Léa Jourdan still resided in the countryside, in her grandmother's house. That the successful, urbane, cultured, sophisticated woman she'd become, working between London and Paris, was just a front, a cover up. She attributed her inability to form lasting personal relationships to the fact that the warm, loving part of her had been left behind.

Her hostesses were startled when their guest polished off her now cold coffee in one gulp and rose to her feet. 'Do you know, I came here hoping that I'd rediscover my real self. But I was looking for the wrong person. It's my mother I should be finding. And I know the very man who'll help me. Thank you for the meal. Thank you for letting me into the family. I'm going to ask Jacques to organise a trip to Corsica.'

Kissing the bamboozled women on both cheeks, she left before they could think of anything to say. Amelia found her voice first. 'Emilie, you know that wacky baccy you smoke sometimes round at Marc's?' Her sister was startled. She didn't realise that Amelia knew about her occasional sorties off the straight and narrow. 'Did you put some in Léa's food?' Puzzled, Emilie shook her head. 'Why, Amelia? What on earth makes you think I'd do such a thing?'

'Well, I have absolutely no idea what she was going on about, looking for herself when she should be looking for her mother and going off to Corsica to find her. I just wondered if that was the sort of silly nonsense that stuff made people say.' The younger sister grinned, then giggled as she replayed Léa's mystifying farewell. 'Would you like to find out how pot makes you feel?' she suggested timidly.

CHAPTER 6

Chez Jacques closed its doors for an hour and a half on Sundays so the family could sit down and eat together. As the aperitif customers started to drift away Jacques spoke quietly to Eveline. 'You and Corinne are welcome to stay and eat with us but if you would rather.......'

She smiled, kissed him on the cheek, gestured to her new lover. She'd been sitting with Adele, Lucien and Marc, following Eveline's every move with the attention of a cat watching a goldfish swimming round and round in its bowl. The two women left together, hand in hand, no attempt at discretion.

A contemplative smile played around Joe's lips when he joined Jacques behind the bar after he had been to Lucie and Sandrine's table. They'd beckoned him over to settle their bill, he'd stayed chatting for a while.

'Well?' Jacques asked. 'I've just been asked if I could persuade you to give me the afternoon off. They, Lucie *and* Sandrine, would like me to join them for lunch and then maybe some '*après dejeuner*' relaxation.' Jacques' eyebrows lifted. He said nothing, waiting for his brother to elucidate.

'Or....' Joe's voice and mannerisms changed as he transformed himself into a parody of Lucie, the tilt of the head, the challenging stare emphasising the undisguised intent of the invitation. 'Or, if you're not comfortable with that Joe, perhaps you and Jacques would both like to spend some time with us, tonight, after work?'

Seamlessly dropping back into his own persona, Joe addressed Jacques directly. 'Lovely Lucie has designs on you, big bro.' Jacques' eyes flew skyward. Sighing melodramatically, he smoothed down his immaculately coiffured hair. 'Again,' he breathed. Then added. 'And Sandrine?' 'Actually, I think she's a bit out of her depth. I suspect she thought it was all a good, girly giggle while they were plotting a threesome over a bottle of bubbly. But when Lucie actually made the suggestion, as suggestively as she could, Sandrine coloured up, definitely started to squirm. She's a nice, ordinary woman, a good mum, not a schemer or looking to be a good time girl. And above all, what she really wants is whatever's best for Benoit.'

The two men were standing side by side, Joe significantly taller and larger. But they had the same square, solid stance, feet slightly apart, shoulders back, their benign expressions giving nothing away as their eyes travelled over the emptying tables. They could have been discussing the layout of the room rather than a potential sexual encounter of the not every day kind.

Jacques took the money from a departing customer, wished the group *bon appetit,* returned his attention to his brother. 'I'll pass on the foursome, if you don't mind. I think I've got enough on in that department for the time being.'

He cast a wry glance at Marie-France, squatting with her back against Doc's knees, demonstrating to Jacqui and Angelo how to lure Jambon to lie down from a sit. 'But what are your thoughts, little bro? If you're up for some double trouble, you can, of course, have the afternoon and the evening off.'

Joe stretched his neck, rolling his broad shoulders as though to relieve them of the weight of the decision he was having to make. 'Well, I'll definitely stay here and do the lunch. Unless...'

Registering that he'd dismissed Eveline, Joe wondered if Jacques might want to consolidate his newly established, long anticipated, intimacy with Marie-France.' 'Unless you're thinking about yourself and the boys and Marie-France......'

Jacques tipped his head back, letting out a 'ha', the closest he got to laughing out loud. 'You think I might want to play at happy families? Come on Joe. The nearest Marie-France might get to presiding over a family meal would be to sit on the floor with eight puppies to make sure they all get a go at the communal food bowl.'

Joe grinned at the image his brother's words evoked. Jacques continued speaking in his usual, calm, controlled manner. 'If there's anything nuclear about our family, Joe, I'd say it's you and me and the boys, wouldn't you?' The grin on the younger man's face became a beam of happiness. 'In that case, I'd better get my pinny on and start preparing some food.'

He put his arm around Jacques' shoulders, ruffled his hair, gave him a wifely peck on the cheek, before sashaying to the end of the bar. Lucien, putting on his jacket on the other side of the room, scowled at the mincing man's performance. 'It's people like that who give people like us a bad name,' he complained to Marc, delving into his pocket for the money to pay their bill. '*Cheri*, you don't need people like that to give us a bad name. You're more than capable of doing it yourself,' he replied placidly. 'So let's go and pay up and let them get some peace to play whatever their games are while we decide on a few of our own.'

Jacques called Joe back. 'Hold on, little bro. Your ladies are waiting for a reply to their invitation. What's it to be? Afternoon and evening?' Joe folded his arms in the definite 'I've made my decision and I'm sticking to it' pose he'd developed when he was smaller as well as younger than Jacques. 'I'm going to give them both a miss. It probably sounds a bit daft and out of character but I'm not sure I like being.....'

He hesitated, uncertain about how to express the unfamiliar sensation. 'Manipulated?' Jacques suggested. Joe nodded thoughtfully. 'Mmm. Now that's a word I normally like the sound of but in this case.....'

He tried to keep his voice light hearted but Jacques discerned the genuineness of his dilemma. 'Actually Joe, for what it's worth I think you're right. It's all very well being treated as a sex object if that's what you want, but I think you deserve a lot more than that, as a human being, as well as a chef. On that subject, shall we ask Doc if he wants to eat with us? He doesn't seem in any rush to leave for his usual lunch at the hôtel.'

They looked over at the older man, massaging Marie-France's shoulders as she comfortably used his knees as a back rest. 'Do you know, Jacques. I think I could learn a thing or two from Doc.

He doesn't seem to put any effort into it but he's certainly got some sort of a way with the women, hasn't he?' 'Mmm.' Jacques' eyes smiled. 'Good to see her back on form, isn't it? Little minx.' Marie-France, evidently stuck in her squatting position, was giggling helplessly as Doc tried to haul her upright.

Jacques strode over and unceremoniously lifted her on to her feet while Joe courteously explained to a relieved Sandrine and a disappointed Lucie that he had family commitments, so wouldn't be able to accept their most kind and interesting invitation. He escorted them to the door, kissed them both in farewell, locked out the world for the short time the popular bar's schedule allowed.

'Right boys, hands washed, table set. Mum's busy but Doc's staying. Jambon can stay if she behaves as well as Galla. So can Marie-France but she needs to behave as well as Galla too. Joe, I'll give you a hand in the kitchen.'

The entrée was made up of leftovers from the previous night's extravaganza, to be followed by the same main dish as Léa was eating at the Blanchards. Emilie had discovered that there was more of Eric's lamb than she remembered in the freezer and shared it with Joe, although the recipe was his own. The kitchen was very much his domain but today he was pensive. Jacques sensed that he needed to get something off his chest.

'Jacques.' 'Yes, Joe.' 'You remember that time after you'd welcomed Eric into the family, your family, when you confronted father about how he treated you after Eveline left and explained how important Marie-France was to you?'

Jacques put down the pile of plates he was about to carry through to the table. Joe's thoughts needed his full attention. 'I certainly do remember, Joe. It was the most frightening thing I've ever done in my life. I knew I was running the risk of losing you, all of you, even Marie-France. Especially Marie-France.'

He performed a slow intake and exhalation of breath, as though calming himself against the memory of the fear he'd experienced that evening. 'It had to be done though. I knew that we couldn't move on, any of us, if the air wasn't properly cleared. Of course, Marie-France's accident rather complicated the outcome.'

'But what about now, with mum and dad moving back to Corsica instead of staying here. Are things alright between you?'

'Yes, Joe, they're fine, as good as they can be. It's right that they should have their own place, their own space. In some ways dad and I are miles apart but in others I think we're too much alike. Too controlling, some would say.'

Joe peppered the roast potatoes with turmeric and tipped them on to a serving plate. Jacques waited, sensing he hadn't reached the crux of the matter that was bothering him, although he had a very good idea what that was. 'And me?' Joe asked. 'I mean, I know you've just said that we're the nuclear bit of the family and all that but with Marie-France being here too and...'

Jacques peered into his brother's anxious hazel eyes. 'Joe, you are you and Marie-France is Marie-France. I don't want either of you to be, or to behave, like anyone else. As long as there's no lying or pretending, no subterfuge, I don't see why we can't all co-exist. Do you?' Joe breathed a noisy sigh of relief.

Jacques recognised that there was still a mutual attraction between his brother and Marie-France. Considering the sort of people they both were, it might well one day demand consummation. But not yet for a while. He picked up the pile of plates, remarking conversationally, 'But if we don't hurry up and get this food on the table Angelo will probably fade away from starvation, Jacqui will die of boredom, and Marie-France will give up on both of us and persuade Doc that she needs some more personal attention than we seem able to give.'

CHAPTER 7

'Well?'

Joe had wished them goodnight. The bar was clean, tidy, empty, except for Jacques and Marie-France sitting by the balcony door watching the night. She jumped at his question but didn't repel the touch of his hand on her shoulder. 'Well?' she echoed. 'How, Jacques, does one follow a night like we had last night?' 'Oh, that's easy. Come on.'

He held out his hand, relieved she wasn't rejecting him as he'd feared she might, sensing her antipathy towards any commitment that might hint of domesticity. He led her towards the stairs. 'Wait there,' he commanded, went behind the bar, reached up to the back of a top shelf, brought out a bottle and two glasses. 'After you, madame.'

He followed her up the stairs. At the door of the bedroom they'd shared for the first time the night before, he handed her the bottle and glasses, telling her to go in, he'd be there in a minute. She sat on the edge of the bed, surprised at how nervous, how gauche she felt. She seemed to have become a different woman. No longer the lusty, enthusiastic seductress she'd been before her accident but a shy, almost inhibited being she didn't recognise. Before she could give herself the talking to that she thought she deserved, the man she was waiting for, the man who was so different from any other she had been with, and they were many, came into the room and presented her with ...a book! 'Claude Michelet. The first volume of his Vialhe saga. Have you read it?' She shook her head, puzzled about the relevance of a novel as a follow up to the previous night's passion. Jacques took the bottle and glasses she was still clutching, as though they were cuddly toys to comfort her in bed, and put them on the dressing table. 'I thought you might find it entertaining. It's the fictionalised story of the history of a paysan family, tracing their lives through the twentieth century. Eveline said she found it a good read. I prefer an unchallenging thriller myself, preferably on an e-book reader. Much tidier.'

While he was talking he'd taken the book round to the far side of the bed, the side nearest the balcony doors. He opened them a fraction, knowing her craving for fresh air, even in the relative chill of a December night, put the book down, poured a small glass of amber liquid from the bottle, put that beside the book. 'Quality, not quantity,' he explained. 'Now, what would you prefer as nightwear, tee shirt or shirt?'

He opened a drawer filled with his neatly folded clothes, looked at her. She realised she was supposed to answer. 'Oh, tee shirt I think. Easier to get on and *off*.' She emphasised the last word, trying to make it sound as suggestive as her body was telling her she should.

His mouth twitched into an almost smile as he made his choice and handed it to her. 'Right then. You use the bathroom first. Anything you need help with?' She shook her head mutely, wondering if she'd dreamt the sensual activity of the previous night. Maybe it had been a blip in time and now they were back to where they'd been for the past few weeks, her the disabled patient, him the patient carer.

Dressing herself in Jacques' tee shirt in the en suite, she was immediately aroused by its fresh softness and the way it smelt of him. She went back into the room. The duvet was folded back on the bed, revealing invitingly clean sheets. The pile of pillows she'd used to make herself a secure nest since she'd been back from hospital was propped up against the headboard on the balcony side of the bed, beside a lesser number on the other side.

'In you hop. I'll be with you in a tick.' For only the second time in their shared lives she listened to him peeing, washing his hands, brushing his teeth. Quite surprised he didn't have a shower at night as well as in the morning, she decided that probably in the heat of summer he did.

He too was wearing a tee shirt. She almost giggled in relief, having conjoured up an image of him emerging from the bathroom in striped flannel pyjamas like her father wore in the cold winter nights on Skye. When he wasn't out on the hills lambing, out on the hills, with her, setting the scene for the way she would live her life. 'What am I doing here?' she asked herself. 'Waiting in his bed like a meek newlywed.'

She'd been married once, long ago when she was too young to know any better and had retained a clear notion of the difference between being clasped in passion and clutched in possession.

Jacques smiled, really smiled. Her heart leapt into her throat. Most people, profligate with this facial expression, use it carelessly, with varying degrees of sincerity, in any and every situation. But for Jacques, straight faced, deadpan Jacques, this was a demonstration of intimacy, a warmth of feeling reserved for those who were really special. Once or twice she'd caught a glimpse of it fading on his face as he turned away from his sons. Occasionally the ghost of its affection showed when he looked at Joe. Now, in this precious moment of time, he was smiling openly, without reservation, at her. She folded back the duvet. 'Hop in then.' She parodied the words he'd used earlier. 'After all, it is your bed.'

Propping himself up on the pillows, he raised the glass he'd poured for himself, waiting until she raised hers before proposing the toast. 'To a life that's as smooth as this forty year old armagnac.' Once again she felt relieved. An unacknowledged dread had been hovering in the background of her mind, fearing he was going to say something that could be interpreted as acquisitive. Here's to us. Together at last.

A memory came to her. Jacques standing at the front of the church at Rab's funeral. Rab's funeral? Almost a year ago now, it sometimes felt like a blink of time, sometimes like eternity. She pulled her mind back from that precipice, focussing on the memory Jacques' toast had elicited. 'To Rab!' he'd said, raising a glass in lieu of an elegiac speech. She'd appreciated then what an exceptional man he was. She recollected various occasions when a spark, or a chemical reaction, or whatever it is that stimulates desire, had passed between them. How she'd resisted its pull, sensing that he did too, afraid that the physical attraction would take over, devour their relationship, so that when it burnt itself out, as lust, in her experience, usually did, there would be nothing left and they'd have lost something far more precious than the transient pleasure they'd gained. She turned her head, looked at him sitting up beside her, as neat and cool in bed as he was behind the bar. Too cool perhaps, for his own comfort. The chill December breeze was making his nipples stand out through the smooth cotton of his tee shirt. She ached for him with every fibre of her body but understood now what he was doing. He wanted to preserve their unique relationship, to allow it to express itself but not exclusively sexually, so that it did not consume them, destroying the rest of who they were when they were together. With a wistful smile she chinked his glass. 'To a smooth life,' she agreed.

They sipped, appreciated, chatted desultorily about nothing much for a few minutes before he flipped open the e-book reader. She picked up the book he'd selected for her, balanced it on her raised knees. *They abandoned the sunken path and the shelter of the thick brambles* she read and was soon immersed in the *paysan* life of the early twentieth century. It wasn't long before he closed the e-book reader and placed it beside his glass on the bedside table. Leaning over to kiss her on the lips, she felt the intensity of his self-discipline as he drew back before she became irrevocably responsive.

'I sleep as well with the light on as I do when it's off,' he murmured. 'Read for as long as you like.' He knew her so well, including her restless nocturnal habits. Putting all his pillows but one on the floor he lay down with his back to her. Within seconds his steady breathing told her he was asleep. She carried on reading until she realised she'd not taken any meaning from the last page her eyes had scanned. Abandoning the book to the bedside table, marking her place with the bar mat he'd provided for the purpose, she considered lying down to curl up against his back but decided that her inevitable fidgeting when she couldn't maintain the position would disturb his sleep. Dozing comfortably propped up on the pillows until the first light of day, she was instantly awake when she felt him getting out of bed. 'I've spent plenty of nights with plenty of men without having sex,' she remarked. 'But rarely in a proper bed and never with a man I want as much as I want you.' His priceless smile washed over her. 'Well, I can't let you loose on the world in that frame of mind, can I? Come on, out of bed and support yourself on the dressing table. Let's see if we can spice up those exercises that Jean-Paul has you perform so chastely.'

She didn't even consider whether her hip ached as she sprang up and assumed the position, as she did for the physiotherapist. 'I've always been surprised that Jean-Paul lets you keep your clothes on,' Jacques commented, pulling the tee shirt off over her head. 'It's far better to observe your muscles closely when you're exercising, to make sure they're moving smoothly and naturally.'

To Marie-France's surprise she was embarrassed when she saw her reflection in the mirror. Totally assured and confident about the functioning of her body, she'd rarely had the opportunity or need to observe it in action. Not many mirrors in barns and outhouses, where most of her couplings had taken place. She averted her eyes from the skinny woman facing her. Jacques, naked now, moved behind her, encircling her with his arms, placing his hands over hers where they rested on the polished wood. 'Look at yourself,' he whispered in her ear. 'Look at us.' She gasped when he entered her, instantly fully aroused, came within seconds, as did he. 'Right, *ma cherie*, into the shower with you,' he instructed, as soon as their breathing had slowed. 'I don't want you greeting Uncle Eric smelling of sex, though I'm sure he wouldn't mind.'

They kissed their way into the shower cubical and soaped every centimetre of each other's body, staying under the gushing water for far longer than Jacques' normal timed allocation of sixty seconds. He dressed her, with all the touching and caressing he'd forbidden himself from indulging in when he was acting as her carer, insisting that she strap up her arm. 'A reminder that you should still be a little cautious.'

He kissed her before they left the bedroom they had now shared for two nights. She understood instinctively that she'd need to return there to receive any further overt expression of intimacy. Jacques was a circumspect man when it came to displaying emotion in public. They started downstairs as a couple but by the time they reached the bottom he'd become deadpan Jacques Luciani, bar owner and *homme d'affairs,* but strictly in the business sense and she was...Marie-France.

CHAPTER 8

Normality, in as much as she knew what that meant, was sneaking back into Marie-France's life. Eric Roumignac, the farmer she was forming a business partnership with - she wasn't really sure what that meant either - arrived at *Chez Jacques* just as she'd finished her breakfast of coffee and croissant, to collect her and the geese in his aged but pristine Sinpar Renault van.

'I considered leaving a drake and a couple of females here, any animal life adds to the ambiance of a place as far as I'm concerned,' she told him. 'But Pierre Calvet and his team of builders will be starting work after the New Year. They're going to have to access the house through the garden and it could all become a bit hectic, so I'll have to make do with the chickens. They'll be safe enough in their run, although until the work starts I'm going to let them range throughout the garden. It'll be good for them and they might scrat up a few bugs and beasties that I don't want overwintering. Do you think we'll get all the geese in the van in a oner? There are far too many of them to keep but I thought it would be better to do the cull up at the farm, if that's alright with you?'

She chattered on, unperturbed by the monosyllabic replies and nods of her taciturn companion. They were comfortable together, these two, in the agricultural world they shared.

Getting the geese into the back of the van could have been accomplished in a much shorter time than it actually took, but Marie-France wanted to give bored Galla a chance to use her herding skills rather than luring the birds with grain and picking them up bodily, the method, left to himself, that Eric would have employed. She rigged up a ramp, sent her dog 'away tae me' and 'come by', getting her to take the flock of geese around the garden once or twice to get them moving as a group, finally ordering her dog to 'walk up' and 'push' them towards the narrow entrance that was the door of the van. That's where it got noisy. The geese, unnerved by the unknown vehicle, resisted and flapped, facing up to the dog and the people trying to funnel them in. Eric didn't object that a job that could have been effectively done in a fraction of the time was prolonged. He didn't object to anything Marie-France suggested. She'd brightened up his life far more than she appreciated, just by being who she was. Along with the rest of the people who cared for her, he was so relieved that at last she was recovering from her injuries, mentally as well as physically, he would have granted her the sky if it was his to give.

Joe, attracted by the hissing and screeching, the yapping of the safely enclosed pups, the quick fire shouting of orders as mistress and dog worked together trying to control their unruly flock, came down to see what was going on, thinking he would be a side-line spectator. But when he saw his still less than agile friend lurch towards the last of the wing flapping birds, narrowly avoiding falling as she tried to grab it, he unwittingly became involved. 'Straddle it from behind and pinion its wings,' Eric instructed gruffly. He too had experienced a surge of concern at Marie-France's near tumble.

'Now what?' Joe, no stranger would believe he wasn't the older man's son, they were so similar in looks, was holding the protesting gander, trying to avoid the vicious looking beak writhing around on the end of the long, powerful neck. 'I'll open the van door, you put it inside as quick as you like. Galla will stop them all flooding out again, won't she?' Eric asked Marie-France sternly. 'Of course! She's done a great job, considering she hasn't done any serious work for months. A solitary animal is always problematic, even to a Superdog like my Galla.'

Some people might have sounded defensive, Eric obviously just wanted to get the job done, but Marie-France was too exhilarated at being herself again, even if she was still a bit creaky, to take her partner's gravelly remarks as criticism.

'Right, let's get this lot up the hill. Jules is loading the trailer with the wood we cut yesterday and Elie's doing the milking but I don't like to leave them alone too long. Wouldn't do you any harm to come up some time to give us a hand while you're only cooking for the family, Joe. The exercise would do you good.' Joe sucked in his not insignificant girth and grinned. 'What are you suggesting, half-uncle Eric?' This easy going man was another person who brought more pleasure than pain into the lives he touched.

Eric didn't reply, just patted his newly discovered nephew fondly on the back, and folded himself into the driver's seat of the laden van, while Marie-France made her way round to the other side. Galla took her usual position in the footwell at her mistress' feet. Fidgety Jambon, who hadn't been in a car before, was firmly held on her lap.

They didn't talk on the way up the potholed lane to the farm. Marie-France remembered how she'd tried to engage her prospective employer in conversation the first time they'd travelled the route together. He'd made it clear then that driving and talking were mutually exclusive activities and she'd respected that ever since.

They pulled into the muddy farmyard. Eric suggested they park up, open the door of the van, let the birds make their way out in their own time. Without any pressure the flutter from van to ground wouldn't cause them any harm. 'Let's give them a couple of days to settle in before we decide which ones to despatch,' he suggested. To those not of the stock management world this might have sounded cruel, incongruous at least. Marie-France knew as well as he did that the geese were stressed by their displacement. Stressed meat is not as good as that from a relaxed, well cared for animal, as these birds would be by the time they'd been allowed to forage freely around the house to supplement the extra grain rations they'd be given until the time of their killing, to be carried out as calmly and painlessly as possible.

'Come into the house for a couple of minutes,' Eric suggested. 'There are a couple of things I want to talk to you about.'

He'd intimated a couple of days previously that he had some concerns about the young men who were working for him and was looking forward to Marie-France becoming involved again. Managing males, of any age, was certainly one of her finely honed skills.

My Beau, the two year old Beauceron dog that had been Eric's mother's, waiting proprietorially on the door step, gave them a calm welcome, recognising Marie-France, who'd been involved in his training. 'Your old boy gone?' she asked, referring to the aged dog that had always been around before. 'He has,' Eric confirmed. 'A couple of days after mother died. As if he couldn't be bothered asserting his authority over My Beau to keep his top dog status, he took himself off into the barn, made himself a comfortable nest, curled up and slept away, much as mother did. He had a good life and a good death. Glad I've got My Beau to take his place. A farm isn't a home without a farm dog.'

While the humans talked the canine social conventions took place. Galla and My Beau, well acquainted, greeted each other by sniffing nose to nose, then had a quick circle round each other. Jambon - Marie-France had him on a long rope lead to allow him to explore without any risk of escape - had yet to learn the social niceties. He rushed straight up to My Beau. The older dog curled its lip in warning, but not too seriously, merely a pale imitation of Elvis Presley. Jambon immediately got the message, lay down submissively, rolling over on to her back as My Beau sniffed her thoroughly, asserting his seniority. He drew back, affecting a total lack of interest. Irrepressible Jambon righted herself, approached the older dog again, bowing, head down, front legs outstretched, in what was clearly an invitation to play. My Beau gave a half-hearted growl deep in his throat, suggesting that to cavort with the youngster would be beneath his dignity. Jambon backed off, but not very far, then tried again, darting forwards, dancing around, submitting whenever My Beau approached. A two year old dog is only a grown puppy and after a couple of minutes, when their respective hierarchical roles were firmly established, he joined in the game, darting, running, cavorting.

The watching humans smiled. 'They'll be alright then,' Marie-France observed, picking up the rope she'd dropped so it didn't inhibit the natural dog behaviours. 'But I'll bring her inside otherwise she'll cause havoc out here.' 'Let's take My Beau in too, so they can get to know each other under supervision,' Eric suggested. 'Galla can stay outside and get used to being here.'

Marie-France had only been in the farmhouse kitchen half a dozen times before but on each occasion had been struck by how neat, tidy and organised it was. Eric's mother, who'd died not long ago, had played a part in the farm's day to day running but hadn't lived there until the last few days of her life and didn't involve herself in her solitary son's domestic arrangements. Marie-France knew it wasn't the old woman's death that had caused the change that had come over the place. Her nose wrinkled fastidiously at the smell. She'd grown up with open fires and wood burners and thought that a room felt heated just by the way the wood smoke hung in the air. This stale odour was different.

'Cigarettes and spliffs,' Eric explained. 'He smokes nonstop.' He gestured towards the bed under the stairs that his mother had slept in as a child and died in as an old lady. Marie-France saw a pile of *mégots*, tab-ends, on the floor beside it, as well as dozens of empty beer bottles scattered in an ever widening circle.

'Elie?' she ascertained. 'How often does he stay here?' 'Most of the time, this last while. I get the feeling he's not welcome at home.' 'But haven't you spelt out the house rules?' The burly farmer shrugged, seemed to diminish in size, aging in the process. 'I'm no good at managing people,' he murmured. 'Suppose that's why I'm on my own. Give me a herd of cows or a pack of dogs and I can usually keep them in order, but lads like him, I don't know where to start.'

He looked so weary and demoralised that Marie-France couldn't decide whether she wanted to take him in her arms and offer comfort or shake him by the shoulders - not that she could have reached them without standing on a bench - and tell him to get a grip. She did neither, understanding that he needed her to take control.

'You said Elie was doing the milking, didn't you? I'll go and see him right away.' 'The milk yield is down.' Eric's voice was grave. The welfare of his animals of far more consequence than his own. 'Especially the goats. It's hardly been worth Paulette picking it up for the past few days.'

With a nod of understanding Marie-France made her way determinedly towards the stable. Still using her cane, almost out of habit, she'd replaced her arm support because of the ache induced by her excess of confidence with the geese. She fixed a smile on her face as she got to the stable door and stood for an instant listening to the sucking and wheezing of the old fashioned milking system and breathing in the farmyard smell, more agreeable to her than the most expensive of manufactured perfumes. 'Bonjour Elie,' she called out, peering down the length of the stalls, where the cows stood swishing their tails, munching at hay, placidly waiting for their turn to have the milk suctioned out of their full udders.

He was leaning up at the far end, a cigarette clamped between his lips. He pushed himself off the wall but made no move to come and greet her, just gave a surly nod, as if she was invading his personal space. 'Elie, I don't care what damage you do to your lungs in your own time but you cannot smoke in here. The fire risk is too great,' she said, still keeping her voice light and pleasant.

He looked at her with heavy, baleful eyes. She thought he was going to argue but at that moment the milk stopped running from the cow he was standing beside. He dropped his cigarette to the ground, glared at her defiantly, stubbed it out, removed the suckers from the milked cow, attached them to the next cow in line.

'Don't forget to clean the udders, before and after milking, and make sure the cloth is washed out and well disinfected,' Marie-France reminded him. 'It's unpleasant for the beast and extra work and cost for us if she gets mastitis.'

Elie shrugged again, wiped the udders cursorily before dropping the cloth back into the murky looking bucket of water. 'And don't forget that the first few milk spurts go into that little blue cup with the sieve in it,' she reminded him. 'Apart from being good practice for detecting mastitis the poultry benefit from it being added to their grain. Fattens them up beautifully.' She hoped that if she explained the whole process to him he might become more interested in the job, rather than treating it as a one-off chore.

Watched quietly while the milk started flowing from the cow, she noticing how completely detached Elie was, treating the animal like an inanimate object rather than a living, breathing beast who would respond to a calming voice and a gentle hand. 'It's always tempting to let the bucket get full of milk before you carry it over to the cooling shed,' she remarked, trying not to sound too harping. 'But you'll spill less if you take over two half-filled buckets rather than one full one.'

The surly young man glared at her, picked up the bucket, almost full to the brim, sloshed some of the warm, yellow milk into another bucket, spilling a significant amount in the process. This was the last cow to be milked and he pushed her away, roughly pulled off the suction cup and stomped off with the two buckets to the shed on the other side of the yard, where the cooling machine was whirring and humming, waiting for the latest contribution.

While he was away Marie-France, telling herself she must keep cool and cheerful, tried to think of a strategy that would help her get through to this unhappy, aggressive youth, who'd previously been puppy-dog complacent beneath a half-hearted hard man exterior. When he came back into the stable she was crooning to the goats, already tethered in their milking stalls. 'Have these little monsters been giving you a hard time?' she asked cheerfully, pulling gently on a pair of soft, white ears. 'Eric tells me they're not being very generous with their milk. Perhaps we can milk them together and I'll see if I can find out what's going on.' 'You can do it yourself, for all I care,'

Elie replied, sticking an unlit cigarette between his lips. Marie-France's patience was running thin but she decided to give him one last chance to cooperate before challenging him outright about his behaviour. 'That's not really the point, is it? It's you that needs to learn to work with the animals, if you want to keep this job. And as I know how to do it you'd be as well to try and learn from me. Now come here beside me and we'll try this little madam together. You'd better let me have the stool because if I try and squat down you'll have to haul me back up if I get stuck.'

He leered at her and muttered, 'Yeh, you'd like that, wouldn't you?' 'What did you say, Elie?' she asked, all softness gone from her voice. 'Nothing,' he murmured, sulkily. 'Right then, last chance. Let's get this girl milked.' 'This girl?' he mimicked. 'It's not a girl, it's a fucking goat. And just as stupid as any other female.'

He bunched his fingers into a fist, aimed a blow at the soft eyed animal, hitting it on the side of the head with enough power to make it stagger. Marie-France was on her feet instantly. 'Get out,' she hissed. 'You're not fit to be anywhere near any animal.' 'Get out yourself,' he retorted, as the whisky he'd swigged on his way to the cooling shed fired up his courage. 'You're just a woman. You can't tell me what to do.' 'I might be *just* a woman, but I am every bit as much your boss as Eric is and I'm telling you to get out of this stable right now.' Her eyes flashed in anger as she faced up to him. Barking out a humourless laugh, he took a step towards her. She became uncomfortably aware that although he was young and slight he was a good head and shoulders taller than she was.

'So who's going to make me get out then? You?' He loomed over her but she stood her ground, even when he lit the cigarette and blew the smoke directly into her face. As always, when in any sort of trouble her first thought was Galla. She knew she'd be mooching around in the farmyard, either watching or moving the poultry to satisfy her need to be in control. Before Marie-France could produce the whistle that would bring her dog running, an unexpected voice rang out from the doorway.

'Well, Elie. What a brave boy you're turning out to be, just like the rest of the menfolk in your family, always ready to beat up on a woman, eh?' Paulette Aubry had arrived to collect the milk. Not seeing anyone around she made her way to the stable, to see if she could give a hand. 'What do you know about my family?' Elie retorted belligerently. 'Everything. I went to school with your mum, remember, and put vinegar on her bruises when her father, your grandfather, beat her. I could never understand why she took up with the class bully, your dad, but when she finally decided he'd hit her once too often she came to live with me until the commune found her a place of her own. She put all her energies into making your life as good as she could but now it seems you've turned out just like all the other men she's known. Including, I suppose, the one she's living with now. Poor Colette, what a disappointment you must be.'

This accusation seemed to exacerbate Elie's temper rather than calm him down. He took another step towards Marie-France, as though to finish the job he had psyched himself up to do. 'That's right, show us how tough you are.' The threatened woman, surprised by the vituperative words, wished Paulette would stop goading the drink and drug fuelled youngster. 'Mind you, even though she's only half your size you'd never have dared to have a go at her before, would you, when she didn't need a stick to walk and had two strong arms to fight back. You really are the lowest of the low, Elie Durand.'

This insult did make some sort of impact on the young lad. He remembered the first time he'd come into contact with Marie-France, after she'd chased him, Jules, Benoit and Guillaume, through the streets of Labeille. He also remembered, rather belatedly, her connection with the powerful Lucianis. This stimulated another idea in his bellicosely muddled brain. He faced Paulette. 'Anyway, why are you standing up for her? You don't like her. None of the women do. She's come into the village and taken jobs that should have gone to the locals and...' He paused so his next vitriolic statement would have maximum impact. 'And she's taken the men too, and not just one at a time!'

His triumphant declaration didn't have time to wing its way into the air before an icy voice snarled a response. 'Get off my farm, right now, and don't ever set foot on my land again.' Eric Roumignac's muscular figure filled the doorway, obscuring Jules, standing just behind him, horrified at the words his friend had spoken.

'Jules, go and get the boy's bag, stick as many of his empty bottles in it as you can. He may as well take some of his rubbish away with him as he won't be coming back to clear up. And then you go with him, lad, to make sure that if he falls over and hurts himself he doesn't do it on my land. In fact, take the rest of the day off, I need to get a few things in order here.'

Jules threw an accusatory look at Elie before leaving to do as he'd been instructed, fearing that his troubled friend had just lost him the job he was beginning to enjoy. As well as insulting the woman he still had a crush on.

Marie-France had lowered herself back down on to the three legged stool during Elie's outburst to Paulette, clutching her stick like a comforter. Even in the dim light of the stable her freckles stood out darkly in the alabaster paleness of her puzzled, anxious face. She looked tiny and defenceless, like a pixie that's lost all his magic powers because the world has told him he's a fake. Eric's barely controlled, simmering anger roiled towards boiling point when he saw how all the exuberance had been sucked out of her. He took a menacing step towards Elie. Faced with this powerful, fuming man, he seemed to shrivel, as his bravado evaporated. Avoiding Marie-France as though fearful he might inadvertently hurt her and bring the rage of her protector down on him in a hail storm of blows, he shuffled out into the daylight, keeping his eyes lowered, as though searching for a speck of hope in the soiled straw covering the roughly concreted floor.

Eric spoke again, his voice rasping with the effort of controlling his so rarely lost temper. 'Paulette, if it's true what he said about you, if that's the way you think about Marie-France, then our association, our friendship, is over too.' The irate man hadn't heard what his neighbour had said to Elie, only the youth's ranting reply.

Paulette shook her head. Speaking calmly, she finally managing to pour some balm on the aggravated situation. 'I'll admit, Eric, that I did feel resentful about Marie-France for a while. But after you explained why you'd given her this job it was obvious that you were right. There isn't anyone available locally with her skills. And as for the work she does *Chez Jacques,* well, she can hardly be accused of keeping the locals out of a job there, can she, considering the way Jacques has employed Elie and his pals. And as for the rest, well...'

She shrugged her shoulders dismissively as though it was none of her concern whether the other women thought the incomer was taking their men. Her husband, Nicolas, openly admired Marie-France for her unconventional attitude to life but Paulette didn't feel her marriage was in any way threatened. She turned towards Marie-France, still sitting on the stool, a stunned expression on her face. 'I'm sorry, Marie-France, that you had to hear that rubbish and be subjected to Elie's cowardly display of what he thinks of as manly behaviour. His mother, Colette, has had a difficult life but she's always tried to do her best for her boy. I know that he, in fact both of them, are having a really hard time with this new bloke and his mate, who seem to have inveigled their way into their home. Not that that is any excuse for the way that little shite treated you. Are you okay?'

Marie-France shook her head as though to dislodge any memory of what had taken place. 'Sticks and stones and all that,' she said brightly. 'But I'm glad you turned up when you did, Paulette. As you said, I'm not quite fighting fit yet. Thank you for standing up for me.'

Getting to her feet, the two women shook hands as though to consolidate a new allegiance. 'One-handed milking must be a bit tricky,' the goat farmer remarked. 'I'll do it for you.' Paulette Aubry, a down to earth, practical woman, was glad to be able to offer to do something useful. 'And you two look as though you could do with a cup of coffee or something stronger. Are *we* okay,

Eric?'

His anger had ebbed away, or maybe it was clinging to the lad who'd caused it as he slouched off down towards the village. 'Of course, Paulette. We're fine. And I apologise for speaking to you so discourteously. I was a bit upset.' 'Not surprising, Eric. You've had a lot of disruption in your life. If there's any way we can help you get back on an even keel, just let us know. Nicolas wouldn't be at all pleased if the hunt activities were curtailed because you were overworked.' Paulette's husband, as well as being a volunteer *Sapeur Pompier,* was an enthusiastic member of the local *chasse,* of which Eric was the president.

Relieved that the crisis seemed to be over, and content to leave the goats in the care of an expert, Eric shepherded Marie-France over to the house. As soon as she was inside the door she took off her arm support. 'I never thought I'd hear myself say that a house was more in need of a clean out than a stable, Eric, but in this instance, I think yours is.' Looking at the remnants of Elie's rubbish, she giggled helplessly. 'Having said that, I don't think I'm the person to do it. House cleaning is definitely not one of my specialities.'

Eric smiled down at her affectionately, pleased to see the colour back in her cheeks and the sparkle back in her eyes. 'It'll take me two minutes. I'm used to doing for myself. Do you think you might be capable of pouring out two coffees? There's a pot on the stove that should still have some in it, unless that boy drank that as well as everything else he could get his hands on.'

When Paulette stuck her head around the door to say she'd finished with the goats and given them and the cows a helping of hay to keep them contented until they were turned out, Eric and Marie-France were sitting on opposite sides of the big farmhouse table, deep in earnest conversation.

'You see, Marie-France, it was quite different with Pierrot, the lad who helped me before. He'd been coming here since he was a babe in arms and had grown into the job, so he knew what needed doing without being told. But even Jules, we'll not even mention the other one, can't use any initiative, he just hasn't a clue what the simplest job involves. If I ask him to clean out the sheds, for example, I have to explain where everything is kept, where to put the manure, where to get the fresh straw, how much to use. It takes three times as long telling him about it than it would to do it myself. And I can't get on with anything else.'

'I understand, Eric, really I do. It's like a duckling who hasn't learnt how to swim. He needs to follow someone around until he gets hold of the routines. But now I'm back in action it should be a lot better, especially as he'll be able to do the physical stuff that I might still find a bit tricky. Are you prepared to give him another chance, if I promise not to go AWOL again? He's a good kid and willing. But I think we should make it very clear that he's only here to do specific jobs, in the first instance, just for a couple of hours a day. I suggest helping with the milking and shed cleaning, including the poultry. When, if, he proves he can work independently we can take a view on whether to increase his hours. Or not. Then you and I can get on with the rest of the work without interruption. What do you say, partner?'

'I say it's great to have you back where you belong and why don't we turn this coffee break into an early lunch of bread and soup then take the dogs out and have a good blether while we're on the move. You can ring Jules and tell him to be outside *Chez Jacques* in the morning when I come to collect you, so you can do the milking together.'

Galla drove the beasts out into the top pasture, they set off to walk down to the tree line at the bottom of the farm. Marie-France was puzzled when she tried to close the gate, and frowned at the frayed piece of rope that seemed to be the only means of fastening it.

'That's the very sort of thing I was talking about, with the lads,' Eric explained, looking slightly abashed. 'It should have been replaced as soon as it broke, but it never occurred to either of them to do anything about it themselves or even to draw it to my attention. Mind you, I'm guilty of laziness myself, I suppose. Since my old boy died I quite often leave the gate open and let the cows make their own way into the milking shed. The gate not being fastened hasn't been a problem, if it's not actually open they just stand and wait. Patient beasts, cattle.'

Not for the first time, Marie-France felt a wave of compassion for this kind, equable man. He'd experienced so much turmoil in such a short space of time, including losing the dog that had been his constant companion for the past twelve years. Even having My Beau, his mother's dog, to keep him company, he would still feel the loss. A new dog never takes the place of one you've been close to. It has to find its own.

CHAPTER 9

They set off down the sloping swathe of land towards the treeline, agreeing that as it was her first walk over rough ground they shouldn't set their sights too far. As they strolled, Galla, the adult canine, walked sedately beside her mistress. My Beau, next in seniority, was allowed to make his own way, as long as he didn't stray too far. Jambon, the podgy, irrepressible pup, was on a long rope lead, keeping her with the party but encouraging her to respond to the recall command issued when she stretched her restraint to the limit. Eric and Marie-France talked. They talked about land use, about crop and pasture rotation, about the advantages of having enough land to be able to leave some fallow rather than constantly using chemicals. Eric pointed towards the area of woodland where the fuel for the winter after next was being cut, so it would be well seasoned when the time came to burn it, extolling the virtues of his self-sufficiency, in this, as in so many other aspects his life.

Not even the smir of rain that started to fall could dampen their spirits. They walked, talked, planned for the arrival of the sheep, once she'd persuaded him that they should get their new stock from Christian, the sheep farmer who was going to take one of the pups that his dog had sired.

'Do you know about the Clun Forest race?' she asked him. 'No, but I think I'm just about to find out,' he replied benevolently, putting out his arm to steady her as they went down one of the steeper inclines. She grinned, nodded her thanks, accepting his help readily, without inhibition. 'Well, they are hardy, adaptable, good foragers, and great lambers, sturdy, wide pelvic structures. A good reputation for fecundity too. A multi–purpose animal, meat, wool, and milk. Although the Aubrys have got the milk side of the business pretty well covered locally with their

Lacaune. We don't want to go into competition, do we?'

'No, certainly not. We don't want the work and commitment of more milking either,' Eric agreed. 'So why Clun Forest then, rather than the Suffolk mixes that are common around here?' 'Their meat is exceptional but more than that, so is their wool. It doesn't have the black fibres in it or the kemp, like the Suffolk, so it can be used for hand-spinning. Don't look at me like that, Eric. I've no intention of sitting by the fireside spinning away like an old witch. But Martine, Serge's daughter, might. She makes the baskets that we sell on the market with the eggs. Not that she's into witchcraft,' she giggled, 'But she's very into handicraft and as the mayor is so keen on promoting anything local she might well get some sort of grant to develop the home spun wool idea.'

'Do I detect Jacques' voice behind those words?' her companion asked. 'He's the entrepreneurial one, isn't he?' 'You're right, of course. He asked me what the difference was between one sheep and another when I was thinking about breeds. Being him, he picked up on the wool idea. But it's nothing to do with him, what breed we decide on. He's very clear that the farm decisions are up to us and he'll only get involved in the business side as much as we, or rather you, want. This is your farm Eric, and as you know, the partnership is neither here nor there as far as I'm concerned.'

'But you would like to get some of these Clun Forest sheep?' 'I would,' she agreed. 'Not only because of all the attributes I've already tried to sell to you but because they're pretty too. They've got lovely brown faces. 'Why didn't you mention that before? I'm always a soft touch for a pretty face. Why else do you think you're here?' he said, a smile playing around his lips.

She flung back her head and laughed gleefully, under no illusion about the prettiness of her looks. When men were attracted to her it wasn't because she was pretty; it was because she wanted them. Eric laughed with her, enjoying her unrestrained response to his teasing.

'So that's one item of business we can report on at Jacques' meeting on Wednesday. New sheep. Clun Forest. The next thing to consider is how many. I suppose that depends to some extent on the amount of extra land you want to take on. And that involves discussion with the Blanchards and Léa, doesn't it' 'Amelia phoned me yesterday afternoon, although I must say, she didn't sound altogether herself. I think they must have pushed the boat out because Léa was there for lunch and had rather more to drink than usual. She sounded almost giggly!'

The thought of straight-laced, straight-faced Amelia giggling made Marie-France want to do the same but she restrained herself to directing a sunny smile at Eric to encourage him to tell her what his cousin had said.

'I didn't get all the ins and outs, Amelia was uncharacteristically vague, but the upshot is that they're taking the farm off the market for the time being. We don't have to make any definite decisions about the land for the time being and can use as much or as little of it as we wish. Amelia seemed very pleased when she told me.'

'Have you heard about Léa?' Eric asked. 'Léa? What about Léa?' Marie-France had seen the Blanchards' attractive cousin speaking earnestly to Jacques the previous afternoon, hadn't thought to ask him what about. 'She's on her way to Corsica, to see my father. Amelia said something about Léa going to see him because he would help her find her mother. She really was very unclear, not like Amelia at all. But anyway, I know my father will be delighted. He developed a real soft spot for little Léa, as he called her.'

'And what about you, Eric, and Léa?' Marie-France wondered if Eric had developed a bit of a soft spot for Léa himself. 'Me? Oh!' A blush reddened his already ruddy face. 'Well, do you know, my rather too observant little friend, I've discovered that one is never too old to develop an adolescent crush! I just hope I didn't make too much of a fool of myself. Which reminds me, do you think my attendance at this meeting of Jacques' is really necessary? Can't you speak for us both, partner?'

Marie-France understood Eric's reluctance about sitting in a room talking about subjects like sheep and land that belonged outside in the open air. She had reservations herself about the formality of this partnership. 'I don't think you need to worry about it, Eric. Any time I've been to what Jacques calls a business meeting it's involved a bit of chat, usually about stuff we've all talked about at other times. Then Joe lightens the mood, as he's so good at doing, by producing some new nibbles or drinks he's created. Jacques just likes to do things the way he feels is right.'

'He likes to be in control too, doesn't he?'

Marie-France felt the warm glow spreading over her cheeks working its way down her neck, and further down, right down, as she remembered the first night she'd spent in Jacques' bed. He certainly took control then.

Eric was too absorbed in his own thoughts to get a glimpse of hers. 'He's a very ambitious young man, Jacques. It was his idea, you know, this partnership of ours. He talked to me about it when you were in hospital. I wasn't entirely sure why it's was so important to him until I worked out that it was about keeping you around.'

The conversation broke up for a while as Marie-France untangled the lively pup. She'd wrapped her training rope around a tree while trying to chase after My Beau. Eric had followed his train of thought in another direction. 'But I'm under no illusions about Jacques' priorities in life or in business. When it comes down to it everything he does is for his children.' Marie-France's stomach heaved. She felt as though she was going to be physically sick. If Eric had referred to Jacques' 'boys' the word probably wouldn't have had any impact. But he hadn't. He'd said, 'his children'.

Ever since she'd been sexually active Marie-France had been on the contraceptive pill. When she wasn't sure about a man's past, his provenance, as she tended to think of it, she insisted, in the most beguiling way, that he use a condom. She was in absolute charge of her own body. Until she had her car accident and was hospitalised for weeks. Most of her stay in the establishment she'd hated so vehemently for its stuffy airlessness had faded into an unpleasant blur. But one scene came back to her, as clearly as if it was in the present.

The reluctant patient very rarely summoned help from the staff, preferring to manage for herself, as she always had. On this particular occasion she'd panicked. Gilou, the nurse coordinating her care, arrived almost immediately, realising it must be something serious for her to have used the buzzer. On the bed with her knees bent up towards her chest when he arrived, she looked genuinely frightened, for the first time since he'd been caring for her. 'What's up, Marie-France?' he'd asked.

Standing in the drizzle in the open air she once again heard his calm, caring voice. Incongruously, she remembered the way the sunlight streaming through the window made the hairs on his strong arms glint like bronze. 'I'm bleeding,' she'd whispered.

One of the major worries after her accident was that the van she'd been thrown out of might have crushed her, causing internal injuries. The scans and examinations had all been reassuring but when she'd seen the blood in her knickers she thought they must have missed something after all. Gilou helped her to lie back on the bed and examined her. 'Trauma often upsets your cycle,' he'd said. 'When did you have your last period?' To his surprise the fear on her face was replaced by undisguised hilarity. 'My last period?' she replied. 'Oh, about eighteen years ago, I think. I'd completely forgotten that I haven't been taking the pill since I've been in here. Oh, Gilou, I'm so sorry to waste your time. You must think I'm a complete idiot.'

A smile beamed softly from his perceptive eyes. 'Not at all. Nice to feel wanted for a change. But this is maybe a good opportunity to let your body have a break from contraception. I don't think you'll be interested in any of that sort of activity for a few weeks, anyway, do you?'

And she hadn't of course. The only activity she'd been interested in was getting her body back into working order, walking, dressing, becoming independent.

Passionate, freedom loving Marie-France had never, in her whole life, had unprotected sex. Until the night before last with

Jacques. Controlled, controlling, fastidious Jacques. He knew for a fact that she wasn't on the pill because he'd been in charge of her medication from the moment she was let out of the hospital. And controlled, controlling, fastidious Jacques would not have *forgotten* to use a condom. It would have been a decision.

Marie-France's breath was coming in short bursts, her heart thumping like an over amplified drum. Eric didn't hear it. He was distracted by another noise. 'That's unusual. The bikers don't usually come up here in the winter. The engines sound too loud for trial bikes too.' They were almost back at the farmyard and the sound of the motors cut through the damp air like the intense buzzing of bees around their hive.

'Seems we might be getting visitors.' There was a hint of anxiety in Eric's steady voice. Anything out of the ordinary could become a matter for concern when it disturbed his mundane life. Just as they reached the gate two powerful motorbikes roared into the yard, splashing and skidding through the mud. My Beau, as was his job, started barking at the strangers. Galla, not having been told to do so, stayed quiet, slightly unnerved by the noise of the engines. Jambon yapped excitedly, pulling at the rope as her mistress wound it in.

'Take the dogs and go into the house,' Eric ordered. The two leather clad drivers were dismounting, the pillion passenger descending from the back of the first bike was Elie. Anticipating a situation that would be best handled calmly, Marie-France complied immediately, scooping undisciplined Jambon into her arms, commanding the other two dogs to follow.

Galla had driven the cows back up the hill ready for evening milking. Eric pushed the unlatchable gate shut to keep them on the other side. He strode towards Elie and his black suited companions. 'Well?' he asked coldly. 'What are you doing here? I thought I told you to stay off my land.'

'So this is the old man who gave you a doing, is it Elie?' The bearded, sallow faced man whose bike Elie had been on, took a threatening step towards Eric, who was peering at Elie's bruised and badly scratched face. 'I never touched you Elie, and you know it.' He spoke directly to the cowed youth, ignoring his companions, as if hoping that by not acknowledging their presence they might disappear. They didn't. The one who'd spoken, evidently the leader, stepped towards the burly farmer.

'If my woman's lad says that you beat him up then that's good enough for me,' he sneered, his words thick and viscous with intoxication. 'And for no good reason,' he continued 'Considering the woman he was going to make out with wouldn't have objected anyway, from what we've heard.' 'Well you heard wrong, so just get off my farm and don't make any more of a fool of yourselves than you already have,' Eric retaliated, his voice gravelly with barely controlled anger.

The ringleader laughed mirthlessly, a harsh, nasal, unpleasant sound that tarnished the purity of the afternoon air. 'Oh, come on, old man. It's common knowledge she's the town bike. Elie just wanted a ride, same as everyone else. But he's young and doesn't know his way around a woman's body yet, so me and my buddy thought we'd come and give him a demonstration of how it's done. Get out of the way, old man. If you behave yourself, we might even let you watch too, seeing as you probably can't get it up yourself anymore.'

This was too much. Eric's control snapped. He stepped aggressively towards his tormenter but the younger, innately violent youth attacked first, delivering a blow to Eric's guts that made him double over in pain. Winded, he reached out blindly, holding on to his assailant to try and keep himself on his feet. With a mocking laugh, his leather clad opponent drew back his fist and smashed it into the older man's face. Eric went down, felled like one of the oak trees he'd been sawing up for firewood. Elated with his victory his attacker prepared to finish the disabling job with his boots, calling on Elie and his other, more reticent companion, to come and join in the fun.

'Stop, right there!' If he'd been a dog, any dog, he would have complied immediately when he heard the tone of Marie-France's command. But he wasn't a dog, he was a drink and drug fuelled oaf. Distracted, he didn't give the prone man lying at his feet the kicking he'd planned.

'Ha, so you've saved us the bother of coming to get you,' he leered at her. 'Well isn't that nice of you. We'll take you right here, in the open air, and then we'll be on our way. Elie, get your trousers down. It'll not take me long to get her in the mood.'

He started to stride towards the petite figure. She raised the rifle she'd been cradling in her arms like a huge, rigid snake, pointing it in his direction. 'I told you to stop,' she said, in a chillingly calm voice. The other biker hung back, as did Elie, even in his befuddled state becoming less sure of himself, remembering that Marie-France was stronger and a lot more physically capable than her appearance suggested.

'Let's leave it, Xavier. You've hurt the old bastard and I don't think I fancy her anymore anyway.' 'Oh come on Elie! The fun's just started. You're not frightened of the silly cow, are you? Look, she can hardly lift that gun. There's no way she could use it.'

Even in the midst of his bravado Xavier jumped back as the shot rang out and zinged off the mirror of his bike. But he soon recovered himself. 'So maybe she has got the strength to pull the trigger,' he jeered. 'But there's no way she's gonna to have the balls to hurt anyone.'

A second shot boomed out. The goose squawked and staggered backwards for a metre or so with the force of the bullet that hit it squarely in the brain, then ran in a circle, flapping its powerful wings before collapsing in its death throes. Even Xavier was alarmed by this unexpected display of wanton killing. Before he could recover himself enough to decide what to do Marie-France called out to Eric, who'd managed to crawl over to the fence and was hauling himself painfully to his feet.

'Eric, stand back!' She took a couple of steps towards the house, still keeping the gun levelled directly at the stunned Xavier. Pushing open the door, she released My Beau, clamouring to get out. Galla, not being a hunt dog, was cowering nervously at the sound of the gunshot. Marie-France called her calmly. Immediately at her mistress's side, she was directed towards the gate. 'Galla, jump!' Marie-France instructed. All the dog's nervousness had gone now she was focussed on work. She did as she was commanded in one, elegant leap. The next instruction sent her behind the cows. She was told to push in a voice that told her to get the herd moving. Unused to being hassled the usually docile beasts clustered in agitation against the gate. It swung open, letting them spill into the yard at a run. Marie-France removed Jambon's lead. The gutsy pup was soon yapping and dancing excitedly, joining in what she perceived as fun. The farmyard was transformed into a farcical circus impression of a cattle stampede. Marie-France sent Galla backwards and forwards, driving the usually placid cows at a run, round and round the disoriented, scared intruders. My Beau raced about in excited opposition, leaping and dancing in response to some innate message telling him that he too should be doing something with these beasts. Plucky Jambon, barking continuously, dodged in and out of legs, swinging tails and hissing, squawking, flapping geese.

The sound of the 4 by 4 pulling up at the entrance to the farm was completely drowned out by the orchestrated bedlam. Jacques and Joe tumbled out of the vehicle, followed by a pallid, bruised-faced woman and another of a similar age who clutched Jules's arm as he stumbled out in her wake.

'Elie! Come here, this instant!' the first woman called, raising her voice to a shriek to try and make herself heard above the cacophony of the pandemonium. Xavier's pal, reluctant about the whole escapade from the beginning, managed to nip through a gap in the agitatedly circling animals and made it to his bike. Xavier tried to do the same. Marie-France, seeing that help had arrived, started getting the animals back under control, catching hold of Jambon. Still winded Eric did the same with My Beau. A slightly flustered Galla was ordered to return the equally flustered cows to the field. The first of the bikes roared off just as a patrol car and Sandrine Duval, the local gendarme, arrived with another police officer. Elie's mother clung on to her son's arm as he made a move to get on the other bike, the one Xavier was heading towards. Joe, standing tall, his powerful shoulders held back to emphasise his muscular chest, stepped in front of the smaller man to block his escape. Sandrine Duval's partner shouted 'You! Stop right there!' His words were lost in the blur of what happened next. Xavier strode determinedly towards Joe, pulling something out of his back pocket as he moved. Jacques stepped between them. In an almost balletic motion he smoothly and apparently effortlessly manoeuvred Xavier to the ground. When the gendarmes reached his side he was standing with his foot on the wrist of a hand still trying to clutch at a glinting, long bladed flick knife. Looking down at the spread-eagled man Jacques disdainfully hissed a single word into the eerily stunned silence. 'Amateur!'

Joe's face had become wintry white. His hand automatically went to his cheek, tracing the ragged scar, the result of a previous encounter with a knife in an episode that had nearly killed him.

Sandrine's colleague recovered himself first, bending down to remove the blade from Xavier's twitching hand before nodding to Jacques that he should step away. The officer hauled Xavier to his feet, took him to the police car to spread his hands and feet, searched him, fishing out a wallet stuffed with notes, an identity card from one pocket and a plastic bag half filled with a white powder from another. He handcuffed the disgruntled man's hands behind his back while Sandrine read him his rights, informing him that he was being arrested on suspicion of attempted assault intending to cause grievous bodily harm. And for possession of illegal substances.

'But what about her?' the unrepentant lout protested, nodding towards Marie-France, who'd put the safety catch on the rifle and placed it on the millstone. 'She tried to kill me. She should be arrested too.'

Marie-France opened her eyes wide, a picture of innocence, declaring, in a little girl's voice that everyone present knew was not her own. 'I didn't try to kill *you*. I was just getting tomorrow's dinner ready for the chef.'

Joe, still stunned by the horrifying sense of déjà vu that had overwhelmed him when he saw the knife in Xavier's hand, rose to the occasion. Doffing an imaginary cap, he fell in with her attempts to lighten the situation.

'Thank you, *madame*.' He frowned over at the muddy body of the sacrificed goose lying lifelessly in the middle of the churned up farmyard. 'Though I'm not sure the health and safety standards are quite up to scratch.'

Eric had got My Beau under control. Looking deathly pale and clutching his ribs, he joined the group of people. Glaring at Xavier, he growled, 'If she'd been trying to kill you, you'd have been good and dead, even though your brain is a smaller target than that goose.'

Sandrine looked at Eric's bruised face. 'I don't want to be accused of drawing unjustly hasty conclusions. Eric, can you tell us who did that to you?'

Eric confirmed the obvious with a nod and 'him,' before turning to Elie's mother, still hanging on to her deflated son, worried he was going to try and make a run for it and make an already bad situation worse. 'Colette, I didn't touch your boy, I swear,' Eric said earnestly. She nodded. 'I know, Eric. Jules told me.'

CHAPTER 10

After Eric dismissed the two youths earlier in the day, Jules followed Elie at a distance, furious not only at the way his friend had spoken about Marie-France, but also because of the very real possibility that his behaviour had lost them both their jobs. Elie stopped, reached into his pocket, tipped a pinch of cocaine on to the back of his hand, sniffed deeply and noisily. Almost immediately his dispirited mood changed into exuberant euphoria, as though his walk was one of victory rather than defeat. 'Good riddance to the old bastard, that's what I say,' he crowed. 'Why would I want to go back there again anyway, doing all that filthy work for nothing.' Jules, now beside him, didn't say anything, knowing how unreasonable Elie would be if he remonstrated. He sighed, thinking regretfully of the cash Jacques handed over to them every Friday night, calculated on the basis of how many hours they'd worked at the farm.

'And anyway, the old sod was just jealous because she fancies me more than she fancies him.' This was too much for besotted Jules. 'Who fancies you? Marie-France? Don't be so fucking stupid.' ''Course she does. You should have seen the way she cuddled up when she was pretending to show me how to milk that stupid goat. Begging for it. Probably fed up with all the old guys she's been humping up till now.'

Jules wasn't naturally aggressive. The last time he'd been in a fight was at school, when he, Elie, Benoit and Guillaume had tussled with an opposing gang. The young Jules had inflicted lesser wounds on his opponents than the thrashing he received from his father, still living at home at the time. He surprised himself even more than spaced out Elie when his clenched fist made contact with the bony structure of the other lad's cheek. Elie staggered back, straight into a patch of thorny brambles that slashed at his hands as he tried to cling on to them to haul himself upright, scratching across his face as he fell back in. By the time he crawled out Jules had fled, to avoid the inevitable escalation he knew he'd not be able to handle. He wandered around aimlessly for a while before deciding he may as well go home, telling his mother when she arrived back from her cleaning job that Eric had given him the day off. In the middle of the afternoon his mum's phone rang. He could tell by the anxious tone of voice she used to fire questions back to the person she was speaking to, at the same time as glancing over at her son, that he featured in the conversation.

'No, I don't believe it either,' his mum said. 'Wait, I'll ask Jules. Don't ring off Colette.'

Colette. Elie's mum. Jules started to prepare his defence. 'What happened at Roumignac's farm this morning?' his mother asked. 'Well...' Not sure what sort of detail he should go into, he was completely taken aback by his mother's next question. 'Did Eric Roumignac hit Elie because he caught him trying to have sex with Marie-France?'

Jules almost laughed at this hysterical travesty of the truth. 'No, mum. That's not what happened at all. You know how Elie gets when he's pissed. Well, he started bad mouthing Marie-France. Paulette Aubry was there too, she stood up for her. Eric told him to get off his land and never come back. He told me to go with him, to make sure he really left. On the way back, he started talking rubbish, so I hit him.'

'*You* hit him? Did you hear that, Colette?' she asked into the phone, holding it up to her ear to hear the reply. 'Right, come over to mine. We'll go and tell Jacques, he'll know what to do.'

Still slightly dazed that he hadn't been given into trouble for fighting, Jules followed the two women, Elie's mum looking very much the worse for wear, over to *Chez Jacques*. His mum explained to the Luciani brothers that Elie had arrived home saying that Eric had beaten him up. The violent shit of a man Colette had hitched up with, and his pal, had headed off up to the farm to sort him out. Neither of the women felt they could repeat exactly what Elie, flying higher than any kite and egged on by an equally high and unusually congenial Xavier, had said about Marie-France.

'My car's parked in the square. Joe, go and get it. Colette, Sophie, you come with us. You too Jules. I'll phone the gendarmerie. This character sounds as if he should be managed by the professionals.'

Jules said he'd seen the patrol car pulling into Blanchards garage. Joe reached the garage just as it pulled away. An anxious Amelia, hearing Eric's name, handed him the keys to the 4 by 4. Sandrine Duval, the gendarme, received the message about Jacques' call seconds later and followed the Toyota up the familiar track to Roumignac's farm.

After Jules' mother had repeated what her son had told her, Joe strode over to the hangdog youngster. He flinched as the big man put a beefy arm across his shoulder and tipped up his face so he could examine it. 'Not a scratch! Well, Jules, if you have to fight that's the best way to come out of it.'

Sandrine Duval instructed Elie to lean on the car and spread his legs so they could pat him down. Xavier, still uncowed, despite the handcuffs, looked over and muttered something unintelligible. 'What did you say?' Sandrine asked sharply. 'Nothing,' he returned with an unpleasant smirk. 'He said, it would be much more fun if the *flic* spread her legs for him.' Joe translated the Marseille slang, using the exact intonation patterns, voice and demeanour of the original speaker. Reverting to his own voice, still speaking in *argot*, he added an unintelligible comment of his own.

'And *he* said, 'dream on, she's more of a man than you'll ever be.' But I'm sure he meant no disrespect,' Jacques remarked, casting a cautionary look at his loose tongued brother. 'None taken,' Sandrine replied, giving Joe a surprisingly pleasant smile. 'Add 'using provocative language to the arresting officer' to the charge sheet, would you Gilles,' she instructed her colleague. 'And read Elie, Elie Durand, his rights.'

She held up the bag of white powder she'd taken from his pocket. 'Sorry Colette, I'm afraid your lad's gone too far this time to be let off with a warning.' Elie's mother nodded her reluctant understanding.

'Right, we'll leave you in peace and get these two locked up out of the way. I'll come back to take statements from you all later. Colette, you might want to consider talking to us about *your* injuries. Eric, maybe you should get yourself checked out. *A bientot.*'

The air hung heavy with stillness after the Megane's engine puttered off down the track, leaving the people looking like the stragglers who'd forgotten to go home after a bad party.

'Well us farmers don't have time to stand around looking tragic. The cows and the goats will give up on us entirely if we don't get them milked soon.'

Eric tried to draw himself upright in response to Marie-France's rallying call but she could see he was still in a lot of discomfort. 'Eric, I suggest you go into the house and check yourself out' - she knew the last thing he'd want was to be fussed over – 'But will you leave your overalls as well as your boots on the step. This is a good moment for the nephew who looks so like you to see if he can fill them, temporarily. I presume you can manage without him in the bar, Jacques?'

Jules was the only one disappointed that she hadn't suggested he stay and help. His mother was anxious to get him home and Jacques was relieved, not only that Marie-France hadn't asked *him* but also because he knew she'd be in safe hands. Elie's mother was too busy agonising over her own son to think about her friend's.

'Right!' Jacques mirrored Marie-France's no-nonsense tone. She was surprised when she identified a flicker of anxiety in his eyes. Was she at last learning how to read her inscrutable lover?

'Come on, I'll run you home,' he said to the two women and Jules. 'I'll come back later to pick you up,' he told the others. 'Eric, if you do decide you want someone to look you over give me a ring and I'll bring Doc up with me.'

'Take Jambon back with you, Jacques. She's had enough excitement for one day. And don't tell Angelo that I broke all the rules and let her run riot, will you?' She smiled at him reassuringly. He'd have much preferred to keep Joe and her safely with him but understood that the two of them being together was the next best thing.

'Not quite up to your usual style but at least they fit, just,' Marie-France commented when Joe appeared dressed in Eric's discarded overalls and boots. He grinned, patted the straining front zips, stood to attention. 'Well, little one, I await your command. This is all completely new territory for me, you know.'

Relaxing for the first time since the sounds of the cars had died away, Marie-France returned his grin and led him over to the shed housing the machine that cooled the milk. 'Same rules as in the kitchen, hygiene, hygiene, hygiene,' she explained. 'Although it looks as though standards have dropped a bit since the last time I was in here.'

Joe looked around with surprise at the stainless steel sink work tops and containers of various cleaning stuffs, including powder for the washing machine tucked under the draining board. The shiny, free standing milk cooler took pride of place in the centre, perched on four spindly legs like a giant's saucepan, a stack of wide topped buckets leaning up against it, as though they were taking a rest before being put to work.

'The cooler could probably do with a thorough clean before we fill it, as could the buckets. There are plenty of clean cloths on that shelf. If you could set to work on that Galla and I will go and bring in the cows.' She picked up a plastic container of cleaning solution and handed it to Joe, who immediately took it to the light and started reading the dilution rates. More of her tension started to ease with the relief that she had someone who could get on with the job competently, without supervision. A phrase to do with the difference between men and boys came to mind but she hastily supressed it. She didn't want any thoughts about any men or boys inveigling their way into her consciousness for the time being. Nodding approvingly as Joe washed his hands before making up the sterilising solution, she joined Galla, waiting at the door. The two figures walked off together through the fast fading light of the dull December afternoon.

The cows and the goats installed in their habitual order, munching contentedly on the hay, Marie-France left Galla in charge and went back over to the shed to get the udder wash. She took two of the half a dozen newly cleaned buckets, upside down on the draining board, picked out a couple of the clean cloths neatly folded on the shelf. Joe was giving a final rinse to the now sparkling cooler. Again, Marie-France nodded her approval, suggesting that once he was finished he could bring the rest of the buckets over to the stable. She plodded back across the yard, the buckets seeming incongruously clean as she picked her way around the worst of the muddy puddles.

Only minutes later Joe's big form loomed at the open doors. He stood quietly listening to her crooning to a cow in the mixture of Gaelic and French she used to soothe the animals as she fitted the suction cups, sure she was soothing herself as well. Somewhat warily, he took a step into the stable, taking note of the equipment and the procedure. Half a dozen cows, milked two at a time, the milk going through pipes into a stainless steel churn on a trolley plugged in to an aged looking electrical socket. When the milk finished spurting from the first two cows Marie-France methodically emptied the churn into two buckets, dividing it equally so they were both half full.

Joe spoke for the first time, the sound of his quiet voice causing no disturbance to the calm atmosphere. 'Let me guess, that gets poured into the cooling machine in the shed? A job for a big strong man like me, rather than a pip-squeak female like you,' he teased.

She was happy that the light-hearted banter they indulged in while they were working together in the bar or the kitchen felt just as appropriate here, in her workplace.

Joe picked up the buckets, carrying them effortlessly over

to the shed while she pushed the mobile milking machine along to the next couple of cows patiently waiting, chewing a mouthful of hay, idly swishing their tails, twitching their ears, occasionally peeing into the gulley that led out into another gulley outside the stable door that directed the liquid towards a slope, where it was carried by gravity down into the land.

Once the remaining cows were milked it was the turn of the goats. 'No machine for them?' Joe asked as Marie-France sat herself down on the rickety three legged stool. 'No, it's not worth it for just two and actually, it's a job I really enjoy. Very relaxing, as long as they're relaxed. No point trying if their stressed. Watch yourself!' she added with a grin, as the beast he was standing beside lifted its tail. He moved just in time to avoid the stream of steaming urine.

Joe watched her for a while, leaning against the pretty, ear twitching animal, squeezing and warbling her multi lingual sweet nothings. 'I see what you mean. Any chance I could have a go?' he murmured, almost whispering as if he didn't want to break a magical spell that had been cast in this hallowed ground,

Marie-France, knowing the gentleness of his hands, intimately, suggested he put them over hers, to feel the action. He squatted down behind the stool, encircling her with his arms while his hands covered hers. She leant back into his solid, warm body, imagining the comfort she could find there. But malevolent whispers started up in her mind, echoing Elie and Xavier's words about her. Then she remembered Eric's comment about Jacques and children and her belated realisation about her careless attitude towards their sex. Trying to appear casual she leant forward, as if she was just shifting her position. Joe stood up to give her space.

The milking finished, he cupped his hands melodramatically around one of the goats' head, as though protecting its ears from the calumny he was about to pronounce. 'Goats' meat is becoming very trendy at the moment,' he said in a stage whisper. 'It would be a great specialty to be able to offer in the restaurant. Any possibility of it coming on to the home-produced menu?'

Marie-France tilted her head, hearing familiar footsteps approaching. 'I don't see why not. Let's ask the boss what he thinks.'

The title left her lips spontaneously, making her realise she'd come to a decision about one of the matters that had been preying in the background of her mind.

Eric stepped almost jauntily through the door, dressed in clean overalls, the washing machine wasn't reserved for animal hygiene, and a pair of dusty, cracked but too good to throw away, boots. The injury to his face, caused by one of the bulky rings his assailant had been wearing, cleaned up now, looked more like a heavy scratch than a gash, an inflamed blotch in an iodine jaundiced cheek.

'How are you Eric?' Marie-France and Joe asked simultaneously. 'I'm fine, apart from a case of severely dented dignity. You've no idea, Joe, how unnerving it is to be rescued by a gun toting leprechaun!' His nephew grinned. 'I can imagine. But tell me, what actually happened?'

'Well, just as that lout was about to put the boot in she came out of the house with my rifle...' 'What did she say, exactly?' Joe interrupted. Marie-France frowned, not understanding why Joe was asking for such details. Eric understood though.

'Of course! The latest Luciani story in the making. I'll provide the gist and you dress it up. It just so happens that I've brought a bottle of house *rouge* over to keep out the autumn chill. Sharing a bottle during milking, a tradition that goes back to my parents' time, has recently fallen out of use. Time we re-instated it. Marie-France, you sit back down on that stool. We'll leave the beasts inside tonight, give them a treat to help them get over the trauma of their day. And we'll finish this bottle, to help us get over ours. So, Joe, you'll want the tale from the beginning. Well, we'd just arrived back from our walk when the bikes arrived...'

'The peace of the afternoon was shattered by the roar of two powerful bikes careering into the yard?' Joe suggested. Eric beamed, started to enjoy the reconstructed memory of the events as much as he'd loathed the reality. 'Get off my land!'

Eric commanded in a ringing voice, but the hoodlum, dressed in black leather from head to toe, stepped forwards and caught him unawares, pushing him to the muddy ground.'

Eric nodded his approval at Joe's words, but his face grew solemn as he remembered the fear he'd experienced when he heard Xavier calling to the others to come and join in the fun, knowing he wouldn't be able to protect himself or, more importantly, Marie-France. He had no intention of repeating what they'd said about her, or what they'd threatened to do to her.

'So, you were lying on the ground, expecting a good kicking in retaliation for the thrashing you were supposed to have given Elie. Marie-France appeared, holding your rifle. What did she say? What did you say, Marie-France?'

Warming to the game now, well aware that Joe wasn't as fatuous as he made himself out to be, she was impressed with the way he was encouraging them to turn a harrowing event into an entertaining tale. Maybe this was what stress counsellors did, although the medicine and the situation was hardly clinical. 'I suppose I said, stop right there, or something like that.'

'That's exactly what you did say,' Eric chipped in. 'I remember thinking that it was a shame he didn't have as much sense as the dogs, he'd have done what he was told. Although I must admit, when he said he didn't believe you'd use the gun, I thought myself you were bluffing. Where on earth did you learn to shoot like that?'

'In a misspent youth up in the Alps, sitting on hillsides potting rabbits, mainly. Although I did get the occasional deer which brightened up my diet no end.'

Neither of the men had heard her talk about her summers alone with the sheep in the mountain pastures but Joe didn't want to get diverted from the present story he was constructing. 'So, when did you realise that she actually could shoot, Eric?'
'When she winged the mirror of his bike. I knew that was no fluke.'

'A bullet zinged against the wing mirror of the ruffian's

precious bike, distracting his attention from Eric, who managed to scramble to his feet? Then what? Did you really shoot that goose in cold blood, little one?'

Eric flung back his head and laughed at the squeamishness of this city raised young man. 'The only way to shoot anything is to do it in cold, calculating blood. And that she certainly did, even choosing one of the ganders we'd already identified for slaughter. It's a shame to waste a skill like that, Marie-France. Would you consider joining the *chasse?'*

'Maybe,' she agreed, imagining the pleasure of walking through the woods, potting the occasional pheasant or pigeon. 'But I'd need another dog. Galla, along with most border collies, is too sensitive to be comfortable around guns. She coped surprising well today, all things considered.' 'That's the next bit of your tale, Joe, when she orders Galla to jump into the field and push the cows through the closed gate.' Joe's eyes brightened at the opportunity for impersonation this presented. 'Tell me the exact words you used,' he commanded. ' You don't speak to Galla in French, do you?'

The dog in question was lying in front of the stable doors, pulled almost closed to keep out the darkening evening. She lifted one ear and two eyebrow-like markings at the sound of her name, then let out a bored groan, and a puff of air from her lips, expressing her mild exasperation that no one was giving her anything to do. She became mildly interested when she heard *her* commands being repeated by one of the people she now thought of as part of her entourage but relaxed after her boss signalled they were not directed at her.

'You've certainly got my father's gift of impersonation, my lad,' Eric said, after they'd finished laughing at his camped up impression of Marie-France creating the mini stampede. 'But now it's your turn to tell us exactly what happened, over at the cars. One minute that lout was trying to escape, the next he was flat on his back, with Jacques, as unruffled as ever, looking down on him. I'd have thought if anyone was the fighter it was you. Where did he learn to do that?'

'Martial arts. We both went as kids but I only played at it. Jacques went into it really seriously, the philosophy of control and everything. It became a way of life for him. Still is.'

Joe became sombre, visualising the knife in Xavier's hand. He'd not had time to appreciate that his brother may well have saved his life. He'd also not had time to wonder, until this moment, whether that disdainful word 'amateur' was actually directed at him. Marie-France was lost in her own reveries. A lifetime's devotion to the mastery of control? That explained a lot about the man who'd so recently become her lover.

'And what language were you and that punk speaking? It certainly wasn't Occitan,' Eric remarked, referring to the local patois he was familiar with. 'Marseille argot, although not real street talk. He's not tough enough to make it as a hard man or a dealer there. Obviously a rich kid, like us.'

With a toss of his head Joe evoked his absent brother. At that very moment, Jacques pulled into the farmyard, driving his own car for once. He got out, waited patiently for My Beau, left outside to do his alerting job, to finish barking, was subjected to a thorough sniffing to establish that this was a familiar allowed to advance. Jacques started walking towards the square of light seeping around the stable doors. They were pulled open, two bulky figures framed in the entrance, their shapes so similar they might have been mirror images or butterfly wings. 'I'm later than I anticipated,' he explained, as Eric and Joe relaxed, revealing Marie-France perched on a stool behind them. 'Unexpected delivery. Everyone all right?' 'We're all fine.' Eric, master of the house, replied for them all. 'Except that we've just emptied this bottle. Shall I open another?' 'Another time perhaps. I've left Eveline in the bar and Angelo's getting anxious. The villagers are making up their own, ever more exciting versions, of what went on here. He's beginning to think something bad has happened to you two because you haven't come home. Having said that, if you want some company tonight, Eric, I'd be happy to volunteer Joe to stay with you.'

Marie-France staying was obviously not an option, as far as

he was concerned. Eric shook his head. 'I'll be fine, Jacques, thank you. In fact, now I think of it, I'm really looking forward to having my house back. Anyway, Joe would never fit into that little bed under the stairs.'

Marie-France, detester of confined spaces, would never cope with that little bed either. To be the one to stay in it was certainly not an option for her.

During the short drive back to Labeille, Joe, sitting in the front passenger seat, muttered under his breath, rehearsing his version of the day's events, so he'd be ready to entertain the aperitif drinkers. Marie-France, Galla at her feet, sat quietly in the back. Once or twice Jacques glanced at her reflexion in the rear view mirror but her eyes weren't looking for his, they just stared pensively out into the early evening darkness.

They arrived back at the bar, everyone was agog, waiting for the details they knew vociferous Joe would provide, unlike his guarded brother. 'An authentic Grandfather Jacques' tale,' Joe assured Jacques. 'All exciting highlights and good, cleanish fun. Let the boys listen too. It'll let Ange get into the spirit of the thing so he can tell his own pals and forget that he was worried. Another Luciani legend in the making. But don't worry, you and I have been given very minor parts.'

CHAPTER 11

Everyone brought their drinks and found their places, at the bar or squashed around tables, a much fuller house than usual on a pre-Christmas evening. Joe stood up and took centre stage. 'I know you're all anxious to hear the full, unexpurgated version of today's events,' he began. 'Without any of the Chinese whisper adaptations that have no doubt been sneaking about the village.' The story he told was about as far from the truth as any Chinese whisper could have made it.

'You all know Eric Roumignac, of course, who, it so happens is also a Luciani, my uncle, no less.' Cautious cheers of welcome for the local man. 'And Marie-France and Galla don't need any introduction.' The cheers were more committed this time, quickly followed by a murmur of disappointment that the village heroes weren't present to take their celebrated bow.

'So, where to start?' Joe said diffidently, as if he hadn't got his delivery almost word perfect. 'Ah, of course. It all started when Eric gave one of the local lads a chance to earn a bit of pocket money by doing a few odd jobs around the farm. Eric's been a bit short handed recently, since his little helper decided to take an unscheduled holiday in hospital.' Smiles, tuts of sympathy for Marie-France.

'Well this boy was getting a bit too big for his boots, though not nearly big enough for Eric's. He decided to push his luck and play at being a grown up.'

Elie was not named, referred to only as 'the boy', rather an understatement for a seventeen year old. But it gave the flavour of Joe's account the naivety he was striving for. 'Eric found him in the barn, puffing away at one of the fags he'd nicked from his mum's new boyfriend. More of him later. Incensed at the incendiary possibilities' - groans from the crowd at the verbosity

– 'Eric told the boy he couldn't be trusted to obey the rules and would have to leave the farm straight away. And not bother coming back.'

Fair enough. Quite right. Stupid kid. The audience muttered among themselves, happily going along with the anonymity of the offender.

'But what Eric didn't know was that the boy, deciding he needed a drink to go with his fag, had nicked a bottle of Roumignac's best, well-aged *eau de vie* from the *cave.* That, as you will all appreciate, is not child's play.'

Chuckles of appreciation, mutters of strong stuff that.

'So, when the boy left Roumignac's farm he didn't go just quite as straight home as he might. In fact, he went right off the straight and narrow and fell into the ditch. He had a short nap before hauling himself out, straight into a clump of brambles, which one might believe had been specially sharpened for the occasion.'

Joe had decided to leave Jules out of the story entirely, knowing he wasn't innately a fighter, not wanting him subjected to the inevitable challenges if he was portrayed as the hero of the tale.

'By the time the boy reached home he was in a sorry state, scratched and bedraggled, hung over and embarrassed, especially when the punk who was his mother's new boyfriend was the only one in the house. 'Somebody hit you, kid?' this unsavoury type asked, giving the boy the inspiration for a way to make himself a victim rather than a fool. 'The old man I've been helping out gave me a doing because I wasn't working fast enough,' was the feeble reply he came up with.'

How ridiculous! Eric wouldn't hurt a fly, not a human fly anyway! Eric's skill and accuracy as part of the local hunt was well known and admired.

'Well the punk, an entirely unpleasant kettle of fish, thought this would be a good opportunity to impress the boy's mother, to maybe help him get into her.....'

Joe just paused long enough for the salacious grins before

adding, 'to help him get into her good books!' This was, after all, a family tale. He waited for the appreciative guffaws to die down. 'I'll not have anyone knocking my woman's brat, I mean son, about. Let's go and give this old man a doing,' the punk said.

A few of the longer standing customers protested. Eric's not old. A mere youngster. Not even sixty.

Joe waited for the complaints to subside before he continued. 'The boy's mother had arrived home by this time. She protested. She didn't believe that Eric, who she'd known all her life as a kindly, fair man, would have hit her boy. But the punk, all fired up with illicit substances, hustled the boy out on to the back of his powerful Harley Davidson.'

Joe had also decided to delete Xavier's friend from the action. He'd got away and didn't seem to have played much of a part anyway.

'Now, take yourselves up to Roumignac's farm. Imagine the peace of the afternoon, that dusky time when every sound is magnified until a cat's purr can sound like a lion's roar.' Joe's audience held its breath, leaning forward to catch his whispered words. A tin tray crashing to the floor shocked them upright in their seats and his growled impression of a motor bike roar filled the hushed bar. 'Eric and Marie-France, his little helper, and Galla, of course' - cheers from the canine fan club – 'were bringing the cows in for milking when this raucous sound rent the air.' 'Might be trouble,' chivalrous Eric predicted. 'Marie-France, you go into the house. I'll sort this out.' Most unusually, she did what she was told.'

Appreciative chuckles from those who knew of the impetuous young woman's antics from the past.

'Eric stood in the muddy farmyard, waiting for the threatening bike to arrive. When it did, he was appalled to see the boy get off with his face all scratched and bruised. He'd heard talk about the violent reputation of the punk and presumed he'd beaten up the boy. He rushed over to see if he was badly hurt, straight into the fist of the cowardly lout who was with him. Poor Eric wasn't prepared. He fell to the ground, gasping for breath at the shock as much as the pain.'

That's terrible! Poor Eric. What a bastard. The sympathy was genuine.

'Eric didn't stand a chance. He was down in the mud waiting for the kick that he knew would follow the punch, now he was such an easy target. A voice rang out. 'Stop right there!' The punk looked up and saw a tiny woman clutching a heavy gun.'

Marie-France to the rescue, the audience sighed in unison.

'The foolhardy punk laughed. 'Ooh, I'm so frightened. Be careful you don't shoot your foot off with that big thing, you silly cow." Joe's Marseille accent, coarse and strident, painted a picture of the streets and gutters that no words could ever achieve.

'Marie-France, that's who the little woman was, didn't say a word. She just loosed off a shot that whistled past the punk's ear, shattering the mirror on his precious bike. 'You'll pay for that,' he growled, completely forgetting Eric in his rage as he strode towards the gun toting woman. Another shot rang out. This one made the point far more emphatically, blowing the head off an unfortunate goose, that squawked and flapped and splattered the shocked punk with great drops of vermillion blood.'

'He'll be serving his steak 'vermillion' instead of 'blue' in his posh restaurant,' one wag called out. He was quickly hushed so the story teller could continue.

Joe, grinning good naturedly at the interruption, lowered his voice, to draw his listeners in again. 'Eric was on his feet by now but Marie-France wasn't finished. 'Eric, open the gate,' she called out.'

Not all the company understood, and turned to their companions for a translation of the Occitan that Joe had coming out of Marie-France's mouth.

'Galla, away tae me, come by, lie doon, walk up,' Joe called next, his perfect caricature making it obvious who the speaker was, his explicit gestures expressing the gist of the foreign words that *none* of them understood.

'Marie-France! Marie-France!' Someone started up the

rhythmic chant. Someone else extended it. 'Marie-France and Galla! Marie-France and Galla!'

The whole bar filled with the vociferous intoning of the names, loudly accompanied by handclaps and the banging of glasses on tables.

Marie-France had been sitting outside on the balcony, apprehensive at first, worried about how she was going to be portrayed in relation to the explicitly sexual nature of the threats she'd been subjected to. Even more worried about the image the village already had of her, according to what Xavier, the punk, had said. As Joe's narration advanced she realised that he didn't know about the character assassination, Eric had left it out of his account completely, and she began to enjoy his entertaining version of the nasty events. She stood up, calling Galla to heel just as Angelo came to get her. He and Jacqui opened both the balcony doors and formed a guard of honour for her and her famous dog.

The cheers erupted in anticipation of the famed bow that people were sure was about to be performed. They weren't disappointed.

With Galla close beside her Marie-France stepped into the room, gave a discreet gestural command. Together they acknowledged their fans, the woman inclining her head, the dog, by folding her front legs and raising her backside, doing the same. The connoisseurs of this act, knowing more was to come, cheered even louder. The performers took another couple of steps, Galla rose up on to her hind legs and dipped her head while Marie-France gave a flourishing bow from the waist. The tumult was only shushed into silence when someone called out, 'Come on, Marie-France, you tell us what you said.'

She gave a mischievous grin to Joe before she repeated the commands. This time she spoke in Gaelic, not the Scottish English she'd so carefully taught him.

He assumed a dramatically puzzled expression, cupped a hand around an ear. 'What did you say?' Angelo piped up before she could reply.

'She said....' He repeated the commands, using exactly the same words and intonation as Marie-France herself. They'd decided to train Jambon in Gaelic!

Angelo's turn to be clapped and cheered. Joe, more than happy to share the stage, lifted him up and sat him on the bar. Next, with a wicked smile, he lifted Marie-France up and planked her down beside him. People were trying to outshout each other as the offers of refreshment flooded in.

'Yeeha!' Joe's cowboy holler sliced through the noise, reminding the company that the tale he was telling hadn't finished. As the unruly crowd settled down to listen, Jacques and Eveline moved amongst them, taking orders, serving drinks.

'Fortunately, Galla understands everything that Marie-France says, in whatever language, so she jumped into the field and drove the cows into the yard, pushing them round and round the punk and the boy until they fell over with dizziness. The people not the cows. At this point reinforcements, Jacques and I, arrived with *les flics* in hot pursuit. All we had to do was open the car door so the baddies could be bundled in and taken off to be put behind bars, where we hope they will languish for as long as it takes for them the realise they should never mess with this family again!'

It wasn't long before the customers spilled out on the forecourt, recalling pertinent phrases, chatting and cheerful after the unscheduled *apero spectacle*. They weren't really fooled by Joe's levity. A motorbiking thug beating up someone, anyone, was never a light-hearted matter. It was common knowledge, too, that poor Colette had got herself into yet another abusive relationship. And that Elie, who for a while looked as though he might make something of his life, with the Lucianis' support and against all the odds, had been drinking, drugging and drifting his way back down into the mire. Jules hadn't been mentioned so no one mentioned him now. He wasn't at the gathering because his mother had kept him at home. He hadn't protested, still shocked at Elie's arrest and racked with worry about the uncertainty of his standing in relation to Eric, the Lucianis and especially Marie-France. Benoit and Guillaume, his friends from childhood, who'd listened to Joe's imaginative telling of events, went to see him the next day. He gave his more accurate account of what he'd witnessed, making the most of Jacques' expert performance when he disarmed Xavier, protecting big Joe from being knifed, again. They agreed that as Joe had left this action out of the story entirely, it was evidently something that shouldn't be spoken of, except of course in the strictest confidence. Out on the streets and behind the villagers' walls another thread wound its way around and into the Luciani legend.

CHAPTER 12

Chez Jacques' doors were locked at half past nine, later than was usual on a drab December evening. Joe prepared a light supper to have *en famille* before the boys went up to bed. Marie-France's performing high rapidly plummeted. She picked at the food then left the table, using the remaining pups as an excuse. Four of the eight had already gone to their new homes, one was being picked up the following day and Marie-France intended delivering Jazzy, reserved for Christian, the sheep farmer owner of Galla's mate, in person. Jambon and Janus were being kept, to be trained on Eric's farm. After they were all fed, exercised and settled for the night she came back up the steps and sat down on the balcony of the house next door, to try make some sense of her tangled thoughts.

Of no fixed abode. A designation that to most implies deprivation, neglect, loneliness. To Marie-France it spelled out freedom, independence, fulfilment. For all her adult years she'd moved around the country, shearing here, lambing there, harvesting somewhere else, sleeping in barns and outhouses or in the back of the ancient Land Rover now languishing in a field on her parents' croft in Skye. For all her adult years she'd lived an itinerant life, taking pleasure where she found it. Until almost a year ago when she'd come to this little village to set up home with a man who was dead when she arrived. She'd stayed because Jacques had let her take over the lease to his house next door to the bar. And then she'd become involved, she wasn't sure how, in his business. Then he'd more or less declared to his family that she was the most important person in his life. In all fairness, Jacques couldn't be blamed for the accident that for a while had completely stripped her of her independence. Nevertheless, the notion that he'd taken advantage of her reliance to increase his hold upon her started to fester, burning unpleasantly in the pit of her stomach. While she was in hospital he'd persuaded Eric Roumignac that he shouldn't just give her a job, the job she wanted and was so capable of doing, but that they, she and Eric, should form an official, legal partnership. Eric himself, she was convinced he was actually quite happy muddling along as he had for years, had told her that he thought Jacques' suggestion was more about keeping her around than a sound business proposition. Keeping her, manipulating her, possessing her. That was it, that's what Jacques was doing, trying to make her one of his possessions! Well, she wouldn't have it, she wouldn't be possessed, she wouldn't stay in this community that was judging her according to its own petty standards of morality. She'd have to buy a vehicle. Not a problem. She'd sign back on with the agency that had always found her work. The lambing season was about to begin so she'd be readily welcomed back into the fold, the sheep fold where she belonged. She'd show him, Monsieur controlling Jacques Luciani, that he couldn't control her! And if he had made her pregnant during their unguarded coupling, she'd get rid of it, his unwanted brat, at the earliest opportunity.

Marie-France was renowned for her ability to problem solve, to look at a situation and take all practical steps to resolve any difficulties that might be muddying the waters of the lives they were affecting. Usually, when she'd set her mind on a course of action, she felt positive, raring to go. The huddled woman clutching a thin jacket around her skinny body, shivering in the cold of the night, clenching her teeth as she stared out into the darkness, didn't give that impression at all.

Jacques didn't imagine for one second that Marie-France would trot dutifully up the stairs to his bed night after night for ever. At the very least he expected that sometimes she'd make her way up one more flight to Joe. Nevertheless, he was saddened to see, after they'd only spent two nights together, that she was sitting dejectedly outside on the balcony, Galla at her feet, staring out at nothing. Once the bar had been readied for the morning Joe went out for a village prowl, too over-stimulated by the events of the day, and his retelling of them, to settle to sleep. Jacques selected two fleeces from the coat hooks by the kitchen door, put one on himself and carried the other, along with two glasses of cognac, out on to the balcony.

Galla opened her eyes, didn't lift her head, only raised the markings that were as expressive as any eyebrows, immediately recognising one of her people, no need to react further.

'Alright?' Jacques asked quietly, pulling over a table to put the drinks on and a chair so he could sit beside her. His mouth dried up with fear at the baleful look she gave him. He'd anticipated she'd be upset but wasn't prepared for the fury flashing in her grey green eyes.

On the way back from Roumignac's farm Jacques had heard, in painfully explicit detail, about Xavier's carnal intentions towards Marie-France. The punk, as Joe had so appropriately christened him, had been fired up by Elie's self -defensive assertations about her sexual behaviour, cobbled together from snippets of gossip gathered and exaggerated into fantasies by some of the youths he'd taken to hanging about with. Colette, sitting in the back of the car with her friend, told her about how the violent man had ranted and raved, goading his reluctant companion and Elie into falling in with his sadistic plans. She spoke loudly enough so that Jacques was bound to overhear. He understood that to be her way of letting him know about the threat to Marie-France, without having to suffer the embarrassment of telling him directly. Jules, sitting tensely in the front seat, pretended he wasn't listening.

So Jacques now knew that it was actually Marie-France who'd been the focus of that afternoon's attack. Knowing too about the fight or flight response that such an attack could arouse, he'd prepared himself to talk her out of running away. But it seemed rather as if she was going to counter attack. And that he was the target.

She took a gulp from the glass he pushed towards her, by her expression he wondered if she was going to throw it in his face.

She was chewing her cheeks as if trying to restrain herself from spitting out the words gathering in her mouth. He gave her an opening.

'Difficult day today,' he said mildly. That was enough to unleash her simmering venom. 'Difficult day? Difficult year, more like. I should never have believed I could live among people. I don't belong. I don't know why I ever thought I could. In fact, I don't know what I'm doing in this village at all!'

Jacques' heart started pounding. He felt the panic rising to his throat but didn't allow it to choke him. At least he was getting some idea of what was troubling her. But he wouldn't address that yet. A roundabout route would be the better trajectory.

'Oh?' he said calmly. 'What about your partnership with Eric?' 'Oh yes! My partnership with Eric. The one you persuaded him to offer, to keep me here. I'm not going into a partnership with Eric, or anyone else. He doesn't need me. In fact, all I've done is brought complications into his life, poor man.'

Jacques listened, overtly impassive, but his brain was frantic, filing away the information she was giving him, desperately trying to work out how to counter her negativity. 'I see,' he murmured. 'Have you told Eric?' 'No, not yet. But I will, tomorrow. I'm sure he'll be greatly relieved.'

Her words were still bitter. Jacques became increasingly sure that the bile in them was primarily aimed at him. 'Mmm. Well while we're talking about partnerships, perhaps it's time we got a few things cleared up about ours, if that's what it is.'

She stiffened, clenched her fists. He wished she would hit him, it would be so much easier to subdue her physically than it was to negotiate around her disordered thoughts. 'What about our *partnership*, as you might think of it?'

The emphasis she put on the word made it sound as if the idea of anything between them was totally unpalatable. His next words seemed inconceivably inappropriate. 'I wonder, Marie-France, if you've ever considered getting married again.'

She almost choked. Was he really so insensitive, so stupid, to propose to her when she'd as good as said that she was leaving?

The smooth voice broke into the jumble of confused, vitriolic thoughts that she just couldn't sort out into words.

'But if you have, thought about getting married that is, I'm afraid it won't be to me. Eveline and I are not going to divorce. It keeps everything far more straightforward and secure for the boys if we're still legally man and wife, in terms of inheritance and such like. Of course, our marriage will merely be a legality, not a lifestyle, but everything we have, houses, business, etcetera is in joint names. Neither of us sees the point of complicating that by making our separation legal. And neither of us feels the need to make any commitment other than an emotional one in any future relationship.'

Any future relationship? Did she come into that category? And what about the needs of the person in any future relationship? What if they did want to make more of a commitment than just an emotional one.

At this point she called her perverse inner rantings to a halt. Hadn't Jacques actually just relieved her of one of her psychological burdens? She returned her attention to his infuriatingly calm voice. 'The most important thing, of course, is that nothing muddies the water for the boys' future.'

Eric's words about Jacques' total focus on his children exploded in her brain. Her blood started to boil again as she remembered the potential outcome of their unprotected sex. 'Another thing I've wondered about, Marie-France, is if you've given any thought to having children?'

Her pulse rate went from nothing to a hundred quicker than her maiden-name-sake, Arthur MacDonald, reputed to have been the first man to take a car to that speed. She almost gasped out loud with this proof of the conviction she'd sometimes had that Jacques was a mind reader. Again, his steady, unemotional voice didn't waver. 'But if you have, considered having children, that is, I'm afraid that it won't be with me. I had the snip after Angelo was born, even before I knew how he was going to turn out.'

The loving warmth when he talked of his son was tinged

with humour. Humour? Was he laughing at her, taking the piss because he knew she'd have been worried? She forced herself to look at him directly for the first time since he'd sat down beside her. Her breath caught in her throat at the passion shining from his eyes. The formality of his previous speech had evaporated when he spoke again.

'Marie-France, I have never wanted anyone, or anything, as much as I want you. I'm not just talking about sex, although I have no complaints on that score. What I want is you, the Marie-France-ness of who you are, your individuality, your love of freedom, your total disregard for convention.' He lent forward and covered her hand with his own. She was so transfixed by the way he was looking at her and what he was saying that she didn't even think to pull it away. He'd become the man he'd always been for her. Someone to confide in, to trust.

'My total disregard for convention, as you put it, seems to have earned me a rather unsavoury reputation. Do you know what they are saying about me, Jacques?' 'They who? No one of any worth or significance judges you at all. That was made patently clear to me by people's reactions after you'd had your accident. You've no idea how difficult it was to follow your instructions and keep everyone away. Doc, for example. I felt I was well qualified as a medical practitioner by the time I'd remembered the answers to all the questions he sent me in with. And I had to memorise every detail of your progress chart, just to make sure that the hospital staff were not being parsimonious with the truth when they said you were getting better. It was Doc who put me in contact with Jean-Paul for your physio and he suggested that Geneviève could come in on a daily basis so we could get you home. And then there was Yves, sending almost daily messages with Mathieu, demanding that he should be informed instantly if there was anything at all that he could do to help.'

'And as for Pierre Calvet,' Jacques continued. 'When he heard what had happened he came to tell me that he'd work overtime himself to make sure the facilities were right, so we could get you back as soon as possible.'

Pierre Calvet, the builder? She'd never even spoken to him since Rab's funeral. Why would he be so concerned? It had never occurred to her that Rab's boss might have felt some responsibility for the death of one of his workers. Or that he might harbour compassionate feelings towards the bereaved girlfriend who'd been left behind.

Jacques hadn't yet finished with his identity parade of caring people. 'Dominique was in every morning with a different selection of pastries and such like that Georges had baked specially, hoping they'd tempt you to eat. Janine arrived regularly with cantal cheese and goat's milk yoghurts, in case we didn't know they were your favourite. Serge offered to give a lift to anyone who hadn't got their own transport and wanted to visit you, until we explained that you wouldn't want to see them. Eveline and I nearly fell out, because she was convinced that I was being over-protective and wouldn't *let* anyone else come to see you. Joe and I did fall out. He told me I was a selfish bastard thinking I was the only one who loved you. I almost expected him to change my name to his, as your official partner. And Margaret McPherson phoned me sounding very concerned, but I haven't a clue what she said.'

They exchanged a smile in acknowledgement of the garrulous Scotswoman's chatterbility.

'And as for the boys, I caught Jacqui and Matt planning how they would get to the hospital on public transport, convinced that you must really want to see them. As for Angelo, well he had a full blown tantrum because I wouldn't let him put Galla and the pups in the boot of the car so you could look out of the window and see them. And Benoit, Jules and Guillaume were falling over themselves trying to help in any possible way so you wouldn't feel they'd let you down. I should have noticed then that Elie wasn't so much a part of the gang as he had been. But I had other matters on my mind. You. So, are you still bothered about what they, whoever they are, are saying about you? Because I'm not, and neither are any of the other people who care for you.'

Marie-France gazed at him in wonder. In less time than it had taken her to drink a glass of cognac this inscrutable man had dispelled all her apparently insurmountable problems. As she studied his handsome, solemn face she became aware that the fire that had been fuelling her hate towards him had changed its course and was now directing its heat to a completely different part of her anatomy.

She decided, quite consciously, to employ some of the calming strategies she used so successfully with her dogs when they were upset, knowing that their effect was as quietening for her own emotions as it was for them. Firstly she turned her head away - a direct look could be interpreted as confrontational. Normally, her next gesture would be to yawn, usually this produced the same response in the dog, a reflex that would help it to relax. Clamping her lips to supress the yawn that started in her jaws as soon as she thought about it, she decided that in human terms the association with bed, which was what she was trying to play down, was rather too strong. Next? Lip licking, a good, non-threatening canine exchange. She imagined licking her lips, imagined Jacques following suit. Her heart thumped like an enthusiastic tail on a reverberating wooden floor. Perhaps it was time to accept she was a woman, not a dog. A woman who didn't want to stay calm at all.

Jacques had been staring into space, chiding himself for his failings towards Elie. He turned immediately at the sound of her husky voice. Her smile was impish, her words a teasing invitation. 'If you really are prepared to take me for what I am then now's as good a time as any, don't you think?'

The tender smile, starting in his eyes, slowly finding its way to his sensuous lips, drove the last fragments of her unhappiness back into the shadowy recesses of her mind, where they lingered for a breath before expiring with a vanquished sigh. He stood up and held out his hand. Her eyes glittered. With an almost imperceptible shake of her head she reached out, catching hold of the loose cloth of his jacket, using it as leverage to help her to her feet and to pull him towards her as she backed into the sturdy wooden table. It was her turn to take control.

'Let's see if this furniture that you bought especially for me is as strong as it's supposed to be,' she grinned, rummaging through the layers of his clothes until she found his belt, which she dexterously unbuckled.

Lifting her until she was balanced on the edge of the table, controlling, controlled Jacques Luciani let out a long breath of blissful defeat.

CHAPTER 13

The festive season arrived. Marie-France was still in Labeille, still in the Luciani family's life, still working at Eric's farm and still in Jacques' bed.

The *en famille* Christmas meal, in which Corinne, Eveline's longer than one night lover was included, was a quiet event. The big festive celebration, attended by most of the village, took place in *L'hôtel de La Gare* on the night of the thirty first of December.

The previous year none of the Lucianis had been there. Jacques had been slumped in the depths of lonely misery, trying to exist without Eveline and the boys. Joe was partying in *L'Il de Reunion,* unaware that his family had been split apart. This year they all studied the menu together, Jacques sent some SMS's, received prompt replies and was all set to reserve a table for eleven.

'How do you make it eleven?' Jacqui asked. Jacques counted off on his fingers. 'Starting with the youngest and working up. Angelo, you, Joe, Marie-France, mum. Don't know Corinne's age so we'll put her next to mum. It's where she likes to be. How many is that?' 'Six. You next?' 'Yup. Me. That's seven. Emilie, Amelia, Eric, Doc. How many is that?' 'Eleven.' 'Well, there you are then. Eleven it is.'

'Ten.' Marie-France's voice was quiet but determined. 'Sitting round a table for hours on end with too much food in a room full of people is most definitely not my thing. Count me out.' 'Too much drink too?' Joe suggested, in a half-hearted attempt to persuade her. 'I don't know if it's escaped your attention but she lives in a bar, to which she has the key,' Jacques commented crisply, keen to let her know she wasn't under any pressure, from him or anyone else.

She flashed him a grateful smile. 'Right, that decides it. I'm staying here.'

'Can I stay with you?' Angelo had at first been excited that he was included in the prestigious outing, especially when he knew that lots of his pals would be there too. But Marie-France's words had obviously struck a chord. For all that he could be hilariously entertaining he wasn't really a crowd person either.

Marie-France looked to Jacques. She sensed that this was a significant occasion for him personally, to be seen with his reunited and reconstituted family and didn't want to encourage his youngest son to stay away.

Jacques looked to Marie-France, wondering if she would prefer to be alone. 'If you really don't want to come, that's fine by me, Ange but it all depends on...' 'I can't think of anyone else I'd rather end the year with,' Marie-France interjected. The saying of the words made it true.

'Nine it is then.' 'Shame grandpère couldn't be here,' Joe remarked, expressing the very thought that was burling round his brother's brain. Neither of them had realised how much they'd missed the larger than life man that had played such a big part in their young lives, until reminded by his recent visit. They were conscious of an unfillable vacuum now he'd gone.

'Wonder how Léa's trip went,' Joe mused. Like a bolt out of the blue it struck Jacques that it was totally ridiculous that they didn't know, that in these days of instant communication they'd lost contact with someone who was dear to them just because he was too deaf to speak on the phone. He made a resolution - what better time to do it? – that in the New Year he'd put in the effort to organise his grandfather's access to the internet. But for now, he had to organise the bar for the regulars arriving for their aperitif.

New Year's Eve, after a warm-up drink in the bar, the party of nine glittered off into the night, leaving Marie-France and Angelo to get up to whatever mischief they'd planned.

People were already converging on the hôtel and the Luciani party joined a chattering queue. There was no code, for dress or anything else. Most of the women dressed up and most of their men followed suit, although there were few of those. Apart from the occasional jacket, the prevalent male attire was trousers and shirts in varying styles and colours. Many, but not all of the women wore dresses or skirts, some very short and trendy, others very formal and long. Necklines ranged from the revealing plunge to the modest throat-hugger. Eveline and Corinne fell into the formal category, wearing the dresses they'd removed from each other on the first night they were together. Jacques and Joe were trendy, deciding they might be mistaken for waiters if they wore evening attire. Everyone who was anyone was there. Everyone who wasn't, the majority, was there too. The seating plan made no allowances for status or wealth, only for the size of the groups who wanted to gather together. The dining room was packed with blocks of tables, arranged with just enough space between to allow for the circulation of the squad of waiters and waitresses. Jules, Benoit and Guillaume were part of the workforce hired for the night, the hôtel profiting from the skills they'd acquired *Chez Jacques* in the summer. Elie, waiting for his case for drug possession to be heard, had been taken away from the village by his mother to stay with friends while she tried to plan a new beginning for their lives.

The evening was as packed with food, people and noise as it was supposed to be on the one night of the year when all the different cliques of the village congregated in one place. The Luciani table was a particular source of interest, as people remembered back to Jacques and Eveline's arrival in the village and recounted, with varying degrees of accuracy and goodwill, what had happened to them since.

They seemed such a respectable couple. So sad for Jacques when he was on his own. Fancy sitting at the same table with his ex-wife and her fancy woman? It's great to see them all getting on together. They certainly don't live what I'd call a conventional life. It's great for the village that they're here. Did you hear what happened at Eric Roumignac's and what was said about….?

Marie-France was conspicuous by her absence, made even more so when one of the handful of workers from the shoe factory on the outskirts of the village was persuaded to go and talk to Joe. 'No Marie-France?' she asked, more interested in the missing woman's notoriety than her welfare. Joe, quite high in the notoriety stakes himself, saw an opportunity to agitate the melting pot. 'Marie-France? Oh, she decided to spend the night with her fiancée.'

Before he could be subjected to any questioning he turned to Jacqui, as if to continue with an engrossing conversation. 'And he said and then she said and then he turned round and she said...' he gabbled, using a few words of Marseille patter that his nephew might understand. Whether he understood or not, it gave Jacqui the excuse to let out the huge guffaw that had been clamouring to escape ever since his uncle's purposefully provocative statement.

Fiancée? But I'd heard that Joe...Well I thought it was Jacques...Who could it be?' Who's not here?'

Everyone round the Luciani table had heard about Angelo's proposal to Marie-France in the car on the way to Roumignac's farm, when she'd explained the meaning of the song she'd taught them. Joe started to hum the tune of 'Mairi's Wedding' under his breath and soon a la-la, la-la version rang out. Dominique and Georges were sitting at a neighbouring table with Janine from the mini supermarket and Inès, the emotionally labile florist. Dominique gave her husband's hand a squeeze. 'Isn't it wonderful to see them all so happy?' she gushed.

Back at the bar Marie-France and Angelo were happy too, snacking on the finger food goodies that Joe left for them in the fridge and teaching some new tricks to Galla. The one involving her carrying a bottle of whisky in her mouth but presenting her tail to the hung-over victim instead was abandoned when her multilingual mistress remembered that the expression 'hair of the dog' would be lost in translation.

As soon as the food part of the evening was over and the

debris from the platters of sea food, foie gras, magret de canard, pommes *forestières*, sorbet and endless other courses had been cleared away, the more general socialising began. Jacques took his digestif with him on his rounds, stopping at every single table to exchange the season's greetings.

Some families never went to *Chez Jacques* because the café culture wasn't part of their lives, but the rumours about the activities of its prominent proprietor and his family reached the most isolated homes. Attending fêtes and other village gatherings gave their occupants the opportunity to catch up and to observe.

'Looks like he's canvassing.' A reasonable supposition. The local councillors, a mix of farmers and business people, were elected from the community, the mayor selected from their number. Jacques, a relative newcomer and entrepreneur had the right credentials to present himself at the next local elections as someone prepared to take on some civic responsibilities.

The *municipals* aren't for another two years. The end of *Madame Le Maire's* first term. I've heard he's an ambitious young man, and already pretty influential in certain quarters. The first time he was here he did the rounds with his wife. I'd heard they'd split up, but isn't that her sitting at the table?

Eveline had declined Jacques' invitation to accompany him, on the basis of their business partnership, preferring to keep a low-ish profile with Corinne.

'*Bonne année et bonne santé!*' Yves Moreau and Dr Martin stood up to shake Jacques' hand, standing aside while he kissed their wives. 'Marie-France?' Geneviève asked, anxious at the absence of her former patient. 'She's fine!' Jacques replied reassuringly, knowing that the concern was genuine .'And Angelo's looking after her, so Jacqui tells me,' Yves boomed with a knowing smile. The two boys, joining forces as soon as they were allowed, were doing a socialising tour of their own.

Jacques moved on. He and Yves, in regular contact, didn't need to converse at length. The shoe factory table next. Jacques politely moved from person to person shaking hands, giving the standard greeting, skilfully avoiding any questions that might satisfy the blatant curiosity Joe's remark about Marie-France had stimulated. He stopped to chat when he reached the boss of the factory, also the chairman of the local football club. 'Thank you for the cash, Jacques.' - loose change went into a collection box at the back of the bar - 'but we miss your training sessions. Any chance of starting up again?'

After Eveline left him Jacques had given up everything except the bar. Since then all his energies had been directed at re-establishing his family life, which included Marie-France. Now he felt a surge of reinvigoration. 'Why not? It's time me and my boys got a bit of exercise. I'll be in touch in the new year.' He tied the first knot in his mental handkerchief.

'We've got a new section. Rugby. Yves Moreau is doing the training.' 'I'll enrol my boys in that,' Jacques responded. 'Time they learned some gentlemanly manners.'

A party of noisy pompiers called him over. They stood up in almost military fashion to greet him. 'Sounds as if you gave a convincing performance up at Roumignacs, putting down that aggressive lout.' Jacques identified the speaker as the *chef* of the cadets, younger brother of Sandrine Duval, the gendarme. Before he could construct a suitably non-committal reply, Joe, also doing his rounds, joined them. 'Lifelong training in martial arts,' he remarked. 'Although in Jacques' case it's more art than martial,' he added, knowing his brother wouldn't want to get a reputation as a fighter. 'Thought so. I believe it's good discipline. Wouldn't do this rowdy crew any harm to get a taster. Don't suppose...?' 'I'll ask around. There must a club not too far away who could put on a demonstration.' Another reminding mental knot was tied. 'In the meantime...' Catching sight of Jules, he beckoned him over. 'A round for this table, on my tab,' he commanded.

A group of local worthies greeted him next. 'Your name is still on the fête committee list,' one of their number remarked. 'Any danger of you turning up to the meeting next week?' 'Every chance. Send me over the agenda, would you?' Jacques replied. 'Good. Madame Roux is retiring as chairperson. We thought of putting your name forward to replace her.' Jacques nodded his thanks for this recognition of his worth. Before he could move away they were joined by Pascal, the chef, of the culinary variety, of the hôtel, also a committee member. 'Does Joe's restaurant mean we can't combine resources for tourist events in the summer?' he asked, after acknowledging Jacques' compliments for the meal they had just eaten. 'Not at all. I don't anticipate any rivalry between us. The remit of our two establishments is completely different. In fact, I was wondering if we might extend our joint activities, put on some events in our garden, one of your extravaganza *aligot* and *saucisse* creations, for example.'

L'hôtel de La Gare, geared up for the workers' all year round *menu du jour,* only had the capacity for half a dozen tables outside. 'But you'd be better off discussing that with my brother. I believe he's got the notion to try out some novel ways of using local goats' meat. Why don't we co-opt him on to the committee?' He was already talking like the chairman-elect.

'Only two more days of peace, then we start on your house.' Pierre Calvet, the builder, was presiding with his wife over a large, rumbustious group of young men and women. A generous employer, this event was one of the perks he gifted to his workforce and their partners. Jacques did the tour of the table, asking after the plasterer's new-born baby, commiserating with the mason whose father had recently died. It was Benoit he summoned this time to deliver the round of drinks. 'I expect I'll claw back some of your bill in after-work refreshments,' he joked. 'But coffee will be on the house.'

'Might not look like his grandfather but he's made of the same stuff.' Albert Aubry seemed to have emerged from his retirement chrysalis as a social butterfly. He watched Jacques' straight back as he walked away. 'I wouldn't want to cross him anyway, ' he remarked, cackling at the idea that anyone would notice if he did oppose them.

Nicolas smiled over at the old man. This was another family

enjoying a reformation.

The less resilient, not exclusively the oldies, started to drift away home. Tables and chairs were pushed back, the discotheque flashed and crashed its way into action.

'Think I'll stay on for a bit.' Joe had settled beside Inès, in the seat that Georges had vacated when he'd scuttled back to the lair in the boulangerie he so rarely left.

'Dad, Mathieu's dad says I can go back to his, if that's okay with you.' 'Sure Jacqui. Enjoy yourself.' His normally cool son was already red faced with heat and dancing, if that's what the jumping up and down the youngsters were engaged in could be called.

For the non-discoing revellers it was the end of the night, really the beginning of the morning. Eveline and Corinne wound their arms around each other and headed for Marc's empty flat - he and Lucien were celebrating in style in a classy gay club in town. Jacques was alone when he let himself into the bar. Marie-France wasn't in the bed that they both still referred to as his, so he carried on up the stairs to the boys' room. She was curled up around Angelo, on the floor, surrounded by all his favourite toys and books. For once she appeared to be deeply, peacefully asleep. He stood and watched them for some minutes, his heart aching at the poignancy of the scene. He fixed it in his memory, a beautiful memento to gaze on in moments of solitude. When he tiptoed out of the room and down the stairs he wasn't unhappy that he'd be spending what was left of the night alone. She was here, she was safe and she had his son in her arms. What better omen could he hope for at the start of a New Year?

CHAPTER 14

'You can keep your Toyota, my *DGD* is on her way!'

The second day of January. The bar unnaturally quiet, the calm before the storm of building work, to begin the following day.

Marie-France had just taken a call from her mother. They'd spoken briefly after the bells, or, more accurately, after the pipes. In the village on Skye where Marie-France had been born it was the wail of bagpipes that welcomed the New Year. '*Bliadhna Mhath Ùr* from your dad and me,' her mum wished her. 'No time to chat now but I'll phone you, not tomorrow, too hectic with the village dropper-inners, the day after. I've got something exciting to tell you.'

What her mother had to say was indeed exciting. Marie-France's eyes sparkled as she told Joe and Jacques how her cousin, Rory, who'd been working in a garage in Glasgow, returning to his roots on the Isle of Skye, noticed the Land Rover languishing in a field. After much crawling about, skiddling in oil, proddling of panels and wiggling of wires the zealous mechanic had decided - in spite of it being a bit of a rust bucket, with a hole in the floor under the driver's seat and a drooping door that refused to shut, even with the most forceful of slams and curses – that it was a shame to let something as superficial as body work put an end to the active life of a strong-engined vehicle, even though it was well over twenty years old. Since then he'd been dashing away with a soldering iron but Marie-France's mother hadn't said anything about her cousin's project, not wanting to raise her daughter's hopes until the much-loved vehicle's resurrection was complete.

'But now she's as good as new and they're going to drive her over but we've not to worry about accommodation because they've been in touch with Marc and he's found them a cottage on the outskirts of the village they can rent cheaply, because it's out of season, for a month at a time.'

She stopped to draw breath. Joe and Jacques looked at her as if they hadn't understood a word she'd said. 'What did she say?' Jacques asked his brother. 'We-ll, I think I heard Marc's name and maybe *màthair*, which I have a notion might be Gaelic for mother, possibly something about *un cabanon* but apart from that, I haven't a clue.'

'Oh!' Marie-France cocked her head to one side, looking like a cheeky robin, except her hair was red rather than her breast. She played back in her head what she'd just said, giggled. 'I wasn't speaking French, was I?' 'Not much English either, as far as I could tell,' Jacques commented dryly. 'Definitely no Occitan or Marseillaise,' Joe added, grinning. 'Whoops! Sorry about that. I always do get a bit linguistically confused when I'm talking to *màthair*, I mean maman.' 'Not half as confused as we do after you've been talking to her. So, are you going to let us into the secret of what's made you positively luminescent with excitement,' Jacques asked.

She started again, explaining as she went along. '*DGD*', the letters were pronounced as French, 'Is the name of my Land Rover, the one I left in Skye because I thought she was dead.' '*DGD*? Well that's obvious,' Jacques muttered. 'Oh, sorry. *DGD*. *Deux Graisses Dames*. She's an eighty eight. The Land Rover, that is.' 'I see,' Joe murmured reflectively. 'Well, that's as clear as chick pea juice.'

Marie-France sighed in exasperation. The detail was getting in the way of the news she wanted to convey. 'My Land Rover is a short wheel base, an eighty eight. In bingo, which is a game like *loto*, they call out the number 88 as two fat ladies, because of the shape?' 'Right! But what makes it an eighty eight?' Joe, always interested in vehicles, genuinely wanted to know. 'It's eighty eight inches between the back wheel and the front.' Jacques tapped on his tablet and converted for Joe, 'Two metres, give or take an *inch*.'

He said the last word in supercilious English. Marie-France impatiently tried to take back control of the conversation. 'Anyway, the specifics don't matter. What's important is that my parents are driving my Land Rover down from Scotland. It'll take them a good few days, and then they're going to stay here for a while, in a little house that Doc found for them, courtesy of Marc, on the edge of the village. They're really good at keeping secrets, aren't they? I didn't even know mum had been in touch with Doc.'

She was sparkling in joyful anticipation but before Jacques could relish the sensation of his lover looking so happy his phone rang. He walked to the other end of the bar to take the call while Joe grilled Marie-France, asking about other words he'd picked up on. What a Rory was, for example.

'It must be mother's day,' Jacques remarked, as he returned to their company. Joe frowned. A dutiful son as well as a chef, he knew that this widely observed fête was celebrated at the end of May. 'That was mum,' his brother explained. 'Oh, it was a quick call for mum.' 'Mmm. All I can say is I think we must be very wicked.' Joe looked from Jacques to Marie-France, grinning provocatively. 'Alright for some,' he remarked under his breath. 'All of us,' Jacques clarified. 'That sounds fun.' Joe and Marie-France chorused in unison. 'They say there's no peace for the wicked,' Jacques explained with exaggerated patience. 'And we're not going to be getting much. Grandfather wants to come for another visit. Where on earth are we going to put him?'

Jacques frowned, imagining the banging and clattering starting up next door the following day, wishing he could wave a magic wand to instantly summon the extra accommodation that would be created when the restaurant and the living quarters above it were completed.

He looked from Joe to Marie-France and back again, but found no inspiration in their mystified faces. Joe reacted first. 'Don't see the problem. We don't have an injured midget to cater for this time and we know grandfather is more than capable of climbing any number of stairs.'

Marie-France was only recently out of hospital when Grandfather Jacques last visited, installed in a specially adapted bed and room downstairs in what was soon to be the restaurant. Not having seen the eighty four year old man for some time they hadn't known if *he* was fit enough to climb stairs. That was when Marie-France moved into Jacques' bed, although it wasn't that long since they'd been in it together. She became aware that perhaps this was part of the problem. 'I can sleep anywhere,' she declared. 'This time last year I'd bedded down on the balcony.' 'Now stacked to the gunnels with building blocks and cement,' Jacques reminded her. 'I don't sleep in my room all that often anyway, so you two can move into it if you want,' Joe suggested. 'No, I won't have you left to roam the streets of Labeille, Joe. God knows what you'd get up to,' Jacques replied severely. Marie-France decided this was a good opportunity to make the point that she and Jacques were not an inextricably bound couple. 'I could go to Eric's with the all the other young bitches. I've spent the greater part of my life sleeping in outbuildings anyway.'

The cellar where Galla had given birth to eight puppies was also part of the building site. The three that remained had been re-housed at Roumignacs' farm. The brother's exchanged relieved looks. Marie-France's words of self-deprecating humour demonstrated that she was not going to be cowed by the malevolent gossips. 'Or you, Jacques, could move back in with Joe. Or on to the bed settee in the *salon*,' she suggested.

It was taken for granted that Jacques' once marital bedroom was the only one fit to be offered to guests. 'Or I could move in with the boys,' Joe offered. 'Or *I* could move in with the boys!' Marie-France echoed, picking up on his teasing tone. 'Or *I* could go and sleep at Eric's!' Joe added. 'Although I'm not sure I'd fit into that little bed under the stairs.' 'Or I could go and sleep in Doc's cottage in the woods,' Marie-France proposed. 'Except I don't know where it is.'

'I didn't know Doc had a cottage in the woods.' Joe hadn't been around at the time of Doc and Marie-France's flirtation. 'I could come and look for it with you, although I'd have to take my teddy in case I got scared.' 'Or I could sleep on *your* balcony, Joe,' she suggested. 'Or we could all sleep in my room, together.' His eyes met hers conspiratorially, as though this was definitely an option to be seriously considered.

'Okay, okay, I get the point,' Jacques sighed, feeling the need to stop the conversation before it got any further away from him. 'We'll figure something out. Anyway, we're maybe panicking too soon. Mum said pépère has sent me an email.'

The thought of their low-tech grandfather communicating by email was almost as momentous as the announcement of the visit.

'Who's panicking?' Joe and Marie-France said together, giggling like disrespectful school children in front of a pompous teacher. 'Haven't you two got some cows to milk, or something?' Jacques responded. Still chuckling, the terrible twosome chivalrously held the door open for Eveline, who'd just arrived after depositing Angelo at the school gates.

'Or I could go and stay with Eveline and Corinne,' Joe called back over his shoulder.

'Or *I* could go and stay with Eveline and Corinne,' Marie-France countered.

'Or we could both go and stay with Eveline and Corinne,' they sang out together.

'What's that all about?' Eveline asked Jacques, as Joe shrugged into a warm jacket, trying to persuade a giggling Marie-France to fit herself in as well. 'Grandfather is coming for another visit.' 'Oh? Where's he going to stay?'

Long suffering Jacques put his head in his hands. Marie-France and Joe whooped out joyfully into the chilly morning. Watching them clamber into his Citroen saloon, Jacques thought back to the conversation he and Joe had the morning after the attack at Eric's farm. Jacques repeated what he'd learnt from Elie's mother about Marie-France being the real target of the assault. 'I might not have let him down quite so gently if I'd known,' he said, trying to temper the anger gathering in his younger brother's eyes. Joe responded with a rather weak smile.

'Oh, by the way, I haven't thanked you for saving my life, have I? Thank you.' 'You're welcome. You'd probably have blocked him yourself anyway but I didn't want to take the chance. At least I managed that okay, but too much other stuff has got away from me. I should have seen something coming with Elie. I just presumed everyone was happily coping with the lads but Eric clearly wasn't.'

He paused, mentally replaying his conversation on the balcony with Marie-France. 'She was all ready to pack her bags and go, you know, after she heard what people in the village had been calling her.' He didn't need to say her name for his brother to understand who he was referring to.

Joe reached out, rested a long-fingered hand gently on Jacques' forearm. His voice caressingly soft, he murmured, 'But she didn't go, Jacques, presumably because of the way you reassured her. And you can't take responsibility for everything that happens within your sphere. But you're right, we do need to think things through, in relation to the lads, Marie-France, Eric, everybody.'

Jacques, noting the 'we', understood, with a bit of an internal jolt, that the little brother he'd always nurtured, protected, advised had finally come of age and was declaring himself a full, active, decision-making partner in all aspects of Luciani family life, including its associates.

'What are your thoughts?' he asked, in acknowledgement of this realisation. 'Okay. The village lads first. We took them on in the summer because there was plenty of work. At this time of year there's not enough to keep us, by which I mean you, me, and Eveline, busy.'

'Guillaume isn't a worry. Amelia is organising for him to enrol on an apprenticeship scheme, so he'll be with them for some of the time for practical work when he's not at college,' Jacques offered. Joe nodded approvingly. 'I'd wondered about going down that route with Benoit but I think he needs more experience before he commits to restauration. I'm going to discuss the possibility with Sandrine of him spending some time with one of my contacts in Marseille.'

Jacques raised eyebrow suggested that perhaps that wasn't all Joe was going to 'discuss' with Benoit's attractive mother. All he received back was a crooked grin.

'And Jules?' Jacques asked. 'It doesn't seem right he should feel he's being penalised because of Elie's misdemeanour, especially when he stood up for Marie-France but...'

Joe interrupted with surprising vehemence. 'Puppy love is all very well but he's getting a bit old for it now. In any case, who knows what ideas have been seeded in his fantasies by the sexually explicit stuff he heard in your car. I'm not saying for one minute that he's like Elie, but I think he needs to mix with his own age group and mature along with them. I can't imagine Marie-France will be very comfortable having him too close for a while either. And Eric has certainly had enough of unqualified helpers. I learnt a lot, that evening when I stayed up at the farm. Us sophisticated city folks have the notion that farming is all muck and unskilled hard labour, but that couldn't be further from the truth. Everything that happens is as organised and coordinated as any well run hôtel. The clients are animals rather than human, but their requirements are every bit as demanding. To see Marie-France working at her real job was a revelation. And to see her and Eric together in that situation was quite an eye opener too. If we are going to lose her to something as commonplace as settling down it will surely be with him, or someone of his ilk. They think the same, move the same, react the same. And it's all so calm, focussed, disciplined.'

'She was married to a farmer,' Jacques interjected. 'But it only lasted six months or so.' 'Doesn't surprise me. She'll have thought that was what she wanted and then immediately started wondering what, or who, she might be missing out on.' It occurred to Jacques that the reason Joe understood Marie-France so well was because they were very much alike. Was his little brother getting restless too? 'Like you, you mean?' Why dance around the cooking pot when he could get straight to the point. His directness was rewarded with an appreciative smile.

'Exactly. Which is why I'm going to try my hand at farming.'

They agreed that Joe would run Marie-France up to the farm every morning in Jacques's increasingly beat-up car, until the Toyota 4x4 they'd ordered through Blanchards' garage arrived. This would save Eric one journey a day. Joe would then stay on to help out with the milking, at least until Marie-France was confidently back to full strength, again freeing Eric up to get on with other work. It was an arrangement that suited everyone, letting them all benefit from a period of stress-free routine. But the peace, as Jacques had remarked, was about to be shattered, but even more thoroughly than he imagined.

CHAPTER 15

'Léa, my dear, you look every bit as wonderful as I remember.'

When Jacques made the arrangements for Léa's visit to Corsica, on the afternoon after her meal with Amelia and Emilie, his mother acted as an intermediary because his grandfather's poor hearing made the phone too difficult for him to use. Louise explained that someone would meet her but hadn't specified who. She was pleased to see Grandfather Jacques himself standing at the arrivals gate at the airport. The distinguishedly silver haired man, easy to spot, towered above most of the other waiting people.

He raised her hand to his lips before kissing her on both cheeks. She hadn't given any indication as to why she wanted to visit him. In the bar, Jacques, frugal with words as always, fended off his mother's questions, saying only what Léa asked of him, passing back only what he heard his grandfather say in the background. Now, Grandfather Jacques asked nothing, simply took her well-travelled case out of her hand, offered her his arm, led the way to his car.

'You gave no indication of how long you intended staying, my dear, or indeed if you wanted me to arrange accommodation, so I haven't. I live rather out in the sticks but if you want me to find you a hôtel en route that will be no problem. On the other hand, although Bernard and Louise, my son and daughter-in-law, are living in the guest wing of my place at the moment, I do rattle about in the rest of it. There are two spare bedrooms, so unless you are concerned about the potential impropriety...'

He let the rest of the sentence hang in the air, she grasped it with a smile. 'I'd be delighted to rattle about with you, if it wouldn't be an imposition. It is you, Jacques, I want to spend time with.'

He beamed his delight, patted her hand, trying, and failing, not to see her mother in her beauty. He did acknowledge to himself a *soupçon* of apprehension about the reason for the visit. He'd given a rather contorted version of his past in relation to her mother, feeling the need to be parsimonious with the truth in order to protect his newly discovered, illegitimate son, Eric.

They chatted about nothing in particular as he drove. The beauty of the scenery once they were out of Ajaccio. The steep drive up into the hills. How everyone was well when she left them, back in Labeille. When they reached his brother's farm he pointed out the building that was his home. And another, still in the early stages of construction, being built for Bernard and Louise.

Opening the front door with a flourish, he directed her to a large, airy living room with a magnificent view down into the valley they'd just driven through. Within minutes there was a casual knock at the door, followed by a female voice shouting '*coucou!*' Léa was introduced to Alba, Jacques' niece who lived with her husband in the old farmhouse with her father, Marcel, Jacques' younger brother. Louise came through the door leading to the guest accommodation where she and Bernard were staying. 'We've already met. How are you, Léa?' The women were intrigued as to why this elegant, sophisticated female had decided to visit. The only explanation the old man had offered, he didn't know any more himself, was that she was the daughter of an old friend from Marseille that he'd lost contact with after the war.

Hearing Léa was going to stay, Louise went off to find linen, Alba to make sure the spare room was tidy and aired. Jacques filled the silence they left behind. 'Now, what about food. I usually make supper for myself but...' 'I would be very happy to join you, Jacques, both in the making and the eating of supper.' 'An apero before we start cooking?' he suggested, as soon as the guest bed had been made up and Alba and Louise had taken the hint that their presence was no longer required.

Léa launched straight into the speech she'd been preparing

ever since she'd decided to make this trip. 'Jacques.' - he noticed she'd dropped the 'Grandfather' everyone used to distinguish him from his grandson in Labeille – 'I want you to tell me about my mother.'

It was as he'd supposed. What else did they have in common? The uneasy knot tightened in his stomach. How was he going to maintain his assumed air of detachment about Monique? Her daughter, the image of her mother, was resurrecting all the strong feelings he'd kept closely guarded for decades in the depths of his romantic heart, the heart which leapt in his chest at her next forthright words. 'But this time I want you to talk honestly, truthfully, as Eric's mother did to him.'

Jacques frowned. What had Solange told their son about the complexity of his relationships in the past, the very distant past? 'Eric?' he asked, to give himself time to think, wondering if it was because of an attachment she'd developed for his son that she'd come to visit. 'Your son has inherited your good looks, Jacques, but I sense he got his straightforwardness from his mother.' Solange's image filled Jacques' mind. Plain looking, plain speaking. He said nothing, waiting for Léa to elucidate. 'Before she died, Eric's mother told him about the circumstances of his conception. Knowing I was coming to the village, she decided he'd be better off learning the real truth from her rather than any permutation of it I might have heard from my mother or from Jean Guerin. She also told him that the reason she'd never spoken about his father, you, when he was small, was because she'd also slept with Jean and couldn't be sure whose child he actually was. Until the resemblance made it crystal clear.'

Jacques' eyes clouded as he imagined the confusion, maybe even pain, such a confession from a mother might induce, even in a grown man. A perceptive woman, Léa quickly interpreted his look of consternation. Her next words were reassuring. 'Eric Roumignac is one of the most well-adjusted men I've ever met in the whole of my exceptionally well peopled life. Well grounded, I'd like to say, as a farmer should be.'

She waited for the smile in Jacques' eyes to acknowledge the simplistic *jeu de mots*. 'His childhood, with his grandparents as his mother and father, was as stable as any could be.' Another shared smile, quicker this time, at a further play on words, a transparent attempt to lighten the situation. 'When he learned that you, his fantasy hero, were his father, he put his mother's actions into context, without disturbing the security of his past. You have nothing to fear about the mental well-being of your son, Jacques.'

'I'm not sure I can imagine anyone daring to put Solange into context,' the old man joked, observing, in a more sombre tone. 'You seem to have got to know my son far better than I did, Léa.' 'That's because you didn't have the opportunity to be yourself with him. You were too busy playing the part you thought would protect his, and everyone else's feelings. And you continued the play-acting with me too, when we spoke about my mother, didn't you, Jacques? But Eric told me, and I quote his actual words. 'It wasn't *my* mother Jacques Luciani was in love with Léa, it was yours.' So now, Jacques Luciani, I want you to be completely truthful with me.'

Sitting back to let him assimilate all that she'd said, she thought she saw the glint of incipient tears gathering in the corners of his astute, brown eyes. He took a drink, nodded, encouraging her to continue speaking while he composed himself.

'Do you remember when I told you about mother taking me away from Labeille?' He nodded again, abruptly, just once. He'd tried not to torture himself with that disturbing account of what seemed like cold heartedness in a woman he remembered as warmth personified. 'I've come to realise that whenever I think about my mother it's with a child's mind. I'd like you to introduce me to her as an adult.' 'My dear Léa, I can think of nothing I would rather do. Ever since we had our little chats I've been thinking how sad it was that such a vibrant, such a very special woman as your mother, should be dead and remembered by her only daughter as hard and selfish. Far from the truth, at least during the time I knew her. But I got a strong sense when we first met that you didn't want to know anything about her. What's made you reconsider?'

Léa took a sip of kir, stared through the picture window. Or rather at the actual picture the window framed. 'The first thing that made me wonder if I should re-examine my view was when someone who'd actually known her, Albert Aubry, told me not only that all the boys in the village fancied her but that she was an extremely courageous woman. He linked four names together. Mother's, yours, Eric's mother's and Jean Guerin's. Maybe that's another person I should be reconsidering. Then, the same day, Amelia and Emilie showed me a photograph album containing pictures of a past I'd never connected to at all. But, actually I think what really made me think was something Emilie said.'

She cast her mind back to the Blanchards' salon. The pictures that had been taken out of the album, pictures of an aunt they'd never seen or heard mentioned. How sad for grandmère, to have had to hide one of her children away like that,' Emilie said.

Repeating those words, Léa explained that it dawned on her that not only had her mother's existence been obliterated from Labeille, she'd obliterated her too. 'It's as if she never existed. And then I remembered how you looked at me, obviously seeing my mother. I put that look together with what Eric said about you being in love with her and decided that you were the one person who could help me get to know her. So here I am. What was she really like Jacques? And what did she do that was so brave?'

Jacques took a deep, deep breath, as though to draw in his memories from the dust motes dancing in the last of the sunlight.

'We met in Marseille station,' he began. 'In fact, *we* met there, Léa, you and I. You were with her, standing on the platform with a suitcase and bags and baskets. A hassled young mother wondering how she was going to get herself, her daughter and her luggage safely on the train. I lifted her on to the train but we didn't travel together, that time. I was too busy worrying about whether I was doing the right thing, to give a thought to any woman.'

His memories flowed more fluently once he'd placed himself right back in the past. He told Léa about his first visit to Blanchards' cottage, how he'd helped Henri with the wood, how Léa's grandmother had fed him and given him a sack of food to take back for his family. Jean came into the tale when he made his entrance at Roumignacs' farm and asked Jacques to source some false papers for the young men of the village. 'When I travelled on the train with Monique I became aware what an attractive woman she was. And when she, er, demonstrated her attraction for me.'

He paused, wondering how, or if, he could explain to her daughter about the feelings Monique had aroused in him. She recognised his dilemma. 'Jacques, I am sixty seven years old. I've lived what in those days would be called a libertine life, although by today's standards it would probably be considered quite tame. What I'm trying to say is, tell it as it was Jacques. I don't want to be spared any embarrassing details or have whatever happened dressed up like a Daphne Du Maurier novel. I want to know the real woman, don't forget.'

He nodded, let his mind drift off again, and recounted exactly what had happened on the train when Monique fell against him. Completely absorbed in his memories, wallowing like an ecstatic hippo in a mud bath, he wasn't really recounting events for Léa but re-living them for himself. When he reached the end of that emotive episode he dragged himself back to the present. 'I've never thought about it before but I see now. It was danger that aroused her. The excitement of it spread throughout her whole body, made her absolutely irresistible. And if it hadn't been for a couple of bounty hunters I wouldn't have resisted at all!'

His version of the cancelled tryst with Monique was told in his well-practised, amusing, raconteur style, with himself as the dupe. But he became solemn when he reached the woods with Solange, remembering the pain of his injured leg, and the shattered tranquillity as they cowered together, hiding from men whose sole aim was to enrich themselves.

'Do you know, Léa, I think that was the only time during the war when I actually considered that I might die. And because the fear made me realise how precious my wife was, I was desperate to live, to prove to her how much she was valued.'

He moved the story on, describing how Solange and Jean saved his life, the few days he spent recovering in the maquis camp. 'They were brave young people, Léa, prepared to put up with such hardships. Not just to protect themselves but to fight back, to make the effort to create the sort of society that I wanted my son, Bernard, to grow up in. Jean inspired them, you know, with his passionate belief in *liberté, egalite, fraternité.* He made the words real, made them mean something that was important enough to suffer and die for.'

Sensing him making the journey back again, looking for his younger self, she waited quietly for what he might say. 'I realised how selfish and self-centred I was. My only consideration had been to provide for my own family and, by doing that, to further my own interests. I'd given little or no thought to what I believe today they would call the bigger picture.'

Solange, an unsophisticated, innocent girl from the country, had opened his mind. Ready to sacrifice her youth to become one of the many ordinary people not prepared to submit passively after France's military defeat, she gathered fragments of information, like his mother collected scraps of material to sew together to make a rich, warm quilt. He, Jacques Luciani, knew he could contribute to the web that Jean and his like were spinning with those gleanings, a web that would surely someday become wide and strong enough to trap and destroy the parasites exploiting their country. Solange, when she accosted him in the woods, had aroused him, but not in the way that he'd anticipated, considering the service she'd asked him to perform. Jacques, an incurable romantic, still found it troubling to think about the young girl from Labeille giving herself to him, out of duty rather than desire. To avoid betraying Solange's memory, her trust, by describing anything that had taken place in the woods, he said nothing about it to Léa. In any case it was Monique, *her* mother, not Eric's, she was interested in.

'Your mother, like you, was a strikingly beautiful woman. She used her body, not in the sense of prostitution, but as a weapon. When she came into my bar in Marseille, she often did in the course of our work in the resistance, the whole place brightened up. She shone out like a beacon of hope when most people were locked in misery and deep despair. Always made-up, dressed in stylish clothes. She kept them stylish too, altering them so they fitted, however thin she became because of the scarcity of food. What a tiny waist she had. I could have put my hands around it and joined my fingers in prayer.'

Léa noted the 'could have' but didn't interrupt for fear of dispelling the spell he was casting. 'She was charming to everyone, even the *boche*, it would have been dangerous not to have been. She came into the bar, sometimes on her own, sometimes with her in-laws, your grandparents. She and I flirted, as though we didn't know how to be discreet. Other people, even my own wife, believed we were having an affair. I often left the bar shortly after she'd been in, no doubt feeding into the gossip about our supposed affair. We encouraged that supposition in the hope it might provide a smokescreen for why we were so often seen together.'

A supposed affair rather than an actual one? But it wasn't her mother's love life Léa was interested in at the moment. She wanted more information about the courage Albert Aubry had spoken of. 'But why did she come into the bar? And why were you seen together? What did she actually do?'

Jacques was somewhat bemused at the question. It seemed impossible to him that she, Monique's daughter, a child of the occupation, didn't know about the resistance.

'Your mother used to receive information from a number of sources, Solange being one of them. Sometimes it was oral, sometimes written down. She took that information and passed it on, usually to Jean, who decided what to do with it.'

He leant forwards in his chair and looked directly at her for the first time since he'd started speaking. 'If your mother had been searched, if they'd found any of the papers she carried, if they'd even suspected that she was part of the resistance, she would have, at best, been shot on the spot. I say, at best, because the alternative was too terrible to contemplate. The Gestapo were completely pitiless when they wanted information and the methods they used to torture it out of people well...Jean gave us all cyanide pills to take if we were captured. I was as terrified of the thought of taking it as I was of being caught, terrified that I wouldn't have the courage to swallow it. Thank god I never had to find out.'

His saliva had dried up to the extent that his tongue was sticking to the roof of his mouth. He went to the buffet to pour another drink while he got control of unexpectedly strong feelings. Léa wondered if she'd asked too much of him. Perhaps he shouldn't be putting himself back into such dark times. By the time he sat back down he was the affable, articulate man he'd been before. 'In a way the occupation was a sort of liberation for your mother, and for other women like her, able to become something, someone, completely different than they could have been in peacetime. I'm not saying she actually enjoyed it, the hardships and the danger were extraordinary, but in a way she thrived on the adventure, on being able to do something other people couldn't do, in her own way, to use herself on behalf of others, for a cause.'

Léa thought about how her mother had died, killed when she crashed the motorbike she raced about on, determined to be the first to get to the scene of whatever news story she'd been told about. Wasn't that the same characteristic Jacques was describing?

'Her laugh was unlike anyone else's I've ever heard, so clear and strong and tuneful. She could have been a symphonic orchestra all by herself.' He'd returned now, into the past, to summon up its reality. 'One time Jean sent her to tell me to meet him immediately. She'd come into the bar on her own and ordered a cognac, the code for an urgent meeting. He'd just started giving me my instructions, I was to head off a courier whose mission had been compromised, and we heard that wonderful laugh ringing down the alleyway we were huddling in. Jean dived into one doorway, me another, just as Monique, in the square we'd just left, dropped at the feet of two German officers. She was teasing them because they'd frightened her and made her tip her shopping on the ground. A typical Monique thing to do, to warn us of danger by getting into the middle of it herself. She got away with it, on that occasion as on many others. The *krauts* were so charmed by her that they knelt down and helped her pick up her things, totally unaware that if they'd looked at the back of her belt rather than at her cleavage they'd probably have found one of Solange's neatly written papers of collated information.'

Léa's mission had been to discover her mother but the more Jacques talked, the more she found out about the other people Monique was involved with. Jacques himself and Jean, the man she'd despised. Someone else she'd wronged perhaps?

'You mention Jean a lot. Obviously he was an important part of what it was you and mother were involved in.' 'Jean? Oh yes, without Jean I wouldn't have been part of the resistance. I'm not so sure about your mother, though. She was more driven than I was. In fact, it might have been Monique who introduced Jean to Marseille. Solange definitely wouldn't have been there without him. Actually, now I know about them, together, I wonder if she was there because of her personal feelings for him. Not that that made her any less brave. I never approved of him taking her to Marseille, I thought she was too young, too naive. Mind you, I don't think he approved of me either, most of the time. But no matter what I thought about him as a person, his part in the organisation of our little group, I think they refer to them as cells now, cannot be underestimated.' 'You don't sound as if you liked him much.' 'I didn't. He wasn't my sort of man at all. Too cold, calculating. But exactly what was needed at that time.'

Jacques gave a short, humourless laugh. 'Mind you, that could be interpreted as sour grapes, I suppose. After all, he was the one who got the girl! Do you know, I never even suspected about Monique and him. Even afterwards, when they'd gone off together – the gossipmongers couldn't wait to tell me, quite malevolent some of them were too – I found it hard to believe. But Monsieur Jourdan - sorry, I keep forgetting he was your grandfather - confirmed it when he came to tell me that their son, your father, was home and that they were all moving out into the country. He was quite vitriolic about Monique, understandable perhaps, although I'm quite sure that he, along with everyone else, believed that she and I were involved with each other and he'd never voiced any disapproval. But maybe that was different, because of the times. Maybe he presumed that once the world got back to normal we'd all become the people we'd been before.'

Now was the time, Léa decided, for the question niggling to be asked. 'So you and mother weren't involved with each other? Weren't you in love with her after all?' 'Ah, now, that all depends on what you mean by involved and love. We were strongly attracted to each other. So very alike, you see. But our physical passion was never consummated, although we had plenty of opportunities when we were cuddling and kissing in public, to throw the Germans or the informers off the scent. It would have been the easiest thing in the world to take a few extra steps and enact the scene for real. But it never happened. I was quite proud of myself, actually. I thought I was honouring the vow I'd made when I thought I was going to die in the woods and all I could think about was how much I wanted to be with Marthe and Bernard. I pledged I would never again be unfaithful to my wife. In fact, I'm going to tell you something that I've never told anyone else. It would completely ruin my reputation if it got out.'

He looked around him dramatically, as though to be quite sure she was the only one who would hear his long kept secret. 'After that business in the woods with Solange, I was never unfaithful to my Marthe, not once.' His infectious grin made him look like a small boy confessing that it was him who'd eaten the last piece of apple tart. Léa smiled back.

After a pause, as though to let his admission settle into the dust, Jacques reflected. 'Looking back, once I knew about Monique and Jean, I realised it was probably her self-restraint, not mine, that kept us in check. Do you know, Léa, even the fact that Monique chose Jean to go off with, to try and make a future, was actually to her credit.' 'Rather than waiting for my father?' 'I didn't know your father. I didn't know them as a couple. But by the liberation they'd already been apart for four years, long years, living completely different lives. And, although she didn't it know then, it was at least another year before her husband, your father got home. She must have realised that she couldn't be the same person she was before, and probably neither could he. Maybe she didn't think it was worth the risk of trying to make it work between them after all that time.'

Léa thought about the photographs she seen of her parents, her mother young and vivacious, him so much older and formal. 'Maybe their relationship was already on the rocks before the war,' she said thoughtfully. 'But what was so creditable about her choosing Jean as her man?' 'She wanted something more in her life than domesticity, that's clear. And she was a very bright lady. So she must have chosen him for what she saw as his vision, hoping, no doubt, that she could be a part of his future, the future he would carve out for himself and for the country. It doesn't sound, from what you told me, as if his ambition was quite as great as she'd hoped. But don't you see, Léa, although you resented her taking you away from Labeille, she wanted you to be part of that future too?' 'She also undoubtedly knew what her brother was like and realised that grandmère wasn't likely to be as devoted to me once he got home.'

She explained to Jacques what both Albert and Amelia had said about Paul Blanchard. Jacques smiled, pleased she was beginning to view her mother in a more positive light, a more adult light, exactly what she'd wanted to do. They seemed to have reached some sort of a watershed.

'Shall we go and get some supper before it's time for breakfast?' he suggested. It didn't take them long to heat the light soup he'd made, hoping she would stay. It took even less time to eat it and they were soon cleaning the bowls with the remains of the bread. 'Will fresh fruit do you to finish off?' he asked. 'It really is fresh too, grown right here on the farm. One of the many improvements my brother and his family have made is to get into the clementine growing business. Marcel and I went our separate ways as young men but were equally successful, I'm glad to say.'

He wasn't boasting, just stating a fact. Léa found herself enjoying his company more with every minute she spent in it. She declined a coffee, agreed that an armagnac would be the perfect way to finish the evening. 'Not that I've finished talking about your mother. Thinking about her has unlocked so many memories I could go on forever. But I promise I won't,' he said, with a sparkling smile.

'I enjoy listening to you Jacques. I'm a writer, don't forget, and it's rare for me to meet someone who really impresses me by painting such vivid pictures with their words.' He inclined his head in acknowledgement of her compliment, storing it in his heart to bring out and consider later. It seemed a long time since anyone had genuinely wanted to hear him talk, apart from that brief interlude in Labeille when he'd realised just how much he'd missed Jacques and Joe, his grandsons, who clearly still loved and respected him as much as they had when they all lived together at the hôtel in Marseille.

Léa and Jacques stayed at the table, face to face, sipping the digestif. After a few minutes contemplation Jacques found the point to start talking from. 'The last time I saw your mother was during the fighting in the streets of Marseille. The resistance had almost done the job of defeating the Germans before the French Forces arrived but it was still a terrifying time. I stayed at the bar, protecting my family was all I cared about. I saw Monique outside, shooting away, just like everybody else, only she was using a camera instead of a rifle. She was right there, right in amongst it, completely focused on what she was doing, daring any bullets to come near her.'

Léa became almost breathless with this absolute connection to her mother, one she recognised, one she could feel. 'It was those photographs, the ones she took during the Battle of Marseille, that became our passport out of France. They made her famous. And Peter, the man I told you about who took us over to England. He wrote the story of my mother's pictures, a personal experience, as close to the action as could possibly be!'

She suddenly felt sad and angry with herself that she'd never even looked at the photographs she'd carried around in their sealed box. She'd surely have got to know her mother much sooner if she had. 'They're in a box, under my bed in my flat in Paris, all the photographs she ever took.' She was near to tears and suddenly exhausted.

'Enough's enough for one night, little Léa. Off you go to bed. By the morning you'll have decided if there's anything else you want to know. I'll wish you goodnight but I don't expect you to sleep too well. There must be so much teeming about in your brain, I'm sure I'll be able to hear it from my room on the other side of the hall.'

CHAPTER 16

Early the next morning. Jacques was up and dressed, drinking his first coffee but waiting for his guest before he breakfasted. As she sat in front of the mirror applying her makeup, having chosen casual slacks and a blouse as clothes appropriate for the day, she remembered his description of her mother's impeccable dress sense. 'Well mother,' she whispered. 'It seems I don't just take after you in looks. I pay attention to my clothes and make-up too.'

Breakfast was simple but exactly right. Coffee, fruit juice, home baked bread, farm made butter and a selection of kitchen made jams. Jacques and Léa didn't clutter up the peace of the morning with chat. It wasn't until they'd finished that she asked, 'Jacques, would it put you or your family out if I stayed on for another night?'

'My dear Léa, your words have out-sung the birds. As far as I'm concerned you are most welcome to stay for as long as you can. And as for my family, well I'm sure they'll be delighted to have me occupied and out of their way for a while.'

After the lunch they cooked together they took a short walk around the farm. 'This is the house Bernard and Louise are having built,' Jacques told her, as they stopped beside what looked like a huge garden shed, the skeleton of its timber frame starkly unclothed. 'A surprise to all of us when they decided to retire here full time. It was generally accepted that they'd base themselves in Labeille to spend a few more years with their grandsons and make the permanent move here, into my house, once I'd popped my clogs.'

Léa waited. Staring into the distance, he seemed disturbed at his thoughts. Or maybe he was just wondering whether to share them. 'Something's changed between Jacques and his father,

143

something profound.'

He sighed and watched a seagull until it disappeared from view. Still Léa said nothing. 'I've lost a big part of myself, being so out of touch with the boys. But I can't do the phone, not now my hearing's so bad. I suppose I'm lucky that's all that's really let me down in old age but…'

Tempted to follow this subject, to talk about hearing aids and email, she once again held her peace, wanting him to trust her with whatever was really concerning him. 'They didn't tell me about Jacques and Eveline splitting up, not until just before we went to Labeille. Louise used to phone Alba fairly regularly but she never even mentioned it to her. I think that's when whatever happened between Jacques and his father took place. Something about the way Bernard handled the situation, I imagine.'

He paused again, sorrowfully, as though in some way it was him who'd failed in his responsibilities. 'They really played down Joe's injuries too, when he was attacked in Marseille. It was quite a shock when I saw that dreadful scar on his face. Poor Louise, to have her precious doll damaged like that. He seems to be coping with it, although I didn't have enough time with him to really find out.'

Léa guiltily remembered the morning after the meal Joe had cooked, when she'd wondered if his scar was artificial, an attempt to make him appear more interesting. She wondered what had come over her, to dismiss the Lucianis so simplistically when there was a wealth of family dynamics that could have much more interestingly occupied her inquisitive mind. They were certainly occupying the mind of the man beside her, who clearly felt he should have been involved.

'Anyway!' Jacques spoke brightly, chasing the shadows from his face. 'You don't want to be bothered by all my family stuff and its far too nice a day to waste being miserable. Come my dear, let's go back and you can subject me to another of your stimulating inquisitions.'

For the rest of the afternoon they sat in the salon and talked.

At least he talked, mainly in response to her questions, which he considered seriously and answered as fully as he could. As the day wore on the information she requested became more specific.

'What was she wearing?' she asked, after he'd given one particularly vivid description of her mother stumbling off the pavement to distract a known informer who was watching Jean suspiciously as he walked hurriedly away. Jacques' eyebrows expressed his surprise at this detailed level of interest. His eyes narrowed, peering into the past. 'It was the height of summer, oppressively hot. A chiffony type blouse. White, over a full, flowery skirt. And a straw hat decorated with a generous sprig of bougainvillea. It grew like a weed in some places.'

'Like this?' She picked up a notepad she'd been scribbling in and made a quick sketch. Moving over to sit beside her so he could see better, he studied the line drawing. 'Almost,' he replied. 'The skirt was a little fuller, perhaps just a mite shorter. And she had a scarf. She always wore a scarf. There are any number of pieces of information that can be conveyed by how its tied.' Léa made another sketch, incorporating his corrections. He noticed that underneath the brim of the sun-shading hat the face was blank.

That evening they went over to the main house to collect some eggs for breakfast. Alba insisted they drink an aperitif with them, curious to find out more about her uncle's mysterious visitor. She learnt only that she was exceptionally pleasant company, with a knack of getting you to talk about yourself while she listened, making you feel that what you said, however trivial, was of great interest. 'No wonder he likes having her around,' Louise remarked, rather snidely, after they'd left. 'He must be in his element having such a pretty, captive audience who hasn't heard all his tales a hundred times over.'

Alba was surprised. Jacques had rarely recounted any stories to his brother's family. Not for the first time, she wondered if the man who'd lived in Marseille for most of his life had left a great chunk of his personality behind, as though it belonged exclusively to his own son's family. She felt a flutter of something approaching sadness for the old man. He'd come to live alone in the house that he and his beloved Marthe had designed in readiness for their eventual retirement. The consensus of opinion was that she'd never got over the loss of her youngest son, Joe's father, and gave in almost willingly after she suffered a massive stroke at a relatively young age. Jacques had only reluctantly moved out of the hôtel shortly after Angelo was born, to give young Jacques and his expanding family more space. Although he was always amenable and polite, he did sometimes give the impression that he felt his life was done.

But that changed overnight after he'd watched the video Bernard brought back from Labeille as a means of introducing Eric. Jacques watched the film with Bernard, mesmerized by the quiet darkness, thrilled by his family's performance, almost overwhelmed by Eric's likeness to Joe, struggling to supress the notion that he was looking at the ghost of his youngest son, Joe's father. Once he was alone the old man had replayed the film over and over until the early hours of the morning but was up, dressed and tapping on the connecting door just as Bernard and Louise sat down for breakfast. 'It's time I made a comeback!' he announced. 'We're going to Labeille. In style.'

'I can't believe you're going along with this,' Louise complained to her husband when the fancy clothes were brought out of mothballs. 'I can't believe Bernard's going along with this,' she remarked to Alba and her husband, after their son Marcel had been tasked with finding and hiring the classic car. 'I can't believe you're encouraging him,' Louise commented, when Alba agreed to young Marcel being co-opted as chauffeur.

But Alba, her husband and Marcel senior were happy to see the excitement brightening the old man's face. It seemed to chase away the tired lines of aging.

'It was amazing!' Marcel reported, when they arrived back home after their extended week away. 'Great-uncle Jacques was a completely different man. Like a film star. You'll see when you watch the video. It's hilarious. And the village is great too. Think

I might go there on holiday in the summer.' After watching the video the young man's mother thought the pretty girl he had his arm around might have had more than a little to do with that remark.

'Actually, the moment I'll never forget was when he stood up to talk at the funeral of his old flame,' Marcel said. 'He was so powerful and dignified. I never even knew he was part of the resistance in Marseille.' 'Why would you?' he mother replied. He didn't know about the part his own grandfather, her father, had played in the liberation of Ajaccio in nineteen forty three either. The first place in France to free itself of the occupying forces.

After that visit to Labeille, the video of Grandfather Jacques' arrival had been watched and laughed over so often that Marcel made another couple of copies in case they wore it out. But the star of the performance soon shrank back into the decline of aging, if anything becoming even more detached, not even cheered, it seemed, by the fact that Bernard had decided to come and live on the island full time earlier than anyone had anticipated.

'It's good to see him looking brighter though, isn't it?' Alba commented in response to her sister-in-law's less than affectionate remark about his story telling. Louise shrugged her shoulders as though her father-in-law's state of mind was of little concern to her. Alba hoped that once they had their own home the tension between her uncle and his daughter-in-law would start to ease.

On the third morning Léa greeted Jacques with a cheeky, 'One more night?' as he rose from his chair to kiss her bonjour. 'I'll pack your bag for you myself when I've had enough of you,' he replied, with an equally mischievous grin.

'She's a journalist. When she discovered that uncle Jacques knew her mother during the war she decided to come and find out what actually went on in Marseille. I think she's writing a book,' Alba reported exuberantly, having stayed to drink a coffee with her uncle and his guest when she went over to get his shopping list. 'I hope she's not expecting any historical correctness,' Louise remarked. 'From the ridiculous stories he used to tell the boys you'd think the whole thing was a corny spy film, with him as the leading man. Léa's mother was probably one of the famous *belles dames*.' 'If the mother looked anything like the daughter, I should think she was, *trés belle*,' Bernard commented mildly, earning himself a scowl, then a conciliatory kiss. His wife was enjoying far more than she'd anticipated having her husband to herself, away from the often unfathomable demands of their complicated offspring.

'Actually, I was thinking of asking Léa if she'd like to stay for Christmas,' Alba said. 'What do you think? I've never seen uncle Jacques on such good form. I'm sure he'd be really pleased.' The invitation was issued and accepted, on the condition that Léa would be allowed to help with the preparations.

On the fourth day the emphasis of Léa's questioning changed. No longer so focussed on trying to get to know her youthful mother, she was trying to get to know the young Jacques Luciani too.

'And what were *you* wearing?' she asked him, after he'd described an incident when he'd been sent to seduce a young woman, to find out if she was an informer as Jean suspected. Léa noticed that whenever he spoke about himself during those times, he became a flippant raconteur, telling an entertaining tale, disguising the reality by looking through a romantic lens. Her question made him pause. He screwed up his eyes to peer at the detail. 'I was quite a dandy, in those days. Like Monique, I thought it was important, a personal act of resistance, to always look my handsome best. Jackets, waistcoats, silk ties and hats were my trade mark, all acquired before the occupation, of course. As accoutrements they were quick and easy to slip over my working clothes of black trousers, white shirt, black tie.' 'And the gangster image, fedora hat and all, that you were wearing in the video they played in Labeille on your last night there. Was that typical?'

He gave her an appraising look, impressed that she should have observed the detail, reminding himself he should perhaps ask her a few questions, if she ever gave him the opportunity. 'The gangster image, in various degrees of flashiness, did have its uses, both during and after the war. But on the occasion we were talking about I didn't want to draw too much attention to myself, unusually. And there were severe restrictions on what we were allowed to wear, although I managed to keep most of my pre-war Italian influence chic intact. But when I went to meet the young lady, who I never got the chance to seduce in any case, I seem to remember I wore a plain dark suit, rather dowdy by my standards. Why all this attention to detail, Léa?'

She shrugged. 'Habit, I suppose. Fashion was a part of my journalistic remit. And when I'm trying to build up an image of a person, like now with my mother, the better I can visualise them, the more I feel I get to know them.' The next morning Jacques was dressed in neatly ironed jeans and a white cotton, open-necked shirt instead of the track suit bottoms and sweat shirt he'd previously worn around the house.

Knowing they'd be together for the days leading up to Christmas, it no longer seemed so urgent to spend every minute talking about Monique. They started going on trips out, taking it in turns to drive, buying their own fresh produce from the markets for the meals they planned together, visiting the local tourist attractions, stopping often to drink coffee or something stronger. At every opportunity she encouraged him to talk, about himself. As he related the highlights from his past he became more and more like the younger man he was portraying. Energetic, witty, sharp. He even started to stand up straight and tall, slipping off the round shouldered stance that was beginning to reduce his height, using his cane more as an extension to his expressive hands than a support to lean on. After their extensive discussions about the occupation, post liberation was a natural place for him to start his reminiscences. Soon his handsome face was glowing with pride, for the achievements of the city that had become his own, as much as his personal successes.

'Do you know, the first ship entered the port with supplies only two weeks after the liberation? That was an incredible feat, considering it looked as if it was so blown up and flattened it would never rise again. Freight was being shifted by rail and road almost immediately. And work started on an underwater fuel pipe which by the following spring was pumping nearly five million litres a day! Can you imagine? Almost as much as the booze I was serving in the bar.'

He'd resorted to his habitually flippant style, which Léa now recognised as being his way of stopping himself from becoming too intense. As she skilfully moved him forwards through his past, the memories became more positive. He recounted his personal accomplishments in a glib, almost self-deprecating manner but couldn't hide the pride he felt about all that he'd achieved. Developing his business, buying up property, making the café-bar the central hub of the hôtel he expanded into the buildings on either side. 'Just like young Jacques is starting to do in Labeille now,' he remarked. 'He'll be successful, with or without my help, but I wish I could be a part of it, even just to experience one more time the buzz of seeing plans come into fruition.'

He was always at his happiest when he talked about 'my boys', his own sons and his grandsons. Although he couldn't hide the enduring misery when he explained about the tragedy of Joe's parents' death. 'Joseph, my youngest, was born just a couple of months after Eric,' he remarked pensively, as if this had never occurred to him before. 'If Bernard, the first, could be described as the *entrée*, then Joseph was the dessert, the *sucré* to follow the *salé*. He was such a sweet, cheerful soul. I wonder where Eric fits in to my filial menu. A bit of both perhaps.'

A little later, after they'd done a tour of the boutiques so she could buy some Christmas present trinkets, he shared an idea that had been turning in his mind. 'She's a wonderful thing, creation, the way she weaves strands of one generation into the next. Bernard was a replica of his mother while Joseph strongly favoured me, in looks at least. And then Bernard's son, Jacques, carried on the po-faced line, although it didn't come so naturally to him. He worked at it, he so wanted to be like his father.'

Léa noticed the mist of sadness clouding his eyes at the gulf that had appeared between father and son. 'And Joe is certainly a Luciani, isn't he? I bet he's the living image of you at that age.' To her surprise, his face didn't brighten into the smile she was expecting. 'I've always worried about Joe, you know.'

She became still, concentrating on the pleasure of the realisation that he trusted her enough to confide. 'Of course, he had the best possible chance, with Bernard and Louise being there for him, straight after his parents' death. But even though there wasn't a scratch on him I still found it hard to believe that a little boy wouldn't suffer any mental trauma after such a catastrophe. He was in the car with them, after all. But Louise spoiled him shamelessly, which I'm sure was the very best thing to do and he grew up as sunny and cheerful as his father had been. Too sunny, too cheerful. Too good looking. Playboy is probably an old fashioned word but it describes him perfectly. He played his way through his childhood, his adolescence, and carried on playing when he was an adult. It's not surprising that he fell foul of Marseille's street life. It's a blessing he got off so lightly.'

'And now?' she asked, to bring him back to her, as he seemed to be sloping off along a dark path on his own. 'Now? Well, I'm still not sure he's found himself, whatever that means. But I do wonder if he's just reached the stage of wanting to be treated as more than just a pretty face, something you must have suffered from yourself, my dear, surely.'

And so they strolled through the days, combing through each other's lives like metal detectorists, examining some of their finds closely, pausing briefly at others before putting them aside to worm their way back into the obscurity of the past.

The Christmas meal was an enjoyable, though quite low key occasion. The family enjoyed the novelty of having an exotic guest who introduced them to the English tradition of stockings and their fillers. The contents of the ones she presented to them were handpicked, personalised fripperies. 'I was going to be really traditional and give you an orange, a handful of nuts and a few squares of chocolate, but I'm glad I didn't,' she laughed, gesturing in the direction of the rows of clementine trees, the mainstay of the farm.

'Another tradition was, still is, the Christmas pudding. It's a fruity, rich, alcoholic sort of cake. But the best thing about it, from a child's point of view, was that it had coins, sixpences at that time, hidden in it, much like *la fève,* the bean, that's put in *la galette des rois* here at Epiphany. Getting a sixpence in the Christmas pudding didn't confer any sort of status, though, not like the person being king for the night. In fact, I seem to remember all the children got one. It must have been fixed!' Only Jacques understood the poignancy of her laugh. She was beginning to realise that her childhood hadn't been completely miserable after all.

He pressed Léa to talk more about the Christmases she had passed in England. She explained that when she was young, Christmas was the most important fête, unlike in France, when, on her first visit as an adult she learnt that *La Réveillon de la Saint-Silvestre* on the thirty-first of December took pride of place. 'Would you consider staying on here for *La Réveillon?*' Jacques asked her, before he went off to bed, leaving her to her now customary session of tip-tapping on her lap top.

CHAPTER 17

The *fin d'année* meal took place around the huge kitchen table in the farmhouse. It went on for hours as everyone did their best to do justice to the seemingly endless platters. Starting with an *amuse-bouche* of *feuilletés et canapés*, followed by *foie gras* with Coquilles Saint Jacques in a clementine sauce. 'A plate of land and sea,' the hostess explained. 'Introduced to us by our very own Saint Jacques!'

Alba had confided in Léa, so very good at confidences, that she'd been nervous about cooking for Jacques and Marthe when they came on their first holiday after she'd taken over the kitchen, when she and her husband moved in to work with her parents on the farm. She'd been afraid she could never compete with the *haut-cuisine* of their hôtel-restaurant in Marseille. 'They soon put me at my ease though, and used to make a point of bringing me recipes, or even actual dishes to try out. It's a shame you didn't get a chance to meet Marthe, she was a lovely woman, once you got used to her straight-faced ways.'

'My Bernard is just like her,' Louise commented. She'd got on well with her down-to-earth mother-in-law, was pleased that her own son Jacques had taken after that side of the family. Although, on reflection, she wasn't sure anymore if that was true. She pushed aside the recollection of the disruptive influence of that peculiar woman, Marie-France on her sons, giving thanks that she and Bernard had made the break when they did, even if it did mean living in the lion's den with the old man for a while until their own house was ready. She watched Jacques teasing young Marcel about all the beautiful girls in Labeille that were missing him, wondering if it was Léa's influence or the onset of senility making him behave more like a playful kitten than a big cat.

The *assiette terre et mer* was followed by a magnificent capon stuffed with Muscat grapes and truffles, served with delicate white grelot onions, sautéed carrots and nutty tasting ratte potatoes. The dessert, clementine sorbet, was the house specialty. There was a different wine for every course, chosen and served by Jacques, dressed up in his hôtelier garb for the occasion.

When finally they made it back to their own quarters, instead of bidding Jacques a chaste good night, as she had every evening previously, Léa reached up and pulled his lips to hers in a kiss as far from chaste as the earth is to the moon. When they eventually parted to draw breath he looked down at her, his eyes twinkling brighter than any star-filled sky. 'Léa Jourdan!' he exclaimed. 'Are you seducing me?' 'I certainly am Jacques Luciani,' she replied, looking up at him with sleepily seductive grin. 'Oh, my dear! Well, I must apologise.'

For a cold moment she thought he was rejecting her. Then she saw the clown she'd learned to recognise peeking out of his gleaming eyes. Looking down into her upturned face, he murmured, 'I'm afraid I'm a little out of practice, my dearest girl. I think we'd better we try that again, don't you?'

When he felt her leave his bed the next morning Jacques knew that the night had been her way of saying goodbye. When he got up she'd be dressed and respectable, her suitcase packed, explaining she'd booked a flight home. Earlier in the week she'd asked Alba for the internet code and had given him a basic introduction to the wonders of the web. They'd share their last breakfast and then she'd probably ask if he'd be so kind as to run her to the airport. Reluctant to let go of the tenderness of their lovemaking, he shuffled over into the space she'd just vacated, still warm from her voluptuous body and fragrant with her scent. As he stretched in contentment he couldn't resist giving himself a brief congratulatory hug. Patting his penis affectionately, he chuckled. 'Thank you, my old friend, for rising to the occasion,' pleased that he still had it in him to perform. But then, she was so lovingly, irresistibly persuasive, a man would need to be dead not to respond. He stretched again, preparing himself to get out of bed, trying to concoct the right mixture of gratitude and affection to greet her with, on their last morning together.

'Room service, monsieur!' Her dressing gown was silk but the way she wore it was far from pure, revealing the full breasts he'd caressed but not seen in the darkness of their first encounter. She put the breakfast tray on a side table. 'But I must warn you, monsieur, that if you accept the breakfast you have to accept *la serveuse* too.'

He sat up in the bed, folded back the bedclothes. 'Come here then, wench. Let's see what kind of service you have to offer.'

In the middle of the morning Louise dropped by to see how they were, stopping short of shouting *coucou* when she saw the guest bedroom door wide open, advertising a pristinely un-slept in bed. Hearing murmurs and quiet laughter from the main bedroom, she crept back out. 'She must be trying to kill the old fool,' she said to Bernard, after reporting what she'd seen and heard. 'At least he'll die happy,' he replied complacently, his expressionless face giving away none of the pleasure he was experiencing at the news that the father he'd thought had yielded to the irrevocable decline towards old age and death was giving life another go.

Jacques couldn't remember a day when he hadn't washed, shaved and dressed. Or eaten lunch. At four o'clock in the afternoon they padded through to the living room in their dressing gowns, but before they made it to the kitchen he sensed a change in her mood.

'Jacques, would you sit down for minute. There's something I want to ask you. But before I do I need you to know that I am securely financially independent.' He felt he had to say something, anything, to stop his clamouring brain from connecting with his too rapidly beating heart, in case they were clutching at a completely erroneous straw. He cleared his throat, which didn't stop the screckle in his voice. 'Me too,' he said, giving a disparaging smile at the feebleness of his utterance.

'Good, that's got worldly matters out of the way.'

She lowered herself until she was poised on one knee in front of him, leaving her gown to fall open. He didn't even glimpse at the expanse of naked thigh, keeping his eyes steadily fixed on hers. 'Jacques Luciani, will you marry me?'

He exhaled a long breath and the tension left him, along with all the lingering remnants of thought about old age and death. 'My dearest Léa,' he replied, joyful laughter gurgling through his words. 'I thought you'd never ask.' He raised her hand to his lips, kissed her palm. For a moment there was a silence, which they shattered simultaneously.

'Champagne!' 'I'm starving!' The champagne accompanied them as they rummaged through the kitchen cupboards where he grudgingly kept some convenience food, in case of emergencies. They settled on a large tin of cassoulet which she heated up while he opened a bottle of good red wine to disguise the processed taste. 'It's actually delicious,' she exclaimed, polishing her plate with the last of the breakfast baguette. 'So are you, my dear,' he replied, predictably. 'But then, you know that already.'

They found some chocolate and nut covered ice creams in the back of the freezer and devoured them as noisily and messily as the great grandchildren they'd been bought for.

Leaving the dirty dishes on the table they moved over to the sofa and sat side by side. Slurping at clementines in *eau de vie*, they talked, long, long into the night. When sleepiness finally overcame them he went over and firmly shut the guest bedroom door. 'We'll live in sin while we can, it sounds so wonderfully wicked!' he said.

Despite their late night they were up early the next morning. They heard Bernard and Louise going over to join Alba and her husband in the main house, no doubt to speculate about the old people's behaviour. They waited a couple of minutes, then followed, rapping lightly on the door before going in to find the two couples deep in conversation. 'Oh! Bonjour, uncle Jacques, Léa,' Alba said, her embarrassed flush confirming that they had indeed been the subject of the interrupted chat.

Jacques delivered their news. Once the newly declared couple had received somewhat stunned congratulations he spoke to his unusually speechless daughter-in-law. 'And now Louise, would you be so good as to get my grandson, Jacques, on the phone and ask him for his internet address. And Louise, please don't tell him anything more than that I'm wanting to arrange a visit. I will send him an email a little later with the details.'

Hearing the authoritative tone in which this instruction was given, Bernard allowed himself a fleeting smile. 'Welcome back, father,' he thought.

CHAPTER 18

'Married? The randy old so and so. When? Do you think it's a shotgun wedding?' Joe seemed ready to explode with enthusiastic delight at his grandfather's news.

'Don't you think that's more Marie-France's style than pépère's?' Jacques made his droll remark confident in the knowledge that it wasn't. She'd been to see Dr Martin, making no secret of the fact she was back on the pill. He accepted this was her way of letting him know that their sexual relationship was not exclusive.

Joe ignored the irrelevant comment. 'But when? When is he getting married?' 'As soon as it can be arranged after they arrive.' 'They? Oh, of course. Takes two to tango. Who is he marrying? What do you mean after they arrive? Arrive where? Here?'

Joe, thirty six years old, one hundred and ninety centimetres tall, weighing almost ninety kilos. To see him jumping up and down bursting with questions like a five year old was too much for Marie-France. She started to giggle. Even Jacques couldn't keep a grin from turning up the corners of his mouth.

Joe, catching sight of himself in the *Suze* promotion mirror behind the bar, beamed at his reflexion then forced himself to perch on the edge of a stool. 'You're doing it on purpose!' he said to Jacques accusingly. 'Doing what?' his brother asked, opening his eyes innocently wide. 'Withholding information. Begin again and tell me in your usual, pedantic way, starting with, who is grandpère marrying?'

'Léa Jourdan.' 'Léa Jourdan?' 'We'll get on much quicker if you don't repeat everything I say,' Jacques said, like the parent scolding the infant Joe seemed to have become. 'And one question at a time would speed the process too.'

Marie-France poured herself a coffee and came out from

behind the bar to sit beside Joe, charmed by the entertaining behaviour of the two men. 'It must have been like this when they were kids,' she told herself, suddenly aware that she was being included, even as just an onlooker, in something that must usually take place in the inner family sanctum. Was that where she belonged?

'Okay. Sorry,' Joe replied, not sounding even mildly contrite. 'Where are Léa Jourdan and Grandfather Jacques getting married and when? Oh, sorry. That's two questions. Where are they getting married?' 'Here.' 'Here? In Labeille? How are they...?'

Jacques relented. 'Grandfather and Léa are going to set off from Corsica in a few days' time. They're driving. In his car.' 'But where are we going to put them?' Marie-France choked with laugher. Joe's question took them right back to the beginning of the morning. 'They could come and join you and me and Jacques in your room, couldn't they?' 'Quiet!' Jacques said sternly. 'I've got enough on trying to keep my wee brother in check without you winding him up.'

She'd been right. They had resorted to their childhood. She zipped her lips dramatically to avoid being excluded. Not that she really thought she would be.

Joe got control of himself. A bit. 'But seriously, Jacques. It was okay when it was just grandpère but with Léa as well?' 'It's fine. Pépère said in his email that he knew we wouldn't be in any position to put them up because of the renovations, so they are in the throes of making alternative arrangements. Seemingly, Léa has been in touch with Marc and he's got a few ideas.

'Oh my God!' Joe shrieked, pretending to pull out his hair. 'What about the wedding breakfast? Or lunch or dinner or whatever it is? What about the catering?' 'That's okay too,' Jacques replied, desperately trying to keep a straight face. 'Grandfather also said that he understood that the restaurant wouldn't be open but was sure the hôtel...' Joe let out an anguished wail, as Jacques anticipated he would.

In his email, their grandfather suggested that if it was too difficult for Joe to cook for them in the current circumstances, he'd quite understand and they'd organise something at the hôtel. As part of his reply, Jacques wrote. 'As for your suggestion that someone other than Joe could do the catering, forget it. Even being deaf you'd surely hear the tantrum he'd throw on Corsica! We'll manage. The kitchen is still fully functioning. I'll close the bar for the day. We'll easily make up for the loss of income from all the well-wishers and rumour mongers flocking in once they know you're here. They can pay for their drinks at the same time as they pay their respects.'

Joe, hastily enlightened before the predicted tantrum took hold, was so relieved he leant over the bar and poured himself a *demi* of beer to cool his shattered nerves. After a few calming sips, something else occurred to him. 'But why's he getting married here, Jacques, and not in the bosom of his Corsican family?' 'Do you remember this morning, when you said mum's call was very short? I suspect it's *her* bosom that's driving him here, in a manner of speaking.' 'Sometimes, brother Jacques, your manner of speaking is obscure, to say the least. What on earth are you talking about?'

Jacques' eyes crinkled, his voice softened. 'Do you remember the special outings pépère used to take us on?' 'On spy training exercises, for example?'

Marie-France watched, entranced, as the grown men in front of her transformed into mischievous little boys. 'Exactly. Like when we went to Le Vieux Port, a place notably packed with wicked ne'er do wells.' 'He bought us caps and dark shades as disguises once.' 'And he put us to work watching the men unloading one particular ship.' 'You had to count the crates of cognac and I had to count the wine.' 'And a man called Louis came over and shook pépère's hand. And then shook ours too.' 'He said to grandpère, 'Have you put your lads to work?' in a really quiet, intense voice.' 'Pépère looked all around him as if he was afraid someone might hear. He nodded his head. Then the man, obviously an important boss, asked him what we'd found out. 'Right boys' pépère said. 'Time to make your report.' 'They unloaded twenty four cases of cognac,' I replied, feeling really proud that we were reporting directly to the top guy. 'And I counted thirty cases of wine,' you said, all cocky because your number was bigger than mine.' 'He shook his head, looking dead solemn and I thought I'd made a mistake. Then he sighed. 'As I thought,' he said to grandfather. 'There are some bad *mecs* operating here. There should have been thirty cases of cognac too. No wonder I'm losing money.' 'Are you losing a lot?' pépère asked, looking as grim as if they were talking about a killing, not theft. 'Well, there are twelve bottles in each case and each bottle is worth fifty francs, so that's...'

'And you, being the smart arse you are, answered in a flash. 'That means you've lost three thousand six hundred francs, just today, Monsieur Louis!' 'That's right my lad. So I have.' Joe's voice assumed the thick Marseille accent he was so proficient in. As he continued he bent over, as though addressing a small, earnest boy. 'But at least now I'm aware of what's happening so I know what to look out for.' Then he turned to grandfather and said, 'I could do with some observant blokes in my *equip.* Don't suppose you could leave them with me for a while, could you?'

'And pépère replied ?' Jacques prompted. 'I'm afraid not, Louis. I don't think their mother would approve.' 'And that,' Jacques crowed delightedly, 'Is exactly the point of the story!'

Joe's brow furrowed. He thought back to where the recollection originated, remembering it had something to do with their mum's bosom. Whatever it was, the meaning was still obscure.

'Think about mum's greeting to us when we got back.' Joe's eyes searched for the memory then twinkled as he parodied Louise's speech, her pursed lips and arms-folded posture. 'I hope, *beau-père*, that you haven't been filling my sons' heads with nonsense. Again.'

Joe started giggling. 'And you said, in that poker-straight voice you'd just started using so you sounded as much like dad as you looked like him. 'It's alright, mother. Pépère bought us brand new caps so nothing dangerous could make it into our brains at all.' I thought she was going to kill you, right there in front of me. You really must have been a most irritating child. Although I didn't see it at the time because you were so clever, as well as being my hero.'

The two men-boys smiled at each other affectionately, oblivious to Marie-France, their spellbound audience. 'But to get back to grandfather and Léa and why they're coming here to get married. Oh, clang! I get it!'

Joe, assuming their mother's welcoming position again, hoisted his chest up into a pair of substantial matronly breasts. 'She never has approved of our grandfather, has she? I don't suppose she'd be overwhelmingly supportive of him getting married. I can almost hear her muttering silly old fool. So that's why he's coming here, to his favourite grandson's territory where he knows he'll be made welcome, whatever he says and does.'

'Mmm. It's great, isn't it? But there's more.' 'More? More what? Zut! She isn't pregnant, is she? I mean, I know she's a looker and certainly a good bit younger than him but I didn't think she was that young.' 'I'm getting worried about you, little brother,' Jacques murmured, putting his hand on Joe's forehead. 'You seem to have gone broody. That is the right expression, isn't it?' he asked Marie-France. She chuckled. 'Well, if he's anything like the hens when they go broody you'd better watch out. He'll peck your eyes out in no time. Maybe you should be finding *him* a wife, Jacques. What do you think Joe? Time to settle down?' she asked challengingly. Her one time lover clasped his hand to his ample breast and looking into her eyes assumed a tragicomic expression. 'Whenever you are ready, little one, just say the word. You know I'm saving myself for you.'

For the minutest blink of time the world stopped, the room went still, nobody breathed. Then she spotted the glint in Joe's mournful, beseeching eyes. In the same instant she saw Jacques relax the fingers that had started to curl into his palm. The two men stared at each other. Joe let the grin spread slowly from his eyes to his mouth. Jacques followed suit, as though he was his brother's reflection. Marie-France looked from one to the other.

The need to touch them, to hug them both welled up in her like a tsunamic wave but she knew, out of respect for Jacques' personal code of not displaying intimacy in the bar, that she couldn't. Another unprecedented thing occurred, on this, the most unprecedented of days. Jacques made his way around the bar, put one arm around Joe, the other around her and pulled them close, then closer, burying his face in her hair while Joe did the same to him.

At that moment, Doc, along with two other apero seekers, pushed his way through the door. 'Must be Happy Hour,' he said, but only to himself.

CHAPTER 19

The eagerly anticipated day arrived. Marie-France's *DGD*, along with her parents, was expected at any time. She'd abandoned Eric to work on his own on the morning they were due, spending the waiting time hopping up and down, popping in and out, peering across the square as though she might have missed them, like a child determined to catch a glimpse of Santa Claus floating soundlessly across the sky in his sledge. A Land Rover can be described in many ways but soundlessness is not one of its qualities. She was out on the forecourt, Joe and Jacques in attendance, well before it pulled up outside the bar.

Her father climbed down stiffly while Joe, gallantry personified, went round to the passenger side to offer his arm to Morag, who giggled approvingly.

'As you can't hug your old girl, will I do?' Angus asked, taking his daughter into his arms. 'Mhairi, you look fantastic!' her mother exclaimed, cuddling up into the action. 'Did she behave?' Marie-France asked, patting the vehicle as though it was a real horse that powered it. She was surprised when Jacques said, 'Why don't you find out for yourself? Come on, let's go for a drive.' 'What? Now? But….'

Not much about his *bien-aimée* escaped Jacques' notice. She could have, physically, been driving herself for a while now. The reason she hadn't must be psychological. 'Yup, right now. Joe, you look after Morag and Angus.' He explained in careful English to the Scots.

'We are going for a drive. We won't be long. Joe will serve you but you do not pay for drinks here anymore. Okay?'

Angus, every bit as perceptive as Jacques, glanced at his daughter's anxious face. '*D'accord,*' he replied, pronouncing the French acquiescence with equal care. 'Right madame, your chariot awaits you,' Jacques announced, not quite managing Joe's aplomb but making his point by holding open the driver's door. He helped her up on to the retractable step, closed the new, rust free door before going round to the passenger side and climbing in himself.

The reluctant driver sat and faffed for a few minutes, adjusting the seat and the rear view mirror, running her hands around the newly leathered steering wheel, still warm from her father's touch.

'Okay, where to?' she eventually asked. 'Eric's, of course.' Straight to the scene of her accident. Fair enough. Why prolong the agony? She engaged first gear, checked for traffic, pulled out.

They didn't speak. Jacques, stretched his arm across the middle seat, watching every flex of her muscles as she hunched tensely over the steering wheel, a tiny figure, like a child in a grownup's car. She drove slowly, even by Land Rover standards, letting the low gearing do the work, so they trundled up the track to Roumignacs' farm with almost no acceleration. She drove straight past the passing place where Eric had stopped on the night she veered off the road, focussed on reaching what she saw as her first goal, the farm itself.

Eric, still unsettled by the business with Elie and Xavier, was visibly agitated by the arrival of the strange blue vehicle. He stood at the door of the henhouse and took a firm hold of My Beau's collar, purposefully heightening the young dog's excitement so when he was let loose his forward bound would be more vigorous than ever. Marie-France, recognising the farmer's understandable distress, thumped the steering wheel to produce a cheerful *bip-bip* of the horn in greeting as she lessened the distance between them. A welcoming beam of recognition creased his weather beaten face. He let My Beau go, quickly calling him to order as soon as he'd performed the statutory few barks he was permitted.

'So, this is it,' Eric remarked, leaning in through the now open door to place a kiss on each of Marie-France's cheeks, reaching across to shake Jacques' outstretched hand.

'Certainly looks more like a tractor than a car.' 'Drives like one too!' she replied happily. 'No chance of us breaking any speed limits. Seems Jambon is keen to meet her as well.'

The pups had been shut into a shed behind a Heath Robinson barrier of planking, which the most adventurous of them had scrambled up and over, dislodging it just enough to let her litter-mates follow suit. 'You've got too many dogs, Eric,' Marie-France laughed. 'But don't worry, now I'm properly mobile my first great adventure will be to take Jazzy to her new home. Actually, I've just had an inspiration about Funny Face too.'

'In the meantime…' Jacques said, in a serene voice that totally belayed the clenching in his stomach at the thought of the freedom her new mobility might offer. 'You're right Jacques, we need to get back down the hill. See you tomorrow Eric!'

Jacques might have hidden his anxiety but she was not so successful. It had been on the return journey down the steep, muddy track that the van she'd been driving went over the edge. Her tension increasing as the vehicle lumbered downhill, she leaned forwards over the steering wheel, gripping it until her knuckles protruded as bloodless, white balls.

'Breathe out. Let it all go,' Jacques' low voice murmured as they approached the bend where the van had gone off the road. He automatically spoke the words that had long been part of his inner repertoire of controlled self-discipline. More recently they'd been used in a different context, during their love making, to relax her, and himself, as they approached the moment of climax, so the ecstatic moment could be prolonged. The effect on Marie-France was instant. With a shuddering sigh she changed down into first gear, took her feet off the pedals. The vehicle crawled forwards for a few wheel turns under its own momentum until she applied the brake. She clenched and released her fingers before resting her hands lightly on the steering wheel then turned her head to look at Jacques, who appeared cool and unperturbed.

'We could stop, right here, and perform a primitive rite of exorcism on the very spot where I could have died. *Une petite mort* would surely do the trick.' Her voice was husky with desire. He took a deep breath, slowly exhaled, allowing himself a ghostly smile before replying laconically. 'Primitive rites are for warm spring nights, not soggy winter afternoons. Anyway, Joe will have smothered your parents in over-the-top jovial hospitality to hide his worry if we don't go straight back.'

Leaning over, she gave him a resigned peck on the cheek. 'Another time maybe,' she said, re-engaging first gear, gently stepping on the accelerator. 'Certainly,' he intoned, as if he was accepting the deferment of a drink until a more suitable moment. For what felt like eternity he'd been impatiently waiting for her to get back to normal but now, presented with this provocative demonstration of her concept of normality, he was beginning to wonder if he'd be fit for the challenge. Serenely, without giving away an inkling of his misgivings, he remarked. 'But for now, we need to get your lot settled before mine arrives.'

Jacques and Joe stood together on the winter-empty forecourt, both of them experiencing slightly mixed feelings as they watched Marie-France driving her parents away, independent, no longer in need of their support. They didn't have time to brood. Léa pulled their grandfather's Audi into the vacant space the Land Rover had left behind. The car had barely stopped before the passenger door opened and a rejuvenated, spritely man leapt out. There was none of the staged formality of his previous arrival in the village, no handshake leading into filial kisses, no posturing at all. Two strong arms encircled the younger men, drawing them into a crushing bear hug. To their surprise, by the time their grandfather had released his hold, Léa had driven away.

'Léa says to say bonjour but she doesn't want to become embroiled in greetings just now. She's arranged to meet Marc at the office and they're going straight to the house, to make sure it's in order for tonight. Heating on, bed made and such like.' The eighty four year old man grinned like an infatuated teenager hinting at nefarious goings on. 'I knew the bar would be quiet at

this time so I thought it would be the ideal moment for a chat.'
'It's more than just quiet, its empty. Come in, pépère.'

The old man put his arms around their shoulders, as if even a few seconds of lost contact were too long. The three of them pushed together through the door into the silent bar.

'Coffee?' Jacques asked, automatically. 'Of course, my boy. But I'll take the first one standing. I've done enough sitting over the past few days to last me a week.'

Jacques detached himself, taking his habitual place behind the bar. Joe stood beside his grandfather. They both presumed the old man wanted time alone with them to talk about, maybe even to justify, the suddenness of his wedding announcement and everything wrapped around it.

Grandfather Jacques downed his coffee in one gulp but his opening gambit wasn't at all what they expected. 'Well now, I want to know everything that's happened to you two since I was last here. In fact, I want to know everything that's happened to you since I left Marseille, when our lives parted. But let's start in the recent past and head backwards.'

'Oh!' The brothers looked at each other. At any other time their minds would have been spilling over with things to tell to their grandfather but now, being asked an open ended question, neither of them could think of anything to say. Grandfather Jacques chuckled. 'Maybe we'd better move on to something stronger than coffee to wet your whistles. Where are the boys, by the way?'

An answerable question, but was it a loaded one? 'They're at school pépère, I didn't keep them home to greet you as you're going to be here ...' His grandfather interrupted, implying that time was too precious to spend it finishing sentences. 'That's fine, Jacques, just fine. As I'd hoped. I want a while to concentrate on *my* boys first, yours can come later.'

'Oh!' For two articulate men Joe and Jacques were giving a good impression of being unable to speak. As though trying to help them out by filling the silence their wordlessness left, the repetitive sound of a hammer drill started up next door.

'I hear the builders have started work. Once they've left for the day we'll go and take a good look around. I never got further than the ground floor the last time and I didn't get a picture of what you're intending to do, probably because I didn't ask for one. Did you have much trouble finding the right man to take on the job?' 'No trouble at all. Only one option, as far as I'm concerned. Second generation local man. I have every confidence in him. Not only is he a good builder he's also a good man. I know that doesn't really matter as long as he can do the job, but it helps.'

Joe thought he was referring to Pierre Calvet's prompt response when they asked him to do the alterations for Marie-France coming out of hospital. But Jacques was thinking further back, right back, to when she first arrived in the village. Pierre Calvet had picked up the bill for Rab's funeral.

'And it helps that he's prepared to listen and try his best to do what the customer wants. Someone more traditional would have rejected Joe's creative ideas out of hand, but Pierre only vetoed the ones that structurally weren't possible.'

Their grandfather was prepared to listen too, paying attention to every word Jacques said. Now he turned to Joe. 'So, you want to do more than produce the food, you want to design the place its eaten in as well. Good.' He nodded approvingly. Joe stood up taller, bolstered by the praise. The old man, reaching out, gently traced the scar on Joe's cheek, giving another approving nod. Joe, rethinking his looks since he'd not been seeing Lucie, had stopped using the toning-down foundation.

'I don't have any problem with makeup, Joe, on a man or a woman. But I think it should be used to enhance one's features, not as a mask to hide behind. I hope this means you're getting more confidence in being who you are. Apart from when you're being someone else, of course.' The two big men shared a laugh in recognition of their shared skill at impersonation.

As if he was working through a mental check list Grandfather Jacques asked. 'And how's Eveline? I seem to remember, Jacques, that you had some concerns about her, something to do with her partner perhaps? That was one of the many conversations we didn't get round to having. Although, in all fairness, on that occasion it was Léa that distracted me.'

Joe gave a bellowing laugh. 'Distracted? That's a bit of an understatement, grandpère. Hardly a momentary distraction though, was it?'

His grandfather gave a sheepish grin. 'Indeed not. Listen boys, I agreed with Léa that I wouldn't talk about the wedding until she's here too but I do want to get one matter out of the way immediately. Before my wife-to-be popped the question' -he paused dramatically to let the words sink in –'she made it quite clear that she is and intends to remain, absolutely financially independent. You and the rest of the family have nothing to fear in relation to your inheritance. As businessmen, if not as grandsons, I would expect you to have given some thought to that.'

He didn't wait for any response, considering there wasn't one to be made. 'So, that's that. Now, where was I? Oh yes, I was asking about Eveline. Is she still around?' 'Oh yes, pépère. Very much so. She and Corinne, one of the young women from the beauty salon, have got together.' 'Ah, now I believe Léa said something of the sort, although she wasn't sure if was for real at the time. To tell the truth, that was one of the few occasions when I didn't quite follow what she was talking about. I'm not sure she knew herself. Something to do with Corinne and her ex-husband?'

Joe took a deep breath, took his glass into his hand, and recounted the tale, in genuine Grandfather Jacques fashion, adding swaggers and swirls and devious machinations, exaggerating his role as fall guy when it wasn't him but Eveline who got the girl. He finished up with a flourish, Jacques saying, in a decidedly menacing voice. 'Now lads, you won't be telling anyone what went on here tonight, will you?'

Jacques tried to look disparaging, difficult to maintain with his grandfather chortling with delight, not only at his story-telling grandson, but also at the other grandson maintaining the Luciani tradition of sowing seeds of mystery around nothing.

'Ha! Well that's certainly a different take on *les belles dames*, isn't it?' The chuckles rose and fell, settling into their chests before Grandfather Jacques brought them back to reality. 'So, Eveline and Corinne have formed a relationship. And are your boys okay with that, Jacques?' 'Fine,' Jacques replied, with his customary economy of words.

'Fine? They're better than fine about it, grandpère, they're as happy as pineapple in chocolate!' Jacques' eyebrows shot up in surprise at this outburst from his brother. 'Carry on,' he said, interested in Joe's take on his nephews' state of mind.

Joe shrugged, slightly abashed, as if he felt he might be speaking out of turn, but carried on anyway. 'The boys and I have talked a lot about the time when Eveline came out, when she took them away. They told me they're okay, quite cool, in fact, about their mother being a lesbian now, now they're back here, in Labeille. And even before, it wasn't really that that freaked them out. What really screwed them up was that they were cut off, not only from their dad but from his orbit, his orbit of influence, I suppose you could say.'

Jacques, disturbed to hear that his sons had talked about that time to Joe, when they hadn't mentioned it to him at all, found his voice and coughed out, 'But Jacqui sorted that one out, didn't he?'

Joe glancing at him, wondered if he was being signalled to shut up. He didn't. 'Yeh, Jacqui sorted it out. And how! Do you want to hear how he did it, grandpère?'

His voice softened into an alluring murmur, designed to lure his listening prey. Grandfather Jacques recognised the technique. 'Of course, my boy. If you have a yarn that wants to be told then tell it you must.'

'I call this one, The Boys Return. It stars two brothers, Jacqui and Angelo. They'd been taken away from their home by their mother. Far from being a wicked witch, she still loved her kids but didn't know how to make them happy. The man who'd always managed their lives had been put under a terrible spell and didn't seem to know what to do.'

Grandfather Jacques glanced at his eldest grandson, expecting him to be squirming with embarrassment, or even anger. He was sitting forward in his seat, listening intently, fascinated as to what Joe, who wasn't even around at the time, was going to say about those distant months, his own personal dark age.

Joe, in true Luciani style, recounted the drama of Jacqui and Angelo's flight from their mother's lover's home as if it was a boy's own tale of daring do. 'Jacqui, the hero of the tale, had always been told he was just like his father. When his dad lost the ability to think and act like himself, Jacqui decided he'd have to do the job for him. In his mind he became his dad, analysing the problem destroying all of their lives. Except his mum's, she seemed happier than she'd ever been before. Jacqui, ten years old in body but many times that in mind, after waiting for his dad to make the move they were all hoping for, decided he'd have to take the matter into his own hands. Knowing exactly what he wanted to achieve, he started planning, every tiny step of the long way back home.'

Jacques travelled back into the period of time he remembered as a vast expanse of emptiness and loneliness. He'd known he was failing the boys but the problems seemed insurmountable and he couldn't unfreeze his mind enough to address them. Ironically, he had just done that, with Marie-France's oblivious help, and was all set to make things right, when Jacqui, who'd been kept waiting too long, made his move. Like a dreadful whisper from the past, he once again heard Eveline's voice. *Jacques, it's the boys. They've gone,* she told him over the phone, unable to keep the terror from her voice.

It was Jacqui's voice he heard now, coming out of Joe's mouth, as he spoke his nephew's words.

'I had it all worked out but I kept on hoping dad would take over. But when I knew we were being sent back to Arlette's, again, I put my plan into action. At first it was easy, kid's stuff, as if I was pretending we were going to have a play adventure. The first hard bit was taking money from mum's purse. I didn't really need it. I'd been stashing the cash that Dad gave us for ages. But

I wanted to let him know that I'd planned what I was doing, that I was in charge, not anyone else, so he wouldn't let mum panic if she'd thought we'd been abducted or something.'

Jacques nodded. That was exactly what had happened. Eveline's pilfered purse was the first of the clues that his son had left for him to follow.

Joe, as Jacqui, carried on speaking. 'And I knew that once he'd figured that one out he'd find the rest of the clues I'd left, because he'd have to start to think like himself again, just like I'd been doing all the time I'd been making my plans.'

It was true. Jacques, shocked and frightened that his kids were in danger, but slightly reassured when he knew Jacqui was in charge, with a plan, not acting impetuously, had started joining up the marks of the dot to dot picture that his devious son had sketched for him. The clothes left behind instead of being taken back to his mum's. The crisps and drinks taken from the store room. The way he'd taken control of Angelo's pocket money as well as his own. Jacqui, through Joe, explained more about his preparations.

'I planned the journey right down to the last footstep, and left the itinerary on Dad's computer so he'd know exactly what I was going to do. I was a bit worried about Angelo. I knew it was going to be a long, scary day, but there was no way I was going to leave him behind, without me. And he was brill, didn't moan or cry or anything.'

The voice changed now, went up a few tones. Angelo had obviously been with his older brother when he confided in his Uncle Joe. 'That's 'coz it was fun. I liked the bit when we ran to catch the train, even though I needed a pee. But when Jacqui told the train man it was our granny's eighty something-th birthday I knew it was a story. Grandmère Louise would never, ever have let us go on a train on our own. But I never got to hear the rest of the story because I did some colouring-in instead. Jacqui said he wanted me to 'coz I was so good at it.'

Joe, the player of the parts, paused. Even he was affected by the poignancy of the scene he'd brought to life. His grandfather, not ashamed to show his emotions, brushed his hand across his tear filled eyes. Jacques, who'd been holding his breath for so long it felt as though his heart was going to burst, let out a long, sorrow-filled sigh. The story teller picked up the pace and jollied them through the first ever bus journey, the trepidation of the vast station and its electronic notice board, Angelo's worry that they were lost, quickly replaced by absolute trust because his brother was so cool. The tension was almost unbearable until they finally reached the moment when the Jacqui character announced, with a hôtel-kitchen sized ladle of poetic licence. 'It's all right, little brother, we've made it. We're home now and they'll never dare send us away again!'

Joe had applied the well-honed Luciani tale-telling strategy every bit as effectively as the man he'd learned it from, using light and fun to disguise dark and anguish. His listeners were too close to this particular anecdote to be taken in though.

After a pensive silence Grandfather Jacques remarked. 'They must have been bleak days, for all of you.' Jacques, only just beginning to emerge from the enthralling web Joe had woven, nodded sombrely but his brother was determined to have the last word. 'Bleak days? Not for me!' His ironic voice sounded more suited to Jacques than himself. 'I was living it up in *l'Île de la Réunion*. No one told me the family had been spilt up into non-functioning pieces.'

The accusation hovered in the atmosphere, as if trying to decide where to deposit its icy reproach. A jovial voice sent it scudding back into the ether. 'But eventually you galloped in on your white charger to save the day, even if it was only by making sure no one starved to death.'

The mood lifted immediately, as the older Jacques intended it should. 'But at this moment, it seems to me, we're more likely to die of thirst than hunger. May I serve you boys a drink, just to make sure I haven't lost the knack?'

'You're quite an uncle, uncle Joe,' Jacques remarked quietly to his brother, while they waited for an expertly pulled *demi* of beer. 'I didn't realise you and the boys were having heart to hearts. I thought you spent all your time together trying to dream up ways to disturb my peace!' 'We do our best!' Joe grinned, sprawling over the lightweight chair, palpably relieved that Jacques had accepted his performance for what it was. A light-hearted chronical of a time in the family history that shouldn't only be remembered for its sadness and grief, but also for Jacqui's triumphant resolution. It had taken Joe hours over days and weeks to cajole his nephews to talk about those times but when he'd finally gathered enough information to construct his version he tried it out on them. Their reaction convinced him of its validity. Angelo jiggled on his seat with pleasurable excitement, spontaneously clapping his hands, glancing at Jacqui to make sure his enthusiasm was approved. His older brother nodded thoughtfully, as though replaying what he'd heard, then smiled, slowly and appreciatively before offering up his hands for a 'give it five' with his uncle. 'Okay?' Joe had asked. 'Fine!' Sometimes he was very like his father.

Watching his grandsons, Jacques senior sighed in contentment. This was what he'd been missing. This was what Léa persuaded him to do, during the long hours when she'd talked, deep into the night. 'You *can* make yourself part of *your* family again,' she told him. 'Don't waste the rest of your life wondering, worrying, pretending that you're an old, empty man with nothing left to give. You know in your heart that the boys, your boys, as you call them, will welcome you. It's not too late for another Jacques Luciani adventure. And don't forget, in this one, you've won the girl before you've even started. I'll be there with you Jacques, every step of the way. There's nothing to lose and plenty to gain. A new beginning in a place that's already special, for both of us, together. Not that we'll stay there all the time. I've got two lovely homes I want you to make your own, and lots of special people for you to meet in Paris and London.' This was the 'more' that he'd had hinted about to Jacques during their exchange of emails. Pépère didn't intend only coming to Labeille to get married. He was coming to stay.

And now he was here and in the first few minutes his

anxieties had already receded. They'd grown up, matured, especially Joe, but they were still his boys, still together, with that special blend of humour and concern that made them such a good team. And there was another generation to get to grips with yet.

'So, Jacqui and Angelo, they'll be growing up by the second, I suppose.' Jacques smiled, not even trying to hide the happiness that being with his grandfather again made him feel. 'Mmm. Jacqui is quite a man already, and so sharp, sharper than your swordstick. If he ever decides to go into business in opposition I might as well give up. And his wit! Wicked doesn't get anywhere near to describing it. People think dad and I are straight faced but Jacqui, when he chooses to be, is blanker than an empty order book. It can be hours later before I realise I've been had.'

'And Angelo?' 'Ange is a completely different pot of soup. Physically he's so like Joe that he's often taken for his son. I must warn you pépère that when they get together they can reduce a piece of granite to jelly with their double act. But he's got another side. He's deep, a worrier, moody too. In a breath he can change and it's like there's a storm brewing in his brain and when that happens he just needs to get out, away from people. Very much like Marie-France. I suppose that's why they spend so much time together, although if asked I bet they'd both say it was Galla, Marie-France's dog, that they wanted to be with. I don't think she knows just how good she is for him.'

'Ah yes, Marie-France. I was wondering if your little girl was still around.' Grandfather Jacques managed to make the 'your' sound plural, addressing the question to the space between his nephews' heads. 'Is she well?' 'Much better than she was when you were here, physically.'

For once Joe didn't react to what could have been taken as a suggestive allusion, considering that Marie-France and Jacques now went up to bed together every night. He knew Jacques was still wondering whether she was as recovered mentally as she'd made herself out to be with her outspoken, risqué comments. The older Jacques looked from one to the other, intercepted the look that passed between them, waited for clarification.

Jacques gave an almost imperceptible nod, Joe adopted what his grandfather already recognised as his story telling posture. 'It all started when Eric, your son Eric, gave one of the local lads a chance to earn a bit of pocket money by doing a few odd jobs around the farm,' he began. He told the same sanitised rendition of the dramatic events he'd told in the bar. When he reached the closing scene with its dramatic final words, 'we hope they will languish behind bars for as long as it takes for them to realise that they should never mess with this family again!' Grandfather Jacques, who'd been sitting on the edge of his seat, broke into spontaneous applause.

'Well told, my boy. You've not only inherited my handsome looks, you've also been blessed with the gift of the gab, a true *sacré battant*. Fancy my son Eric already having his own Luciani legend. But back in the real world, are they both alright?'

Joe gave the question serious consideration. 'I think so. Just. Marie-France is handling it in her usual brazen way, daring the world to think she might be vulnerable. As for Eric, well I'm not so sure. He seems a bit adrift. But then, from what I can gather, his life has followed a steady, predictable path, season after season, year after year until he got involved with us. Then everything sort of imploded, what with learning about you, his mother dying. Marie-France. Well Marie-France is a potential volcano in anyone's life.'

Grandfather Jacques, listening attentively, frowned at this mention of his son. 'I feel guilty about the way I burst into his life and it all turned into some sort of a pastiche of a movie. It's very high on my agenda to spend some good quality, father and son time with him.'

'Talking about sons,' Jacques remarked. 'While we're delighted you're getting married here, I hope there aren't any problems between you and mum and dad.' 'Not at all. Your mother thinks I'm a silly old fool of course, an astute woman Louise. But its only right that they should have some time together, away from me, to concentrate on their own lives, for Louise to really rule her own roost instead of feeling her husband is still a little boy inside, wondering if his powerful father approves. Léa got me to work out that one. A remarkable woman. And here she is. Léa, my dear. Come and join us.'

The exchanged kisses were polite but not effusive. Although she was their grandfather's wife-to-be Léa was still a virtual stranger. One that hadn't made much of an impression when they'd met before.

'Have you brought the house up to your standards?' Grandfather Jacques asked, as Joe went to get her a coffee. 'I didn't need to. Its *impeccable*.'

Eric had been overjoyed when Marc suggested that his father and Léa could stay in Solange's house, especially when he said he'd take responsibility for ensuring it was fit to receive them. From Léa's reaction, Jacques detected Eveline's pernickety involvement in the task.

'I've made a good start getting to grips with some of what's been going on in *my boys* lives,' Grandfather Jacques explained with a grin. 'But now you're here we can tell them a bit more about what's been happening, or more importantly, what's going to happen, in mine. A subject they've no doubt been waiting in trepidation to hear more details about. Our wedding plans, which you've not even discussed with me! She wanted to wait until we were here, so you two could be involved in the planning,' he said as an aside to his grandsons. 'But I'm presuming it will be a quiet affair, nothing ostentatious.'

'Nonsense!' Jacques and Joe physically startled. Had anyone had ever spoken to their esteemed grandfather like that before? Léa wasn't deterred.

'Jacquot!' A pet name for their grandfather? Another first. Léa continued in the same determined voice. 'You know as well as I do that it's ridiculous at our ages, and in this day and age, that we're getting married at all. You also know that the whole village will be buzzing like an acacia tree in flower once it gets out that that's what we're going to do, with people saying that you're just a dirty old man and I'm just a fortune hunter after your money.

And while we're on that subject ....'

She turned to address the dumbstruck listeners. Before she could Jacques stopped her words. 'You don't need to explain Léa. Our grandfather has already reassured us about your intentions on that score.'

She narrowed her eyes, evaluating his manner. Cool, courteous, devoid of emotion, no phony protestations that the matter had never crossed his mind. He went up a notch in her estimation. Honesty's as good a trait as any to build a relationship on.

'Good, as long as that's clear, let's get back to the wedding. As I was saying, it's ridiculous in this day and age that we're getting married at all, so if we are going to do it we should make a spectacle of ourselves and do it in style. And I know for a fact, Jacquot, we've come to the right place for style. Although I will admit that much of the detail of the *soirée* you put on when I was here is a bit blurred.'

She paused, a rose pink flush heightened the tint of her subtly rouged cheeks. Grandfather Jacques smiled fondly, presuming, as did Jacques and Joe, that she was confessing to having drunk too much. In fact, her embarrassment was in remembering the derogatory opinions she'd formed about the young men she was talking to. 'I underestimated you. As well as the food, the organisation, the service and especially the presentation, of yourselves as well as the rest, was quite spectacular. Although I don't know why I would have expected anything less?'

She held out her hand to her Jacquot, elegantly dressed in cream, lightweight trousers, an open-necked burgundy coloured shirt, and a loose fitting linen jacket.

'Am I right in thinking that the striking waistcoats you all wore were very similar to your grandfather's?' she asked. 'As near as we could get,' Joe beamed, gratified by the praise, impressed by the attention to detail 'Joe does the creativity,' Jacques explained. 'Whereas he does the efficiency,' his brother added. 'Well, no matter who does what, the result was most impressive. I think we'd be very foolish not to make use of such talent.'

Now it was Grandfather Jacques' turn to beam, pleased she was so favourably disposed towards his boys.

Jacques had switched into organising mode. 'The alterations to the house next door, where the restaurant will be, won't be finished until Easter. We won't have the facilities before then for a large scale event but I got the impression from pépère that he wanted the wedding to happen sooner rather than later,' he remarked, keen to get down to basics.

Léa nodded. 'I understand that. An intimate family meal here, as you suggested in your email, would be perfect for the private side of the occasion. But as for the public side. Jacquot, are you religious at all?'

He blinked, taken by surprise by the question, hoping his atheism wasn't going to be a disappointment. 'Well, actually my dear, I'm afraid I'm not, not in the slightest.' 'Excellent. Neither am I. So there's nothing to stop us getting married in the village church. It's such a wonderfully atmospheric building. And what better place for the villagers to congregate to take part in the event?' 'I don't understand your logic, my dear.' 'To my mind it's only hypocritical to make vows if you believe that there is someone, or something, to offend. How can you offend someone who doesn't exist? In any case, we'll hardly be unusual. About seventy percent of the French population have never been to church or have had any religious education, but more than fifty percent of them get married in church.'

Jacques' eyebrows arched, impressed at the quoting of such specific facts. She caught his look. 'I did an article once about the French, religion and marriage. A fairly superficial piece, not one to be quoted with any degree of accuracy. Despite the fact that's what I've just done!' Jacques liked her even more.

'But what I don't know, because my only previous wedding took place in England, is what the rules and regulations are here. I've never been motivated to find out before.' She smiled affectionately at Jacquot, beaming beatifically, as if he was already imagining himself strutting down the aisle with his beautiful bride on his arm.

Jacques didn't pause to take breath. This was a role he knew how to play. 'At least one of the partners wanting to get married has to be resident in the *commune* of choice for forty continuous days, proof of which must be presented in the form of a rental agreement, recent bills for example. Marc can provide you with the former, I'll arrange the latter on line. Electricity and water bills. Tell me if you want one of your names on each contract or both on both. The only legal wedding ceremony is a civil one, carried out in the *Mairie*. In this village it is always *Madame Le Maire* herself who performs it, although strictly speaking it could be another state official. The earliest the marriage can take place is ten days after an application, with proof of forty days residence, is made to the *Maire*, by both partners together. The longest time delay is one year after that. A full *Livret de Famille* must be presented for each partner as proof of identity. Nationality, previous marriages, present unmarried status, etcetera. A church wedding is purely a personal, not a legally binding, occasion and it depends on the availability and attitude of the priest. Our man here seems to be pretty easy going as regards to the participants' profession of faith and attendance at church. He'd rather have the church used than not.'

He paused, the first of his mental checklists had been ticked off. As Angelo said when asked in school to describe his father in one sentence. 'He knows stuff.'

Jacques remembered the deputation who'd confronted Marie-France about Rab's funeral. 'Of course, if you do go for the church, you'll have the choir to contend with. They definitely think they are the guardian angels of the place.'

He remembered something else. Taking a minute to construct the sentence in English he'd been wanting an opportunity to use ever since one of his colloquial English learning sessions with Marie-France, he enunciating carefully. 'Their Bach is worse than their bite!'

Léa's laughter pealed out brighter than the bells of the church they were discussing. Jacques left it to her to try and explain to the other two, who could both sound as if they spoke any language fluently but, in fact, understood very little English at all. The ambience changed, became lighter, more friendly as they transformed into a relaxed group of people sharing ideas for a possibly madcap scheme rather than polite, defensive strangers. And Jacquot was certainly warming to the idea. 'A full scale society wedding. I love it. And, as you say, Léa, so will the village. It'll keep them talking until the spring. A free for all, although of course, there will be special places for the special people. Jacques, would you be offended if I asked Eric to be my best man? 'Of course not, pépère.' He was surprised that his grandfather had even considered the honour should be his.

'But what about dad? He's your oldest son. Won't he be offended?' 'Bernard? Oh, don't worry about him Jacques. We had a good long talk before I left the farm. As I said before, everything is fine between us. Your mother put up with me for almost the whole of her married life, not an easy thing for such a down to earth person as herself. And although she's too polite and dutiful to say such a thing directly to my face I know that my presence there, at the farm, was taking a little of the gilt off the pleasure at having Bernard to herself. Marthe and I never had the opportunity to experience our last years together in the way we'd planned. But I've been offered a second chance and another delightful way to end my days, sharing them with Léa and being here with you and your family. It seems only right that your father and Louise should be able to make the most of theirs, without me getting in the way. And as for coming to the wedding, they were quite content when I told them I'd quite understand if they didn't want to be dragged away again. Poor Louise. She's done quite enough pandering to the 'silly old fool', don't you think?'

His voice had become Jacques' mother's when he said the words his grandsons had imagined her saying after their grandfather told them he was getting married again. Jacques' eyes gleamed their amusement and relief that there definitely wasn't a rift between the two older men. Then, his busy mind considered the potential awkwardness for someone else.

'You don't think it might be difficult for Eric, you know, in the church so soon after his mother's funeral and you...' The habitually glib, dispassionate man's speech petered out. It didn't seem right to mention Solange, the mother of his grandfather's illegitimate child, in front of Léa. He didn't know, of course, that Léa knew all about the unemotional circumstances of Eric's conception. As did Eric himself.

'Don't worry about that Jacques. Nobody else will except the busybodies. It will add to their enjoyment of the day tremendously. And the rest, the majority, people who care, will be happy to see other people happy, as they always are. We'll have to get an order in to Georges for a cake as soon as possible. A proper traditional tiered affair, I think, don't you dear?'

Her eyes were sparkling too. This was the man she'd glimpsed when he was talking about the past, the one she had fallen in love with, the one she'd brought back to full technicolour, flamboyant life. She gave an endearing giggle. 'A tiered cake's okay but I do draw the line at wearing white.'

Joe, a practised dresser as well as undresser of women, scrutinised her through hooded eyes. 'Jacqui and Angelo would make perfect pages, especially if they had a train to carry,' he murmured, almost to himself, trying to envisage the detail of what he was imagining. 'You've got a wonderful figure Léa, and the bearing to go with it. You'd look fabulous in something really regal, Marie-Antoinette-ish.' His sensuous fingers were uncurling, as though he was considering feeling rather just looking at the curves of her body. The activity of his own hands sent him a warning to behave. He relaxed back into his seat, but not before his grandfather noticed the movement too. 'Joe Luciani! I forbid you to seduce my woman!' he boomed, the resonant voice carrying his words down to the other end of the bar, where Jacques was serving a passing delivery driver, who looked up and caught his expressionless eye. 'Family get-together,' the imperturbable bar man explained. The customer buried her head in the daily newspaper lying on the bar. Jacques strolled back towards his family in time to hear Joe saying, without a hint of contrition. 'It's not my fault, grandpère, if I've inherited your good taste in women, along with everything else.'

'Perhaps we should introduce a bout of jousting into the festivities, to see who wins the ladies' favours,' Jacques remarked drolly. 'Good idea. Let's have a trial run,' Joe responded, issuing an immediate challenge for a round of arm wrestling, by positioning his elbow firmly on the table. Léa understood that she wasn't the lady in the questioning look that passed between them.

Grandfather Jacques was still contemplating Joe's idea for the wedding outfit. 'A train? What could be better, symbolically? We met on a train, you know,' he said. His grandsons were mystified. They thought they'd met on the forecourt of *Chez Jacques.*

'Do you really think I could carry it off?' Léa directed the question at Joe. 'You carried grandfather off, didn't you?' he retorted, provoking yet another of her tuneful laughs.

Although she'd concealed it as best she could from Jacquot, Léa had been nervous about the way his beloved boys might receive her. Now she relaxed, reassured by the natural warmth they were extending.

'Lucien. That's the name of the young man who made those wonderful films, isn't it? Do you think he could be persuaded to come and make another one? This wedding is developing into an event that really must be recorded for posterity. You'll have to have someone to give you away, my dear. All the parts must be filled.'

'Why not ask Amelia? She's your closest relative here, isn't she?' Léa was surprised that it was staid seeming Jacques who'd made the rather non-conventional suggestion. She hadn't been at Solange's funeral.

Jacques' fertile brain was cooking up as many ideas as Joe's was tasty dishes. 'Pépère, how large scale, do you think, in relation to the village?' 'You have an idea my boy?' 'Mmm. *Madame Le Maire* is always keen to encourage local events. I'm sure she'd let us use *Le Salle Polyvalent* for a reasonable price.

It's a big enough hall to accommodate all the people who'd want to attend. What do you think, Joe, about getting together with Pascal from the hôtel to put on a drinks and nibbles reception for the general public, before the family meal here?'

Joe nodded enthusiastically. He was in his creative element. A *spectacle* to plan for. And the perfect opportunity for the first joint venture with Pascal, a winter warm up to pave the way towards the summer heat.

'Fraternising with the opposition, my boy?' Jacques' response to his grandfather was as comprehensive as an itemised bill. '*L'hôtel de La Gare* is owned by the *Mairie*, at the moment. Pascal, the chef, is a salaried council employee, paying into a pension scheme. There's no way he is going to work on after retirement age.' 'Which I presume is in the not too distant future,' his grandfather said, catching on immediately to his astute grandson's drift. 'Exactly! Another four years.' 'And he doesn't have offspring to take his place?' 'Right again. And even if my boys don't follow in the family footsteps – if he carries on as his is now Jacqui will probably be President of the Republic by the time he's my age and Angelo's current destiny is to become a shepherd – Joe already has the first of a brood of aspiring sous-chefs who'd be ready to work under his auspices.' 'And, of course, Joe is still young enough to produce offspring of his own,' the proud grandfather mused. 'Indeed!' Jacques agreed calmly. Even his perceptive brother didn't detect the picture that flashed across his mind. A packet of contraceptive pills on a bedside table.

CHAPTER 20

'Are you and *màthair* ever bothered by the way I live?'

Marie-France and her father were in the Land Rover on the way up to Eric's farm. They'd left her mother to settle herself in the accommodation Marc had found for them.

'It's a bit pokey and spartan,' the estate agent said, when he'd asked Marie-France to come and approve the place for her parents, a suggestion the barely domesticated woman found rather disconcerting. It was weatherproof, wasn't it? What else mattered?

'It belongs to an English couple. They've done it up as a holiday home,' Marc continued, unaware of his companion's quandary. 'So it's only got the basics, none of the usual homely touches of somewhere that's lived in all the time.'

Marie-France had grown up in a 'but 'n ben' on top of a hillside on the Isle of Skye, the same 'but 'n ben' her parents still lived in, virtually unaltered despite many missed deadlines.

'We'll add on a room before the baby's born.' 'We'll get an inside loo before she goes to school.' 'When I get a job at the mill we'll be able to afford to extend. We'll put in a second bedroom, with stairs going up to it.' 'We'll modernise the whole place before we retire, so it's nice and easy to manage when we're old.'

The baby, Marie-France, was thirty six years old. Angus and Morag were both retired. The cottage on the croft was the same as it had always been. The truth of the matter was that neither of them were bothered about the house. He lived for his dogs and his sheep, when he wasn't working for the Forestry Commission. She was passionate about her garden, when she wasn't working at the woollen mill where they made a range of rustic jumpers for the tourists. Inside they were warm enough in front of the open fire, Morag sitting in the easy chair closest to the grate, a row of single socks dangling over the back, waiting for their partners who'd not made it out of the top-loader washing machine. Beside her chair, near the fire, slippers were put to warm, boots and shoes to dry. On the other side, a mountain of crossword books, the obsession providing the excuse for the unfinished family joke skulking in the bottom of a knitting bag tucked under the seat. An arran jumper. As a newlywed Morag started to knit for her husband, believing they'd be like the young couples in the women's magazines her mother gave her to read before she got married. She created a picture of Angus sitting on the other side of the fire, reading or smoking, while she knitted or darned socks. Or they would eat prettily presented meals opposite each other at a nicely laid table, a posy of flowers wafting scent around the dust free, polished room. Her pictures were washed away with the first rainfall. The panel of the gifted drop leaf table was only opened up at New Year when their neighbours paid the annual call to drink a dram, soaking up the one from the house they'd just come from with shortbread from a tin or slices of shop bought pork pie, convenience luxuries only for special occasions. Morag and Angus ate their everyday food whenever they could find time, wherever they could find a space amongst the clutter. Substantial meals of mutton, rabbit, chicken, duck. And fish. Mackerel, lithe, saithe. Mussels in the winter, crabs in the summer. Salmon and venison, when the poachers were lucky enough to be generous. Eggs, always available from the free ranging hens, sometimes from the geese and ducks kept primarily for introducing young dogs to herding stock, before they went further afield, or rather further a-hillside, to work with the sheep. Vegetables from Morag's seaweed fertilised garden. Potatoes, stored in the outhouse, enough for the year. In the summer fresh crunchy sybies as well as full sized onions. Lettuce, grown in a bed the ducks and geese ranged on right up until the moment the seedlings were transplanted, to reduce the threat of slugs. Beetroot, carrots, peas, broad beans, runner beans, strawberries, raspberries. In the winter, picked when it was needed, purple broccoli, kale, cabbage, brussel sprouts, parsnips. All cooked on an ancient free-standing cooker, fuelled by the bottle of propane gas that Angus hauled up the hill on the tractor. Another of the improvements they'd never quite got round to was making the rough track fit for a car. In the kitchenette - a lean-to tacked on to the back of the cottage - apart from the cooker and the un-plumbed in washing machine, a sink that emptied out into a ditch which carried the water away down the hill. A set of shelves tacked onto the wooden walls housed the crockery and pots and pans used during cooking and eating. In the porch - a later tacked on lean-to where the electrician had the foresight to put some extra power points - a fridge with a freezer compartment on top, used almost exclusively for mutton or lamb, the one meat that it wasn't possible to finish eating directly from the hoof. The family lived in a room never referred to as the living room. The only room, apart from Morag and Angus's bedroom on the other side of the tiny hall and the loft where their daughter, Mhairi as she was in Skye, slept, once she was secure enough to scramble up the rickety ladder. When she wasn't with her father out in the barn helping with lambing or delivering pups. Or sleeping there because it was raining so hard they'd have got soaked if they'd tried to make it back to the house. In 'the room' another easy chair matched the one that Morag sat in. Angus never sat in it, he never sat anywhere for long. It was buried under a pile of clothes, magazines, newspapers, carrier bags, egg boxes and anything else that it didn't seem right to leave lying on the floor.

Marie-France stood in the middle of the living room in the place that Marc had described as pokey. She looked at the table, a dining chair on either side of it and the cottage style three piece suite, arranged around a stripped pine coffee table. And the shelves filled with guide books, maps and holiday reading novels. She walked, without climbing over any obstacles on the floor, pushed through saloon type swinging doors leading into a compact, fully fitted kitchen, with wall cupboards, work tops, floor level cupboards, an electric hob, electric oven, microwave, automatic washing machine, stainless steel sink with a double draining board. 'There isn't any room for a dishwasher,' Marc explained apologetically.

Another door led into a hall with yet another door that led into a compartment with a WC and a tiny wash hand basin. 'The main bathroom is upstairs,' the guide pointed out. 'They've done well to fit in a shower up there, considering the head height. No bath though.'

Stairs! Up to a bedroom with a double bed, built in wardrobes and a dressing table tucked into the eaves, a dormer window above letting in the wintery light. 'What do you think? Will it do?' Marc asked anxiously, becoming unsettled by Marie-France's silence.

'Do? Oh aye, it'll be fine.'

'This will do fine,' Morag said, as Marie-France handed her the keys she'd just used to let them in. 'Once we get a few of our own things about the place,' she added.

It didn't take the three of them long to empty the Land Rover, even though the back was stuffed full, right up to the newly lined roof. The first thing to come in was a cardboard box.

'Doc said there was a kettle and a coffee maker but I've brought the teapot and our mugs. A cup of tea never tastes the same out of anyone else's.' Where there's a teapot and mugs there have to be teabags and left over shortbread. And the rest of the fruitcake and the half empty bottle of ketchup, and a few tins of beans. 'No point leaving food in the house when we're going to be away for so long.'

Next came the outside clothes, jackets, raincoats, fleeces. 'Doc says you do get a winter here.'

Slippers, shoes, walking boots, welly boots. 'Your dad's bound to be spending some time up at the farm.'

Jeans, tee shirts, jumpers, underwear, packed into crackly new rucksacks. 'We intend going on lots of long walks so they'll be useful for carrying picnics and suchlike.'

Bags filled randomly with crossword books, magazines, a portable CD player and the 'Learning French' course that they'd taken it in turns to listen to through head phones on the long journey south. 'No point installing a radio in this rattly old machine.'

The faded tartan suitcase from the loft was there too, filled with sheets, pillow cases, towels. 'The owners would rather you supplied your own linen, if that's all right.' A new, feather filled duvet in the plastic zip-up carrier it came in.

'Feels more like home already,' Morag said in satisfaction, stepping over a couple of bags. 'Once we've had a cup of tea we'll be well settled. And look, Marc's even left us a carton of milk. And a bottle of wine. He really is a treasure.'

Marie-France declined the tea. Angus swallowed his down in two or three long gulps. 'Shall we get a breath of fresh air lass, while your mother's getting the place the way she wants it,' he suggested. By this he meant settling down in the chair to finish the pot of tea with a crossword or three. 'We could go and see a man about a dog,' she replied, eager for an opportunity to get her dad on his own, not exactly to share her worries but to discover if she should have any.

'So are you?' she asked again, a bit louder in case Angus hadn't heard her over the rumble of the perfectly tuned engine. 'Are you and màthair ever bothered by the way I live?'

Staring out of the window, chewing on his lip, he seriously considering the question. She pulled into a passing place. This might be a weightier discussion than she'd anticipated.

'You mean the way you spend most of your life on the move or out in all weathers talking to beasts instead of sitting by the fire, or even an electric radiator, talking to human beings?'

He might have been talking about himself! But that wasn't the side of her lifestyle that was bothering her.

'I've been in one place for a year now.' She hoped to turn his thoughts towards the direction she wanted them to go. Or maybe she didn't.

Again he pondered, running his tongue around his mouth to stop himself chewing on his lip. 'Like your mum, I suppose, having to try and get accepted in a foreign place with a different language.'

She frowned, trying to make sense of this obscure remark. Then she got it. Her mother had come over to Skye from Lewis, a neighbouring island where the accent, and the Gaelic, was as different as would be expected from places separated by a sixty four mile stretch of water.

'It was easy enough, when I was on the move. I didn't have to worry about what people thought about me. I was only bothered that they were happy with the way I did my job.'

Angus nodded, getting the drift of what she couldn't come straight out and say. 'Your mother has done some pretty shocking things in her time, you know.'

This was totally unexpected. Marie-France was trying to convince herself that she might confide in him but it seemed as if he was going to confide in her! She knew her mother was what was known as 'a character', knew she had a reputation for not conforming to all the social niceties. But shocking? Was the daughter's behaviour more like the mother's than she'd imagined? Marie-France wasn't sure she wanted to know, almost laughed it off, moved her hand towards the ignition key so she could drive away from a potentially uncomfortable situation.

Curiosity got the better of her. 'Mum? Shocking? How?' 'Well, there was one occasion, we hadn't been married long. It was a dry, blowy day and I'd been out with the dogs. Can you imagine my humiliation when I arrived back and caught her at it?'

The tri-lingual daughter, still unattuned to the language her father was speaking, didn't pick up immediately on the potential double entendre. Only when she heard her own question did she begin to wonder if she was about to find out that she'd inherited her sexual proclivity from her high spirited mother. Caught her at what?' she asked, and immediately knew she really didn't want to know. 'Hanging out the washing!' Angus replied, delighted at the flummoxing effect his drollery was having on his feisty daughter. 'Quoi? I mean what?'

And then she remembered. The Wee Frees, the pious

Presbyterians, decried all activity except prayer on ...'It was a Sunday!' Angus crowed triumphantly.

Marie-France's brittle laugh betrayed more than just amusement. Her father, who didn't know what had happened at Eric's or what the rumour mongers had been spreading around about her, detected a crack in her well disguised fragility. He seized the rarely presented opportunity to indulge in some paternal guidance. 'Are you happy, Mhari, right now, at this moment in time?' he asked. She screwed up her face, disconcerted by the directness of his approach. He wasn't put off. 'Because if you are, enjoy it. You, more than anyone, should know how precarious life is.'

She waited for him to develop the theme he'd introduced, believing, hoping, maybe, that he'd picked up on what she been insinuating when she'd asked him if he was bothered about the way she lived. He had. 'As long as you don't make any promises you don't intend to keep, the people who care for you will accept you as you are and the others, well, you've got three different languages to use to tell them to bugger off!'

Hadn't Jacques told her exactly the same thing? This time her laugh was clear and uninhibited as it carried the residue of her disquietude out through the open Landy window and away over the valley.

'Right then, let's go and see about this dog,' Angus said, patting her firmly on the knee.

'I'm not going into partnership with Eric after all,' she explained, as they rumbled towards the farm. 'Just as well,' he replied. This was unnerving. What had her observant father observed between her and Eric? Not that she'd ever tried to hide her affectionate feelings towards the man, if that was the right way to describe them.

'There's no point in complicating a straightforward situation with legal formalities.' Phew! He was only thinking about their working relationship. 'And in any case, Eric is a fine looking, strong man with his own farm. If he wanted a permanent partner, in any sense of the word, he'd have got one by now.' Or maybe he wasn't!

CHAPTER 21

When Marie-France informed Eric that their partnership was being dissolved before it was even formalised, she knew she'd made the right decision. He didn't argue, just nodded his greying head once, as though ticking off at least one of his worries.

Jacques argued, but the fact that he was pinioned to the bed as she straddled him and tweaked his nipples, did make his protests disjointed. She'd challenged him with what Eric had suggested, that he only wanted the partnership as a way to keep her around, during the dark days when she was in hospital and he thought he was going to lose her, if not to death then to flight. 'Okay, I accept that charge, ow! But that was before I figured out that it was you I wanted, the real you, not one that I could keep beside me no matter what. Now I'm not so sure!'

He put his hands around her waist, lifted her effortlessly and reversed their positions. 'But seriously, Marie-France, I do worry about your financial security.' 'Why? I don't. I've never had it before so why should I need it now? That's not fair!'

His finger was sensuously tracing her lips, as though wiping away her words as she spoke. She took hold of both of his hands. 'But don't worry. I'm not going to work for Eric for sexual favours.' She paused to let him savour the tantalising idea that she might be doing that for him. 'I'll work for him on the same basis I've always worked, as an agricultural worker, with an agreed wage and conditions. That will keep me right with the tax man. And I'll carry on paying into the pension scheme so that when I'm a little old lady and you and all my other gigolos have lost interest in me I'll be able to buy myself a cottage by the sea and cultivate roses.' He smiled fondly at the ridiculous notion, as he was meant to do.

Eric, recognising the sound of the Land Rover, waited to

welcome them at the entrance to the farmyard, pleased that Marie-France had brought her father to see him so soon. The two men had hit it off when they'd first met and were both looking forward to spending more time in each other's company.

Similar in disposition if not in looks, they shook hands warmly. Angus, eager to demonstrate his newly acquired conversational language followed his bonjour with *ca va?* He was rewarded with a face splitting smile and the response *Ca va. Et toi?* This caused Angus a bit of confusion. The language course he'd been working from, bought by Rory in a charity shop in Glasgow, was rather old fashioned and had only introduced the use of the formal *vous*. The setback was short lived. The concept one Angus understood from the Gaelic, he readily accepted that *tu* and *toi* should be the way old new friends should address each other.

The greeting from the canine world wasn't so ritualised. Angus was surrounded by the three curious puppies, while Galla reserved her welcome for Marie-France. My Beau was kept in order at his master's side. Angus, with gestures and his daughter's help, explained that he was going to take Janus, known as Funny Face, to give her some individual attention 'There's a porch just crying out for a dog in it,' he explained, when asked where she'd be housed.

The three people, the dogs around them, strolled across the puddled yard to the barn that Eric and Joe had thoroughly cleaned and made ready with plenty of clean straw for the dozen ewes they were going to buy. Marie-France did have to translate *vacive,* the word Eric offered when she told her father they'd not yet been put to ram. 'Ah!' the Scotsman said, *'Dionag'.* 'That's the Gaelic word,' Marie-France explained, when Eric screwed up his face at his attempt to repeat it. He hadn't inherited his father's parroting facility. 'The Scottish-English word is even worse,' she said with a grin. 'It's theave.' 'Seve?' Eric repeated, with the characteristic French speakers' difficulty with the 'th' sound. After a few more attempts, which didn't improve his pronunciation at all, Marie-France suggested through her giggles that he try the English-English version, gimmer. 'Too many words,' he groaned, holding his hurting brain in his hands. 'What was the French word again?' Angus asked. '*Vaciva* in Occitan,' Eric said. The whole performance started all over, the words going from French to Occitan to English to Scottish until they were all holding their sides at the joyful nonsense they were speaking.

Marie-France, looking from one man to the other, felt she might just burst with contentment, it was so good to be amongst her own kind, talking about subjects they all understood even if the conversation wasn't exactly flowing.

'What are the stalls for?' Angus asked, pointing at a sectioned off area of the barn. '*Agnelage*,' Eric replied. 'Lambing,' Marie-France supplied.

Angus rolled up his sleeve and graphically acted out a performance of delivering a stuck lamb, twisting his face into an expression of concentrated effort as he pulled. Tapping himself on the chest, he offered his help if it was needed, clearly missing his sheep already.

The three of them walked around to the back of the farmhouse to take a look at the ever changing but always spectacular view. On this dull day the weak winter sunshine was doing its best to dry out the damp earth. A cotton wool clump of clouds had settled in the valley, creating the image of a frothy white lake. Such a sight always made Marie-France restless, filling her with the compulsion to go somewhere else, anywhere else, to explore whatever it was that could be just over the next hill. With a surge of energy she realised that now she could do just that. She had her trusty Land Rover back and could drive away, whenever she felt like it, in search of whatever it was she didn't know she was looking for. Or maybe she should do something a bit more focussed. 'I can get the sheep at the same time as taking Jazzy to her new home,' she told Eric elatedly. 'The Landy will pull your stock trailer without any bother at all. I'll phone Christian later on and organise it.'

To the listening men, she looked as if she was about to take flight and wing her way to the other farm without bothering about a road vehicle at all. Eric brought her down to earth, in the most practical way. 'I've started ploughing the patch where you wanted the vegetable garden,' he said, pointing at the dark red furrows. 'The peas and beans and onions that I sowed in mother's potager in autumn, for family use, are sprouting well but you'll be needing more than that for the restaurant. It might be worth putting some in now.'

They'd decided that it was too much to expect the builders to respect the gardens behind *Chez Jacques* while work was in progress, although both Jacques and Joe were insistent that the 'local as in out the back' concept must be retained, once the work was completed, hopefully for a grand Easter opening.

'This time last year,' Marie-France pondered. 'I'd just arrived, and even though Rab was dead I stayed to do the garden. That was when I learnt about early sowing.' She didn't even register that she was looking to the future with too much enthusiasm to experience any guilt about not feeling any sadness for the past.

Eric offered coffee, his visitors declined. They offered to help taking the beasts back down to pasture. He refused their offer. 'Your mother will be missing you,' he suggested. '*À bientôt,*' Angus said in parting, earning an approving nod and a thumbs up. With the split face pup squirming at her father's feet, Marie-France, who'd not been behind the wheel for months on end, drove over the track for the fourth time in as many hours. 'Not bringing Galla back?' Angus asked. 'No, *athair,* it's expecting too much of her to put up with all the noise of the building work next door.' 'Of course, during the day, but what about at night?' 'Her balcony is out of action and Jacques doesn't allow dogs upstairs. There is a balcony outside his bedroom but...' Her words petered out when she pulled over to pass the time of day with Paulette Aubry, on her way up the hill to collect the morning's milk.

'At least that's one thing I can report back,' Angus thought, knowing he'd be besieged by questions from his wife about their daughter's welfare. One would certainly be, 'And where is she sleeping?'

'It's strange not having Galla around.'

The newly full-of-people day had finally come to an end. Jacques and Marie-France were drinking a nightcap in the bar before they went up to bed. 'It is,' she agreed, wondering if she should broach the subject of his balcony. 'If you don't think the roof overhang on our balcony is enough to keep the weather off, it would only take minutes to rig up a shelter with some of the concrete blocks and a tarpaulin from next door. I'm sure she'd be happier being here with you at night. And I know you would be.' Before she could reply he stood up, holding out his hand. 'Love you, love your dog,' he said wryly. 'You can thank me in bed.'

CHAPTER 22

'I want you to go with her.' Joe knew that what Jacques had to say was privately important when he came right into the kitchen and closed the door behind him.

'But why? Surely her dad...?' 'She won't ask him. I listened to her and Marc talking this morning.' Typically, Jacques didn't decorate the truth by saying he'd overheard.

When Marie-France told him she was going to collect the sheep Christian had reserved for them, at the same time as delivering Jazzy, he too imagined that Angus would go with her. Then he heard her conversation with Marc.

'Your parents happy with the house?' the conscientious estate agent asked. 'Fine, except mum's a bit nervous about being in amongst so many people. Apparently she kept waking dad up to ask him if he'd heard whatever it was she'd heard, or imagined.'

Marc remembered Lucien's reaction, the first night he'd stayed in Labeille, a *commune* with a population of six hundred, much of which was spread about in neighbouring farms. He lived in an apartment in the artistic *quartier* of *la grande ville.* He'd shaken Marc awake, wondering if the place had died, it was so quiet.

'They've always lived in a cottage right on top of a hill. No neighbours, not even a road leading up to it. It took me ages to get used to the people-bustle here too. In fact, I'm not sure I am, even yet.' The faraway expression on her face after Marc left told Jacques that her craving for the open countryside was eating at her again.

'She's going to stay overnight,' he said to Joe. 'She hasn't said as much but I know she'll want to have a night in the barn, like she did the last time, when I left her there.'

The visit Jacques had made to the sheep farm had been the occasion of one of the many false starts to their physical relationship, cut short by the arrival of his parents.

Joe thought for a minute. 'I can manage here fine on my own, you know that. And Angus will be more than happy to give Eric a hand. You go with her,' he suggested.

Jacques shook his fastidious head. 'I can't Joe. I'm just not the man for this particular job. She needs her freedom, to get away, to leave civilisation for a while, sleep under the stars. It's what she's done all her life. But can you see me sleeping in a barn, on the ground, no toilet except the great outside, no *en suite*, not even warm water to wash my hands?'

His brother frowned. 'But Jacques, you know what Marie-France and I are like. If we're together, alone, overnight, I couldn't promise...'

'I'm not asking for promises, Joe, not from either of you. You know as well as I do that it's going to happen sooner or later. But at least if she's with you, well, I know you care for her and that you'll look after her. I really don't think she's fit enough to drive all that way, hitching trailers, loading up sheep, on her own. And even if she is, I would worry.'

'So would I,' Joe agreed, the simple statement confirming what Jacques already knew. His brother's feelings for Marie-France were as sincere as his own. Joe confirmed something else, too with his next statement. 'And, of course, if it's me she's with, she's more likely to come back, isn't she, into your *orbit*?'

He emphasised the word he'd used in his telling of the tale of the boys' return, to let Jacques know he understood that he needed Marie-France in his life, even if it was on her own unconventional terms.

'Hey little one,' Joe called out as soon as he saw her. 'Brother Jacques says you're too wee to go on an adventure on your own, so I'm coming with you!'

She flashed Jacques a smile that may have been relief, or maybe gratitude that he'd presented her with a fait accompli. In any case, she didn't demur. 'Right, in that case we'll go today, then Galla and I can get the sheep down from the hill ourselves and save Christian a job. Dad's already set off on foot to Eric's so we'll pack a few things then go and pick up the dogs and the trailer.'

Her whole being glowed with exhilaration. They were like a couple of kids preparing for a camping trip. 'Bed roll, sleeping bag, primus stove, coffee pot and makings,' she enumerated. 'You'll need to supply your own mug,' she added.

'Plus duvet, pillows, frying pan, sausages, steak,' he added. 'You can't go camping without having a fry up, can you grandpère?'

His grandfather had just arrived to settle himself in the bar for the morning. Smiling in delight that his grandson remembered the times they'd gone up into the scrubland of the maquis for an overnight adventure, he fleetingly wondered how on earth he'd got away with removing them from Louise's watchful care.

The Land Rover was soon packed with bits and bobs, though not as full as when it arrived. They had to leave room for a dog box to contain un-travel trained Jazzy in the back.

'Uncle Joe, don't forget to be very careful of the *belier* will you? It can be a very dangerous animal you know.' Wednesday, the boys were off school. Angelo had met a ram, with almost catastrophic consequences, when he'd been at Christian's farm the previous summer. One of the many tales Joe had extracted from his nephew. 'Don't worry, Ange, Marie-France and Galla will look after me.' 'And you'll look after Marie-France too, won't you uncle Joe?' the little boy replied, looking and sounding as angelic as his name.

Twelve year old Jacqui, sitting at a table with a book propped up in front of him while he drank a bowl of hot chocolate, looked up sharply when he heard his younger brother's clarion voice.

Jacqui had reached the age when he couldn't imagine spending a night with any female and not having sex. The actual sex was part of the imagining, he hadn't yet consummated his fantasies. Some of his pals pulled distasteful faces, denying that their parents could possibly be still doing such a thing at their advanced ages. But Jacqui had heard his mum and

Arlette, her first lover. Seen the way she and Colette held hands and sneaked kisses. Marie-France and Joe's coupling had been the talk of the village. Marie-France and his dad, much more discreet, nevertheless had to be at it as they slept in the same bed. And most recently, his great grandfather and the classy English French lady he was going to marry, couldn't keep their hands off each other. Jacqui had formed the opinion that, in his family at least, you could still do it at any age. Angelo's comment about Joe 'looking after' Marie-France made Jacqui wonder if the wide eyed boy was just quite as innocent as he made himself out to be. The next part of Angelo's performance, and Jacqui was convinced that was what is was, made him wonder even more.

'Uncle Joe. You might get cold and frightened sleeping on your own in the dark. Here, take my teddy bear to keep you warm.' 'Thank you, Angelo,' Joe replied gravely, putting down the cool box to cradle the toy in his arms. 'He'll be able to tell you all about my adventures when we get back.'

Uncle and nephew, so alike they were often taken for father and son, held each other's gaze in a long, intense stare. So long and intense that Jacqui was sure it had been rehearsed. This was a Joe/Angelo special, a routine that left the audience confused as to what they were seeing. Angelo may or may not have been innocent but uncle Joe was certainly winding everyone up.

Marie-France broke the gaze, broke the spell, broke any attempt at sobriety. 'Come on, you great *lummocks*, the day's not going to stand around waiting for you.'

They were gone before anyone had worked out whether she was speaking in English or Gaelic. Whatever she'd called Joe it certainly wasn't French.

'The tow bar on this is adjustable but I'm not sure it's adjustable enough to fit Eric's old trailer,' Maire-France remarked, loudly, to be heard over the Land Rover's engine noise. 'But it doesn't matter. Christian said I could use his rig. We can save him a trip, bring the sheep up tomorrow and take it back empty the following day. Lambing at the moment. Busy time.'

Joe nodded, preserving his voice, pleased that she'd used 'we' so casually, demonstrating that she wasn't feeling she'd been manipulated, as he'd feared she might. Then he had a thought of his own. 'Come to think of it, my driving licence doesn't have the category for pulling a trailer over seven hundred and fifty kilos.' 'Didn't think it would. Doesn't matter. The driving will be a breeze. It's hitching and unhitching, lowering the ramp and stuff I might need help with.'

Joe was even more pleased. Not only was she happy to have him along, she also accepted that she might need his help. He started looking forward to the adventure.

Angus and Eric, closing the gate to the top pasture, having turned the beasts out after milking, looked up when the Land Rover arrived. Galla was in attendance, as expected when there was work to be done. Funny Face was attached to Angus' belt by a long piece of string, like an umbilical cord that had yet to be cut. Jambon was on a rope lead by Eric's side. A shiny, aluminium stock trailer stood in the middle of the muddy-puddly farmyard.

'Has your trailer had a visit from the fairy godmother?' Marie-France asked, greeting Eric with a kiss on either cheek. She'd already seen her father that morning, he received nothing but a smile. 'Told Paulette you were going to get the sheep. She thought you'd be better off with theirs. Much lighter and just a bit more modern,' the burly farmer replied, once he'd considered her question. 'No problem if we don't bring it back until tomorrow?'

He noted the 'we' and glanced at Joe, carrying on with Angus, pretending to hitch himself up like a donkey to the trailer, miming the effort he'd have to put in to pull it, while the Scotsman lashed him with an imaginary whip.

'Joe's coming with me for the ride,' Marie-France explained, rather superfluously. Eric nodded in approval, didn't say anything. He'd been worried about her making the journey on her own too.

'Right then. Let's get going,' the diminutive woman said, climbing back into the Land Rover. 'Guide me back, will you?'

She flung the request at whichever man wanted to catch it.

Eric frowned when she drove the vehicle forwards to get it into the right position to manoeuvre towards the tow bar. He'd presumed she'd be as skilled in this task as in all the others she performed on the farm. But the direction she'd taken looked all wrong.

'She's left handed,' Joe said. Eric's frown became one of puzzlement. 'Took me a while to figure it out when she first started working with me in the kitchen. I couldn't understand why she looked so clumsy and dexterous at the same time. *Gauchère* brains obviously see the world differently.'

Eric didn't have time to consider whether he was more impressed with Joe's observational skills or Marie-France's ability to manoeuvre. She made the cumbersome vehicle pirouette like a tutu-ed ballerina before backing up to within a metre of the trailer. 'Certainly can't fault that, can you?' Joe added.

He stood back and watched the older men playing their part in a routine they knew well. Angus stood beside the tow hitch with one arm bent at the elbow, emulating the tow ball, while the other beckoned, back, back a bit more, until the ball and socket were approximated. Eric stepped forward and effortlessly lifted the lightweight trailer, retracting a lever before he dropped the socket over the ball. Marie-France got out and stood watching as they sorted the electrics, then got back into the driver's seat so they could check that all the lights were working as they should. The younger man nodded, confirming to himself that he'd know what to do the next time. There's not much call for coupling tow vehicles when you work as a chef, even in the wilds of Marseille. He did take the dog box off Eric though, wedging it into the back as instructed. Marie-France lifted Jazzy into her temporary nest. She settled without much fuss, especially when her soon not to be mistress gave her a rock hard piece of cheese that had been festering in her jean's pocket. Galla took her place at Joe's feet. They were off, a cheery *bip-bip* from the horn and equally cheery waves from the two open windows.

'Not quite as speedy as your Merc,' the driver remarked as all the other traffic overtook them on the main road. 'But much more practical for my way of life. I'm like a snail, crawling along with my house on my back.' Joe glanced into the back, estimated that it was about 120 centimetres long and less than 100 centimetres wide. 'Don't suppose you did much entertaining,' he commented. 'Unless you discovered a tribe of midgets even smaller than you.'

She grinned without displaying any trace of sexual tension at his blatantly suggestive remark. 'You'd be surprised!' He accepted her ambiguous retort in the same relaxed manner. They were just good pals, these two, their teasing banter bouncing easily between them, as light-hearted as a table tennis ball hopping to and fro over the net. For now.

A couple of hours, a pee stop for Jazzy and some desultory chat later, they reached the turn-off Marie-France remembered from before. She drove straight up the potholed track to the barn in the high pasture where she'd taken Jacques and the boys the previous summer. That outing seemed centuries ago, back in the days before her accident, when she hadn't given a thought to running and climbing over fences and facing up to rams to protect her own flock of uninitiated townie people. Glancing over at Joe, sprawling out as much as he could in the narrow seat, Galla curled up comfortably at his oldest pair of trainers, she gave a wry smile at the thought that this particular uninitiated townie had come along to protect her.

Christian, sleeves rolled up, was scrupulously washing his hands and forearms in the icy water skooshing out of a tap attached to a rigid pipe carrying mains water. There was a marked difference in temperature between Labeille's valley and these open windswept hills. Marie-France zipped up her fleece jacket before she climbed down from the far from over heated vehicle. The beefy bearded farmer hadn't seen her since the accident. After he'd bent down and placed not two, but three kisses on her cheeks, the custom in those parts, he looked her over from head to toe. 'Everything in working order?' he asked in his booming voice.

'Fine,' she replied, but his attention had already shifted to the light-weight, up to date rig. 'Borrowed,' she explained. 'As is he,' she added. Joe had pulled on the boots he'd bought after he started working at Eric's and now came round to be introduced to Christian. 'This is Joe, Joe Luciani, Jacques' brother.'

The farmer's hand still wet, he pointed his elbow at Joe, who touched it in an alternative greeting to a hand shake. 'Joe? Ah yes, the sauce man or even the saucy man, as my wife calls you. She's forever going on about those tasters you sent up last year. At least, I think that's what she's going on about, but with Francine, you never can tell.'

'Saucy Joe! I like it,' Marie-France said, poking him in the ribs. He doubled over, groaning oh-oh-oh as if he was in the greatest of pain. Christian, who hadn't given him a milliseconds thought since they'd met, remembered Jacques, his stiff formal manners and clean, ironed clothes and wondered if he'd got it wrong when he'd presumed that Marie-France was *his* little woman.

'How is Francine?' the little woman, whosoever she was, asked. 'Fine. She's at market selling her wares at the moment. At least I think that's what she's doing, although she did mutter something about selling her body too if I didn't manage to make it into bed soon.' He roared with laughter. Joe grinned happily. Here was another farmer he wouldn't have any trouble getting on with.

'I presume you're not making yourself all clean just for us. Lambing, I suppose?' Marie-France enquired. 'Certainly am. Just successfully delivered another couple of bags of chops. I like to supervise the first timers so I can give them a hand if needs be. Haven't got enough space to have the whole flock under cover but the weather's quite kind at the moment so they'll be alright on the hill. Now, where's this new pup you promised me?' he bellowed, his vocal volume control not having any other adjustment.

Marie-France opened the back door of the Land Rover and slipped the noose end of a cord lead over the puppy's head before she lifted her down. 'She'd jump if left to herself,' she explained to Joe, wondering why she was being so protective of the fearless little dog. 'Her bones are still a bit fragile for such a high leap.'

Christian, watching while she let the inquisitive pup sniffle and snuffle about the place, didn't approach until Marie-France encouraged Jazzy to her side and raised one finger. Jazzy obediently sat. 'I've taught her the basics but only with gestures so she doesn't have to learn a new vocabulary,' she said, handing Christian the lead. He took it from her and squatted down but didn't fuss the pup as Joe expected. 'She's prettier than Galla, doesn't have that droopy ear. Just hope she's as good a worker,' he remarked. 'Me too. Looking promising so far. Alert, very interested in stock, even passing cats. Early days though.'

Joe remembered the pets of his many and various girlfriends being cooed and chucked under the chin, fed tasty morsels from the table and encouraged onto his lap. Being a sharp dresser at the time, he wasn't at all keen. These country people treated their dogs completely differently, as valued members of a team but still animals, individuals in their own species, not jewellery to enhance their human selves.

'I'd better give Francine a ring and warn her you're staying the night. She'll be mad that she hasn't had a week or so to prepare something special to eat for the sauce man.'

Christian, noticing the bedding in the back of the van, along with the incongruous teddy bear, was actually speculating as to where Francine was going to sleep the unexpected visitors. 'No need,' Marie-France retorted. 'I've brought my own chef. Anyway, we're going to stay up here, if that's alright. I presume you will be too.'

Joe wasn't sure if he was relieved or disappointed that his temptation resisting ability wasn't going to be tested. It occurred to him that the reason she'd agreed so readily to his company might have been because she knew they would be chaperoned by the shepherd delivering his lambs. He wasn't sure if he was disappointed by that either, but he didn't have time to decide.

'Right, I've got a consultation in the maternity unit so I'll have to leave you to it. Your lot are in the small field at the top, they're marked with a splash of red. If you don't think you'll manage....' 'We'll be fine. Joe's not as well trained as Galla but he can do the brute force and ignorance stuff, like erecting a temporary pen against the barn, so they're ready to go in the morning, presuming that's what you intended?'

Christian nodded, scooped Jazzy under his arm, remembered her previous visit. 'The young tup is pretty feisty, have you warned Joe about...' 'It's okay, my nephew has given me the lecture on how to beware dangerous rams,' Joe interjected. 'Your nephew? Oh yes, the wee fellah who was here last time. I wondered who you reminded me of.' 'I know,' Joe replied with an easy grin. 'We could be father and son. In fact,' he looked down at Marie-France with a wicked grin. 'Perhaps it's time Eveline and I came clean and admitted a past misdemeanour. Now wouldn't that put the cat among the pigeons? Or should I say, the cat among the cats?' he chuckled.

Christian, not having much to do with the complexity of human society, looked mystified. 'Jacques' wife, Eveline. She's gay,' Marie-France told him, as if that explained everything. 'Right.' he said. 'I'm off. I'll put Jazzy in an empty stall to keep her out of trouble. It'll give her a chance to get used to my voice if nothing else.'

As he walked away it struck him, but not with any sense of importance, that Marie-France had talked about Jacques' wife rather than his ex-wife. Maybe he had got their relationship wrong. But what did it matter? It was no concern of his.

CHAPTER 23

'See why I wanted to expose her to as much noise as possible?' Marie-France said to Joe, as Jazzy's new owner strode off, singing a loud, tuneless version of 'Marie-France avait un petit agneau'.

They chattered away as they assembled the galvanised barriers to form a small enclosure, Marie-France directing, letting Joe do most of the lifting and pulling while she answered his questions, explaining that the sheep didn't need to be under cover, even in the coldest weather, but it was always prudent to keep an eye on first time lambers. 'Now for the fun bit,' she exclaimed, when she was satisfied with the result.

Galla sat up alertly for minutes on end after they first arrived, ears and nose twitching, recognising a favourite place, where she'd surely get to play the most important game in her existence, real work. She eventually settled down and lay, chin on paws, never taking her eyes off her mistress. Leaping up as soon as she heard the change in tone, she was sitting by Marie-France's side before Joe had a chance to look at the incline of the land they were about to go up. He divested himself of his jacket.

'Let's go!' She recovered the shepherd's crook she'd leaned up against the wall of the barn, pulled out the flat tin whistle she always wore on a string around her neck. Joe thought he might have to modify his long stride to hers but she tramped steadily and confidently over the rough land.

'Home ground!' Joe said to himself. 'I've just discovered what that really means.' She did hesitate when they reached a stile, accepting his outstretched helping hand without any awkwardness. She asked him to pull open the short section of barbed wire at the entrance to the field where the red marked sheep were too, sensibly wary of over testing her newly healed arm. After that, her willing human companion became superfluous.

'Away tae me!' The command was little more than a whisper but Galla raced off to the right, hugging the hedge line, keeping a good distance between her and the young flock, their heads lifting in anxiety when the unknown humans approached. Before the eager dog could get behind them they made a dash for the furthest corner of the field and huddled there, snorting, huffing and puffing their distrust.

Wheet-wheeo-wheet-wheet. Joe, having only ever heard a single toned whistle, was startled by the complex sounds shrilling out into the crisp air. Galla wasn't. She loped up to the dithery group of animals and worked her way between them and the hedge. Even though the sheep were young they were already larger than the dog and she disappeared from view behind them. Marie-France didn't move, didn't stand on her tiptoes to see if her precious Galla was okay or was being crushed by the woolly mass, just issued another command. *Peep-peep* the whistle sang. Then again, *peep-peep.* The flock started to move away from the dog, as insistent as the repeated sound that they should head downhill. The young ram, nostrils flaring, as feisty as Christian had warned, decided to have a go at displaying his dominance over this intransigent incomer disturbing his ewes. Galla didn't give him a chance to make any sort of statement. He turned towards her, she nipped him on the nose. He decided he'd go with the ovine flow after all. She nipped him on the heel, to reinforce that he'd made the right decision.

Galla was on her own ground too, Joe reflected, completely different from the cute dog he knew from the bar, bowing with her mistress or weaving in between the tables and chairs. She was even different from how she was at Eric's. When she followed the cows up from the fields it looked as if they were taking her for a walk, rather than her bringing them in. The mature animals were so used to their established routine that they didn't need any encouragement from man nor beast to get them into the comfortable stalls where they would happily munch hay, lined up like the regulars chewing the cud in the bar.

This Galla was assertive, strong, not far removed from the wolf she was descended from, in the way she crouched and stalked. Although she only nipped, didn't savage. At least Joe hoped so.

The ewes with their male trotted down the hill, Galla pushing steadily from behind. Joe turned to Marie-France to make some facetious comment about her not being needed at all but she was squinting in concentration, watching every movement of every sheep. When one of them made a break for it and tried to run back up the hill a *wheet-wheeo* command sent Galla off to bring it back into the group. Joe realised that even Galla the wonder dog couldn't do the job on her own, no matter how good her instincts were. 'Now that's what I call teamwork,' he muttered to himself, awestruck, almost jealous, at the precise communication between the handler and the dog. Glancing at Marie-France again, he wondered if she'd ever established that intensity of interaction with another human being.

Joe closed up the stretch of barbed wire fencing after they'd passed through and then hurried to catch up with Marie-France, now at the head of the flock, a pied piper who only whistled for one of her followers, the one who pushed the rest.

'All downhill from now on!' She addressed him as though he'd been a part, an active part, of what had been happening ever since she and Galla had excluded him by their partnership. Watching her striding confidently over the tussocky grass, eyes shining, face glowing, not just with the cold but with undiluted happiness, his throat constricted, his breathing becoming even more laboured than the rush had already made it. He'd long been attracted to his little friend but never so compellingly as he was now. He hesitated to say, even to himself, that she was beautiful. Beautiful women usually had flawless or in some other way outstanding features. She was nothing like that. What she exuded was life, a sense of life that promised to share itself with anyone who entered into its magnetic field. Joe had never wanted her as much as he did at that moment. He felt he was going to implode with the strength of the irresistible longing commanding him to take her hand and run with her downhill forever into a future filled with…

'Steady!' As if she wasn't sure he'd understand the command, she repeated it in French, spreading out the syllables of the onomatopoeic word. *'Dou-ce-ment.'* 'Lie down.' she added. Joe was ready to prostrate himself before her but she was once again unaware of his presence. She turned to face the slowing sheep as Galla lowered herself to the ground, a position far from at rest but it stopped her pushing the sheep, who'd gathered too much momentum under the pressure of her powerful presence.

'Okay, walk up.' She brought the dog back to her feet. From a greater distance, Galla once again drove the animals, calmer now the decision about where to go had been taken from them.

'You're out of training, big fellah,' Marie-France commented with a cheeky smile. Joe struggled to control his laboured breathing, relieved that the spell had been broken before she'd become aware that it had been cast.

The barn with its holding-pen extension was in sight, she spoke again. 'Now for the difficult bit. Go and position yourself on one side of the gap we left open. I'll face you on the other side. With any luck Galla should be able to push them through the funnel we create. If they try and break, flap your arms and stamp your feet. Not too vigorously though. We don't want to frighten them to death.'

The sheep, moving at walking pace now, baulked at the sight of the confining space, started to veer off to one side. Marie-France, instead of trying to head them off, as the novice observer expected, took a couple of steps in the other direction. Galla, as if she was her human's mirror image, or a dancing partner performing a *pas de deux*, moved in the other direction at the back of the implied circle. On command, she started to put gentle pressure on the flock again, encouraging them to pass between the two human gateposts. As soon as the leader, not the young ram but the most self-assured ewe, eyed the hay scattered on the ground, Marie-France walked into the pen herself. Picking up a bucket of grain, she rattled it to attract them to the familiar sound and was soon surrounded by twelve eager noses, pushing and shoving, all trying to thrust themselves into the bucket at the same time. As he was closing off their exit Joe noted the bucket holder twisting slightly, trying to avoid contact on her injured side. She clearly wasn't quite as confident about her physique as he'd assumed. Before he could decide whether he'd be a help or and hindrance if he went over to help she tipped the rest of the grain in a wide circle on the ground and pushed through the woollen mass to his side.

'Glad you haven't lost the knack!' The jollity in Christian's thunderous voice sounded forced. He was carrying what looked like a floppy, unstuffed, cuddly-toy pyjama case, the drooping of his massive shoulders expressing his distress. 'Mother okay?' Marie-France asked, acknowledging the dead lamb with a toss of her head. 'Fine. This was the second of two and she's already settled down with the first. Lots of milk.' He paused, evidently considering.

'Got one that hasn't?' She'd followed his train of thought like ducklings waddling after their mum. 'Yup. First timer, triplets.' 'Grafting?' Joe looked from one to the other. He understood the words but had no idea what they were talking about.

'I'll do it. Give me a tick to wash up and put on my overalls. You go in and prepare the foster ewe.' Marie-France knew that even the most experienced shepherds, especially soft hearted giants like Christian, often baulked at skinning a lamb they'd just delivered. She wondered briefly if she'd be more sentimental if she was dealing with her own stock instead of someone else's, without seriously considering that the beasts she'd come to collect would be the nearest thing to her own she'd ever had. The habit of not looking too far into the future was too well ingrained to let her think along those this-time-next-year lines.

Christian nodded gratefully and waited while she rolled up her sleeves, washed and disinfected her hands and arms and fetched a pair of clean overalls from the Land Rover. Joe, still in the thrall of his recent awakening of desire, didn't have time to contemplate whether watching her put clothes on could be as sexy as taking them off.

'Brighten that up for me, would you?' she said, handing him a sharpening steel and a knife with a fixed, twelve centimetre long blade. Still no wiser as to what was going to happen but content to be of some use, he quickly and efficiently honed the steel blade to butter slicing sharpness. By the time he'd finished she'd taken the still warm corpse from Christian, who disappeared back into the barn.

'Lamb in lamb's clothing,' Marie-France remarked to the mystified onlooker, cutting into the loose skin on the inner front thigh of the lifeless new-born then running the knife down the inside of the leg, using her fingers to prise the skin off the body. Joe felt it was rather ghoulish to desire someone in such bizarre circumstances but desire her he did, observing her hand deftly wielding the knife, the tip of her tongue peeping pinkly through her lips as she concentrated on her task. He wondered fleetingly if perhaps his arousal was being piqued by the dubious possibility of being involved in some ancient, rustic, sacrificial rite, an offering of a naked lamb to appease the gods of death. Unlikely. Christian and Marie-France were surely far too practically up to date to indulge in such traditions. He tried to focus objectively as she made a cut at one hock, then did the same with the other back leg before pulling the skin off the back and cutting through the tail, with a precision to be envied by one who envisaged himself as a potential butcher. But why would you prepare such a pathetic, meatless specimen for the pot? Next she cut from the top of the rear legs towards to the front of the navel on both sides, pulling all the skin forwards. The front half came off in one piece. She kept working with her fingers until she reached the neck then carried on in the same fashion down the front legs. After cutting round the neck, taking care not to touch the veins so there was no blood, she made slits above the knees, cut another slit in the rear flanks and fed the rear legs through, ending up with a onesie with readymade neck and front leg holes. Standing up she stretched her taut limbs in satisfaction, just as Christian emerged from the barn.

Joe, impressed at the standards of hygiene since he'd arrived, was rather taken aback when he saw that the farmer, carrying a definitely living lamb, appeared to be smearing what looked like slime around its face and neck. 'Birthing fluids,' Marie-France explained, aware for the first time that Joe hadn't a clue what was happening. 'We're going to attempt to convince the ewe whose lamb was born dead to adopt this one, so we're trying to make it smell like one of her own.'

Christian squatted down and calmly and gently they coaxed the living lamb into the dead one's skin. Once its head and legs were sticking out of the holes it looked as if it was wearing a tailor made outfit to protect it from the cold.

'Well, you learn something every day,' Joe said admiringly, as the shepherd took the alien, as he had just learnt it was called, to present it to the foster ewe. 'How likely is it to work?' 'Pretty good chance. We'll know almost immediately. The mum tends to accept or reject straight away with this method of grafting.'

She went off to wash herself, leaving Joe to return once again into his rational skin as he cast off all his nonsensical notions of sacrifice and desire.

'Here, let me do that,' he insisted, when she started setting up the camping stove to brew a welcome pot of coffee. 'I am the chef, after all.' 'Brighten up the coffee as well as you did that knife and I might just keep you on,' she retorted, handing him the hip flask she'd filled from an armagnac bottle behind the bar.

By the time Christian came out, restored to his usual ebullient self by what appeared to be a successful adoption, the air was filled with an aroma, the best in the world, when caffeine is the strongest craving. Joe had put in extra cups, also taken from the bar, and they perched on the tumble down stone wall to drink, the two men grinning in uncomprehending amusement as she regaled them with a suitably squawking version of *three craws sat upon a wa'*.

Refreshed and reinvigorated, Christian suggested they check over the sheep they'd just brought down from the hill. 'Let's worm them and give them a manicure while we're at it. It will save you a job when you get back.' 'Right! I'll go and get my personalised hoof clippers. It's taken me years to train them to be *corrie-fisted*.'

Once again her companions looked blank. 'Whoops! Been around my folks too long,' she laughed. 'I'm reverting to childhood.' 'Isn't that senility?' Joe asked, ducking the cuff she aimed at his head but not moving quickly enough to avoid a yank on his pony tailed hair. He was once again his equanimous self.

While Marie-France was away Christian flipped the first ewe on to its back, hoisting it into a sitting position, where it stayed put, like a huge stuffed toy at the fairground, waiting to be claimed by the best shot at the rifle shooting stand.

'Show me how you do that,' Joe demanded. He knew this would be a routine task for his rugged little companion but having noticed she was still aware of her physical limitations, he wanted to be able to offer the kind of skilled help she might be prepared to accept. She did. The two of them quickly developed a smooth routine, him catching and immobilising, her administering a measured amount of vermifuge from a syringe into the animal's mouth, inspecting and trimming hooves as necessary. It didn't take them long to work their way through the twelve sheep but by the time they'd finished, Christian, obviously superfluous, was leant up against the side of the barn snoring gently, oblivious to the approaching dusk. Marie-France shook him awake. 'Go home,' she instructed. 'Let Francine hear you snoring beside *her* for once. There's nothing here I can't cope with.'

The tousled man, rubbing his eyes, tried to construct his sleep laden thoughts into a convincing protest, realised there wasn't one, gave her a hug, shook Joe's hand and rattled off down the tortuous track, Jazzy on the seat beside him. The potential lovers were alone. Apart from sheep, lambs and Galla.

'Food?' Joe suggested, his stomach reminding him of his overriding appetite. 'Definitely,' she agreed. 'I'll do a quick round to make sure there are no problems. If you manage to make your cooking smell sufficiently enticing I'll come back.'

She and Galla vanished into the rapidly falling darkness. Joe set to, building a small fire of brushwood, not only to save on gas but also to recreate the camping experience he'd remembered from childhood escapades with his grandfather. After an unremarked period of time she was beside him, ravenous with hunger, elated by the absence of civilisation's constraints.

They ate and drank like the monarchs of the mountains they felt themselves to be. Joe hadn't stinted when he packed up the provisions. Chops - pork, so as not to offend our companions he laughed - as well as the promised sausages and steak. Bread, onions, garlic, thrown into the pan whole, unpeeled, eaten like sweeties, the flesh sucked through the skin. The potatoes, wrapped in aluminium foil and thrust into the embers, were charred and inedible by the time they remembered them, adding yet another gust of hilarity to the many already floating in the night. They talked and laughed, sharing glimpses of their past, but only entertaining ones, discussed future plans, his to do with the restaurant, hers to do with the farm. It was well into the night before the cold started to infiltrate their contentment. After dousing the fire, she sent him off to fetch the bedding while she did a final check on the mothers with their new-borns.

'All settled,' she announced. 'Looks like the grafting's been successful. Time for us to cuddle up together for a couple of hours?' The look accompanying the invitation was explicit. Joe only just managed to catch his breath to stop it escaping as a whoop of euphoria that the night was not going to remain platonic after all.

On the one previous occasion they'd had sex Marie-France had been wild, reckless, joyful, maybe even desperate, although he hadn't thought about that at the time. He hadn't thought about anything except the pleasure they gave each other. Now, he wasn't fazed when she produced a packet of condoms, especially as the chocolate flavouring sent a sweet rather than a restricting message. He too had been party to Gilou's report about her taking time off the contraceptive pill - the nurse hadn't been sure whose woman she actually was, any more than they had themselves. Joe, knowing she was aware that he'd had at least two sexual partners in the recent past – he pushed aside the thought of hers - approved her prudence with regard to sexual health. Yet he was very conscious that she was different, completely different, from the way she'd been before. Her approach calm, even considered. Maybe she was worried about indulging in a repetition of their previous acrobatics because of her hip. He let her set the pace, taking the hand she offered as she led him towards the nest she'd created with their bedding on a mattress of hay. He wondered if she was resisting him, perhaps not as certain about renewing their intimacy as she'd seemed. She held him close, kissing him lavishly but once his passion started to heighten she pulled back, only momentarily, but long enough to let the tension subside. She repeated the sequence, holding, kissing, withdrawing, but this time letting out a long, slow breath. With a blinding flash of insight Joe recognised the technique she was employing. Jacques'. She was trying to emulate his brother's lifetime practice of performance enhancement through inner harmony and control. Joe distanced himself even further from the deeply breathing figure beside him, giving himself time to figure out how his mind was reacting to what felt like Jacques' remote manipulation. Slowly, a calculating smile spread across his face in the darkness.

'Well, brother Jacques, you might be *l'homme d'affaires* but when it comes to affaires of the heart and body I reckon I can match you anytime.' Hugging himself gleefully he rolled over to face her, eager to initiate her into a few performance enhancing techniques of his own. In that instant, a beam of moonlight lit up her face. Concern overcame the jubilant excitement brought on by the notion of picking up the gauntlet that Jacques didn't even know he'd thrown down. He saw by her mortified expression that she'd realised she'd given herself, and Jacques, away. More than that, she was horrified that Joe might think she considered them as rivals. His instinct was to comfort her, to tell her it was fine, that Jacques had sanctioned their being together.

But how could he do that without confirming, maybe even complicating, her fears? Pushing aside all thoughts of Jacques, all thoughts of himself, he tried to focus on her, on the type of woman she was, on what was important to, and about her. Paling under his scrutiny, she opened her mouth to try and explain, although in truth she had no idea what to say. Joe put his hand gently over her mouth, firmly lying her down on her back beside him. Tense and anxious, she expected him to take her to task. He kissed her softly on the forehead then, with a secretive smile, took hold of her hands, put her fingers in his mouth, tenderly sucking at each one as though he was licking the chocolate from the top of an éclair. Her receptive body started to respond to the sensuality of his action. 'Open your eyes, little one. Look at me,' he whispered, as if he wanted her to be sure it was him she was with. She lifted her chin, inviting a kiss, but he shook his head. Still holding her hands, he directed them towards her triangle of red pubic hair, massaging, manipulating them until she understood what he wanted her to do. Familiar with the eroticism of watching someone pleasure themselves, her fingers started to explore, twisting, twirling the wiry hair, parting and probing, titillating the delicate membrane around her clitoris. He leaned up on one elbow and used the back of the nail of his forefinger to trace the areola around one nipple until it was erect, then reached over to stimulate the other in the same way. She reached out for him. He shook his head. 'No one knows you better than you know yourself, my love,' he murmured. Looking into his calm, caressing eyes she realised that nothing had changed. She hadn't, she couldn't, come between the brothers or set them against each other. Far from being compromised, the unique relationship she had with them individually had been strengthened because of the loving trust they had for each other, and for her. Once again she reached out to Joe. Once again he shook his head. With a whimsical smile he replaced her hands on her sex, indicating that he wanted her to continue with her masturbation. Relaxed and confident now, she quickly brought herself to climax, presuming this was the precursor for the sharing that would follow. When the shuddering of her orgasm subsided Joe leaned over her and whispered, 'Never forget, little one, it's your body, and only you should decide what to do with it.' Then he pulled the covers over their nakedness and cuddled her to him as if she was the teddy bear languishing under the untidy pile of their discarded clothes.

Galla lifted her head just once, to identify the unfamiliar sleeping sounds, recognised they belonged to her human flock, curled into a comma to indulge in some contented dreams of her own.

Joe woke the next morning to the smell of freshly brewed coffee. Marie-France was squatting beside him, fully dressed, a steaming cup cradled in the palm of each hand. As he struggled to a sitting position she said, 'You do know Joe, don't you, that I love you both.' 'Of course you do, little one, just like we both love you,' he replied, giving her a serene smile, his voice dark with tenderness and sleep.

CHAPTER 24

They were up, dressed and standing in the chilly grey dawn by the time Christian's pickup came rattling noisily up the track. The peace was even further shattered as he and his wife climbed out, shouting their bonjours.

'Any problems?' the shepherd asked Marie-France, missing the beatific smile she directed at Joe when she replied, 'None at all,' as he was already on his way into the barn.

'I'm Francine, the wife,' the woman, almost as round but not quite as tall as her robust husband, announced to Joe. 'Aren't I?' she said to Marie-France, as if needing confirmation.

Marie-France had almost forgotten Francine's scatty style of communication and hugged her affectionately. On this morning she had enough affection to share with the whole population of the world. Joe held out a hand politely to the new comer, they'd never met before, but Francine huffed it away and gave him a hug too.

'I always think it's the best recommendation when a chef likes his own cooking,' she said, patting his portly stomach 'And you've even managed to put a bit of beef on her too. I wonder why they don't talk about putting on the mutton, or even the pork,' she mused, before addressing Marie-France, grinning at a disconcerted Joe.

'You don't look nearly as bad as I thought you would. When Christian said you'd broken your arm and got a new hip I imagined you with one arm and three legs! Oh, and thank you. My man's in love again, although you'd never know it by the way he tucks her under his arm and carries her about.' Jazzy, left in the pickup, jumped up at the half lowered window, yapping for attention, as if to explain that it was her who was being spoken about.

'Oh, I almost forgot, I brought some breakfast for you and your saucy man. I couldn't think of a sauce to go with it so I hope *jambon cru* and bread and paté and a couple of hard boiled eggs and....I can't remember what else but there must be more than that. Here. You're the cook!' She thrust a bulging basket at Joe, just about collapsing with the strain of not dissolving into giggles. 'You've met Francine then?' Christian bellowed, scooping his new pup out of the vehicle. 'So where's the coffee to go with the grub?'

After they'd hastily eaten as much as they could and shared another pot of coffee, not taking the time to sit down in the wintry chill, Marie-France backed the stock trailer up to the pen. With four people and a dog the sheep were easily persuaded to go up the ramp. A feeble sun was making an effort to break through the clouds as they waved goodbye and started on the even slower return journey, the driver being conscious of the sensitive cargo she was towing.

They barely spoke. What was there to say? The atmosphere between them as clear as the morning air, they were closer than they'd ever been before.

Angus and Eric were mucking out the cattle shed when the Land Rover chuntered into the yard. Funny Face -her official name, Janus, had become lost in the past. Or was it the future? – was tied by a piece of string to her new boss' belt. Jambon, Angelo's pup, was attached to the trailer being loaded with dung. My Beau, leaping up from his customary place on the house step, was quickly called to heel so he didn't get in the way of the incoming vehicle. Joe climbed down, greeted the waiting men, then directed Marie-France as she backed towards the barn, prepared to receive the sheep. The nervous beasts baulked at the new surroundings when the tailgate was lowered but before any of the experienced sheep people, or even Galla, had time to intervene Joe himself jumped up and flamboyantly dragged the lead sheep out, knowing that the rest, being sheep, would follow.

'Glad to see you've been doing something useful with your

time, lad,' Eric growled fondly. 'Certainly have,' he replied, sending Marie-France a sublime smile that his uncle chose not to interpret.

'So have you, I see,' she remarked, looking at the small chicken-wire ring on the other side of the gate that opened onto the top field. Her father followed her eyes. 'Time these pups of yours started on the basics,' he declared. 'Aye, always good to get the basics sorted out as soon as possible,' she agreed, then, for Eric and Joe's benefit, courteously translated her comment into French. This time it was her father who chose not to speculate on the significance of the glance that Joe beamingly received.

Once the sheep were settled and admired, it was the first time either of the men had met the prettily brown faced Clun Forest breed, Marie-France decided she should return the trailer to the Aubry's straightaway. Joe announced himself desperately in need of a shower. 'Keep it,' Eric said as Marie-France leaned in to retrieve the dog box. 'Jacques phoned to say that Pierre Calvet suggested I'd be bound to have a spare one for a mobile home for Galla.'

His pack of hounds howled in the background, as though to remind him that they were waiting for Saturday, the next day for the hunt. Pushing aside, for the moment, the concept of 'mobile', Marie-France shoved the box back into the Landy, ordered Galla, and then, with mock authoritarianism, Joe, into the front. They set off. Together. Again.

On the return journey to Labeille Marie-France began to experience some niggly misgivings. It had been so easy and clear when they were out in the wilds, to melt into the warmth of Joe's assurance that everything would be fine. Between her and him. And Jacques. But would it really? Could it? Jacques Luciani was a proud man, on the way to becoming a well-respected member of the community, serving on numerous committees for this and that. She'd even heard someone wondering if he was going to stand as a councillor, maybe even as mayor. She recognised the strength of his feelings for her – hadn't he declared them to his family? - and hers for him. But what if, her stomach lurched at the thought, but what if he now wanted rid of her, if sending her off with Joe for the night was his way of getting her out of his bed and into his brother's? For a second she wondered if that would actually be so bad. But then she had another stomach clutching thought. What about Joe? What if all he'd said, and hadn't done, wasn't as altruistic as she'd believed? What if he didn't want her? What if she'd managed to lose them both?

A powerful, soft fingered hand massaged the back of her neck. 'Relax, little one. And trust me. Everything will be fine. I promise you.'

Back at *Chez Jacques*, the world exploded around her in a burst of people and activity, surreal in its everydayness. Jacques greeted her and Joe with kisses as usual, as did Angelo, home from school for lunch, which Eveline, who stuck her head out of the kitchen to wave bonjour, was preparing. Grandfather Jacques, installed at the sturdy wooden table that had once been Marie-France's, now functioning as his personal reception area and office, stood up to greet them too. Joe teased Angelo, saying first he was going to paint the faces of all his teddies black because the new sheep were so cute, then telling his wound-up nephew that his esteemed uncle was going to become the next world champion sheep wrestler. Angelo, jumping up and down in excitement, wanted to go and see the new flock straight away but his father reminded him he had to get back to school. The burgeoning shepherd was only slightly assuaged when Marie-France explained about the training ring, promising they'd make a start with Jambon at the weekend. Lunch came and went. Angelo disappeared back to school, an overdue drinks delivery arrived. Marie-France manned the bar while Jacques and Joe carried the crates down into the cellar. The day blurred past until Pierre Calvet popped his head round the bar door, as he did every evening, to say they were off, he'd see them in the morning.

'Will you come with me to have a look around next door?' It was the first time Jacques had addressed her personally since they'd been back. Her nerves, settled with the distraction of the mundane routines, started to jangle again. 'It's easier now to visualise the accommodation,' he explained, as though she was an interested tourist rather than the lover who'd spent the night with someone else.

The only part of the alterations to the house she'd lived in for months – although not much of it - that Marie-France had been involved, or interested in, had been the roof garden that Joe had asked her advice about. Houses, accommodation, bedrooms had never figured in her life. Now she wondered if this was the point of Jacques' request. Bedrooms. Where was she going to sleep? She followed him nervously, wondering if this was how he was going to tell her that, as she was no longer paying rent, there wouldn't be a place for her in the new design.

She barely noticed the changes to the ground floor she'd moved into over a year ago. Jacques led the way up the stairs, stopping at the faded wallpaper-stripped second floor where she'd set up the heated propagators, reminding her that she must decide soon where she was going to sow seeds and bring on seedlings this year. If she was still going to have a garden to plant them out in.

'We're putting two *en suites* in here,' he remarked. 'As well as picking up some summer *chambres d'hôtes* trade, we're hoping to attract an all year round elite clientele who'll come to the restaurant for intimate special meals and stay over in a comfortable bedroom instead of having to drive home. It's a shame we won't be open for Saint Valentine's this year. The ideal time to promote our romantic service.'

The fourteenth of February held a different significance for Marie-France. The day the geese invariably started laying their huge, rich eggs. She wondered if she had a romantic bone in what she was beginning to think was her over-sexed body.

She followed Jacques up the next flight of stairs. What she'd known as the top floor was unrecognisable. The room under the loft that she'd loved for its view over the river and the tree coated hills beyond, had gone, the whole floor one open space. As if they were preparing an exhibition of modern art, or maybe just perfecting how to tag, someone had spray-painted outlines of doors on the plaster stripped walls. The old balcony was still there and she stepped out on to it, grasping at the rusty iron rail as though by holding on to something substantial she might keep herself in *Chez Jacques'* world. She'd just realised with a rush of adrenaline that she didn't want to leave it. Or would it be so bad to just let go and float across the full river rushing its way towards pastures new?

'We're reserving this floor, and the loft space above, for us,' Jacques explained. She startled at the word. 'Us?' 'Yes, the family,' he elucidated, not making anything clearer to her at all. As was her way when she didn't understand enough to question, she said nothing.

'I couldn't imagine anything more exciting than traditional bedrooms,' Jacques continued. 'As you know, I'm a very conventional thinker and I like everything in its proper place.'

Everything and everyone. This was it, had to be. The moment when he'd tell her she didn't have a place, certainly not a proper one. Or maybe that she'd have to make a choice and decide where, and who with, her proper place would be.

'But Joe, as you know, has a far more imaginative and open mind than mine. He came up with a design of multiple spaces, a sort of mix and match of living cum sleeping areas, to be altered according to the needs of the person who takes possession. The boys, well Jacqui at least, has reached an age when he needs a space to call his own. Angelo will soon get used to the idea when he realises he hasn't got to fall in with big brother's notion of organisation. And Joe and I are certainly grown up enough to have somewhere of our own too.'

Her heart began to thump with the relentless rhythm of the hammer drill that had been pounding throughout the day. No mention of her then? She looked around, and as a way of distracting her mind from the subject she didn't want to face, tried to work out how all the rooms he'd described would fit into the area they were standing in. She stared at the painted representations of doors.

'We're going to break through to next door and incorporate all that accommodation into the new plan.' She frowned, trying to visualise what was on the other side of the wall. She'd never been up the second flight of stairs in that building. She'd never been anywhere higher than Jacques' conventional, designated bedroom.

'It's Joe's room at the moment,' her implacable guide explained. 'And beyond that the boys' room, a rubbish filled box room and a bathroom. At least the water is already on this level. It will make the plumbing easier to install in here.' 'Right!' 'As you see, there'll be plenty of room, especially when the lofts are included. Shall we go up?'

He didn't take her hand as they went up the loft stairs, little more than a glorified ladder. He hadn't touched her at all since they'd been alone. Her heart plummeted right back down to the cellar she'd slept in the previous summer, as if it was wondering how that was going to be assimilated into the grand design.

On the one occasion she'd been up in the loft, looking to see if there was anything she could use as supports for her gangling seedlings, it had been as dark, dusty and pigeon-shit filled as would be expected of any centuries-old village house. Now, when she stepped up through the hatch, it was like entering a different world. The whole of the front wall had been taken down. The roof, exposed oak beams with light, pine coloured wood covering the underside of the tiles between them, appeared to be resting on the remaining side, virtually all tinted glass. The extended floor projected out beyond the roof, creating an uncovered balcony. Openings in the connecting wall with the other loft had already been created, giving a forever and ever Alice in Wonderland impression of the space beyond. She'd agreed with Joe that a garden might be possible but never envisaged it could be like this!

Jacques was talking to her again, as if she was a client that he, as an estate agent, was trying to impress with the uniqueness of the building she was considering buying. 'This, of course, will be the garden, a simple summer, barbeque type kitchen on that wall. Although judging by the way Joe's been going on about your trip away I think he's just as likely to want an open fire to cook on.'

The first direct reference he'd made to the time she and Joe had spent together. What else had his brother told him?

'Calvet was impressed by your idea of collecting rain water from the roof for watering the plants and he's found an excellent system which allows for a butt on each balcony, with a valve system to take the overflow straight down into the main drains.'

Marie-France, struggling out of her self-absorption, became aware that her articulate, precise speaking friend was burbling. A quavering tone to his voice that she'd never heard before. Resolute, unflappable Jacques was nervous! Now she was sure. He was psyching himself up to tell her that the position of gardener was about to be advertised because it was no longer available to her.

'And now, the room that's easiest to understand, because it is almost finished.' He gestured towards the forecourt side of the house. Once again, she followed. He slid open glass doors, exactly the same as the ones in the restaurant, the one's creating the impression that the outside and the inside were uninterrupted. A Velux window in the roof framed the first palely twinkling, early evening stars.

'We had to put in a conventional window on the street side but it's triple glazed so should shut out any village noise, especially being so high up. We're just hoping that our green fingered fairy gardener will find it suitable enough to come and nest in, from time to time.'

She discerned a tremor of desperation in his words but in any case he'd given himself away by a performing an audible deep intake and exhalation of breath.

'Jacques? This is for me?' 'Of course, *ma cherie*. It's not quite up to the standard of the barns and wide open spaces you've lived in before, but it's the best we could do to give you a refuge, whenever you feel you need one.' 'Oh Jacques. What can I say?' She blinked away the tears gathering in her astounded eyes.

'That you'll stay, on your own terms, at least for another while?'

He held her then. They held each other, soundlessly, wordlessly, until they'd gathered up their inexpressible emotions enough to speak. 'However, as you can see, it's going to be a while before this place is ready, so in the meantime...'

'In the meantime,' she said with a grin. 'Would you help me get that dog box up on to your balcony for Galla? And I wonder if you'd select another book for me to read. You know what I want so much better than I do myself.'

CHAPTER 25

'We've done our forty days but we've hardly starved and we've not even tried to resist temptation, have we?' Léa took her eyes off the road just long enough to flash her Jacquot a tantalising smile. 'Biblical quotations? You've been thinking too much about church,' he retorted, patting her fondly on the knee. 'You're sure you're not disappointed?' she asked. 'How could I be disappointed with you by my side?' he replied, gently tucking a strand of her blowing hair behind her ear to keep it out of her eyes.

Living together in Labeille without a break for forty days so they could be married there hadn't proved to be any hardship at all. Although the plans for their extravaganza of a wedding very quickly changed course.

Léa found an unexpected ally in teenager Jacqui when, on very little reflection, she rejected Joe's idea for her outfit. 'Marie-Antoinette was married in a silver and white dress that didn't fit her,' she announced. 'There was a gap at the back and the bones of her corset and her petticoat showed though. Now I don't mind being scandalous but not in such an unflattering way.'

'We're Republicans. Why would we want to assist at a royal wedding, even if it is just a parody of one?' Jacqui had been sitting apparently engrossed in his phone. His defiant comment came as a surprise to the gathering.

'Bravo, young man!' his great-grandfather cried. 'I'm glad to hear you not only know your own mind but you're not afraid to speak it, either.' Joe dramatically shrugged his broad shoulders, as if he was mortally offended that his idea had been rejected.

'And anyway, she got her head chopped off!' Angelo, never one to be left out of a conversation for long. Léa laughed, a sound more and more frequently cheering the winter afternoons. 'Well then, that's it. We don't want to give the ne'er do wells an excuse for chopping off my head, do we? I need another image.'

'Do you really not mind causing a scandal, or was that just talk?' Lucien had agreed to take photos, make a video, whatever, as long as he could be in on the planning of the *spectacle* from the beginning. He wasn't interested in money, just fun, and being Lucien, felt no need to mince his words.

'We are a scandal, Jacquot and me, to many people here, so I genuinely don't mind adding ammunition to the charge, but only if it's done with style.' 'Style you can do, lady Léa. If I was a woman I'd envy you your looks. But as I know my man will never be tempted by them I'm happy to admire. Stand up and do a twirl till I get a better idea of the proportions of your bits.'

'How come Lucien doesn't get told off for thinking about touching Léa, like Uncle Joe did?' Angelo asked, his eyes innocently and completely unbelievably wide. His pal's dad, listening in the bar during the first wedding discussion, had told his wife. She told her sister, who'd been overheard by the kids telling…

'Because Jacquot knows that if it came to a duel I would scratch his eyes out,' Lucien screeched, thrusting at Angelo with an imaginary sword. 'Gangster's moll?' Joe suggested. 'Though I'm not really sure what that would entail.'

Jacqui quickly searched on his phone, looked at the results, turned red under his naturally tanned skin. 'Ooh, sexy!' Angelo cried, looking over his brother's shoulder, making sure everyone noticed his adolescent awkwardness.

'Angelo!' Eveline remonstrated. Still somewhat in awe of Grandfather Jacques' elegant bride-to-be, she thought should be perhaps treated with some respect. Léa was the same age as Angelo's grandmother.

'It's alright. I think she's sexy too!' Grandfather Jacques, as sometimes happened when he was in a group, missed the direction of the conversation through his deafness.

Léa's laugh rang out again. Leaning over, she kissed him as a reward for treating her as if she was as young as he made her feel.

'I see what you mean,' Joe said, looking at the images displayed on discomforted Jacqui's phone. Léa coloured up when he placed it in her outstretched hand but she talked her embarrassment away. 'Maybe I'm not as *outré* as I thought I was but I really don't think I could walk down the aisle in black any more than I could in white. Although there's more flesh than material in most of these get-ups. And actually, while we're on the subject of aisles, we're having second thoughts about the venue.'

She'd been with Jacquot to view the church. They sat together in the front pew of the atmospheric medieval building, bathed in the calm simplicity an empty place of worship often inspires, even in those who are not spiritual. Remembering being there with her grandmother, she was filled with a sense of the horror and pain that a true and fervent believer would experience at the thought of anyone treating the house of their god with the cavalier irreverence they were planning.

Now, amongst his family in *Chez Jacques*, Grandfather Jacques nodded his support of the decision he'd left to her to make. 'You can still have a stylish service in the *Mairie*,' Jacques remarked. 'Although the participants will, of necessity, have to be fewer. Invitation only, I would suggest.'

Léa and her man looked at each other tellingly. Evidently another matter they'd been discussing. Jacques immediately picked up on their dilemma. 'Perhaps it would be more enjoyable if the whole thing was less of a public spectacle and more of a private celebration of what, after all, is an important family event?'

He saw the relief flooding into his grandfather's eyes, confirming his suspicion that the old man had been worried about upsetting his grandsons' opportunities to develop their business by making less, rather than more, of the occasion.

'Actually, I've been thinking it over too,' Jacques continued. 'And I think it would be a shame for us, Joe and I, to concentrate on work when we'd rather enjoy the day. Would it upset you if we abandoned the idea of the village reception? There'll be plenty of other opportunities to exploit the hôtel connection.'

'But I'm still going to prepare a suitably lavish meal,' Joe said hastily. 'And, if you're not in too much of a hurry to set the date, it looks as though we'll be able to dine in style. Pierre Calvet told us yesterday that he was ahead of schedule and the restaurant and the rooms above could be ready before Easter, if we didn't mind the leaving the finishing touches, like decoration, electrical fittings and all that, in the family space till later.'

'Apart from this level, there's really not much structural work to do at all,' the builder had explained. 'The rest is mainly plumbing and tarting up.'

'In that case, what I would really like,' Grandfather Jacques declared. 'Is for us to be the first couple to try out your romantic notion of eating, drinking and then going upstairs to bed. What do you think, my dear, an intimate dinner for twelve and then to the honeymoon suite above?'

And so it was decided. Except that the number of diners was reduced by one. 'Once you've done the clever bit in the kitchen you must become a guest, Joe,' Marie-France insisted. 'And you too, Jacques. The boys, Jules and co, not yours, and I will do the work.'

Jacques open his mouth to protest, shut it again when she persisted. 'If you think I'm going to...' 'Sit round a table for hours on end with too much food in a room full of people,' Joe parodied, flinging back his head and sticking out his chest in a perfect caricature of the defiant woman in front of him. 'You can count me out,' Jacques joined in, with the affectionate twinkle in his eye that with increasing frequency ruined his deadpan image whenever she was around.

Officialdom satisfied, the marriage date was set for two weeks before Easter. Léa and Jacquot headed up to Paris where she had a wardrobe of suitable outfits and more than a few bits and bobs she wanted to collect to add a few personal touches to Solange's adequate but spartan house.

They decided to avoid the motorways and take their time,

enjoying the drive through the little towns and villages that, like Labeille, had barely changed over the decades. During lunch on the first day of their journey, he leaned over the table and took her hand in his. 'You do know, Léa my dear.' She bent towards him to listen. He always used her name before 'my dear' when what he had to say was something important, personal. 'You do know that it is you that I'm marrying. It's you I'm in love with, not your mother, not anymore.' 'And you do know, Jacquot dear, that I am marrying you, not your handsome son.'

A fond smile passed between them. He'd confessed to her, back in Corsica, when they were each learning who the other was, that he'd wondered if her love interest was in Eric. She'd readily admitted she found him a very attractive man. 'But now I know you, I realise he's just a pale imitation of the real thing. In any case, I wouldn't want to be accused of cradle snatching.' Eric was almost eight years younger than her.

'Whereas I, my dear, relish the accusation,' he'd retorted, pulling her on to his knee. Léa was almost twenty years younger than him.

They stopped in the early evening, spotting a promising looking *chambres d'hôtes*. Once they'd inspected and accepted the room they leaned against the inside of the door, giggling at the raised eyebrows of their host when they'd asked for a room with a double bed. She'd presumably assumed they were father and daughter.

'They probably think I'm the Lolita that didn't get away,' Léa gasped. 'Lolita Luciani! Sounds like a porn star, whereas Léa Luciani...'

She let the implication hang in the air, where Jacques regarded it with curiosity. He hadn't for one moment imagined she'd change her name to his, being such an independent, modern woman, but was proudly gratified at the suggestion, especially when she expanded.

'Although Jourdan is my family name, since we've been in Labeille I realise that I've never really had a family, not like yours. They're such a wonderful bunch and so welcoming, I wondered if I could make a public statement of belonging, if you and they would be happy with the idea.'

Jacquot, his mind learning to accept the new name as his own, sighed with contentment. Her words added yet another layer to the cocoon of happiness wrapping itself around him.

They set off the next morning after a leisurely breakfast during which they flirted outrageously. Unable to resist their joyful behaviour, their host's expression changed from disapproval to endorsement, especially after they told her they were shortly to be married.

Jacquot took the first turn of driving, he was always more alert in the morning, and by eleven-thirty was cruising slowly along one of the almost identical main streets of the almost identical places they passed through. The *bar-tabac, boulangerie, épicerie, pharmacie* lined up as though they'd raced ahead from the last village to present themselves again, hoping, this time, to entrap a customer. Jacquot, noticing a sign for a bistro advertising a midday menu at thirteen euros, turned off to see if it was a suitable place to stop for lunch. Léa gasped, almost swamped by the gush of *déjà vu* washing over her.

'Are you alright, my dear? We can always drive on to the next village if you don't fancy this one.' 'No, it's not that, it's just...' She wound down the window, closely scrutinising everything they passed.

In the village square, they parked up in front of a municipal plaque bearing a name and some dates. Léa gulped audibly. 'I thought so. Look Jacquot, this is where we came, mother and I, after the liberation. Mother and I and...' *Jean Guerin,* the plaque informed them, had been mayor of Peyrat from 1957 till 2001.

The stunned couple stood staring at the sign as though waiting for it for it to address them. Jean Guerin, the man Jacques Luciani had worked with in the resistance in Marseille during the German occupation of France. The same man who'd abandoned Solange, even though he believed she was carrying his child. The man who'd run off with the beautiful Monique and her seven year old daughter, now staring, pale-faced at this proof of his existence.

Jacques spoke, but in a way she'd never heard before, his voice thoughtful, calculating, ominous. 'The dates refer to his term of office, not his life span.' Léa turned to look at him. 'You don't think he could still be alive?' 'Why not? He wasn't much older than me and I'm still very much alive, as you know.' He straightened his back decisively, as though to demonstrate the fact. 'Come along, my dear, it's ten to midday. We should be able to get to the *Mairie* just as it's closing for lunch.'

She didn't protest. It would have been futile. He was already striding purposefully in the direction the street sign pointed.

The woman behind the counter in the reception area looked up in irritation as they pushed through the door, then glanced at the clock to draw the unknown intruders' attention to the hour. 'I'm so sorry to disturb you madame,' Jacquot gushed. 'But it took me somewhat longer to get here than I anticipated. I don't suppose *Monsieur Le Maire* is still in his office?'

The sign on the entry door quite clearly identified the present incumbent as *Madame Sylvie Petit*.

'*Madame Le Mayor* has just left for lunch,' the secretary replied pointedly. 'Oh! So Jean finally stood aside to let someone else serve his compatriots. I'd forgotten that he must have got old, like me.' 'Jean? You mean Monsieur Jean Guerin, the longest serving mayor of our commune? Do you know him?' 'Indeed, I am proud to say I do, madame. We served our country together as associates during the occupation. Although I'm sure that will sound like very ancient history to someone of your tender years.'

The woman must have been only a few years younger than Léa, certainly approaching, if not passed, retiral age. She didn't know whether to take umbrage at the suggestion that she didn't know her country's history or to be flattered by this old rogue's specious complement. She decided on the latter course, as it gave her the opportunity to find out more about this rather intriguing man. Léa, uncharacteristically, was hanging back, taking no part in the interaction.

'Is Monsieur Guerin expecting you, Monsieur ...' 'Luciani. Jacques Luciani.' He announced himself as if she was sure to be familiar with his name. 'But in answer to your question, no, Jean doesn't know I was planning on dropping by. You see, it was my good wife who kept the contact going between us over the years, you ladies are so much better at it than us men, but since she's passed away, god rest her blessed soul, I've rather let things slide.'

His shoulders sagged with the weight of his bereavement, but as the secretary tutted sympathetically he straightened up again, making a conscious effort to face his empty world with courage. When he spoke, his voice, which had become quavery with grief, was once more strong and melodious.

'And you know madame, I can't even claim to have forgotten his address. I never knew it. It was only by a stroke of mind delving inspiration that I recognised the name of this village when I was planning my route. But I knew it would be easy to find him here.'

Gesturing at the walls of the office, the photograph of another Jacques, Chirac, the President of the Republic, hanging next to an elaborate scroll-like representation of *La Déclaration des Droits de L'Homme et du Citoyen*, he inclined his head towards the older than middle-aged woman in front of him, as though she and her surroundings had fulfilled all his expectations.

'Would you like me to phone *Monsieur Le Maire,* I mean, Monsieur Guerin, for you, Monsieur Luciani?' 'Would you my dear?' Waiting for her to put her hand on the phone, he said. 'But, on second thoughts, it would be wonderful to catch him off his guard, something I never once managed to do when we worked together in the resist...'

He swallowed the rest of the word as though he'd be breaching an official secrets act if he spoke it out loud.

Obviously *bone fide*, the secretary decided. In any case it would be an easy matter for him to find out from anyone in the village where the well-respected ex-mayor lived. 'I'll write down his address for you,' she volunteered. 'No need. Just tell it to me,

237

madame. I wouldn't like Jean to think I'd fallen into the habit of carrying incriminating information on paper instead of in my head.'

If she hadn't been quite so edgy Léa might have laughed at his play acting. As it was she just clutched at his arm, as once more he strode purposefully in the direction that had been pointed out to him. 'Jacquot, are you sure we should do this?' she gasped, struggling to keep up with his long stride. 'I mean, he is an old man and I really don't know what I would want to achieve.'

'I am an old man too, my dear,' he replied, without slowing down. 'And I know exactly what I want to achieve. Leave this to me.' He patted the hand resting on his arm. She had no option but to try and keep up as he continued on his course.

The village they walked through had changed substantially since Léa had been there as a seven year old, immediately after the liberation. All the bombed and ruined houses had been re-built or demolished, but she still recognised some of the streets they passed through. A new building, well different anyway, it actually looked rather jaded, on the site where she'd spent a few, unhappy months at school. She felt herself shrinking, becoming that small, miserable child again.

'Here we are!' Her determined companion, usually so considerate, seemed completely unaware of her jangling emotions. 'It's the same street his parents lived in,' she whispered. 'In fact, it's the same house! Oh Jacquot!'

He wasn't listening. Perceiving the doorbell as being too discreet he thumped loudly on the front door. Only seconds later they were face to face with the man they'd both last seen six decades before.

'Yes, can I help you?' Jean Guerin peered through a pair of bottle-bottom spectacles. The round shouldered posture of his youth had exaggerated itself so he had to make an effort to stand upright and there were only strands of thin, oily grey hair clinging to his scalp. But behind all that he was easily recognisable as the man he'd been, especially the analysing look in his faded eyes.

'Well old friend, don't suppose you ever thought you'd see me again, did you? A ghost from your past come back to haunt you, just when you thought you'd got away with it.'

Jean looked from Jacques to Léa, his gaze stopping in puzzlement for a moment, before travelling back to the large man whose bearing didn't seem as jovial as the honeyed menace of his words.

'I, er, I'm not sure. I mean...' He looked at Léa again, bristling in irritation at his well-remembered, hesitant speech.

'You might have wanted to forget me but I'm sure you haven't, not with your devious, conniving mind.' Jacques, almost whispering, voice like ice, words carrying an ill-defined, sinister threat.

'Jacques? Jacques Luciani!' With the habit of a lifetime the ex-school teacher automatically held out his hand. 'And this is?' He looked with troubled eyes at the woman who seemed so familiar. Jacques was uncharacteristically discourteous in his response. 'This? Oh, this is my next wife.'

He figuratively brushed her aside, dismissed her, as if she was a flibbertigibbet of no consequence, whose presence was obstructing his mission. For the first time Léa glimpsed the man of steel behind the light-hearted, self-effacing tales, the man who'd used more than just charm to achieve what he had in his long, successful, prosperous, life.

'Have you got one, Jean? A wife, that is? Anyone I might know?' He peered over the smaller man's shoulder into the dimly lit hallway, as though the woman of the house might be lurking there, ready to receive him. 'Ah, yes, well., I do have a ... My wife's name is Madeleine. You see Mon...'

Jacques interrupted as though he didn't want to hear the name his old rival was about to pronounce. 'Any children? Or should I say, any more children?'

Jean paled, visibly alarmed, threw another squinting glance at Léa, blinking to black out the idea his mind was trying to construct, then returned his attention to Jacques, towering above him like a malevolent spectre. 'Children? Well, no. My wife, Madeleine and I, didn't....'

Again Jacques cut him off. 'Just as well, perhaps, you always did prefer other people's children to your own, didn't you, what with all those pupils you were so keen to take care of.' He leered close to Jean's face. Solange, Eric's mother, had been one of Jean Guerin's pupils. 'Mind you, I'm not surprised you got rid of my old flame and her brat. Did she ever know you'd been at it with her cousin as well?'

Léa, the brat he'd referred to, found it difficult to believe that this course, crudely spoken oaf was the same personable, charismatic gentleman she was going to marry. But he wasn't, was he? He was playing a part, making up a story that had very little to do with facts. Eric was *his* child, after all, not the son of the old man standing on his doorstep, squirming with guilty embarrassment, glancing down the road, dreading that his wife, the embodiment of his respectable present life, would appear and stumble into his murky past, the murky past he suddenly felt it was important to know more about.

'Um, so Solange Roumignac, did she....' 'Yes, little Solange, who worshipped the ground you, her hallowed teacher, walked on, all the way to Marseille, successfully delivered a baby girl, who survived and grew to womanhood, no thanks to you.'

'Ah, and does she, did she, the girl....' 'I've no idea what the poor little bastard was told about her absent father. Would you like me to ask her? And I could send her mother your love, for old times' sake.'

Two old ladies were making their way up the street. Madeleine, Jean's wife, and her sister, had just been to the shops. Jacques saw the panic in his impotent adversary's eyes. Having no desire to hurt his ignorant, innocent wife, he brought the encounter to an end.

'Well, Jean, I'll not intrude any longer into your parochial, provincial life. I never did believe you'd make it to Paris, you know. Big ideas in a little mind always get stuck where they belong.' As if he'd just become aware of her presence, he offered Léa his arm. 'Come along my dear. Let's find somewhere else to eat, before I completely lose my appetite.' Taking the bemused woman's elbow, he marched her back the way they'd come, leaving Jean staring after them, wracked with the perplexity of not knowing who she was.

By the time they reached the car all Jacques' malevolent anger had dissipated and he was his usual jaunty, charming self. Léa, understanding now why he'd been so effective as a cut and thrust businessman, was glad she was with him and not against. He'd have been a ruthless, formidable opponent.

He held the driver's door open for her and then got into the passenger seat. The adrenaline spurt that had sustained him during his performance had evaporated, leaving him weary but unrepentant. Before Léa pressed the ignition switch he put his hand on hers. It was important to him that although he'd spun a web of convoluted lies to Jean, the woman he loved knew he would always tell her the truth.

'I didn't do that for you, Léa, or even for Monique. I did it for Solange, who would never let anyone fight her battles.'

His words hung heavy in the silence that followed them until, with his characteristic bonhomie, he chased their echo away. 'Mind you, I do think she was far better off without him. He certainly hasn't aged as well as the handsome devil you've taken up with, has he, my dear?'

CHAPTER 26

They stayed that night in a small hôtel on the outskirts of Paris. The next morning Léa took the wheel and drove to her apartment in the 19th *arrondissement*, on the eastern side of the city. 'It's not pretty to look at, from the outside,' she said, without a hint of apology, as they looked up at the modern building. 'But it's what I could afford and one of its many advantages is that there is somewhere to park.'

Léa's home was little more than a studio. Jacques' presence, if not his size, filled it immediately as he moved around, picking up this, touching that, nodding approvingly. In tribute to the reinforced concrete structure that housed it, the apartment was furnished and decorated exclusively in the art deco style, from the two leather club chairs on either side of the chrome and smoked glass table to the marble tub and washstand in the tiny bathroom. Even the latest gadgetry in the galley kitchen was hidden behind a façade of Bakelite, whenever practical. Jacques smoothed his sensitive hands over the high polish of the mahogany corner cabinet, squatting down to trace the outline of the rose basket design on the door. He stood for a while, peering at the copy of George Barbier's *Lady with a Panther*, the only picture hanging on the wall, raised his eyebrows at the swirling pattern of the iron radiator cover with its marble shelf disguising the single radiator, all that was needed to heat the restricted space. Léa watched him move into the bedroom, clearly as at home as she wanted him to be, her smile matching his as he took in the geometric rose patterned wallpaper and the stylized birds, perched and pecking at the garlands on the cover of the welcoming double bed with its plump, feather filled pillows. 'Exquisite,' he breathed. 'Just like its creator.'

Léa had only known him in rural settings, Labeille and his

brother's farm on Corsica and was a little anxious that he might find the hectic bustle of city life daunting. Nothing could have been further from the truth. As soon as they went out into the streets he transformed into the adept man about town he'd been for most of his life, slightly dated in style, certainly, but in a way his image was all the more credible because of that. Like Charles Aznavour he seemed to say, *Non je n'ai rien oublié*, giving the impression that the world he'd lived in with all his hints of its glamour and *politesse*, was actually the real world and that this modern, rushed, casual representation was slightly tawdry in comparison. She asked him, as it was the first time in his country's capital city, whether he wanted to go into the centre and visit all the sights. The monuments, towers, history laden buildings.

'Oh, I don't think so, my dear,' he replied, with the sparkle in his eye she'd come to love. 'They've existed for hundreds of years without seeing me so I don't think they'll suffer from my neglect.'

They selected an upmarket bistro to eat their lunch, reducing the likelihood of fast food seeking tourists. He raised one expressive eyebrow when he looked at the elaborate prices next to the rather plain meals. 'Makes one realise how lucky we are to have Joe, doesn't it? I'm so glad he's not wasting his creativity by having to work within the constraints of maximum profit. They did the right thing, getting out of Marseille when they did.' His boys were never far from his mind.

Léa hadn't referred to Jacques' hostile confrontation with Jean the previous day. Wondering if she'd not been too comfortable with his vulgar performance, he was relieved to hear the amusement in her voice when she remarked, 'Just think, I could have been brought up in that ghastly place, with him as my father!'

The man opposite her, slipping down in his seat, halved his natural size, peering at her myopically over a pair of imaginary spectacles. 'Ah, yes. Well now. The child. What did you, ah, say her name was?' Léa snorted with laughter at the perfect take off of Jean's faltering speech. 'The child? The brat don't you mean?' she retorted. 'I seem to recall you described mother and me as your old flame and her brat.'

Encouraged by her spirited reaction, Jacques stayed in role. 'Mmm, yes, well, Mon…Er, you know, I mean Mad… Er, what did you say my wife's name was?' 'Oh yes, the wife! How did you refer to me? My latest wife, you said, as if I was the last dress hanging on a clothes rail. It's a shame I wasn't wearing one of those gangster moll outfits Jacqui was so embarrassed about. It would have suited the role you assigned me perfectly.' She took a sip of wine to subdue the gurgling laughter in her throat.

'He couldn't keep his eyes off you as it was. He looked as though he'd seen a ghost but couldn't make out if he was being haunted by the future or the past.' 'If there was a ghost about it would surely have been Solange, what with you bringing her back to life and landing her with a daughter instead of a son. How do you think she would feel about that?'

Jacques' eyes opened wide, in a contemplative expression reminiscent of his ever curious great-grandson. 'Do you know, my dear, now I think of it, I have absolutely no idea how she would feel. I didn't really know her at all.' 'Except in the biblical sense!' Léa threw back, determined not to lose the light-hearted mood by letting him drift back into introspective reminiscence. It worked. 'Little Léa! You are sometimes a very naughty girl, I'm delighted to say.'

They clinked glasses, in a toast to naughtiness. But Léa hadn't finished recreating the unfortunate Jean's character assassination. 'Mind you, that comment about him being a little man in a parochial town was a bit below the belt.' 'Exactly where I was aiming,' Jacques interjected. 'I know, but even so, holding the position of mayor for so long is worthy of respect, surely. And from what I've picked up it seems possible that your eldest grandson might be heading in the same direction.' 'Jacques? Oh I doubt it. Jacques isn't interested in the trappings of power. It's real control he wants, without accountability to any electorate, village councillors or other committee member types.' 'And yet, it seems he is constantly being asked to sit on committees for this, that and everything else to do with village life.'

Jacquot gave a knowing smile. 'Ah, but if you look more closely, you'll notice that he only agrees to join them if the chairperson's position is available, or shortly will be. As I say, he wants to be in the position to wield influence, not to be subject to it.'

Léa reflected that she hadn't taken much notice of *Chez Jacques'* proprietor, perhaps because he allowed himself to stay in the shade of his brother's larger than life, entertaining personality. She was interested, now she was going to become part of this family, to discover more of its dynamics. 'How do you think *they* will take it, Jacquot, when they learn that *I'm* going to take the Luciani name?'

She asked the question seriously, hoping he wouldn't give her a fatuous, oh they'll be delighted, type of response. She wasn't disappointed, even though he didn't pause for a second to consider what he was going to say. His boys were a subject he was very versed in.

'Jacques will perform a quick mental calculation to determine whether any of his interests, professional or personal, are likely to be threatened. He'll then make momentary eye contact with me to make sure I agree. It used to be the other way round, get my opinion and then do his mental check, but he's matured into his own thoughts now. After that he'll probably nod, or if he's feeling particularly expansive, he might say something verbose like, 'Welcome to the family, Léa'.' These words were delivered with the same expressionless face and even voice she recognised as his eldest grandson's.

'And Joe?' She was enjoying herself, genuinely fascinated by Jacquot's insight into the mental workings of the young men he'd so influenced in their early lives.

Once again, no hesitation. 'Joe will already have decided how to respond, based on Jacques' reaction. Even if he didn't agree he wouldn't challenge him, not in public at least, about something so intrinsic. He will want to add something sweet to what is generally perceived as Jacques' sour and seeing as you and he already get on so well together he'll probably go over the top and say something cheeky like, 'Oh I've got a new Luciani granny, hurrah!' and give you a rib-cracking hug.' Once again, it was Joe's voice that made this facetious declaration through his grandfather's mouth.

Léa didn't have time to bask in the knowledge that the easy going relationship she'd established with Joe had been noticed and approved. Jacquot moved down to the next generation. 'At which point, if Angelo is there, he'll try and capitalise on his uncle's cheek and take it one step further. Easy, on this occasion.'

Impersonating his little double was easy too. Being with Jacquot was like being at the theatre, but he was much more than a stand-up comic. His characters became the people they really were. 'Well *I've* got a new *great* granny Luciani!' the sturdy little boy announced through his grandfather, attracting everyone's attention like a flowering lime tree attracts the bees.

'And what about Jacqui?' Léa asked, once she'd accepted the kisses and cuddles Angelo was certain to give. Any excuse.

'Jacqui? Ah, now Jacqui is often unfathomable, even to me. He certainly won't check with anyone as to what his reaction *should* be. But he will have some inner criteria to determine his course of action, depending on his mood. He might not respond at all, might look up and say something profound like 'cool'. On the other hand there's always the possibility that he'll do an internet search, in the time it would take me to open my phone, and come up with a set of statistics about how many women in what age groups take their husband's family name.'

As young Jacqui, his grandfather shrugged his shoulders and with an overdose of nonchalance remarked. "So you see, you really are an unusual person Léa.' But beware the hidden barb. You're likely to wake up in the middle of the night calling him a cheeky little sod, having subliminally worked out that his comment was only appropriate for the over seventy fives. Jacqui is the one to watch out for, even his father says so. And he should know.'

And so the afternoon passed. They shared food, drink, stories, each other. They even shared poetry. 'What's in a name?' Léa declaimed, in English, when they returned to the subject of hers. 'What?' Jacques asked, puzzled. She translated, explaining that it was a quote. 'Shakespeare, the English Molière,' she explained. 'Tell me again, in English,' Jacques demanded. After only a couple of repetitions he stared deep into Léa's giggling eyes, declaring from the heart. *What's in a name? That which we call a rose, by any other name would smell as sweet.*

The faded scholar, a long time émigré from Oxford, eating a solitary lunch on the far side of the bistro, pricked up his ears with pleasure when he heard the words of the bard, recited by an old English gentleman in a beautifully modulated accent. 'Unusual these days to hear genuine Received Pronunciation,' he told himself, drinking a toast to the country he hadn't visited for decades.

Eventually the happy couple arrived back at her home. He suggested a sieste would be in order. 'Before we test the bed, Jacquot, I'd better get my mother out from underneath it, so I can finish the final chapter of the 'Discovering Monique' assignment I started when I came to you in Corsica.'

Intrigued, he followed her into the bedroom and watched while she pulled a well-travelled cardboard box out from under the bed, the words, *ma mère*, written in black felt pen on the top. She carried it through to the salon, nervous, no, more than that, scared. She had put off looking in it for so long, for the whole of her adult life. Who would she meet when she finally lifted the lid? The wicked witch she'd believed her mother to be. Or the courageous freedom fighter she'd been introduced to by Jacquot, the man who was, at this moment, watching her with a guarded expression, the man who'd been feeling very unsettled ever since Léa had mentioned her mother being in a box underneath her bed.

Since he'd been talking to Léa, trying to make her see the bright, positive side of her mother rather than the dark, resented woman she'd been carrying in her heart, his own memories of Monique had crystallised. He'd never had to face up to the finality of her death and in a sunny corner of his mind she'd continued to exist for him. But a box, even a cardboard one under a bed, sounded just too much like a coffin. Much as he was reluctant to think of her as gone forever, when he saw Léa's strained face as she cut through the string tied around the box to reinforce the Sellotape that had long ago lost its stickiness, he pushed his own anxieties aside.

'Come along then,' he said jovially. 'Let's see what Monique got up to in that foreign land you grew up in.' As soon as she folded back the flaps of cardboard Léa's panic subsided. She realised that her mother wasn't going to appear in any of the incarnations she had imagined. Monique's image wasn't going to be visible at all. She'd been on the other side of the lens.

Léa picked up a small press cutting paperclipped onto a blank piece of paper to stop it getting lost amongst the layers of photographs beneath it. An entry in the obituary column of the newspaper that had first published her work.

Monique Jourdan 1919 – 1955. Madame Jordan, as she was professionally known, was an exceptionally talented photographer who came to England from France in 1946. She exploded onto the news scene with a series of graphic, daringly close-up photographs, depicting the fighting on the streets of Marseille, one of the bloody battles which took place during the liberation of the south of France during the German occupation. She spent the rest of her tragically short life recording post war Britain, creatively depicting the highlights of both public and private events with a uniquely personal style. She will be greatly missed by all those who worked with her. She leaves behind a daughter, Léa Jourdan. RIP

The paragraph didn't take long to skim through, not many words were needed to describe such a short span of time, bringing home to Léa with a stab, more of guilt than sorrow, how very brief her mother's life had been. She translated for Jacques, who nodded, looked at the dates, shook his head, said nothing. She tipped the rest of the contents of the box out on to the smoked glass table, wanting to avoid making the event seem like the ritual of sharing holiday snaps, handing one over at a time and saying, 'And this is one of......'

The material had been gathered systematically, each wallet of photos with their negatives attached to the article they related to, usually only one of a number of shots was published. Léa picked up a bundle, encouraging her companion to do the same, aware that now she'd realised she wasn't going to see her mother she'd shifted her focus of attention. She wasn't looking for her mother at all, she was looking for herself! But as she peered at photo after photo she began to get the eery feeling that she'd spent so much time as a child wishing herself somewhere else her wish had been granted. She wasn't there, not even in the pictures of one of the few personal events that had been recorded, Peter Knight's wedding.

'But I know I was there,' she told herself. 'I remember it clearly.' Noticing a blurred trace of a running figure in the background of one of the photos, she heard her own childish voice, whinging, when they tried to get her to pose with the group. 'I don't want to be here. You're not my family. My family is in France.' What a horrible, ungrateful child she'd been. So determined to be unhappy.

'Ah! Now I see Monique!' She'd almost forgotten the man beside her, leafing through the photo wallets on his own. She glanced at him in consternation. What could he mean? Her mother had taken the pictures, hadn't she, not featured in them?

'There is always a motif of optimism. Look, look at this one,' Jacquot commanded.

A typical post war scene. A huge, desolate space, piles of stone, the occasional remnants of furniture sticking out of the rubble. A bomb site. Devoid of people. 'See, she's captured the devastation but what she really wants us to see is hope. And there it is, in those pretty flowers, growing profusely, all by themselves. Nature giving life where man took it away.'

The picture was in black and white but the eyes visualised the colour, nevertheless, in the familiar clumps of purple rosebay willowherb, the pink and white foxgloves, the garish red splashes of prolific poppies. Léa didn't have time to consider how blind she'd allowed herself to be in everything to do with her mother. Jacques passed over another picture. 'And this one. The same theme, in a way, but she's got someone giving nature a hand.'

This image was a row of semidetached houses, so familiar it could have been one of the streets she'd walked along every day. One of the houses had been catastrophically bomb damaged. Half its roof gone, the doors and windows boarded up. Clearly no one was living in it. Yet the front garden, in normal times expected to be a well-manicured lawn with a path leading up to the front door, had been transformed into an orderly vegetable garden. Peas and broad beans ready to pick, rows of earthed-up potatoes, onions, lettuce. A bountiful oasis in a desert of destruction.

Jacques picked out another cutting at random, frowned at the English article, asked Léa to explain. 'There was a terrible flood, apparently, in Norfolk. That was in...'

This had been front page news in the local paper. She glanced at the date at the top of the page. 'In January nineteen fifty three. It's described as the worst peacetime disaster to hit East Anglia.'

A series of harrowing pictures of the damage caused by the terrible floods. Léa wondered how her mother got there - surely not on the motor bike which propelled her to her death in the back of a bus - but even in amongst the tragic scenes the photographer had captured a glimmer of hope. A snapshot of a policeman in Sheringham standing guard over a baby he'd placed in a suitcase to protect it from flying pebbles from the gale swept beach.

'Ha! I wonder how she got those little scallywags to laugh like that?' Jacques passed her a picture of a group of grimy, short trousered and short skirted children peering at the camera, or rather at the photographer. As he'd observed, she'd made them laugh uproariously, unashamedly displaying their gappy gums.

'What's the structure they're in front of?' he asked, taking the picture back to look at it more closely. 'It's a bomb shelter,' she replied, nostalgically recognising the place where she too had happily played at houses. *'Bomb shelter?'* He replied, repeating the meaningless words perfectly. 'Oh, sorry!' Léa laughed. 'It's all these familiar sights. I've started to think in English. It's an *abri anti-bombe*, they built them all over the place.'

'Built them?' Jacques asked, puzzled. 'Oh, but of course. There was no one there to stop them. The Germans would have taken a dim view of us putting any time or resources into trying to protect ourselves like that. But did they work? That one doesn't look damaged at all.' 'That was near where Peter Knights, the man I told you about, lived. They were very lucky. Just one stray bomb dropped in the village.'

The memories swished back. She could see the huge hole the bomb had left in front of the church, hear the relief in the voices of the parishioners when they pointed out how easily the church could have been destroyed. She felt her hand being taken by one of her school friends, who wanted to sit beside her during Mass. A pleasant memory. Maybe life hadn't been all bad after all.

'Do you know,' she said. 'I must be a bit other-home sick. I'm going to make a pot of tea. Do you want to try a good quality English brew?'

Jacques didn't hear her. He'd picked up the feature about the Battle of Marseille that had launched *Madame* Monique Jourdan's career. He was instantly galvanised, as he hadn't been since they'd sat down, peering at the places he knew, giving a running commentary, to himself rather than his companion, who didn't remember anything about the city where she'd spent the first three years of her life. He studied each picture, holding it up close to his face as though he wanted to see through into the inside of the bullet pocked houses. Or hoping he might reach out and touch the blood stained bodies to restore them to life. As with all the other articles there was a wallet of unused photographs and their negatives. He tipped this out on to the table and picked up every print, still muttering comments to himself. 'I'd forgotten how flattened Le Vieux Port was.

Incredible when you look at it today. They never did rebuild that row of buildings. Not surprising, seeing the state of it. *Merde,* that's the Boucanier's house! It's amazing they survived when Madame Desmarais didn't. Her place was right next door and looks hardly touched.'

A photograph lay in the palm of his hand. For a surreal moment Léa thought it was Joe, who'd somehow managed to travel through time to take part in one of his grandfather's adventures. She quickly blinked the nonsensical notion away. Of course it wasn't Joe, it was the man he so resembled, whose younger self had been captured for posterity.

The most extraordinary portrait of an exceedingly handsome man, he could have been posing on a Hollywood film set. The background, a row of commercial premises, but not any old, anonymous commercial premises. A hand painted sign above the door he was standing in front of, proudly spelling out that this was Luciani's café-bar-tabac. It could have been an advert, or one of those pub mirrors representing scenes of days gone by, except the bar was closed, robustly closed, shutters at the window, a table wedged on its side by two chairs in front of the door. The man himself, the heroic star, the only person in the shot, was dressed in the everyday working clothes that any barman worth his salt would have been expected to wear. White shirt, black bow tie, black waistcoat, black trousers and polished, lightweight black shoes. But there the image of normality ended. An upright table beside the dashing figure. Laid out on it, like a novel presentation of a new range of aperitif snacks, an unsheathed sword stick and a rifle, one of a number secreted by the Roumignacs, he'd broken down and smuggled into Marseille, putting the stock in with a tied up package of broom handles. One of his less successful entrepreneurial enterprises, he ruefully explained to the guards. Beside these two far from appetising objects there were rows of neatly laid out rounds of ammunition of different sizes, some for the Chamelot-Devigne revolver that he grasped in his outstretched hand. In the other hand, a large hunting knife. He held it threateningly in front of him, as though he'd far prefer to use it rather than the gun. Jacques Luciani's last stand, could have been the title of the piece. He clearly had no intention of moving from his post. Now, in Léa's salon, he appeared to have assumed that stance again.

'I'll go and make that cup of tea,' Léa told herself, tiptoeing out of the room. Not that she'd have disturbed Jacques if she'd stomped. He was totally immersed, back there, outside his bar, re-living the memory word for word.

'The battle's won but the city's in a complete mess!' he'd announced to Marthe and his mother. His father had mercifully died soon after the first bombardments in nineteen forty, fatally shocked back into the terror of his experiences in the trenches during World War One.

Jacques had made it clear to his resistance colleagues that he would not actively join in the street fighting once the French Forces arrived, choosing instead to stay to protect his own. As soon as things started to quieten down he did a tour of the city. 'That massive explosion we heard was the Germans trying to blow up the Transporter Bridge but only part of it fell into the water. The Port looks completely destroyed. Goodness knows how they'll ever get it functioning again. The Germans have definitely surrendered and it seems to be an Algerian division that's taken control of rounding up their soldiers. But now, the greatest threat to us is from our own rats, the ones who've been lurking in the sewers waiting until it was safe enough for them to come out and celebrate victory in their own style, by looting everything they can get their grimy hands on. Alcohol, of course, is a prime target so I want you to take Bernard and go next door to the Mercier's *cave*. Stay there until I tell you it's safe to come out.'

Marthe and his mother complied without any histrionics or melodramatic kisses, as confident as he was that he'd be able to cope, in one way or another, with a few gangs of cowardly vermin.

'Salut Jacques!' Monique's melodic voice floated over from the other side of the street. She was dressed all in black, in one of her husband's suits, but if she'd thought to disguise herself as a man she'd completely failed. A bright cotton scarf tied as a belt emphasised her tiny waist and strands of her blond hair had escaped from the black paysanne beret she wore to contain it, framing her animated face like flickers of sunshine.

'One for the road?' She called, lifting the Bobax camera she held in salutation. 'I'd love to serve you a drink, *cherie*,' he'd laughingly replied. 'But as you see, I have my hands full just now.'

That was the moment the camera clicked, the moment the photograph in the palm of the subject's hand was taken. It rested there unseen. Jacques was replaying the minutes that led up to that moment, from his side of the lens.

He sat straighter in his chair as his body recreated how it felt on that afternoon. Exhilarated, exuberant, he flung back his broad shoulders, grinning challenging at the world as he welcomed the future, his future, the one he'd planned for himself and his family when he'd come to Marseille, the future the war had interrupted, forcing him to channel his prodigious cunning and drive towards defeating the enemy obstructing his plans. He wasn't so naive as to believe that the Germans being chased out of his city was the end of the suffering and conflict. But it was a beginning, the first step on the ladder of a free future. He wasn't even remotely afraid of the fracas he'd prepared himself to deal with. The men he was about to encounter were neither disciplined soldiers or organised criminals. They were chancers, pariahs, the type who came regularly into the bar to try their luck and were just as regularly ejected. Jacques was almost looking forward to a straight forward clash with an enemy he knew he could defeat, probably without recourse to his extravagantly displayed armoury of weapons. When Monique hailed him it wasn't her who'd caused the fire to course through his veins, not this time. It was the reawakening of the aspirations of his ambitious future. He'd taken little notice of the attractive woman then but now, looking at her in his mind's eye decades later, he noticed the tension in her drawn face, heard the wistful note of regret in her clear voice.

His post war future beckoned impatiently but what about hers? Could she resume the banal life of faithful wife and devoted mother, married to a man she'd never even mentioned since she and Jacques had become…What had they become? Friends? A ridiculous understatement. Lovers? In all but the seemingly inevitable physical consummation. Could she have seen that as her destiny? Wife, mother and mistress to a philandering barman, who loved her but not enough to disrupt his family and his future plans.

When she'd shouted to Jacques from the other side of the road, he knew now, she already had a lover. She'd already made her plans. Monique had chosen Jean Guerin to lead her away from the mundane, domesticated life she knew she'd be unable to sustain, towards a future she hoped would provide an outlet for her passionate, creative energy.

'One for the road,' she'd called. But she wasn't asking him for a drink, she wanted a last photograph, a memento of him, of the dangerous escapades they'd shared, of what they'd had between them, of what might have been.

Sixty years later as Jacques watched her raise the camera to her eye he finally understood what she was saying. 'Goodbye, Monique, *ma chère, chère amie,*' he whispered over the years.

CHAPTER 27

Léa came cheerfully back into the room balancing a pot of tea and two gold rimmed, hand painted cups with matching saucers on a polished glass and aluminium tray. Seeing Jaquot leaned back in the leather chair, his eyes closed, for a heart-constricting moment she thought he was dead. Forcing her shaking hands to put the tray down on the table, she leant over him, breathing a shuddering sigh of relief as she saw the steady rise and fall of his broad chest beneath his open necked shirt. Her instinct was to creep away and leave him to sleep, to rest. To rest in peace? Instead she knelt down beside him and took his hands in hers, suddenly acutely aware of the precarious nature of time.

Les amoureux came back from Paris powered by a whirlwind of energy, treating every second of every day as a precious moment not to be wasted. They stuck with their resolution to have a quiet wedding but a spin off from the event attracted a packet of publicity for the Lucianis' new venture.

The village bank manager, who doubled as a reporter for the local newspaper, inevitably heard about the forthcoming wedding. Equally inevitably, he knew about Grandfather Jacques' contact with Labeille during the war. Rather than just contributing the usual, 'so and so, resident of, married etcetera he wrote a short piece under the eye catching title of, *Eighty Four Year Old Man comes back to Labeille to marry daughter of village-born woman he worked with in the resistance.* He gave a brief resumé of their meeting, described in some detail the wedding breakfast that inaugurated the grandson's restaurant and commented on the whimsical first married night in the room above. This article might have slipped into parochial obscurity if it hadn't been for the photograph that accompanied it. Lucien, deprived of pizazz, concentrated on artistic instead. His stunning picture of the glamourous couple, the pose mirroring exactly the black and white background reproduction of Léa's parents' wedding photo, caught the eye of an editor of the parent paper, which had a nationwide distribution. The editor decided to send one of his trainees to see if she could get a follow up article. 'Concentrate on the resistance angle,' he suggested. 'And take a few photos, just in case there's a picture that tells a better story than you can get in words.'

This was the break Rose Laurent had been waiting for. She made an appointment to meet up with the couple at the restaurant the following day.

'Why *Plus 15*?' Mademoiselle Laurent asked, moving backwards to take a snap of *Chez Jacques* and its parallel sister sign hanging over the new restaurant door.

Grandfather Jacques smiled as Joe folded his arms and leant back against the door jamb. If she expected a concise answer to her first question the reporter was going to be disappointed. 'Well now, you might expect that as the bar, *Chez Jacques,* was already successfully functioning before this place was done up, more space was needed, an overflow, on special occasions at least. Where better to extend, for that extra fifteen customers, than the house next door? A simple knock through from one to the other. In fact, if you follow me I'll show you exactly where the connecting door could be.'

He led the bemused woman into the restaurant. Still inexperienced enough to need the security of an image to disguise her real self, Rose Laurent had cultivated a mildly cynical air of 'heard it all, seen it all,' but when Joe stood back to let her go through the door before him her eyes opened wide in amazement. She'd expected the room to be clean and freshly decorated, a rustic look, perhaps, wooden yokes as light fittings and a stencilled tin milk churn in a corner. What she faced was a dining room straight out of a prestigious Parisian apartment. An ornately moulded dado rail ran all around the room at chair back height, separating a rich burgundy coloured, art nouveau lincrusta frieze from the smooth, pale-blue wall above. As a practical concession to modernity, the plastered ceiling was studded with encased dimmable LED light bulbs to cast gentle pools of light around the damask covered tables, some round, some oblong, so they could be combined for diverse groups. Discreet spotlights picked out little groups of chubby, harp playing cherubim hovering over the most intimate tables in the corners. Click-click went the camera.

'But in fact,' Joe continued, as if nothing had interrupted his suggestion that this elegant space might become an extension to the bar. 'My brother Jacques, proprietor of the bar of the same name, didn't feel any need to pack any more sardines into his can. It was more upmarket food he had in mind. That's why we decided that restauration was the way to go. So we did go, out on to the balcony. It's through here.'

He led the way through to the room where departed Rab had constructed the *salle d'eau,* now also departed. The world outside flooded in through the optically illusionist glass as Joe ushered the bewildered young woman towards the place where Marie-France had made her first nest, on the original, primitive balcony. Click-click went the camera.

'But as you can see, only so many tables can be fitted into such an enclosed area. Not a problem in summer, of course, when we cater for the masses in the food garden behind the bar with absolute ease because all the fresh food is provided in abundance by the organic garden next door. As you see, even this early in the season it's beginning to look productive, what with the spring sown peas and broad beans and the alliums all sprouting nicely.'

Joe resisted the temptation to use Marie-France's voice when he imparted this information. His audience looked confused enough already. Click-click. Scribble-scribble.

Joe talked on, seemingly unaware that he was doing anything other than answering the question about the origins of the restaurant name. *Plus 15.*

'But in the winter, when people want to eat somewhere with a suitably warm and erotic, whoops, I mean exotic, atmosphere, an intimate restaurant is the obvious solution.'

'Of course.' A fact she could report on. 'And I understand you offer an all-inclusive package, accommodation as well as food?' '*Mais ouais*! And you might think that package could have had a bearing on the choice of *Plus 15* as a name.' Joe's accent had been drifting closer to Marseille as he spoke. Grandfather Jacques, following in the word spinner's wake, had a notion as to why.

Rose Laurent frowned. A part of her said she should be taking control, asking direct questions, getting on with the interview with the old man and his young bride. But there was something mesmerising about the soft tones of this slightly sinister looking chef. 'I understood that you only have two guest rooms. Surely you can't sleep anywhere near fifteen people?'

Joe smiled. How could she have thought he looked sinister? He was like a big, cuddly schoolboy. 'We are a family concern, as I'm sure you're aware. Three generations of Lucianis in the hospitality business so far, starting with my grandfather, who will shortly speak for himself, and a fourth generation waiting to take over.'

She looked around, expecting a miniature version of this compelling man to materialise through the walls. He'd have liked to but Angelo was at school.

'However, although we are family minded the rooms above are not designed to be child friendly, they're decidedly adult orientated, if you take my meaning.' She did take his meaning. 'Are you telling me that Plus 15 refers to the age of consent?' she asked, prudishly shocked at the insinuation. Was this restaurant actually a cover for house of ill repute?

'No, no of course not!' Joe was so wide eyed and innocently aghast at the improper suggestion, she felt quite guilty for having made it, unaware that her priggish reaction had decided him not to suggest that she might want to look at the bedrooms.

Rose, beginning to feel rather uncomfortably out of her depth, determined to assert herself. 'So, *Plus 15*,' she said firmly. 'What is its meaning?' 'Well, in Marseille, where I come from,' Joe said, standing tall and grinning at his grandfather in acknowledgement that he was plagiarising one of his story lines. 'We add on the number 15 to emphasise how really big something is. Like, 'we've already got dozens of customers, plus 15.' And that's our philosophy. Whatever the customers want, we make sure they've got more than enough.'

'Oh? So it's a saying from Marseille? But why the number 15?' Joe's laugh reverberated round the dining room, out on to the balcony, down into the garden and through to the bar.

'I've absolutely no idea,' he confessed. 'But I mustn't waste any more of your time,' he added apologetically. 'You're not here to talk about the Luciani family's mundane business concerns. My grandfather and his wife have a far more interesting story to tell. And he's so much better at it than me. Please, let me serve you an aperitif while you conduct your interview.'

Grandfather Jacques and Léa were already seated at a table placed in front of a door, Rose presumed so as not to disrupt the rest of the tables already set for the next meal. 'It's rum based, called Le Flamboyant. One of my favourites,' Joe explained, ladling pineapple and mango pieces into wide glasses before taking the cover off a dish of bite sized samosas.

Rose was glad when he left. She'd been taught that to be an effective interviewer one must employ active listening skills, interspersed with incisive questions. The only thing active about her listening so far had been to follow the unnervingly attractive chef about like a processional caterpillar. And as for incisive questioning! Well, she'd still not got a straight answer to the one question she'd asked. Still, it didn't matter. As the chef said, she wasn't here to talk to him. Her assignment was to get a story from the old couple. She was sure that wouldn't pose any problem at all, they'd be desperate to talk to a willing audience, to tell her in great detail all about the past, the time people of advanced years remember best.

Taking a sip of the cocktail, avoiding the lumps of fruit so they wouldn't clog up her speech, she explained carefully to the old folk that she was going to use a machine to record them. She asked her first, incisive question.

'During the war?' the old man replied. 'Oh but that was such a very long time ago. You were just a little girl, then, weren't you my dear?' He gave his wife a lascivious smile. She simpered suggestively. Straight laced Rose Laurent was almost sick. It was all downhill from there. After five minutes during which she didn't get one useable fact she decided the old woman was just as much in her dotage as her even older husband.

'So you're from the village, are you Madame Luciani?' Rose asked. 'Oh, no. I was born in Marseille.' 'But your mother was from the village?' 'Well, she was born here, but she wasn't here during the occupation.' 'So you were in Marseille during the occupation?' 'Oh no. I was here, in the village.' Really, you'd have thought she was purposefully trying not to give any information away, as if she was keeping it for herself.

Rose stood up, thanked them for their time as politely as she could, cursed her luck that her first assignment should be with a couple of dippy dotards and left, clutching a menu and one of the flowers from a table decoration the old man presented to her saying, totally incomprehensibly, 'What's in a name?'

'Let's go through what you got,' her mentor suggested, after she admitted that her trip had been a complete failure. 'I took a good few photos,' she said dejectedly, displaying them on her phone. She was dreading the inevitable question about *Plus 15*.

'Got Marseille connections then,' her companion remarked, after looking at the first one, before picking up the pristinely preserved menu in its plastic folder. 'Got Ile De Reunion connections too, by the looks of this.' 'This one's good,' he added, looking at the picture in the restaurant. 'Classy and intimate. What's the story about the sign on the door?' 'I didn't ask,' she admitted, noticing for the first time the embroidered panel.

'Not ready for travel column or the literary section,' the editor decided. 'Or even the women's page.' He sent Rose back into the office to write a piece for *Places to eat*. The week after it appeared the paper received an exceptionally professionally written, quarter page advertisement, lavishly illustrated with atmospheric photographs, the most exciting one being of the bedrooms.

'If we keep the basic colours neutral we could use soft furnishings and drapes to change the ambiance of either room according to the booking,' Léa suggested when they were discussing the décor in the guest rooms. Grandfather Jacques had been extolling the artistry of her interior design.

'For example, riotously coloured silk and luxurious cushions would transform it into a bordello.' 'While simple, virginal white, mantilla lace could turn it into a nunnery,' Eveline said, with a wicked grin. '*Le Pur et L'impure*?' Léa suggested, being of a literary bent. 'Colette?' Eveline responded, an avid reader herself. 'Do you think she'd object if we used one of her book titles?' 'I'm sure she wouldn't. In fact, I think she'd fit in here generally rather well, considering her somewhat alternative life style.' 'Are you calling me alternative?' Eveline laughed. 'Not just you, my dear. I think the label fits all of us, the whole family, don't you?'

Almost overnight *Plus 15* was booked up for 'those special occasions you'd like to be exquisitely romantic' for months ahead. Discerning diners rushed to 'come to our little village to taste the foods of the world'. Who could resist the challenge? 'Whatever you desire, ask and we'll make it yours.'

A few months later the editor dropped a book onto the bit of the shared desk Rose Laurent called her own. 'Ring any bells?' he asked sarcastically. 'Jacquot, Mother and Me. A novel based on the true story,' she read out loud, frowning. 'The back cover,' her boss directed. Rose turned the book over. A familiar face smiled out at her. The brief biography introduced the author as Léa Jourdan, recently retired journalist who'd worked in both London and Paris.

Léa's book was a bestseller, the 'based on the true story' epithet appealing to many who considered themselves far too literary to read mere romantic fiction. Even so, Madeleine Guerin was surprised to find her husband sitting on the sofa totally absorbed in the book she'd bought for her own entertainment. In all the years of their marriage he'd never read a novel, even one claiming to be based on the truth.

'Léa Jordan,' Jean breathed, when he saw the photograph of the author on the back of the book his wife had left face down on the bedside table. 'Léa Jourdan and Jacques Luciani.'

He started reading. *We met on Marseille Station. The year was...'* and he didn't stop, not even during lunch when he propped the novel up against the condiment set, until the words, *'Jacquot and I are proving that living happily ever after is not an ending reserved for fairy tales.'*

'Alright dear?' Madame Guerin asked. 'Ah, yes, mmm, fine. Just thought I'd, er, see what was so entertaining about these fictional accounts of the war.' 'You were in Marseille, weren't you dear? Did any of it ring true?' 'Oh, well, bits and pieces, you know. Shall we open a bottle of wine to go with the cheese?'

Jean felt a celebration was in order. Not because his part during the occupation had been recognised. Because it hadn't. The man who recruited Jacquot into the resistance was a tall, paysan type, identifiably based on Monsieur Roumignac. Monique led Jacques through the forest and saved his life, taking him to a very accurately described maquis camp. They had a passionate affair during the occupation but, realising that she could never shatter his world by taking him away from his wife and child, she travelled through France, a graphically portrayed journey, and made her way to England where she devoted her short life to photography and her little daughter. The meeting between this daughter and Jacquot was described so tenderly and emotionally, as he recognised his never forgotten mistress but grew to love her for herself, that even phlegmatic Jean had to swallow back the tears. But the best part of the book, as far as he was concerned, was that the schoolteacher, Solange and her child weren't in the story at all.

Thank you for reading this book. I hope you enjoyed it. As a newly published novelist I need all the help I can get. Star ratings to improve my profile with Amazon. Reviews to interest readers in my work. Word of mouth is the best publicity of all. As Oscar Wilde said,

'There is only one thing in the world worse than being talked about and that's not being talked about.'

Talk about me, please.

Annamarie Delaney

Born Irish, brought up English, lived Scottish, now naturalised French

Coming Next

'You'll never change and neither will I'

Disruption in Labeille after the celebration of *la fête nationale*. Jacqui organises the search for a lost girl. Emilie Blanchard gets married. Joe falls in love. Marie-France makes an impulsive decision. *Chez Jacques* is thrown into turmoil.

Makings and Breakings is the fifth book in the series *Tales From Chez Jacques*

Books in this Series

Away Tae Me

Welcome to the Family

Pastures Old Pastures New

No Peace for the Wicked

Makings and Breakings

That'll Do

Other books by this author

Chrysalis to Nightingale